EPIPHANY

EPIPHANY

EPIPHANY

STORIES BY

Ferrol Sams

LONGSTREET PRESS
Atlanta, Georgia

Published by LONGSTREET PRESS, INC.,
a subsidiary of Cox Newspapers,
a division of Cox Enterprises, Inc.
2140 Newmarket Parkway
Suite 118
Marietta, Georgia 30067

Printed in the United States of America

1st printing, 1994

Library of Congress Catalog Number 94-77574

ISBN: 1-56352-164-4

This book was printed by R. R. Donnelly & Sons, Harrisonburg, VA

Cover and book design by Laura McDonald
Cover photograph by Medford Taylor/Superstock

The author gratefully acknowledges the use of quotations from the
following poems: *John Brown's Body* by Stephen Vincent Benét; "The
Tiger," from *Songs of Experience* by William Blake; *Pippa Passes* by
Robert Browning; "You Are Old, Father William" by Lewis Carroll;
"The Windhover" by Gerard Manley Hopkins; "No. 12," from *Last
Poems* by A. E. Housman; "*La Belle Dame Sans Merci*" by John Keats;
"I too beneath your moon, almighty Sex" (Sonnet cxxviii) by Edna St.
Vincent Millay; and "The Slave" by James Oppenheim.

FOR HELEN

ALSO BY FERROL SAMS

Run With the Horsemen

The Whisper of the River

The Widow's Mite & Other Stories

The Passing

Christmas Gift!

When All the World Was Young

CONTENTS

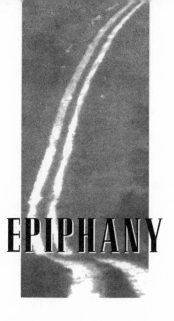

EPIPHANY

THIS IS SATURDAY, JANUARY 5, 1991. NUMBER 231 BEGIN-
ning dictation. *My first patient of the morning is Gregry
McHune, medical record number 079214, thirty-five-year-
old Caucasian male, new patient to this facility, who comes
in because of fever, sore throat of two days duration and gen-
eralized malaise. He has a child who has recently been treated by the pediatrician for strep throat. His wife is a nurse and
insisted that he see a physician. Mr. McHune seems dis-
dainful of this mollycoddling, as he calls it, remarking that
he has been a damn sight sicker than this a heap of times and
has not bothered to see no doctor about it. On specific
questioning, he has not been to a physician in approxi-
mately eight or ten years. He is in my office this morning because
his wife is distrustful of med centers and doc-in-a-box. I was
the only damn regular doctor he could find who was open
on a Saturday and, hell, he has to work during the week.*

*He has temperature of 102, a fiery red pharynx and exu-
date on both tonsils, which are small and mildly cryptic.
Since Mr. McHune is concerned about expenses, I am
going to forego a throat culture and treat this empirically*

*as a strep infection with Pen-Vee-K 500 q.i.d. for ten days.
I have assured him that if he is without fever he can return
to work on Monday. I was able to find him some samples
of the medication.*

*An incidental finding is a BP of 190/102. Mr. McHune seems
unduly defensive, stating that, hell, anybody's BP who had
any sense would be up if he was going to waste a Saturday
morning seeing a strange doctor when he had better things
to do with his time. He further states that his wife is always
taking his BP with one of those contraptions what she
brings home from work and then nagging him to go see about
it, and if I'll just wait till he's feeling better from this damn
sore throat, he'll come back to see me about his damn BP.
I have requested that he ask his wife to log his BP daily and
exacted a promise from him to return to clinic in two weeks
with the record of her findings.*

The doctor was slight, appeared deceptively frail. His
jowls drooped as decidedly as his little pot belly and his
sparse hair had turned white long since—a transition he had
been too busy to mark. He considered, when asked, that it
had been an inconsequential occurrence somewhere between
his bifocals and his hearing aids.

Briefly, he pondered the transcription he had just dictated
into his pocket recorder and decided to let it stand. Maybe
it wasn't as scientific and impersonal a record as the clinic administrator kept diplomatically beseeching him to
produce. The administrator was a younger man, sartorially
perfect, tonsorially resplendent, his speech a soft cadence
of bureaucratic phrases that bespoke years of exposure to
mimeographed federal directives. His phrases were frequently just as obscure and frustrating. When he addressed
the topic of physicians' dictation, he became a bulwark of
dignity, imperial and imperturbable, confidently assured that

so long as patient data were recorded with accuracy, precision and ponderous dullness, then the threat of litigation, albeit still a specter, was no more than that.

The doctor had sputtered. "I've not been sued in forty-five years and malpractice premiums keep going up anyhow. I can't live under the threat of a potential lawsuit from every patient I see if I don't happen to order the right lab test on the first visit or if I fail to mention tsutsugamushi fever as a possible diagnosis."

Mocking the administrator's formal speech structures, the doctor had boldy admonished him, "I'll not spend the rest of my life fencing myself in tighter and tighter with federal guidelines or insurance regulations that accomplish nothing except hindrance of patient care and an increase of my personal frustration level. Too rigid adherence to a set of virtues can lead to worship of false idols, and I am not yet prepared to bend my knee to the trinity of Medicare, Malpractice and Medical Records."

The urbane administrator had allowed himself one blink and only a slight shifting of gaze before his silky reply. "There is always the possibility that a health care provider in this clinic, even granted that he is one of only two family practitioners in the group and very important to the operation and successful function of that group, might conceivably be denied the continued use of electronic devices which, of course, belong to the group for the purpose of dictating patient data to the medical transcriptionists for inclusion in the patient chart as part of the medical records of the group, if he should adopt a resistant attitude toward conformity with the uniform policies established by this group."

"You're saying you'd take away my recorder, aren't you?"

"In a word, yes."

"You win, you win. I'll conform. Be uniform. Hygeia, Panacea and Aesculapius are this moment superseded by Mal-

practice, Medicare and the Federal Government. Their banner says, 'Conformity! Uniformity!' Their slogan is, 'Backward! Downward!' From now on I'm a slave. Out of here,
I've patients waiting."

When the administrator carried a point and won an issue,
he could relax into human English. "Dr. Goddard, you're a
trip! A challenge, sure, but also a trip. Thanks. I'll let you get
back to work."

Mark Goddard loved his pocket recorder. He thought about
his earlier career when every bit of information in a patient's
chart had to be written in his cursive hieroglyphics, a labo-
rious and tedious chore at the end of the day, frequently lacking in detail and more often than not indecipherable by
anyone other than himself. Dictation was quick, easy, efficient, and resulted in accurately typed records. The ladies in
medical transcription were modern day genii, he thought, sitting all day with headsets and typing as rapidly as he could
speak, their efforts being entered into a computer and then
printed out for his review before permanent inclusion into
the charts. In addition, the information was stored in perpetuity
in the computer.

"I don't like computers," he once grumbled to a younger
doctor. "They're too powerful. I have the conviction that if
I came up too close on one unawares, I might be snatched into
some obscure data bank and disappear like Rip van Winkle;
not to be heard of again until some fumbling high school graduate, who has never really learned to read, punches the
wrong key, and I'm all of a sudden resurrected into a generation
even more foreign to me than this one."

"Bullshit," expostulated the young gastroenterologist
who sported a shock of untamed black hair through which
he frequently ruffled impatient hands when talking. The hair
reminded Dr. Goddard of the topknot of high-stepping
roosters of his rural youth. "You know we couldn't run this

place without computers." He laid an arm across the older man's shoulder and added in affectionate brashness, "You're so full of it lately I keep expecting your eyes to turn brown."

Mark Goddard laughed. "At my age, sonny boy, I have a built-in distrust of any system that incorporates such items as floppy discs and software. That's getting too personal."

"We couldn't run this place without you, either."

"Thanks. I hope it's years before you have to try. I'll admit that giving up my pocket recorder would be like going backwards from antibiotics to calomel or from Lasix to phlebotomy. Get out of here before I sink to telling you how I walked to school through the snow with wolves snapping at my heels."

"Watch the brown, Doc."

"Out! I've patients to see."

This is Saturday, January 19, 1991. Number 231 beginning dictation. My first patient is Fred Eubanks, medical record number 000548. Impression: Laceration, right knee, sustained ten days ago while splitting wood. Tetanus toxoid was administered, the wound repaired in our Immediate Care Department and it has healed by first intention. Sutures are removed and patient is dismissed from further care.

"Next patient, Gregry McHune, medical record number 079214. Patient had complete recovery from his pharyngitis and has returned to the clinic with a diary of daily blood pressure readings recorded by his wife. They range from 170/104 to 150/100. His pressure in the office this morning is 196/110. After discussion with Mr. McHune and refusal on his part to undergo any laboratory tests or other diagnostic studies, he has agreed to a trial of medication. I have given him Tenormin, 50 mgm from the sample closet. He is to take one daily, abstain from alcohol, use salt sparingly and return to clinic in two weeks.

Gregry McHune's voice was soft, not only Southern but slurred to the back of his throat, the cadence interrupted on longer sentences by short gasps of replenishing air drawn between dusky teeth permanently stained to a bluish grayness.

"Wonder where he was raised," thought Mark Goddard. "That accent's not Georgia, not even Thomasville, and those teeth aren't all the result of tobacco. Must have been dosed too enthusiastically with tetracycline before we discovered what it does to children's teeth."

McHune's face was small-featured, as smoothly taut and impersonal as the radiator ornaments of early automobiles fashioned to split onrushing wind. His eyes were tawny, hooded in repose, full of amber light, constantly guarded. When he spoke he blared them wider open and his forehead became corrugated with earnest wrinkles. Always there was a watchfulness, a wariness in his eyes. Looking directly at someone, with no shift whatever of lateral gaze, he still gave his listener the impression that he was aware of even the faintest peripheral movement and was prepared.

"Prepared for what?" thought Dr. Goddard. "He's like a cat. Ready to pounce."

The simile pleased the doctor. He surveyed the young man's nondescript hair, not gray, not brown, closely and evenly cropped like a pelt above the swept-back forehead; was conscious of the litheness of the lean body, the poise of long straps of muscles as tensely patient as stretched springs.

"Cat's not in it," amended Mark Goddard. "This man's like a panther."

McHune watched as the physician rechecked the blood pressure. He did not look at the cuff, the pumping bulb, the pulsating needle of the glass-faced manometer; he watched the doctor's eyes. And he waited.

"I'm getting the same thing the nurses did, Mr. McHune.

And basically the same reading as your wife has done at home."

The eyes waited. Steady. Unflinching.

"I think we have to go on medication for hypertension. And there are some tests I'd like to get done this morning. A little later, I think we definitely should schedule a complete physical for you."

"I knew it," came the flat-toned response. "As sure as I'm sitting here I knew it. Let me tell you one thing, Doc. I'm a pore man. I've got a wife and a youngun and it takes all us both can scratch up to make ends meet. The only reason I come over here today was because I promised my wife. And I also promised you that I would. And there was something about you sort of got to me, if you know what I mean. Like you was looking at me instead of just my damn sore throat and was seeing something besides thirty-five dollars for a damn office call. It may just be your way; I don't know because I never saw you before two weeks ago, but I can usually size a man up pretty damn quick, you understand? And you acted like you cared."

"I do," interposed Mark Goddard. Carefully. Quietly. "Is there any reason I shouldn't?"

The eyes flared golden, the voice was thick as syrup. "Hell, no. I'm as good as the next one. I don't hold myself to be no better than most, mind you, but not near as mean as some I've known. I always try to do what I know is right, and you can damn well believe I know what's right and what's wrong. Just because I'm worth caring about don't necessarily mean that everbody does it, if you understand what I mean."

"I think I understand. What does that have to do with your blood pressure?"

"Well, goddamn, Doc. A man's supposed to pay his debts. I know that's right. A real man ain't supposed to make no debt he can't pay. I know that's wrong. I ain't going out on no damn limb for a bunch of tests I can't afford. Now that's just the damn way I am and if you can't accept that I guess I might as well quit wasting your time."

Mark Goddard thought, "I'll be damned if I sink to asking him if he has insurance, and I'll not even stoop to looking on that computerized sheet in his chart to find out. This is between me and the Cat." Aloud he said, "I accept. Relax."

The doctor grasped a knee between his hands and leaned back into thin air, expertly balanced on his stool. In a deliberately musing tone, he continued, "You know something? When I started out we didn't have all those 'damn tests,' as you call them. The only treatment we had for high blood pressure was phenobarbital and a low-salt diet. We charged three dollars for an office call then, and that was high. This was way before you were born, and no one even thought of suing a doctor if somebody died in kidney failure without a serum creatinine recorded in the chart. Come to think of it, we didn't have creatinine levels available then. Even in a hospital all we could get was a BUN and we expected that to be high if there was albumin in the urine."

"You might as well be talking Greek, Doc." There was a quick flash of the darkened teeth. "Hell, for all I know, you probably are."

"I'm just talking common sense, Mr. McHune, but when all is said and done the Greeks were also fluent in that language. What I'm getting at is that I'll step back in time and treat you without the tests if you'll promise to come back when you're supposed to."

The wary eyes flickered ever so faintly. "You got a deal, Doc. I'll come back. Why don't you just call me 'Gregry'?"

"Thanks. Is there supposed to be an *o* in your name? Have I finally caught the computer in a spelling error?"

"Everbody asks me that, but 'Gregry' is what's on my birth certificate. Maybe my mama couldn't spell so damn good, but you can't lay it on no computer."

"One other thing, Gregry, and we'll get back to the blood pressure. Where were you born and raised? I know it was in the South, but I can't quite place your accent."

"Many folks as you got out there waiting, you'll not get no dinner, Doc. You ask all your patients these questions?"

"Only those who are interesting, Gregry."

"Well, I ain't exactly what I'd call interesting, but I was born in California. That don't count, though, cause when I was three I went to live in Kentucky and my granddaddy raised me."

"You were an orphan?"

"I am now. I wasn't then."

There was a pause. The eyes stared into Mark Goddard's. Were they defensive? Or defiant? The doctor waited.

"My daddy was in the Korean War. I hope you understand it wasn't really no war, it was what they called a 'confrontation' at that time." The voice high-stepped over some syllables like a saddle horse negotiating tree-fall. "My granddaddy said anything with that many folks choosing up sides and shooting at each other was a damn war, and it always seemed to me my granddaddy knowed what he was talking about. Anyway, my ma sent me to Kentucky when Daddy went over, and then he come home all shot up and a plumb mess. She'd get me when she could but we didn't never have what you'd call no regular home; just moved around from one city to another according to whatever VA hospital they thought might be able to help my daddy. I was always glad to get back to Kentucky and I considered that my home. That satisfy your curiosity?"

"Let's call it my interest, Gregry. Sure. I wasn't wanting you to tell me anything you didn't want me to know."

"You need'n never worry your head about that, Doc; I sure as hell won't. I promise you that."

Dr. Goddard laughed. "All right. Now let's get back to treating your blood pressure. I'm sure you know about eating as little salt as possible."

"I don't never eat no salt to amount to nothing. My wife sees to that."

"Good. What about alcohol?"

The voice was as cautious as the eyes. "What about it?"

"How much of it do you use?"

"Lord, Doc, I don't measure it. I just slosh a little on me if I get scratched or cut myself shaving now and then."

"Come on, now, Gregry. You know I mean how much do you drink?"

"Alkyhawl?"

"Yes."

"I don't drink it at all. I may not be educated but I ain't no fool. That stuff'll kill you. I knowed a fellow once what drinked down two pints of it and he went stone blind and died a-screaming; from his kidneys locking up on him. Least that's what they said; I never seen him myself. You couldn't hire me to drink that stuff."

"Good. If more people with high blood pressure had that attitude, my job would be easier."

The wrinkles in the forehead relaxed, the eyes took on extra light, the voice was almost theatrically casual. "Course I drink a six-pack of beer every night."

"What?"

"And usually a twelve-pack on Sariday and Sunday."

"Gregry McHune, you know perfectly well beer is alcohol. I am educated, but I ain't no fool, either."

The laugh was as soft and gurgling as a brooklet rising from hiding beneath winter leaves. "Had you going for a minute there, didn't I, Doc? You'll have to 'scuse me; I just had to test out what kind of fellow you are."

"I'm the kind who is trying as hard as he can on a Saturday morning to accommodate a patient's request not to spend money on laboratory tests and treat his blood pressure at the same time. Do you drink hard liquor?"

"Not unless me and the old lady go to somebody's house and they ain't got no beer. And that don't happen more'n oncet or at the most twicet a year; we stay pretty much to ourselves."

"Well, now, Gregry, I want you to leave off all alcohol for the next two weeks. It'll be hard for you to do, I know, but it is very difficult to regulate blood pressure if a patient drinks alcohol. Do you think you can do it?"

The eyebrows shot upward. "I'n do anything I set my mind to, Doc. Hell, the damn stuff don't mean nothing to me nohow; I just drink it so's I'n sleep."

"How long have you been drinking this much?"

"Eight and a half years."

"How long have you had trouble sleeping?"

"Ten and a half years."

"It's going to be hard, Gregry. I'm not preaching at you, but it's important."

There came a shrug, the eyelids widened. "Hell, you don't know what hard is, Doc. You ain't talking to no damn child, you know. I'n go longer'n two weeks without sleeping. I'll take you on."

"Great. No salt, no alcohol. I'm going to give you a prescription for a drug called Vasotec. We'll start with a small dose and see how you respond. It's a little expensive but it has few side effects."

"There you go, Doc. I told you I'm a pore man. I can't afford no damn expensive medicine."

Mark Goddard whipped his stool around and rose. "Wait here; I'll be right back."

He hastened to the supply closet and began searching the shelves, extending his neck to utilize his bifocals. His nurse

approached behind him. "Can I help you look for something,
Dr. Mark? You have a lot of patients stacking up out there."

"Thanks, Lucy. I have it. I know I'm running behind, but
I can't help it. I think this guy really needs me, and I can't rush
him."

Back in the treatment room, he handed Gregry McHune
two small boxes. "We didn't have any samples left of Vasotec,
but here's another drug that's good. This is Tenormin and it's
in a form so that you have to take only one a day. Take one
every morning and don't forget, you promised to see me in
two weeks."

"I won't forget, Doc, but hell, you didn't have to do this.
I'm a pore man, but I ain't no damn charity case."

"You're accommodating your habits and wishes to mine,
Gregry, and I'm trying to accommodate mine to yours. I'll
see you week after next."

"I'll sure be here." There was a pause, almost of embarrassment. "I ain't never run into no doctor like you before."
He hesitated. "If you care, I care."

"Thanks, Gregry. One thing I'd like to point out to a clear-
thinking, perceptive young man like you who is poor. If you
can afford beer and all the cigarettes you're obviously smoking, you could afford diagnostic tests and prescription drugs."

The shoulders squared. There was fire somewhere behind
the eyes; they glowed like lanterns. "Hell, Doc, now you've
took up preaching."

Mark Goddard's laugh was an abrupt bark. "Had you
going there for a minute, didn't I, Gregry? Like I told you,
I am educated but I'm no fool. You'll have to 'scuse me; I
just had to test out what kind of fellow you are."

"I'll just be damned! You won't do, Doc. See you in two
weeks."

This is Saturday, February 2, 1991, Anno Domini, and with

*this momentous observation Number 231, better known as
"the old doc," is delighted to be able to raise both his voice
and his recorder and begin dictation. Good morning!*

The transcriptionist removed her headphones. "Hey,
Kathy. He is in one of his moods on this tape. On a tear;
feeling feisty. Might as well get ready to send copies of
everything he says this morning to the administrator. He told
us to watch him."

The administrator was not dilatory. Within hours he con-
fronted Dr. Goddard. He was smooth and his fluffy blanket
of bureaucratic syntax dissipated any sharp chill of criticism,
his tone deferential, unctuous. Dr. Goddard recognized confrontation, however, no matter its guise, and shook off the
sensation of being oxygen-deprived and drowsy into which
the administrator's speech occasionally lulled him.

"Dr. Mark, I'm sure you remember the Risk Prevention Seminar in which you participated last year and the importance
that was stressed at that period in time of choosing precise
and accurate terminology in dictating patient encounters, taking care at all times to be professional in observation and to
be sure of minute anatomical and physiological proficiency
in delineating that terminology in an effort to avert any
possible distortion of meaning in case the physician should
ever be faced by an adversarial and antagonistic attorney in
the process of litigation, the entire purpose of the Seminar,
as you remember, being to reduce the overhead of the entire
clinic by lowering the insurance premiums of the participating
physicians."

Mark Goddard shook his head like a swimmer regaining
the beach. "I also remember someone who came before you,
the latches of whose shoes I am not worthy to unlace. He said,
'Brevity is the soul of wit.' What's on your mind? Spit it out."

"This. Defend it."

Dr. Goddard tilted his head backward for focus and read from the proffered paper. "*Gregry McHune MR 07924. BP 140/92. Patient discontinued Tenormin because of side effects. Begin Dynacirc 2.5 mg. b.i.d. Patient promises to return to clinic in three weeks.*

'I too beneath your moon, almighty Sex,
Go forth at nightfall crying like a cat.'"

Calmly and pedantically the doctor replied, "This needs no defense. Those are the first two lines from a sonnet by Edna St. Vincent Millay, who may be unknown to you young people but was probably the most widely quoted and certainly the best-loved poet of my generation. Her first published work was a long masterpiece called 'Renascence' and appeared when she was only seventeen. I've heard that she was red-headed and that as a student at Vassar she once danced buck-naked in the snow on her dormitory roof and . . . ."

The administrator's sigh was arrestingly audible. "Dr. Mark, you know very well that's not what I mean. Although I'd like to have the time some day to learn about this poet, my chief function is to operate the affairs of the clinic and to be sure that all the physicians are attending their patients within accepted parameters of medical care. That includes transcriptions on the charts. How would this look in court?"

"Hell, it's not ever going to court. I started to dictate

'Tiger! Tiger! burning bright
In the forests of the night,
What immortal hand or eye
Could frame thy fearful symmetry?'

But I decided Millay's sonnet was more appropriate. This patient reminds me of some giant cat who is only tolerating his trainer and his cage. Do you want me to dictate what he actually said?"

"That might be more appropriate, but you would have to be word accurate."

"And specific," shot back Mark Goddard. "His first words to me were, 'Doc, I only come back because I promised, and my granddaddy taught me it's wrong to break a promise. Those goddam pills you give me has messed up my sex life. I like you fine, but if I've got to choose between having a stroke or limber-dicking my life away like a gilt in a hog-wallow, I'm done with you.' He also told me, 'For the first time in my life I'm ashamed of my own dick. You ever try to poke a marsh-mallow into a piggy bank? Just goddam it to hell, Doc!' It took me thirty minutes to settle him down, change his medicine and extract another promise of return. That note is a masterpiece of succinctness."

The administrator's eyes closed overlong and expressed rigidly attained patience as eloquently as his tone. "No more poetry, doctor. Please. No more poetry in the office record. I'll let you get back to your patients."

Mark Goddard took a deep breath and let it roll. "I'll freely confess that his language was more graphic and explicit than the poetry I chose and that it might be much more meaningful to a potentially adversarial attorney, should one ever by the remotest chance happen to review this record, but my chief concern was that I be able to remember what he said without exposing the ladies in the transcription room to such a coarse concept of the problem. My granddaddy taught me it was wrong to talk like that in front of ladies, and I am sure Mr. McHune's granddaddy did the same for him."

"I'm leaving, doctor. I'm leaving it with you, but please, no more poetry."

This is Saturday, February 16, 1991; number 231 beginning dictation. First patient this morning is Gregry McHune, record number 079214. Patient's BP is down to 150/90 and he reports even better readings than this at home with occasional diastolic values in the low 80's. He is gratified to

*be experiencing no side effects. It has now been four weeks
since he had any alcohol and he requests sleeping pills for
intractable insomnia. After some discussion, I have per-
suaded him that his problem may very well be due to underlying depression and he has agreed to a trial of Prozac. He
is to return to clinic in three weeks.*

"Gregry, this blood pressure is really improved. It's not under
perfect control yet but we're getting there."

"It's been running as low as 140/86 or even 80 when the
old lady takes it at home. Runs up to 96 or even 100 when
I get mad, but goes back down when I cool off."

"No side effects from the Dynacirc?"

"Whatcha mean by that?"

"You've had no more problem with erectile dysfunc-
tion?"

"Hell, I'm here, ain't I? Which reminds me, I guess I
ought to apologize to you, Doc, for the way I talked to you
last time."

"What do you mean?"

"Well, yelling at you and using a word like *limberdicking*
and all like that to a man as educated as you are."

"I had heard the term before, Gregry; not, I confess used
as a noun-verb, but even James Kilpatrick would have been
accepting of it used in such an appropriate manner. Com-
munication is the important issue, and I've no objection at
all to its being vivid."

"Whatever you say, Doc, but to answer your question, I
ain't had a bit of trouble getting up a bone since I come off
that other medicine. In fact, the old thing gets so hard now
a cat couldn't scratch it. Things is fine in that department."

"So much for vivid speech this morning, Gregry. Tell me,
what are you getting mad about that runs your blood pressure up?"

"Well, Doc, much of nothing, to tell the truth. I've just got a real short fuse and I'm likely to fly off the handle and commence to yelling about things wouldn't bother no sensible man at all. You know what I mean? All the time I know it ain't reasonable, but seems like I can't help it. The old lady says I should say something to you about getting a pill for my nerves. But hell, she don't know everthing; I personally think what I need is something to make me sleep. I come off that beer like you told me and now I can't even get to sleep first part of the night. At least when I drank my beer I'd go on off to sleep, even if I did wake up later at two or three and lay there looking in the rafters till daylight."

"Gregry, it occurs to me that you may be depressed. Insomnia, inappropriate outbursts of anger, tension, anxiety, disturbed sleep pattern. Do you feel depressed?"

"Hell, Doc, you ain't been talking to my old lady, have you? You sound just like her. Next thing I know, you'll be on my ass about smoking."

Mark Goddard smiled. "That's coming, Gregry, but later; I don't want to push my luck. Of course, I haven't spoken to your wife. You're not only a master of vivid speech but an artist at evasiveness. Let's get back to the question: Do you feel depressed?"

The golden eyes stared wide and unblinking. For a second they seemed to deepen. "Goddammit, Doc, sometimes I get a lump in my throat and feel like crying for no reason at all. Sometimes I look at my wife and my kid and realize how lucky I am and then, Wham! I feel as sad as if I was at a funeral. It don't make no sense atall; I got nothing to be sad about. I got a good job, a house, the best old lady in the world and a little boy you wouldn't believe. And you're goddam right I'm depressed. What else you see in that crystal ball of yours, Doc?"

"It's not I, Gregry. You're the crystal ball; I'm just looking in it. I think I can help. Just wait a minute."

Doctor Goddard made another trip to the sample closet and returned.

"Here are some more of your Dynacirc pills I found; the drug rep was by just yesterday. And here," he paused, "are some other pills I want you to take. We won't know whether they'll work until we try. You take one early every morning and take it regularly. It will be at least a week or ten days before you notice any effect, so be patient. If you get real excited and antsy, overly nervous or jittery, or have any other reactions that puzzle you, call me. Otherwise, I want to see you in three weeks. If for some reason you can't take the pills, bring them back to me, for they're very expensive and I can pass them on to someone else."

Gregry McHune accepted the proffered small boxes and looked at them gingerly. "Prozac? Prozac? That somehow rings a bell. What they supposed to do, Doc?"

"It's a drug designed to combat the chemical imbalance that we call depression. It builds up gradually in your system and I hope it will make you sleep better and eventually help you to have a more level and uplifted mood. It's not a 'feel good' or 'happy' pill. You might sell one on the street but you'd never sell the second one. There's a package insert there that lists all the possible side reactions. You and your wife read over them and if you notice any ill effect, call me."

"Prozac! Hell, Doc, I knew I'd heard of that. It's the one what's on TV and everwhere that's supposed to make folks kill theyselves. I already told you I don't like to take medicine."

Mark Goddard leaned forward and looked straight into the staring eyes. "Hey, Gregry McHune. I've been treating you for six weeks now and doing my dead level best to help you, and that without any laboratory tests and not one prescription you had to pay for. I have humored you and catered to your wishes whenever I can and even come

close to violating some tenets of good medical practice in
the process. If there is any doubt in your mind that I know
less medicine than Oprah Winfrey or Phil Donahue or
some wet-behind-the-ears smart-aleck news reporter who
thinks he can stumble up on a Pulitzer Prize if he just
keeps indiscriminately turning over enough rocks, then
maybe I'm not the doctor for you."

Mark Goddard held his breath, realizing that he had
flung down a glove he hoped would not be retrieved.

Gregry McHune's eyes never shifted; he exhaled slowly and
replied in a flat tone. "I'm gonna try you one more time, Doc;
I'll take the pills. Hell, man, I didn't mean to ruffle your feathers or get you up on your dew claws or nothing like that. You've
always played straight with me and we ain't never blowed
no smoke up each other's ass, if you know what I mean. I don't
want you to get the idea that I care less about myself than
you do. I'll take your damn pills."

"All we can do is try them, Gregry; they may not help at
all. Don't let it get out on the street, Sport, but I am frequently
wrong."

Gregry McHune laughed. "You won't do, Doc. I don't believe
there's another'n in the world like you." His farewell handshake was a loose grip accompanied by a single formal
pumping of the forearm—almost, Dr. Goddard thought,
like the unaccustomed effort of a shy first-grader. "I tell you
one thing you're right about. Oprah and all of them other folks,
to say nothing about them news reporters, is hell bent on setting folks against each other; they got everbody suspicious
of everbody else; they's what I call 'shit-stirrers.'"

"Good analogy, Gregry; it'll give me something to think
about. See you in three weeks this time; and don't forget to
have your wife check your blood pressure. Read the insert
about Prozac and whatever you do, don't drink any alcohol
while you're taking it."

As Gregry McHune walked toward the cashier's desk, Dr. Mark Goddard approached him in afterthought and spoke softly over his shoulder. "Or beer," he added.

Gregry's face crumpled in glee and his voice gurgled in soft laughter. "You won't do, Doc; you just won't do. You don't never turn nothing loose, do you? I'm outa here."

— ∎ —

Good morning, lovely young ladies lurking in the distant bowels of the record room with your headphones in place and your fingers tapping madly along while your lovely eyes are glued to the flicker of phosphorescent figures on that compelling and controlling computer screen. It is Saturday, March 9th, the sun is shining brightly, it is good to be alive, and you will never in a hundred years guess who this is beginning his dictation as bright-eyed and bushy-tailed as Frisky, the squirrel. Our first patient today, right on time and gratifyingly responsive to both treatment and interest, is none other than Mr. Gregry McHune, medical record number 07214. The patient reports that his BP at home has ranged from 130 down to 124 systolic and from 90 down to 84 diastolic. In the office today it is 126/82 and I am overjoyed. Plan of Treatment: Continue the Dynacirc and abstinence from alcohol. Return to clinic in three weeks. In addition, Mr. McHune reports that he is sleeping better, is more tractable and agreeable in the workplace and that his wife has told him in no uncertain terms to get some more of those pills. Plan of Treatment: Continue Prozac and return to clinic in three weeks to check on that also, provided that all goes well.

> *'Morning's at seven,*
> *The hillside's dew-pearled; . . .*
> *God's in his heaven—*
> *All's right with the world.'*

End of dictation. Thank you.

The resultant flurry in the transcription department did not on this occasion reach senior management. When Maryanne left off laughing, she called to her colleague, "My God, Kathy, you won't believe him this time. Let me rewind this tape and you listen. I can't believe any seventy-year-old carries on like this. He's crazy as a loon but it makes me feel good just to hear him. See if you think we have to notify the administrator about this one."

Kathy's response was immediate: "Maryanne, of course not. We don't have to type that first part; it's just a salutation to us. At least you can tell he's been in our department and knows there are real people in here. Some of the doctors I've typed for over the years didn't even know I existed. Dr. Goddard is downright cute as far as I'm concerned, and I don't want Mr. Bentley squelching him."

"Well, Bentley's the one who hired us and you know what he told us about poetry. There's no way you can get around that last line being poetry, for I remember having to read it in tenth grade English."

"Maryanne, it doesn't rhyme, and in the unlikely event the administrator even notices it, you can just play dumb and say you didn't know it was poetry."

"'Dew-pearled' doesn't rhyme with 'world?' Here, you type it. I'll get another one."

"It wouldn't work; he knows I'm not that dumb. But if you leave it off, Dr. Goddard will notice when he signs his dictation and be in here to make fun of us."

"Ah, go on back to your desk. I'll type it in for Dr. Goddard and take my chances with the powers that be. Didn't you love that part about 'the flickering phosphorescent figures on that compelling and controlling computer screen'?"

"I liked the part about 'lovely young ladies lurking in the bowels of the record room.' I've always wanted to lurk. Where does he get all that stuff? He's just plain cute. He really is."

Mark Goddard had not felt cute when he grasped his pocket dictaphone and dictated Gregry McHune's record; he had felt ecstatic; even a little triumphant.

Gregry's eyes were as watchful as ever, but there was a new brightness in them.

"Doc, don't you even come in here and set down lest you feel as good as I do."

"I feel great, Gregry. Tell me about yourself."

"You take my dad-blamed blood pressure and then you tell your own self about myself."

In the expectant silence, the puff of the inflating bulb and the hiss of escaping air from the cuff were as dramatic as a pointing drum. Gregory McHune again refrained from watching the pulsating needle, forcing a sense of ritual into this moment. As Mark pulled down the Velcro strapping and folded his instrument, even that action was tinged with drama by the tenseness of the waiting patient.

"Well?"

"Gregry, I can't believe it! Your blood pressure is down to 126/82. That's in normal range in anybody's book."

"That ain't all, Doc. It's been running that or even a little better at home for might near two weeks now."

"That's marvelous. The Dynacirc is not bothering you?"

The reply was laconic, careful. "Don't reckon it is. Ain't took none in a week."

"What?"

"The samples give out and since the pressure was doing so good I figured to wait and see if it went back up before I bothered you. Ain't that all right?"

"You can't argue with a sign post or with success, Gregry. What about the Prozac?"

The eyes remained feline, but the grin was wolfish. "I figured if I waited long enough you'd get around to asking that. I didn't want to come on too strong and commence to bragging because I figure a doctor with the big head would be more than I could stomach, but I'll tell you what my old lady said."

"All right, Gregry, what did your wife say?"

"She told me to get my butt back in here and stay on them pills or not to bother bout coming home."

"You mean she threatened to leave you?"

"Hell, no, Doc; you don't know my wife. She lined it out several years ago and made it clear that she might sometimes make me wish she would leave, but she wouldn't oblige me by actually doing it. That woman ain't no quitter. She's done stuck by me through too much."

"I take it, then, that she thinks you're doing better on the Prozac."

"Doing better? God, Doc, first thing she says when she comes in from work ever morning is, 'Have you took your Vitamin P yet?' She sees to it that I get it."

"She thinks you're sleeping better?"

"She don't know much about that except on the nights that she's off. You see, I work days and she works nights and that way we don't have to take the young'un to no day care center. She's not said nothing about my sleeping; she just brags on the way I'm acting around the house, says I'm even-tempered and don't prowl and pace no more, says I've calmed down and am fun to be around again."

"What do you think?"

"Well, now, to tell you the truth, Doc, and to bring this whole thing down to earth, I don't feel all that much different myself. I reckon she's right that I don't have as short a fuse as I did and things don't bother me at work like they did and seems like I get along better with people, but I'm still Gregry McHune."

"Of course you are. I wasn't trying to change you, Gregry."

"The hell you wasn't."

Mark Goddard's voice was sharp. Decisive. A little indig-

nant. "I most certainly was not. If there's one thing I have finally managed to learn in this world, it is that no one can
change anyone else."

Gregry's brow wrinkled above the widened eyes. "Hell, I've
learnt that too, Doc, and I 'spect I ain't more'n half as old
as you are. But I've also learnt that most folks don't never
give up on trying. Wives sure as hell don't, and if you don't
you're the first doctor I ever heard of who has give it up. Ain't
no use for you to blow smoke up my ass by saying you liked
me the way I was." His voice slowed. "No more'n I liked
myself."

There was a flicker in the eyes that reminded Mark Goddard of the sudden white flag of a startled doe. Very carefully,
he replied. "But I did, Gregry. And I do. Like you the way
you are. With no changes. And that's no smoke." He paused.
"Do you like yourself better?"

"Well, now, I never once came out and said I didn't like
myself, did I? You know, we're getting way off the subject
of whether I'm sleeping better. I'm here to tell you there ain't
no question about that; I ain't woke myself up yelling in over
a week now, and I've sure got more energy ever morning."

"Sounds like the Prozac, the Vitamin P, is doing what I hoped
it would. Do you miss drinking beer with your friends?"

"What friends?"

"I thought you told me you were going out and drinking
beer every night."

"What I told you, Doc, was that I drunk beer every night.
As I recollect I also told you me'n the old lady stay pretty much
to ourselves. I never told you I went out drinking beer with
my friends. Hell, Doc, I ain't got no friends."

"That's hard to believe."

"You can believe it. I've always been a loner. Specially the
last ten years, I'd say."

"What about the guys you work with?"

"Oh, I get along all right with them. We pass and repass, but we don't socialize. We ain't what you could call friends."

For a second Mark Goddard thought Gregry McHune was going to blink, but the moment passed. "Hell, Doc, I reckon you're the closest thing I've had to a friend since my granddaddy died. Except my wife, of course. She's the best friend I've ever had in my whole life."

Mark Goddard had interacted with patients for enough years that he could release a suspended breath with no sound. "Gregry, that's beautiful. I've known several men who were able to say that about their wives but they were all much older than you, had been through a lot of fires, a lot of bad times. You're a rich man."

"Even if I ain't got no money?"

"Maybe, Gregry, it's especially *because* you don't have any money."

"You're getting a little deep for me, there, Doc; I'll have to think on that one." The stained teeth flashed. "Anybody ever say your eyes ought to be brown?"

Dr. Goddard followed the lightening of mood as effortlessly as a trout rising in a dappled pool. "It has been mentioned, Gregry, always crassly." He laughed. "But it'll never happen. As you say, you think on it. I realized years ago that thinking must be very painful, or so many people would not avoid the process."

The eyes never left Dr. Goddard's face but there was merriment in them. "You'n just kiss my ass, Doc. I mean to tell you, you won't do. Trying to get ahead of you is like trying to piss off the back of a moving pickup without getting wet."

"I'm glad I remind you of your grandfather, Gregry."

"Hell, I never said you reminded me of him, Doc. You're always putting words in my mouth. I said you was the closest thing I'd had to a friend since he died. But come to think on it, and not to avoid none of that pain you talking about,

I guess the reason is that both of you have made me feel like
you give a shit."

"Well, Gregry, I guess that's as realistic a definition of friendship as a thinking man could ask. I'm proud to be included
in that list."

"You gonna write me a subscription for that Prozac?"

"I'll have to, Gregry; I'm out of samples. Ronnie's real good
about stocking me up on them, but I think every doctor in
the clinic is handing them out."

"Who's Ronnie?"

"The drug rep."

"Drug rep?"

"Yes. What your granddaddy and mine, too, for that
matter, would have called a drummer."

"I gotcha. When you want I should come back?"

"One month, Gregry. Four weeks. Leave off the Dynacirc,
but get your wife to keep checking your blood pressure
until I see you again."

"How long you aim for me to take this Prozac, Doc? She
told me to ask."

"At least six months is recommended. Maybe a year. Or
even longer if we need to; it's not habit-forming. But whatever you do don't stop taking it abruptly, and, Gregry, don't
drink more than an occasional beer while you're taking it."

"Hell, Doc, I don't even think about no beer any longer.
The old lady likes me better with Prozac than beer."

"Good."

"And, Doc."

"Yes, Gregry?"

"You're right. I do like myself better."

"See you in four weeks, boy."

Gregry turned and bestowed his pump-handle handshake
on Mark Goddard, but the grasp was firmer.

"Thanks for everthing, Doc."

Mark Goddard broke the gaze and fished the tape recorder from his pocket. "Out of here and let me get to work." His tone was pseudo-imperial, but his heart was singing.

Gregry McHune returned to clinic in three weeks instead of four. Dr. Goddard read the nurse's notes before entering the room. T 103. BP 120/80. Wgt 162. P. 100. C/O cough x2d, fever, and chill.

"Gregry! Good morning. What in the world has happened to you?"

The eyes blared but the luminescence was noticeably less. "Don't come at me this morning, Doc; I'm sicker'n a cat what's been eating streaky-field lizards. I thought it was just a cold, but when my fever went up to l03 last night after I had that chill, the old lady told me to get my ass over here, that I more'n likely got pneumonia."

"Are you coughing anything up?"

"Gobs of it. Greener'n a gourd. I tell you, Doc, I ain't felt this bad in I don't know when."

Dr. Goddard palmed the diaphragm of his stethoscope to warm it. "Slip your shirt off, Gregry, and swing around so I can listen to your chest."

The man pulled a flannel sweatshirt emblazoned with a Georgia Tech logo over his head, and compliantly twisted in his chair.

"That's fine. Now, open your mouth and breathe in and out. Deeply."

As the physician leaned over the back of his patient in search of rales, his attention was diverted by two tattoos, primitive and blue. On the left shoulder was a cross from which hung an awkwardly twisted Christ, drops of blood dripping blue from a spiculated crown. In the foreground, propped starkly against the foot of the cross was an envelope. The postmark sported "Heaven, U.S.A." around its periphery but a

muddied, illegible date in its center. The address itself, however, was very clear. "Gregry McHune, Esq." Directly beneath
the name, in even larger letters, was a facsimile of a stamped
directive: "Moved. Left no address. Return to sender."

On the right shoulder, as crudely crafted as seventh grade
bathroom art, was a supine female figure, legs drawn up, legs
spraddled, head obscured by two upright breasts, genitals gap-
ing wide and surrounded by hair that Mark Goddard noted
to be darker and thicker than the beard of Christ on the opposite shoulder. To the side of one leg was traced a bottle, replete
with cork, labeled "XXX." By the other, carefully placed so
that nothing obscured the flagrant center, was a pair of dice
showing a one on each upturned face, a five and a two on
the sides. Beneath the composite was a banner furled in
three folds, obvious vehicle for a three word motto, devoid
of print, shriekingly unfinished.

The doctor carefully made no comment, worked his
stethoscope alternately upward, reached finally Jesus on
one side, Lillith on the other, let the stethoscope dangle
from his neck.

"Gregry, you have rales in the right lower lung. I want to
get a chest x-ray."

"What you think, Doc?"

"I think you have pneumonia."

"Well, hell, Doc, you think I got pneumonia; my old lady
thinks I got pneumonia; I don't know no two people I trust
more'n y'all. How come you need a x-ray? Just treat the damn
stuff. I know good'n well, old as you are, you ain't always
had to get a x-ray on ever case of pneumonia you treated. I'm
always reading and hearing about medical costs going up and
this has got to be one of the reasons. Hell, I trust you and your
ears and your brain and your judgment. Let's don't waste no
money on a chest x-ray."

"I'll just be a son of a bitch," breathed Mark Goddard.

"What'd you say, Doc?"

"I said, 'Let me see what antibiotics I can find in the sample closet, Gregry. I'll be right back."

"Atta boy, Doc. I knew I could count on you. Trouble with some doctors is they got so much education they've forgot they had good sense."

This is Saturday, March 31, 1991. Number 231 beginning dictation. First patient is Gregry McHune. Medical record number 079214. He has all the signs and symptoms of acute lobar pneumonia that I learned in 1947 on the wards of Grady Memorial Hospital under the joint tutelage of a visiting consultant named Dr. L. Minor Blackford, who was as old as God, and the head of the Internal Medicine Department, Dr. Paul Beeson, who was as demanding of me as God. In obeisance to these two gentlemen and in accession to the request of the pragmatic Mr. McHune, trusting the sense, the intelligence, and the judgment with which I have been endowed, I am electing to treat the patient without radiological confirmation, thus saving seventy-two dollars and striking one puny blow at increased medical costs. Be it noted that when I studied at the feet of Dr. Beeson, the antibiotic available at that time would have been aqueous penicillin injected at four-hour intervals into alternating buttocks by student nurses who had no idea in those days of the dangers of sciatic neuropathy. Today I have given the patient some samples of Augmentin. He will take these 500 milligram pills by mouth every eight hours with food in the economic security of his own home and call me at my home tomorrow with temperature readings. If he progresses as expected, I will check him at the office again in one week and he will return to work shortly thereafter. What hath God wrought? Addendum: In honor of the historicity of this occasion, I am reverting to my original fee schedule when I first opened practice and charging the patient three dollars.

On Wednesday morning, there was flurry in the record room.

"Oh, my God, Kathy! Listen to this tape. There's no way we can bail him out of this one."

"Oh, my God! You're right, Maryanne. Hand it here and I'll take it to Bentley myself. Who is this Gregry McHune anyway? He sure sets old Dr. Goddard off."

Late on Monday afternoon, bidding his last patient of the day farewell, Mark Goddard looked into the grave countenance of the impeccable administrator. "Why, hello, Dennis. I rather thought I'd get to see you today. How are you doing?"

"Hello, Dr. Mark. Do you have a minute?"

"I'm through for the day, Dennis. Have a seat and relax. What can I do for you?"

Dennis Bentley took a deep breath. "Dr. Mark, there are certain metes and bounds within the discipline of permanent medical records that must not, given the litigious atmosphere under which we operate in the present day and age, ever, ever be transgressed. The peril of giving personal offense to you is very painful to me but is overshadowed by the responsibility I have to all of the physicians in this clinic in order to protect them from actions of any partner that might in the eyes of hostile attorneys or incredulous jurors appear irresponsible . . . ."

"Dennis!" interrupted Mark Goddard. "Do you have the slightest concept that I love you? Cut the crap and get to the point."

Dennis Bentley's eyes slipped left and then right; he took another deep breath and held out his hand. "Give me your dictaphone, Dr. Goddard."

"Sure, Dennis, but first listen to this tape I dictated Saturday morning before I left the office.

"*Attention: Transcription Department. Delete the previous dictation on Gregry McHune, medical record number 079214, and substitute the following: Patient has temperature of 103, productive cough, and fine crackling rales in the right lung base. Impression: Early pneumonia. Plan of Treatment: Augmentin 500 qhs with food. Patient to call me tomorrow for progress report and return to clinic one week for follow-up. No work until I see him again. BP 130/82. Continue present meds.*

"Do you still want to snatch my dictaphone?"

"Now, why did you do that, Dr. Mark?"

"Hell, Dennis, I haven't seen you in a week and I missed you; I knew that would bring you running. Then, too, it's the same impulse that made the Pope raise all the urinals in the Vatican to keep the Cardinals on their toes. Want to go to supper with me and the wife?"

"Thank you, no, Dr. Mark. Some other time. I need to get over to the record room and lower those urinals."

"Okay. Some other time then. Good night . . . . Say, Dennis!"

"Yes, sir?"

"Have fun, Son. You're supposed to."

"Sure, Dr. Mark. Whatever you say."

— ∎ —

Saturday, April 7, 1991. Number 231 beginning dictation. First patient in what bids to be a very busy morning in clinic is Gregry McHune, medical record number 079214. Patient feels perfectly well, has had no fever since 24 hours after beginning antibiotic therapy. He has a residual sporadic cough, otherwise is asymptomatic. Lungs are C&R to P&A except for scattered coarse rhonchi in the right base. His BP is 120/82, his sleeping pattern remains improved, his mood is level. Take Augmentin three more days; continue

*his Prozac; see me again in one month. I have advised
him again to break his tobacco addiction.*

Doc, last week I thought I was going to die and I more'n
likely would of done exactly that if it hadn't a been for
you and my old lady; this week I feel good as I ever did in
my whole life, and if it hadn't a been I promised you, I'd a
gone back to work on Monday. Check me over and let me
get outa here."

"Sure, Gregry. Slip your shirt off. Breathe in and out.
Through your mouth. Fine."

Again Mark Goddard faced the tattoos, was faintly
embarrassed by them. Lacking the time to address sincere questions and minus the mood to be flippant and casual, he
studiously avoided mentioning them, although they covered a significant area and impelled attention.

"You still have a few noises in that right lung, Gregry, where
your pneumonia is healing, but I think if you finish your ten
days of Augmentin you'll be all right. I think it will be safe
for you to return to work on Monday. I'll give you a note to
that effect."

"Thanks, Doc."

"Your blood pressure is unbelievably stable. I want you
to continue your Prozac."

"That's right. Don't you mess with my vitamin P, Doc. The
old lady says she'll lie, cheat or steal to keep me in that medicine."

Dr. Goddard smiled. "No problem, Sport. I told you I
want you on it for at least a year. By the way, Ronnie was
here a couple of days ago and I have some more samples
for you."

"Doc, you don't know how much I feel I owe you. I
don't aim to sound like no beggar, but those samples you give
me really do help out. My only brother got kilt last month

in a car wreck and the welfare people put his two-year-old twins in our custody and every little bit helps out."

"What? You have two extra children in your house now? You hadn't told me that."

"You never ast me."

"Why do you have them? Where is the mother? Aren't there any grandparents?"

"She's a crack addict, Doc, and don't nobody know where she's at. And to tell you the plain truth, the hell she's caused, nobody much gives a good goddam. Her mama already has three chirren what belong to another daughter and her only sister lives in a trailer in Florida and has got the emphysema so bad she has to be hooked up to oxygen all the time. Wasn't no other place for them babies to go."

"So now you have two-year-old twins that you're looking after while your wife works! I'm like her, don't you dare skip the Prozac. It's truly a miracle drug if it carries you through that increase in stress."

"Aw, hell, Doc, it ain't so bad. It's more'n made up for by them babies; they's the cutest little things you ever seen. Both of 'em redheaded boys, and just this week we got both of 'em broke from shitting in they little britches. So we're making progress. Least we ain't got to buy diapers no more."

"Gregry McHune, you are an epiphany. I am constantly amazed at the resilience of the human spirit and humbled by the manifestation of unanticipated gallantry."

"I don't understand all them words, Doc, so I ain't exactly clear what you're saying, but the same to you, I'm sure. You know you done become to be the best friend I got outside of my wife, don't you?"

"I'm honored, Gregry. Presuming on that assertion, let me push my luck. You worry about finances; yet you continue to buy cigarettes. You have witnessed the slow strangling death of emphysema in your own family; yet you continue to torture your own lungs. I have never seen a person smoke long enough without being required to pay for it, and I have never seen the bill rendered when the patient was willing to settle it. You have a lot to live for, and cigarettes are not worth dying for. Think about it. Try to break this addiction to tobacco."

"Hell, Doc, I never aimed to bring all that on. You know what? Your waiting room is packed this morning and you barely gonna have time to doctor, you sure as hell ain't got time to take up preaching. My granddaddy told me more'n oncet that a urge to preach was same as a itch to meddle. You want to see me in a month?"

"Yes, Gregry. Just remember I have only one thing to push, and that's your health. I make no money from corpses."

"Hell, if you treat many folks the way you do me I don't see how you make a living nohow. You make precious little off of me. I'm outa here. You get to work."

In May, Dr. Goddard arose to one of the delightful mornings that steal earlier and earlier upon the land after the spring equinox, thinking that Lowell had been a month late in his proclamation of perfect days but that June was probably essential to his rhyme scheme. He stepped out into the tingling grass-wet dawn, into light evolving quickly from soft grayness into muted rosiness and then into sparkling silver. He thrilled to the flutes and whistles of bird song and noted the soft sibilance of tiny wings dipping and darting through air that seemed to him too thin and clear to support even their feathered weight. They must, he fancied, be tossed like darts from some gleeful hand out of Heaven. He sucked in great draughts of flower fragrance, reveled in the coursing of his own blood, and whispered aloud, "Dear God, this is magic."

After a while he went inside, showered, watched the news, and went to the office.

Gregry McHune! What brings a workaholic like you out on a Tuesday? Are you feeling all right?"

"A little weak and no appetite yet but I'm feeling great, Doc. I come by early in the week cause the old lady got a day off and I ast my boss for a day of vacation time. We decided soon as I seen my friend, the doctor, we'd get the kids together and take 'em on a picnic."

"Well, Gregry, your blood pressure is 120/80 right now. I don't need to tell you that's normal. I also don't need to ask about the Prozac; you're obviously doing well on that. I think a picnic is a marvelous idea. You wouldn't have even thought of one a year ago, would you?"

"You got that straight, Doc. I'd a been setting at home sucking on a six-pack and nursing the black ass. A heap of things has changed."

"Where are you planning on having your picnic?"

"Soon as them two-year-olds get up from they nap we going bout fifty miles down the road toward Warm Springs. I hear tell they got free picnic tables on Pine Mountain in Roosevelt State Park, and the days is got long enough now we'll loll around and eat supper and still get home before dark."

"It's a pretty place; I've been there. Have a good time. I want you to keep watching your blood pressure and let me see you again in two months."

"You think I'm doing that good, Doc?"

"You well may be. I don't understand everything I'm seeing, but it's worth a trial. Your wife can check your BP and if it goes up significantly, call me."

"Is that all, Doc?"

"That's enough, isn't it?"

"Not quite, I don't think. I told you you'd done got to be my friend as well as my doctor, didn't I? Well, a guy looks out for his friend, pays attention to him, if you know what I mean, and seems to me you ain't just exactly what some might call your usual meddlesome, bossy self. You ain't bouncing around this morning like you was just sixty years old and could run the life of any and everbody stuck they head in the door. Seems like you're down or something; if you wasn't so educated I might even call it a little touch of the black ass in you, but I know it's got to be something fancier than that." The voice made a soft skip-step in cadence; the eyes blared wide; a definite twinkle shone briefly golden. "Perhaps you don't like yourself too well this morning, Dr. Goddard."

Mark Goddard laughed aloud. "'Physician, heal thyself.' Thank you, Gregry; I deserved that. You are a most perceptive young man." He deliberated over his watch dial a moment. "To tell you the truth, your terminology, although crassly graphic, may be as accurate as anything I could conjure up from the medical texts. When I got up this morning, I spent some time in my garden, totally convinced of the perfection of the Universe. Then I went inside and found my wife watching the gospel according to Gumbel and made the mistake of joining her. I began reflecting on the skill with which the visual media manipulate public opinion and decided that the ubiquitous electronic box, with its satellite feeders and its edited film, has become Plato's cave; that we are once again chained together in a row; that we are forced to look at reflected figures on the back of our cave until we accept the shadows as reality."

"Wait a minute, Doc. You talking about TV?"

"For the most part, yes."

"You done about left me behind, you know. Remember who you talking to and tell me in plain English what's eating at you."

"We're brainwashed."

"We are?"

"Yes!"

"Who?"

"All of us. Everybody! You! Me!"

"Who's doing that?"

"That's what I'm telling you, Gregry. The glib, authoritative, pseudointellectual, pseudoliberal TV anchormen with their shallow, shifting values and their satrapy of twinkling, hair-sprayed, short-skirted sob sisters, all of them panting after success and whoring for recognition."

"You done lost me again, Doc. I sure love to listen to you, but I just be goddamned if I believe anybody's brainwashed you."

"It's close, Gregry."

"I can tell how you feel, but I ain't yet figured out exactly what you feeling that way about, if you know what I mean. What jerked your trip-wire, so to speak? Gimme a for instance."

As Mark Goddard opened his mouth, Gregry McHune added, "In everyday English, Doc."

"Oh, get off my back, Gregry, and stop pulling my leg; you understand every word I say. I guess what's got me in a bad mood today is the fact that I've let the TV commentators make me feel like a racist, when I know full well I'm not one."

"Now, I understand the words, Doc, but I don't know where you're coming from."

"I was watching the replay of the replay of the latest riots in Los Angeles and having to look at the rerun of the rerun of the rerun of that black man being beaten by police-men, and all of a sudden I realized that I had a surfeit, a belly-ful if you will. I am sick and tired of eighty percent of the attention of this country being directed to a fifteen percent racial minority, with the ding-donging everlasting harangu-ing away that any time black people do anything wrong they should receive immediate absolution; that they are only rioting and stealing and plundering because they are perse-cuted by American white people and they consequently should be accorded special privileges and consideration since their ancestors were oppressed.

"Hell, Gregry, this entire continent doesn't have anybody on it whose ancestors somewhere weren't oppressed; that's why they came to America in the first place. And if you want to get racial about it, look at the Orientals, the Koreans, the Vietnamese; they haven't been here a generation yet and they got here with the extra barrier of not knowing English, and already they are spelling champions and it's hard to find one on the welfare rolls.

"And the Japanese. If anybody wants an example of how the American Government has discriminated against a racial minority, look at the confiscation of property and internment we imposed on the Japanese in World War II. But at the time it seemed the thing to do. How much do you know about that? You can't remake history.

"Also you don't hear any Chinese whining and rioting and raising hell because they were starved and beaten and kicked around when the railroads were built in California. Our books are so full of laws not only to protect blacks but to favor them, that if I were a black person I'd be ashamed to look a Vietnamese or a Japanese or a Cherokee Indian in the face."

"You're hot, ain't you, Doc?"

"You're mighty right I'm hot. You cannot prove any theorem when you begin with two false hypotheses: Number one, that if you're black you've been mistreated; and number two, if you're white you're a persecuting racist. What then is the inevitable conclusion? It's that, subliminally at least, I am responsible for inducing the riots in Los Angeles. Well, I'm not! I know Blacks as individuals, not as a mob, and they are great friends and proud people. I'm not any more responsible for those folks breaking windows and stealing TV sets than my black friends are. Just because I am covered with white skin does not mean that I hate black peo-

ple. We live together in harmony in this county. I have
never in my life physically abused any African-American, and
I'm sure you haven't either."

Mark Goddard paused for confirmation. Gregry McHune
was staring at him, his eyes non-committal.

"Doc, that ain't what I call 'em, but I know what you mean."

"And the homosexuals, Gregry. Now, there's another
minority I'm tired of seeing glorified. They can't help it, and
I've had a lot of friends through my life who are homosex-
ual, but dammit, they didn't flounce around and flaunt it. I
wish they'd all get back in the closet and quit raising hell for
the nation to accept their deviation as an 'alternative lifestyle.'
And TV has now got you feeling guilty if you don't go
along with that. That's what I mean by we're being brainwashed."

"Well, maybe you are, Doc, but I ain't."

"What do you mean, Gregry? You've never physically abused
a gay or a black, have you?"

Gregry McHune was as motionless as an alerted doe.
Only his eyes manifested life. Mark Goddard thought they
looked imploring.

"Not unless you want to count that one I kilt, I ain't."

"Come on," scoffed the doctor. "You don't mean to tell
me you killed a gay."

"I don't know nothing about his sex life, but he was
blacker than the far side of hell, and you ain't got no call for
to let them TV folks make you feel guilty about nothing. Them
niggers hate us worse'n you ever thought about hating them."

Mark Goddard winced. "That's the N word, Gregry, and
that's enough to make them hate us. It's taboo around here,
unless you're black yourself. I had a friend a long time ago,
before 1954, who said there wasn't anything in the world that
would have made him madder than being one except for somebody to call him one. You're not sitting there telling me you

killed a black man and expecting me to believe it, are you?"

"You can suit yourself about that, Doc, but that coon's deader'n a doormat, and it sure wasn't no accident. I done time
for it."

"You what?"

"They sent me to jail. I served eight years."

"Tell me about it, Gregry. Right now."

"Well, it was on Christmas Eve and I had went by Sears
Roebuck over in Buckhead to pick up a Christmas present
for a friend and they didn't have what I wanted. The lady got
on the phone and said they had one in a store on the south-
side over close to East Point and they would hold it for me,
but they was closing in haffa hour. I jumped in my old car
and made it over there and to this day I don't remember paying a lot of attention to where I parked, I was so set on getting that present on time. This great big black guy comes up
to me in the parking lot out of nowhere and stuck a .45 right
between my eyes.

"'Gimme your money,' he says."

"'Fuck you!' I said."

"Then, Doc, I seen him tighten his finger on that trigger
and I seen the light in his eyes and I ducked my head to one
side. I mean quick. The bullet grazed me just above my left
ear and all along the side of my head. I reached down to my
leg for my gun and he lowered his and shot again. I seen by
his eyes which way he was aiming and was able to twist enough
so's that one went through my shirt, but I knowed I wouldn't
get another turn at bat. I stuck my pistol right in his chest and
blowed him from here to kingdom come."

"You had a gun?"

"Sure, Doc. My granddaddy told me always to carry a gun
on me, especially if I was going to be in town. He was the one
what taught me to shoot, and he always said, 'Gregry, don't
never pull your gun less you gonna use it.' That's the first time

I ever drawed on anybody, Doc. And come to think of it, it was the last time, too. I've always minded him."

"What happened?"

"Well, hell, Doc, I went home. I looked around the parking lot and remembered real quick what part of town I was in. Wasn't nothing to be done for that bastard what tried to kill me; he was laying there deader'n hell. Way I looked at it, it had been him or me and he was the one what started it. Christmas by then, of course, was done ruint for both of us but, everthing considered, I'd a damn sight rather been in my shoes than his. I wondered for a minute what my granddaddy would've told me to do now, but he hadn't never carried me this far along with his advice; so I just got in my car and left before I drawed a crowd. Seemed like the sensible thing to do."

Although Gregry's eyes were fixed with unblinking and brooding intensity on those of the doctor, Mark Goddard sensed they were focused on a point well beyond the back of his head. He sat still and quiet. Gregry drew a long, faintly audible breath.

"You know, it was a funny thing. I set there in my little old living room-kitchen watching TV all night. I drinked six beers in a row and didn't get drunk or yet the least bit sleepy, never even felt 'em. I kept watching and watching TV, but I never seen a blessed thing on that screen. TV never brainwashed me that night, Doc. All I seen was that man's eyes looking at me and him a-falling. A-falling down and away right in front of my eyes, Doc. He never crashed backwards like they do in the movies; he just got limber all over and slid down on spraddled knees like he was a-melting on down into the ground and in a minute wasn't going to be nothing but a puddle. I thought his fingers wasn't never going to turn loose and let his gun drop, but they finely did. And all the time his eyes was a-looking at me and you could tell he knowed what I had done and knowed what was happening, that he was, by God, dying. That was over eight years ago, Doc, and I can still see him as plain as day and his knowing eyes."

Gregry McHune rose from his chair. His voice was no less authoritative for being even, soft, almost without inflection.

"Stand up, Doc."

Mark Goddard obeyed silently.

"Look at me, Doc." The eyes were hypnotic. "This is the way he done. He fell off just like this, slow and easy-like, right in front of me and as close to me as I am to you. A-looking at me all the time, like I'm a-looking at you. I'n see it right now plain as I could then, him a-falling and him a-knowing. This is the way he done."

Mark Goddard broke the spell by reseating himself. Gregry McHune interrupted his flaccid pantomime and followed suit.

"My God, Gregry," the doctor breathed.

"You'n say that again, Doc, over and over. I have. But," he held up a finger, "don't you put in to feel sorry for me. I never would have got into all this but you ast me had I ever physically harmed one and it jerked my trip-wire." The mouth opened wider and a short laugh bubbled softly through the stained teeth. "And course, that come on from me inquiring ever so politely, thank you, what had jerked your trip-wire this morning. One thing sure leads to another, don't it, Doc? Guess that'll learn me about meddling in your private business."

Mark Goddard took a breath to reply, but Gregry held up a silencing finger once more. "Let's get down to the nitty-gritty, Doc. You was saying that TV makes you feel guilty about the way them folks is treated. I want you to know I don't feel guilty. Not one bit. It's a load on you to kill a man, but I keep telling you about them eyes. They was a-knowing, Doc, them eyes was knowing, but you know what else? Them eyes was hating, Doc. They was full of hate like you never seen in your life and I hope to God you never will. If he'd of had the strength to pull that trigger again, I wouldn't be setting here. I don't feel guilty, I feel grateful. I'm grateful at least I never hated that guy. I kilt him and I'm glad if one of us has to be dead, it's him. I feel grateful out loud to my granddaddy ever day I live.

"And you for sure and certain ought not to feel guilty, Doc. Let me tell you something. When you see one them gangs busting in a store window and one of them black dudes running off with a TV set, it ain't cause his granddaddy was a slave, or cause no black man got whipped up on by white police, or because he thinks his civil rights been violated; it's because, by God, he wants a TV without having to pay for it. Now that's my opinion and it's sure as hell true. I done lived with more of them than you'll ever meet, Doc, and you can carry that opinion to the bank."

"Lived with them, Gregry?"

"I told you I done time, Doc. Hell, yes, I lived with them. You have to, in jail. Seventy percent of the prisoners in this state is black, Doc, and eighty percent of them is queer, and that's another thing you ain't got no call to let TV brainwash you about. Them guys might not can help being homo, but they can, by God, restrain theyselves from acting on it. That goes to the bank, too, Doc."

Mark Goddard's tone was wary. "Gregry, you're accumulating quite a savings account for me."

"Now don't get started, Doc. I ain't done yet. As you can probly imagine, I studied a heap about what had happened, and that's when I done my wrassling with what it pleases you to call guilt. That black man didn't know me from Adam's off-ox, but he was aiming to steal my money I'd worked hard for and to blow my brains out in the process. Now that was what was wrong, Doc, and in my eyes, what everbody should oughta feel guilty about is stealing and murdering. All I done was keep him from doing it, and in the process keep that guilt off'n his back. So in a sense I done him a favor as well as my own self. Not to mention society or whatever you want to call it. I ain't felt guilty since I spent all night thinking about it.

"And when I look around at my wife and family and realize how much I'm finally enjoying being alive after all I been through, and that's thanks to you and that Vitamin P you dish out, then I ain't the least bit sorry for what I done, Doc. And you ought not to let them TV folks what lives with blow-dryers get to you. It'd make me dizzy to calculate the money they make and they don't know chicken salad from Shinola, if you want to talk nice about it. You let one of them get held up or raped and mugged and you'd get a different tune out of 'em."

"I'll put that on my deposit slip too, Gregry. Did you go to the police on Christmas Day?"

"Hell, no, I didn't. I went to work the day after Christmas. If I hadn't done nothing wrong and I hadn't committed no crime, I didn't see no sense in making no big to-do over it. I went about my business like any sensible man would do and I didn't even think about going to the police. Turned out weren't no need to anyhow. Two weeks after Christmas they come to me."

"They did?"

"Yeah. In the evening whilst I was watching TV and drinking a beer. They was right nice, too, in they own way, and so was I, in mine. They knocked on the door and said, 'Did you kill a man in the Sears parking lot on Christmas Eve?' And I said, 'I sure did,' and told 'em what happened. One of 'em said, 'Why hadn't you told us about this before now?' and I said, 'Hell, you never ast me.' Now, Doc, if them ain't the words of an innocent man I ain't setting here."

Mark Goddard nodded accord. "Gregry, those are certainly the last words I would expect to hear from the lips of a guilty man."

"Thanks, Doc. One of them police even said to me, 'We'd never a found you if you'd got rid a that car and not left it parked out there in the street sticking out like a sore thumb. A witness seen it leaving the parking lot.' And, I said, 'Hell, man, I didn't have nothing to hide. Take me on in.' So they did. Leastwise they told me to follow 'em on down to jail in my car. And, Doc, that's when the education of Gregry McHune begun."

"Education?"

"Right. That's when I commenced to carving out a whole new life. Hell, I hadn't never even had a parking ticket or been stopped for speeding or nothing. Closest I ever been to the law before was back in Kentucky. Ever four years the sheriff come to my granddaddy's home electioneering, never bothered to notice my granddaddy no other time. That sheriff had skin like a baby's butt and pink cheeks and curly black hair always looked like he'd sneaked in and spent some time in Bettye-Jo's Beauty Box agetting it set. He could keep the sharpest crease in his britches you ever seen. And shiny shoes? Man, I mean he was flat out a dude. Mr. Metters, that's what I called my granddaddy cause that's what Miss Lila, his second wife, called him till the day he died, would cut hisself a chew of Brown Mule and offer the plug to the sheriff as nice and friendly and polite as you please and listen him out and solemn promise he'd vote for him.

"Soon as he left, Mr. Metters would spit out his cud of baccy and one time he told me, 'Gee-boy, whenever somebody asts you to vote for 'em, be sure to tell 'em you will. Ain't no way nowadays they'n tell how you mark that ballot when you get in that voting booth. When you in there you'n do what you damn well please, but ain't no call to get a candidate fretted ahead of time. They all sensitive as briers about who votes for 'em and who don't. Most elections ain't nothing but popularity contests no how.

"'Twelve years ago I come within a gnat's ass of telling that dandified young whippersnapper that I wasn't about to vote for no spoiled brat that I knowed had slept in the same bed with his mama twell he was sixteen years old, and then when he got his first job working for State Revenue had shot an unarmed man in the back and kilt him cause he was running from a liquor still and about to get away. Been a big mistake had I run my mouth. He oncet had a deal with one of the Tomlins across the creek who was running liquor, and then he double-crossed and stole from him. The Tomlin boy tells me, "I know I'm a crook, but hell, that Sheriff's a damn dishonest crook." Now you think on that, Son. When a Tomlin calls you a crook, you're low-downer'n a mole's navel. Look at him now. Done turned into a little Hitler and got more power than anybody in the county and crazy for more.

"'Ain't nothing in the world can turn out to be as mean and full of revenge as a mama's darling if he ever gets a little authority. He's bent and determined to have his own way in everthing and with everbody. Gee-boy, allus tell a candidate what you think he wants to hear and then vote independent.' Now, that's all the experience I'd had with the law, Doc, till I got carried to jail that night in Atlanta, Georgia."

"Well, Gregry, Kentucky sure sounds interesting. I'd like to hear more sometime about your grandfather, but you've wandered off the subject. We were talking about your education. Did you go to training school or something?"

"Hell, no! I went to prison. For eight years. I'm talking about Jewish prudence, the court system. I mean I learned a heap about all that. Mr. Metters used to look at some of the teachers in Kentucky and tell me you could educate a fool and he'd still be a fool, and that's true enough, I reckon, but, Doc, you're looking at a man what had the fool educated *out* of him. The hard way."

"Yes?"

"Right. They took me down and ast me questions like you wouldn't believe. Told me first I had the right to remain silent. I told 'em again that I didn't have nothing to hide and also that I had been raised not to tell no lies except about politics, and, Doc, I told my guts. It was the first time I had talked to a living soul about it and, tell you the truth, it felt good. Only part I left out was about the eyes. They never ast nothing about his eyes and I never told 'em. I figured they wouldn't understand that part nohow.

"I reckon I talked to them for two hours, and I was sure careful to explain about self-defense and all that. Those two cops, they called theyselves detectives, was real nice, looking back on it. Called in a magistrate and I guess I was lucky there. Mr. Metters said once that magistrates was like little kids what was trying to play like they was judges when they didn't have the education for it, the which our chief magistrate back in Kentucky sure enough couldn't even read and write and on top of that didn't have no common sense neither, for he'd been married three times. I got a good one though and he charged me with carrying a concealed weapon and let me go home on bond.

"The police told me not to leave the state and all that, advised me to get a lawyer. I told 'em, hell, I didn't need no lawyer cause I hadn't done nothing wrong and that I wasn't going nowhere but back to work the next morning. And you know, Doc, I felt pretty good about things? I sure didn't feel no guilt about carrying that gun, the which it was concealed, of course, cause you'd look like a sure enough idiot if you walked around with one strapped around your middle, and me and them cops had worked everthing out real smooth, I thought. Yessir, I thought everthing was settled although it didn't do a dad-blamed thing about them knowing, hating eyes till I'd had about four beers."

"What happened, Gregry?"

"Well, a heap happened, Doc. First off, I got myself engaged. I'd run into this girl who was working in the Waffle House to pay her way through nursing school at a place called Clayton Junior College. Name of Sharon. But something about her reminded me of all the good girls I had knowed growing up, and I remembered a line from some Bible verses I learned in church one time with my granddaddy, and I called her Rose right off the bat. Been my private name for her ever since."

"John Steinbeck," whispered the doctor.

"How's at?"

"*The Grapes of Wrath*, I think. Steinbeck had a wonderful character named Rose of Sharon."

"Well, I got mine from the Bible, and she was a wonderful character in Atlanta. She come from a farm close to a little bitty country town called Metter, Georgia, and that reminded me of my granddaddy. I had told her so and we had been passing and repassing with each other and after they sent me home on bail seemed like everthing was going my way and I got up the nerve to ast her out. She talked real nice and proper and used good English and all that but wasn't the least bit stuck up, and hell, Doc, I flat fell head over heels, as they say, for Rose of Sharon, a condition I ain't never recovered from in all the years since and hope I never do."

"You're fortunate, Gregry. In fact, you are blessed."

"You'n save them words for somebody what don't know it, Doc. She's one of the few women I ever met who can listen and one of the extremely few who will. I'm usually pretty close-mouthed, always have been till I run into Rose and then here lately, you; but I bout talked her ears off. And you know what, Doc? She said she loved me. Said she wasn't going to advise me about no lawyer, I was a growed man and could make my own decisions, and that she didn't know a thing to do about them eyes long as I helt it down to four beers, but that she loved me.

"Lord, I thought I was going to bust. I went out and bought her the nicest finger ring I could afford, cost me $249.99, plus tax, but it had a set in it you could at least see, and that without too bright a light. She moved in my place and we was aiming to get married soon as she finished nursing school and could get some time off for a little trip. Then I went through what I guess they mean when I hear 'em talking about 'continuing adult education' and everthing went to hell in a bucket. Don't never allow yourself to get too happy, Doc, cause you're sure liable to hit rock bottom soon."

"Peaks are frequently followed by valleys, Gregry."

"Sounds like we're saying the same thing, Doc. I'll think on it."

"Your education?"

"Right. It was just beginning. You might say I had so far just been to the first day of classes and now school was fixing to start. I decided, since everthing was going so good with Rose and all, that I might as well lay out a little money on a lawyer. Not that I felt I was guilty of nothing serious or nothing like that, you understand, but just to be on the safe side, a little insurance against bad luck, if you know what I mean. I ast around, got me a good one and went and talked to him. Give him $200 retaining fee,which means it kept him on my side if I needed him, the which that was a heap of money, but I figured if I was aiming to become a family man I could just count on some expense and some responsibility, the two of 'em pretty well going hand in hand if you think on it, Doc."

"The lawyer, Gregry."

"He said I had a point and might come out all right, that the charges could be defended, but best to wait and see what the grand jury done. Now the grand jury is something I hadn't never had no experience with atall and, God willing, will never have again. They sit up and listen to the

D.A. and the police and any witnesses they want to, except they don't never lay eyes on the accused nor listen to his side of the story or nothing. They supposed, my lawyer said, to consider the evidence and decide probable cause and if they is enough evidence of a crime to warrant prosecution. Lawyers can talk as fancy in they own way as doctors can in theirs.

"Anyhow, the grand jury met and here come the police again, put handcuffs on me, scared Rose half to death, and hauled my ass to jail. Said I had been charged with murder. You better believe I hollered for that lawyer then. I was mad enough to fight, kept yelling to them police it wasn't murder, it was self-defense, but they pushed me to the car and yanked my head down and throwed me in the back seat real efficient and businesslike as if they couldn't hear what I was saying or else didn't give a rat's ass. Back seat of that police car didn't have no door or window handles on the inside and they was a heavy steel mesh twixt the front and the back; it was a regular sweet little prison cell on wheels, Doc. I felt like I was smothering and then I felt like I was going to shit and then I was going to puke up and then I broke a sweat, and all in all it was one helluva ride. Worse'n anything you've ever put a guy through, Doc."

"I haven't put you through much, and there are those that would disagree with you, but go ahead."

"The lawyer told me to calm down and not discuss my case but to be respectful to everbody I seen and to cooperate and he'd be back to see me after I was processed. Now that word by itself is enough to scare the living hell out of a farm boy what's dressed hogs and shot venison, Doc, but I remembered Mr. Metters telling me if I ever got in a tight or into something over my head and didn't know what to do my ownself to listen to somebody what knowed more about the situation than I did. I figured that was the case right there between me and that lawyer so I'd follow his directions, besides the which he had a level eye on him and $200 of my money in his pocket. I stayed quiet as I could and said 'yessir' and 'no sir' to everbody spoke to me them first two days, even the trusties what swept the floor. Mr. Metters also said one time that a man don't learn nothing by talking, he learns by listening."

"I'm listening, Gregry."

"You sure as hell are, Doc, and I hope I'm learning you something. This was a whole new world for me and I know you got no idea atall about it, like I myself didn't know I was fixing to be in that world and have to live a whole new life in it. The lawyer come to see me regular and he jowered with the DA back and forth and after a week of me being locked up and wearing them orange cotton uniforms and them little scuffy flats that no self-respecting queer would be caught dead in at the grocery store, he laid it out to me. He said I'd been indicted for murder, which that was a capital offense, and that he's arranged for me to plead guilty and I wouldn't have to serve but eight years. He walked out while I was still ranting and said he'd be back in three days, that he figured it'd take that long for me to calm down and start thinking straight. It took him four more trips and two conferences with Rose. I tell you, I wasn't what you'd call easy in those days, Doc."

"I can imagine."

"We argued back and forth, in and out, up and down, and I have to say he listened to everthing I had to say and to this day I am convinced that he done the very best he could for me. Finely I seen he had about reached the end of his patience; he said, 'Gregry, I keep telling you that you have been indicted for murder and that is a capital offense and in the state of Georgia you just might get sent to the electric chair. I understand you are convinced it was self-defense and so, for that matter, am I, but you know the racial balance in this community as well as I do and any jury we could pick in this county is liable to be biased against you to

start with. You are gambling with your life and I personally think eight years in prison for a plea of manslaughter is
preferable. You are a competent adult, however, and I can't
tell you what to do. I can only advise you.'

"I studied a minute and told him, 'I'm innocent of murder or manslaughter. I'd be pleading to a lie. My mind is made
up. I want to go to court. What I want is justice.' You
know what my lawyer told me, Doc? He said, 'Gregry, for
God's sake wake up and smell the coffee. If you want justice, go to a whorehouse. If you want to get fucked, go to
court.' He most certainly did. He told me that right out of
his own mouth.

"You can believe that jerked my neck and made me figure he was on the inside and knowed more'n I did and I better, by God, remember Mr. Metters and listen to him. I had-
n't never had nothing explained to me that plain before. You
ain't never seen a man change his mind fast as I did."

"That's unbelievable, Gregry."

"I've no doubt my whole life is from where you set, Doc,
but to me and a heap of others it's real as dirt. The lawyer
arranged for me and Rose to get married because she wouldn't
have it no other way. Had a preacher, too, wouldn't settle for
no JP. She graduated from nursing school, first in her class
she was, and next day I stood up before the judge and got
assigned to my honeymoon. I tell you, Doc, you don't mess
with no judge. If a sheriff is like Hitler, a judge is like God
Almighty at the Second Coming. He don't have to take no
shit off nobody. He ast me if I understood what I was doing
and he ast me if I had made any bargain with anybody
about sentences and all that and I looked him in the eye and
lied like a dog and said, 'No, sir,' and he give me eight
years. Just like that."

"Honeymoon, Gregry? That's a philosophical way of
looking at it."

"Well, that's what it was. See, what I had married was not Rose of Sharon; it was prison and I couldn't get no divorce for eight years. For a week I was locked up tight in one jail whilst they filled out papers and interviewed me ever now and then. I set around and talked to the other prisoners, or rather listened to them talk, and I learnt everthing they is worth knowing about Jewish prudence and what life in prison was really going to be like. Some them men was real jailbirds, been in and out, mostly in, all they lives. One of 'em told me soon as I got out of maximum security I might as well make up my mind I was probly going to get raped and not by a man of my own color, if you catch the drift of what I'm saying. All of a sudden I seen the next eight years laying there before me like a deep dark hole in hell, Doc, and I was plumb scairt half to death.

"I never said nothing, but I made up my mind to two things. I made up my mind that no matter what happened I was going to survive. I didn't know how, but I was going to survive and come out of prison and get back to Rose of Sharon. I was not, by God, gonna die in jail. The other thing was: Nobody was going to touch me. I figured that anything what anybody said to me wasn't going to get no fight or even a rise out of me because, if you're tough enough, words out of somebody else's mouth is they own farts and may stink for a little while but can't really dirty you. The wind will blow them away. But I swore that nobody, by God, better ever lay a finger on me. Anywhere. Any time. For any reason. Now, you just quit looking at your watch, Dr. Goddard. I got a few more things to tell you and them sick folks can just wait a little longer. This is between me and you."

Mark Goddard felt a little defensive for getting caught feeling pressured. He was very conscious of the demands on his time and through his years of practice had always been reflexively responsive to those demands. It was ingrained in him that he could not slow down or rest until his office was cleared of patients. "Gregry, you're right about there being sick people out there. Let me check on them for a few minutes and you sit here and wait for me. Are you sure this isn't making you late for your picnic?"

"Wasn't aiming nohow to leave till after dinner, lunch you call it, Doc. The old lady's got some things to do this morning and has took all the younguns with her. I got another thing or two I want to tell you now as we done got started on all this. I'll wait."

"Gregry, I've been fretting over your blood pressure, your insomnia, your depression for months now. Did it not occur to you that these events might have had some effect on them? Why hadn't you told me all this before?"

The eyes were alert and feline; there was possibly a twinkle of mirth in their yellow glow. The voice was as soft and inflectionless as ever. "Hell, Doc, you never ast me."

"Touché, Gregry McHune. I'll be back."

He rapidly saw and treated three sore throats, one follow-up for diabetes, two follow-ups for hypertension, one case of sinusitis and one common cold for which he prescribed antibiotics, unwilling to take the time to educate and argue.

He told his nurse, "Judy, if you have someone real sick, interrupt me or get the other doctor to see him; Mr. McHune needs to talk to me some more." Aware of Judy's quizzical look, he added, "And to tell you the truth, I need to hear him talk some more."

Back in the treatment room, Gregry McHune shifted in his chair and laid down his magazine as Mark Goddard casually seated himself.

"Pardon that interruption, Gregry. I appreciate your calling my attention to those other patients; I had completely forgotten myself."

The reply was laconic. "No call to apologize but I will point out twasn't none of me looking at his watch. You know, Doc, Mr. Metters used to tell me, 'Gee-boy, watch out for anybody you see wearing one them wrist watches; next thing you know he's liable to take up playing golf.' He was right about don't never pull your gun less you're aiming to shoot, but nowadays everbody, including me, has took to wrist watches and I 'spect even he would have to admit they're right handy."

"Right, Gregry. My grandfather carried a pocket watch also, but we're caught up in a faster, more frantic lifestyle now and need to know the hour and minute more frequently that our ancestors did. What happened after your month in maximum security?"

"They sent me to another maximum security, Doc, is what they did. I thought for awhile I could talk 'em into sending me close to Atlanta to a open facility so I'd get to see Rose now and then if it ever come around to them letting me have visitors. I'll never know what they was aiming to do cause all of a sudden everbody quit acting nice and I become a four-star vicious convict, which meant that you are now a animal in the jungle and you got no right to 'sociate with human beings. It also means ain't no judge, no jury, no warden, no guard, nobody in Jewish prudence anywhere is ever again going to believe a goddam word you say and so you might as well save your breath; all because I stabbed that dude."

"You stabbed a man?"

"Damn right I did."

"Did he die?"

"Nah, although the way he hollered and carried on you'd athought he was fixing to. I tell you, Doc, the law's idea of self-defense just don't jibe with mine atall and nobody would even listen to my side of what happened. All they wanted was a explanation of where I got the fountain pen in the first place."

"Fountain pen?"

"Yep, that's what I still call it, a fountain pen. Just like that ball-point you got there in your pocket. That's what I stabbed him with.

"The warden in that prison had a rule, Doc, that if you was walking down the halls, 'corridor' he called it, you had to have the tip of your shoulder touching the wall else the guards would raise hell. I never seen no sense to it myself because them halls are some of the widest I ever was in, but that was the warden's rule and it was his prison, and I sure as hell didn't want to attract no attention and I most certainly didn't want the job of lining out the way that bunch of animals was going to live. Like I say, it was his prison and his hall and his wall and his rule and I regarded myself as a temporary visitor just passing through. I was walking along all by myself with my shoulder touching—had to lean a little to do it—and this dude come up behind me walking fast and said, 'Coming by.' I said, 'Come on, then,' and, Doc, as he went by me he reached out and run a finger up the inside of my left leg just below my ass."

"What? What did he do that for?"

"Well, if you want concrete evidence, Doc, we'll never know, will we? Cause he never said a word and I didn't neither. I just grabbed my fountain pen and quick and fast, hard as I could, I stuck it in his arm. Just below his shoulder. Rammed it all the way to the clip what holds it in your pocket. He screamed for all the world like a rabbit oncet that I seen a fox catch back in Kentucky. Went running down the hall with my fountain pen sticking out yelling for the guard. You never heard such a ruckus in your life.

"And you know what, Doc? They put me in solitary confinement for a week. They call that particular prison a diagnostic and correction center and I learnt right quick that far as I personally was concerned, I was shorted on diagnostic but got the lion's share of correction. Never listened to my side of nothing, they didn't. Acted like that n . . . . black man wasn't nothing but a pore, mistreated victim and and I was a vicious perpetrator, and I learnt some more about Jewish prudence. That solitary'll run you crazy if you let it. Have to make like you're a bear doing what they call hibernating, or else a caterpillar laying up in one them cocoons, and just let time pass you by."

"Well, I'll be switched. A sort of willed catatonia."

"Pardon?"

"Never mind. But, Gregry, what you keep referring to is 'jurisprudence.' Just for the record."

"Right. I know it. That's what I said. 'Jewish prudence.' You slowing me down, Doc."

"Excuse me, Gregry. Go ahead."

"After I came out of solitary, this bug-eyed guy sided up to me in the exercise yard and give me another short course in my education. He was what you call 'habitual.' He'd violated parole I don't know how many times and he was going to be an old man or else it was going to be a cold day in July before he ever saw the outside again. I mean he flat out didn't give a damn. Ast me how many years I had drawed and I told him eight, and he said I'd serve ever one of 'em now and not to look for no early release for good time. Said I had done wrote the wrong kind of letter with that fountain pen and I better quick team up with his crowd or them spades would cut my throat. Said what I had done would quick spread all through the system through the underground grapevine, the which folks was honor-bound to pass news on like they got it and not to take away from it nor yet add to it. Said no matter where I got sent the blacks would be looking for me and hating me cause I had clobbered one of the brothers what was big and bad and had a sure enough gang spread out behind him even if he did swing both ways. I told him I had already experienced some of that hating and that it had changed my life right enough and I sure didn't want another dose of it.

"I thanked him kindly and told him I reckoned that nevertheless I'd make out all right by myself and didn't need to join no team. He dragged on his cigarette and said, 'So. Gonna be a lone wolf, huh? You'll learn quick enough to side with your color, kid, or they'll be writing your next of kin before a year's out.'

"I told him I'd made it on my own ever since I was fifteen and come out the hills of Kentucky for the last time, that I'd been by myself all my growed-up years and lone didn't figure into it cause I'd never known anything else; I just didn't have no stomach for joining no club based on color cause, to tell the truth, I'd really knowed more white sonbitches in my day than black ones. Told him that I knowed about percentages and would say up front I'd knowed very few blacks at all along the way but I didn't at the present time want to judge all niggers by the two what so far I'd had the most intimate contact with. 'If you know what I mean,' I said, all nice and polite, 'but I do appreciate your concern for me.'

"He told me quick enough he wasn't no goddam Christian missionary, that he thought I was tough enough to be of some value to the group and that I'd learn. And when I did, to tell whoever was around what was white and tough that I knowed Sparky at Jackson. That was his handle in the group, he said, cause he'd cheated the chair so many times. Give me the cold chills, Doc, it did; just talking to that man. But I remembered about learning and I listened more than I talked. You gotta watch, too, if you're going to learn, Doc. Listen and watch. Especially in the woods. Or yet in the jungle."

"Gregry, I'm glad you survived."

"That makes two of us, Doc. Last time I seen Sparky was in the yard the day before I got shipped out to Reidsville. Said, 'Kid, I done sent word about you're coming and you already got a friend there. They know about you.'

"'You still ain't call that concern?' I couldn't help asting him.

"'Nah,' he says, 'just payback for the pleasure you've give me.'

"'What the hell you talking about?' I said.

"'You don't know it, but I'm a real music lover, kid, and I was in the infirmary the day that dude you engraved come screaming in with your pen sticking out of his shoulder like a knot on a pine limb. If you think he hollered when you stuck it in, you shoulda heard him when they pulled it out. He hit B above high C and held it for at least a minute. That was sweet music to my ears, kid. It still rings in my soul.'

"I blowed a little smoke myself and said, 'You really hate niggers, don't you, Sparky?' and he said, 'Hate? Nah, I don't hate 'em—no worse'n I do rattlesnakes. I don't mess with them at all unless they cross my path. Don't misunderstand me, kid, I got some hate in me all right, but it's too big and important to include niggers.' He was an interesting man, Doc, and, looking back, I reckon he holp me a lot."

"He sounds interesting, Gregry. Did you run into him again?"

"Nah. He broke out about a year and a half after I was sent to Reidsville and had hisself a real spree. Stole six different automobiles along the way, raped four women and kilt two of them before they caught him. You mighta read about it, Doc. He got it in the head when the sheriff whose deputy had caught him was transporting him, by himself, mind you, to a safer jail. Let him have it out on a side road. The sheriff swore Sparky had got his gun away from him and he shot in self-defense. I been in the back seat of them cars, Doc, as I told you, and they ain't no way in hell a body could get nothing away from nobody back there. You know words are funny, Doc, and you can twist 'em around to make them suit you. 'Habitual' is one thing, and sure fit Sparky. He was asting for it, way I look at it. He was sure a heap smart'n that and if he had wanted to stay alive he never would have broke out in the first place.

"I reckon his hate finely got the best of him and he had to give in to it. And one way of looking at it, that sheriff saved us taxpayers a heap of money that day on that side road. But 'self-defense?' Come on, Doc. Anybody believe that is still looking for a virgin to marry. I ain't got no grief for Sparky, but everbody with bat brains better watch out for that sheriff. You know, Doc, you ain't got to like somebody to learn from them."

"I found that out in a much more formal setting for education than you experienced, Gregry. Were things any better for you after you got to Reidsville?"

"Better? Now that's a word can mean a heap or can mean nothing atall, Doc. Like a man I knowed oncet, somebody ast him how was his wife and he said, 'Compared to what?' Prison is prison, Doc, and I ain't never thought about 'better' in relation to it. All of 'em use the same things to scrub the floors or to wash the uniforms or the dishes or to disinfect the mattresses; so all of 'em got the same smell to them, if you know what I mean. It's a jailhouse smell and part of it comes from the men what's in there, black and white together, all of 'em either scared or mad or both. It's a jailhouse stink and it gets in your nostrils and your hair and your clothes and it goes with you ever step you take. I guess Reidsville—I always called it the Big T cause it was the Tatnall Correctional Institute—was better than most on account of most of the time I was outdoors and forgot the smell, sort of sweet and sour and flat all at the same time, when the wind was blowing in my face."

"Outside?"

"Yeah. First fellow I seen when I hit the ground at the Big T was a guard what I had knowed back four five years before at work. He knowed how good I was with machin-

ery and motors and he told me he was putting in to have me
as his head mechanic. Big T is one big farm, Doc, what I mean
is I don't know how many thousand acres, and they raise everthing they eat and then some. Heap different from forty acres
of tobacco in Kentucky, but I'd done learnt if you've seen one
truck or one tractor you done seen 'em all and I really could
fix most anything. Just takes time and patience. So I landed
this assignment right off where all day long I was out in the
fields keeping machinery going all over the whole farm,
even had my own truck to drive and everthing. The guard told
me to watch out for trouble and stay out of it and I could keep
that job long as I was there. I wasn't no trustie or nothing like
that but I had the run of the open fields all day long and only
way I really knowed I was in prison, I reckon, was when we
got locked down at night. So, yeah, Doc, I reckon things was
what you might call better at Reidsville. Leastways for a while."

"A while?"

"Right. Nothing good lasts forever, Doc; I'm sure you done
learnt that on your own a long time ago, but I'll just point
it out to you again for the record, so to speak. I run into Sparky's
contact right off. He was called Gingerbread Man and he sort
of put in to take me under his wing and all like that. He pretty well lined things out the way it turned out to be, too. You
see, everthing revolved around seventy percent was black and
thirty percent was white. He told me only way to survive that
many coons or jigaboos or jungle bunnies or brothers or mothers or whatever you might want to call 'em, long as we're worrying about words, was for the whites to stick together.
Said you had to watch out for the guards, too.

"The blacks didn't like the guards no better than the
whites did but they'd suck up to 'em when it suited 'em and
they was bad to snitch if a white was involved. Snitching is
one the worst things you can do in prison, Doc; it'll get you
to Stony Lonesome in your own cell some careless evening,

or even around the corner of a empty corridor in broad daylight, if your name ever comes up on the snitch list. I watched
and I listened and I learnt, but I patient and kindly told the
Gingerbread Man I aimed to look after my own self. He said
that was my business but that everbody in the house knowed
what I'd done to that dude in Jackson and that was a crime
against a Brother and I was marked for trouble. Said for me
to watch for it and stay out of it. I told him he'd commenced to talking like a guard but he didn't know what I was
referring to and so he never laughed. Ain't much laughing goes
on at the Big T, Doc."

"I can imagine, Gregry."

"Course I knowed there was a heap of trouble there and
I was constant on the lookout for it to get personal with me,
so to speak. I walked alone and I kept to myself and I was
careful to obey all the rules and sometimes to stick up for myself
and not take nothing off nobody because if you ever do, that's
a sign you're letting down and ever stray dog in the woods'll
be at your throat. Well, sir, no matter how sharp an eye you
got, or how keen a nose, trouble can be right on you and you
don't even recognize it till it's might near too late. I reckon
I'd done got so cocky I had commenced to relaxing a little,
and that's a mistake, Doc. Most places in life a man ought
never to let down his guard; your survival depends a heap of
times on being so finely wired you can move faster than the
next sonbitch."

"Did you get in big trouble at Reidsville, Gregry?"

"Nah. I'm setting here, ain't I? But it was close. On the down
side of a real cold morning, I'd been outside working on a
tractor had got stalled in the middle of the field way over on
the far end of the farm. They was a big old metal barn out
there and in one end they had a shed with a pot-bellied stove
where you could get warm. It was, like they say, colder'n a
witch's tit that morning and I had about froze myself to death

thinking just one more minute I'd have that old tractor running. You know how you'll do when you concentrating on
a job you're doing. Finely I said to hell with it till I get
warm one more time. I stepped in the shed and they was a
buncha guys around the stove. Had such a good fire going
they'd backed off in a big circle around it. About eight or ten
of 'em, some of 'em standing with they backs to it and a few
of 'em setting down spraddled out facing it. They was this
wooden box setting there empty 'thout nobody on it and I
never thought nothing about it, just set down and leaned
fowards holding my hands out like this to the stove to warm
'em like you do when you first come in from the cold.

"This great big black guy I'd seen eyeing me ever now and
then in the dining hall and in the day room, and it sure hadn't
been no friendly looks I had got from him, come up and says,
'I believe you sitting in my seat.' I looked up at him and he
wasn't smiling and I wasn't neither and I just as easy and polite
as you please said, 'I ain't seen no fucking reservation with
your name on it.'

"'I see,' he says, and walked off and I thought I'd faced him
down and turned back to the stove. Well, sir, he come back
from a corner with a two-by-four and swung it into my face.
It hit me right across my forehead and laid both my eyebrows
wide open. Peeled one of them to the bone and it fell down
over my eye, the which I couldn't see out'n it and I thought
the bastard had done put my eye out.

"Knocked me backwards off the box, but by then I had
realized that trouble was on me and I done a back roll,
grabbed a pitchfork what I'd spotted when I first set down,
and when he come lunging at me again with that two-by-four
hollering payback time and he was gonna kill me, I rammed
that pitchfork, which it had a longer handle than his reach,
plumb into his upper thigh about two inches below his
spraddle. Ever tine went in solid, too, what I mean; I had to

jerk with everthing I had to yank it back out and him yelling like I'd kilt him and falling backwards onto that hot stove. Knocked the stove loose from the pipe, he did, and the stove fell over and they was hot coals all around him. Looked like something straight outa hell, Doc. Sounded like it, too.

"All them other guys had backed theyselves off to the wall and I backed myself out the door holding that pitchfork in front of me and got in my truck and drove myself to the infirmary, ableeding like a stuck hog. Sewed me up pretty good they did, and you can't hardly see the scars less you look close. Even if Rose does say it has permanent changed my expression when I look straight at somebody. You can't have everthing, Doc."

"The scars are barely noticeable, Gregry. A plastic surgeon couldn't have done better, and your expression suits you to a T."

"Well, I heal fast, Doc, I mean I really do. That damn n . . . . coon laid up in the infirmary two days and his leg swole up so bad from infection setting in they had to send him to the hospital for ten or twelve days to get antibiotics in the vein and a year later he was still limping. But me, I was back on the job with all my swelling gone in less than a week. I always have healed fast."

"Physically, you mean."

"There you go, Doc. Can't let a opportunity go by to stick it to somebody, can you? And me taking all this time to try and help you get over feeling guilty about mistreating black folks."

"Forgive me, Gregry."

"That's okay, Doc. We all make little errors in judgment now and then. I want to tell you about how bad things was at the Big T after that and then I'll let you go and I'll get on with my picnic.

"Remember I done told you about everthing going round

and round that 70/30 mix. Well, sir, it didn't take more'n two days of me facing them black faces with hating eyes to realize that I had done played whaley, whatever that means; but it's the nicest way I can think of saying it. Hell, Doc, I hadn't stuck that pitchfork in that man cause he was black; I done it cause he was trying to kill me, and I would have extended the same courtesy, so to speak, to any white sonbitch had treated me that way. But them fellas didn't see nothing but color and they took it personal and they thought they was tough and they was ever one of 'em out for revenge.

"I mean to tell you, I was in some more kind of a spotlight. Two days of turning round and round while I walked and looking over my shoulder ever time I took a bite at meal time and laying awake on my bunk at night hoping some black guard hadn't just happened to overlook locking my cell door, and I looked up the Gingerbread Man. Had to promise a heap of things didn't exactly set well, but at least things was better than they was and I settled down to a fairly reasonable chance of coming out of Big T alive. I didn't like having to take on the fight of some the guys in our club because some them was the meanest mothers you ever seen and lowdown white ain't a damn bit better than lowdown black, but I aimed to survive and if that's what it took, I felt like I had to go along with it."

"Club, Gregry?"

"Sure. We only had one. The blacks had three or four and they was so jealous of each other that it made ours stronger, if you know what I mean."

"You got those tattoos in prison, didn't you, Gregry?"

"How in hell you know about them tattoos, Doc? That's right, you must of seen 'em when I had the pneumonia. That one on the right shoulder I got at Reidsville as a condition of joining up with the Gingerbread Man. I reckon you seen and understood the three things we swore by. You

seen the whiskey and the dice alaying up against her leg, did-
n't you, Doc?"

"Yes, Gregry, it's pretty graphic and I think anyone could
recognize the objects."

"They stand for liquor, gambling," he lowered his voice,
"and pussy, Doc. White pussy."

Mark Goddard refused to wince. "The banner underneath it, though, is vacant, Gregory. It looks as though
some words were supposed to be there. A motto maybe."

"You're right. Supposed to say 'White Boys' Club,' but time
they got that far I had balked. It went against the grain to get
tattooed at all—them things is so permanent, Doc—but I did-
n't see no sense atall in spelling it out. If a body could read,
then 'White Boys' Club' would of been all he needed and if
the woman, the liquor and the dice was for folks what
couldn't read, then the ones what could would certainly
get the message, too. Just seemed like overkill to me, Doc,
and I managed to talk 'em out of it."

"Gregry, I'm not feeling guilty about the riots any more.
It may not last beyond the next anchorman's editorializing
questions, but right now I don't feel the least bit guilty. In fact,
I'm not sure exactly what I do feel, but I know beyond any
doubt that I have to get back to work or I'll be handed a guilt
trip by about twelve or fifteen different sick people before
lunch. Remember: Continue your Prozac and see me again.
Let's make it in a couple of weeks, not months."

"Back in control again, ain't you, Doc? But I had you out
from behind that wall for awhile, didn't I? I seen it in your
eyes. Ain't education funny, Doc? If you watch and listen and
ain't too hidebound about who your teachers is, you sure going
to get one. I've learnt a heap from you, Doc, but I feel like
this morning I've learnt you a thing or two."

"Indeed you have. You've truly had an education along lines
I never dreamt. Thanks for sharing it with me."

"That ain't all of it by any means, Doc, and I'll be forced to share some more of it with you next time I see you. Now we got the stopper out this bottle, I got the urge to pour it all out."

"I'll look forward to seeing you again, Gregry. You've told me several times that I was your friend. Well, friendship is a two-way street and I want you to know that I regard you as a friend of mine, also."

"Well, thanks. In that case, effen it's all right with you, I'll just start calling you by your first name to make it official. Names is important. Everbody got a new one when they come into the White Boys' Club. Gingerbread Man, for instance, was called that on account of his CB handle when he was hauling dope. You know, 'Run, run, as fast as you can, You can't catch me, I'm the Gingerbread Man.' I was known as the Secretary. On account the fountain pen, you know. Get it? What's your first name? Mark? Well, we got to make it more personal than that. I'm gonna call you Marco from now on. Yessir, ole Marco Polo. Cause you an explorer, too, in one sense of the word. If you catch my drift."

Dr. Goddard gave an involuntary start, but then a grin rearranged his wrinkles and he extended his hand. "Done," he said.

Gregry McHune, with the wide yellow eyes and the soft chalky voice, looked at the outstretched hand for only a moment before he clasped it tightly and held it. No flabby, loose-jointed, pump-handle motion this time, rather a firm strong grasp. "Friends," he said. There was a wonderment in his voice. Then he, too, broke loose a grin. "And we don't need no tattoos to prove it to nobody else, do we, Marco?"

This is Tuesday, May 13, Number 231 dictating. Next patient is Gregry McHune, medical record number 079214. Patient returns for followup. BP is 120/80. He is doing well on his Prozac

*and is even planning a picnic for the afternoon with his fam-
ily. Plan is to continue the Prozac and maintain him off blood
pressure medicine altogether. Return to clinic in two weeks.*

Mark Goddard sat in thought for a moment and then clicked
his dictaphone back on.

*"Maryanne, Kathy, whoever the snitch doing my dicta-
tion for today, please type the following as a letter and
return it to me.*

'Dear Secretary Gregio,

*This leaves me feeling fine and hoping that all is well with
you. I picture you basking with your family and a fine
lunch on some hillside in Tuscany. Cathay is a strange and
wonderful land, but my journey has not been fraught with
more perils or challenges than you have faced without leaving our country of birth.*

*I anticipated attaining some measure of renown as an
explorer, but it seems to me that every man, every day,
albeit unsung, is an explorer within himself. If he forces himself to watch and to listen, it is inevitable that he will be rewarded with insights and judgments based on fact as it is presented
to him, and what else can constitute an education? Indeed,
what is an education? Also, who, from what lofty pinnacle,
can define "civilization?"*

*Perhaps all answers of worth hinge on a precise question
being asked at some particularly rare and precious moment,
in which event one is led immediately to acknowledge the existence and consider the influence of a Higher Power.*

*What I am trying to say, Gregio, is that you have this day
sure learnt me a heap if I ever get it sorted out. I think.*

I thank you.

Your friend,

Marco Polo.

Now, that," said Mark Goddard, "is cryptic enough to baffle F. Lee Bailey and Barbara Walters put together, should it ever see the light of day. And the fact that it's in the chart may twist Dennis Bentley's knickers, but he'll never figure it out. I, on the other hand, will forever have this as recall of today's conversation. 'Fuck you,' indeed. I can't believe he said that. And to somebody who was holding a .45 cocked between his eyes. And I sure can't believe everything that happened to him later. What a world!"

▬ ▪ ▬

On Wednesday afternoon the administrator appeared, polite, urbane and conversationally circuitous. "Just a moment of your time, Dr. Mark. Between patients, if you will. I know you're busy and I have plenty of time. I thought I'd drop by and deliver this to you in person. It's not a great issue, for you've not previously been remiss in that area at all, but we established a plan, a policy if you will, some eighteen or twenty months ago, that physicians would not dictate correspondence on the same tapes with patient encounters. Don't misunderstand me, it is perfectly acceptable to dictate letters, we expect it and encourage it; indeed, there is no objection to dictating an occasional personal letter. The issue revolves around the same principle upon which a good business is always founded, economy of time and money. The transcriptionist has to interrupt her sequence of typing when she comes upon a letter, change her machine for the letter format, print it separately, and then change back to medical record form. The time involved in this is itself considerable and, considering what we are paying transcriptionists per hour, the cost is unnecessarily formidable. That is why we asked all physicians some eighteen or twenty months ago to confine all their correspondence to a separate tape and never to mix it in with transcription of records. We had also, incidentally, instructed the transcriptionist to report any such infraction to administration so that we could request uniformity of compliance from the physician involved . . . ."

"Enough, enough, already yet, as the yankees say," smiled Mark Goddard. "*Mea culpa*. Forgive me this once and I will go and sin no more. Thanks for bringing me the letter. Did you read it?"

The question induced the slightest of hesitation in the administrator's reply. "I only scanned it enough to see that it was a personal letter and had nothing to do with patient care. Or anything else, for that matter, that I could discern."

"Right," said Mark Goddard. "I'm glad you reminded me of that rule; it had completely slipped my mind. I'll get on back to treating sick folks. Thanks for dropping by." As the administrator turned down the hall, he called to him, "Hey, Dennis, have you ever considered that administrators are like good wives and good secretaries? They're hard to fool and they're hard to find."

The man turned and re-entered Dr. Goddard's office. "Thank you. You know, the business world today turns a significant amount of focus upon the action-oriented management team. Appropriately, the results-processing team leans heavily upon the strategic plan and thereby achieves the desired actions. There is a litany of strategic issues that exist today in the health care environment. It is not the listing of these issues that is so important, but that the issues be clearly identified. There is only a limited degree of understanding of the issues within the health care industry; moreover, the industry is far from a consensus on how to resolve these issues."

Mark Goddard, his mouth agape, drew a long breath to interrupt, but as the administrator held up a palm he noticed that the nails had recently been manicured. He remained silent.

"Dr. Mark, the dynamics of a strategy-driven management team gives credit to the notion that a well-executed plan is a possible source of success. Too often, extensive efforts are channeled into the development of a strategic plan, only to have the plan sit dormant while the organization fumbles its way through competitive challenges."

"My God, Dennis, I'm going dormant myself and beginning to fumble. Get to the point."

"Maintaining a strategic-driven focus appears to be a formidable challenge. Between internal issues and external forces, an organization can easily fall into the crisis management mode. For an effective implementation of strategy-driven management, the entire management team must be managing the organization toward very clear goals."

"Excuse me, Dennis, but if the goals are very clear, they're the only things that are in everything you've just said. You know how it offends me to hear the words 'health care industry.' What are you trying to say?"

"We should never fail to recognize that the clarity of our goals depends upon the vision of the strategic plan. While it is very easy to accentuate a positive management style, we must always be mindful that success starts with a good plan. I plan for you not to muck around with the transcriptionists or our medical records."

"I hear you, I hear you. Dennis, if you were my secretary I'd fire you; if you were my wife, I'd divorce or kill you; but in this day of bureaucratic paralysis, you're a damn good administrator. I love you. Get out of here."

"Thank you, Dr. Mark. Have a good day."

"I'll have any sort of goddam day I choose," said Mark Goddard, but he said it *sotto voce.*

Two weeks later, dashing between patients, Dr. Goddard found a stick-on note from his receptionist gummed to his desk. "Telephone Call: 'Tell Marco the Secretary is tied up today but will come in to see him on Saturday morning.' Is there something going on around here I don't know about? Or can this be explained by the moon being full? The caller would say no more but sounded very much like G. McHune. Nancy."

Mark Goddard scribbled beneath it, "To find out for sure, you'd have to work Saturday," and transferred the note to Nancy's desk while she was busy on the telephone wand. She read it wide-eyed, mouthed "Forget it," and like a perfect lady dropped the subject. "A man's a fool who thinks he can hide anything from a wife or a good secretary," thought the doctor.

On Saturday morning, Mark Goddard found himself anticipating Gregry McHune's visit with an eagerness for which he chided himself. "You're letting personal curiosity get in the way of concern for the patient, and what would William Osler or Paul Beeson say about one of their medical students who did that?" He caught himself up short. "Hell, neither of those scientific giants would have ever listened even this long. What would Carl Whitaker or John Warkinton say? They taught me in psychiatry not to get involved in the real-life problems of patients, and I haven't. At least not beyond furnishing free samples and a few things like that. At least Gregry has never tried to borrow money from me."

He bustled through the remainder of his morning schedule with careful attention to each individual's problem, disappointment at Gregry's no-show relegated to the periphery of his conscience.

At eleven-thirty, the receptionist, whose black tresses, flashing eyes and perfect features distracted people momentarily from recognizing her efficiency and intelligence, approached him, her rigidity about rules leavened by accommodation for several years to a physician who flagrantly flouted so many of them when he thought it justified by circumstances.

"Dr. Goddard," she said, not quite repressing a note of disapproval in her voice, "you still have seven patients who had signed in to see you before deadline and that Gregry McHune is at my window insisting that I register him. I explained that our cutoff is at 11:00 on Saturdays, and he says that he knows that and has been sitting in the lobby since 10:30 deliberately waiting until he was sure he could be the last patient to see you this morning. He insists that I ask you. What do you want me to do?"

Mark Goddard responded very quietly, "Register him, Melinda." He faced the faint flicker of disappointment in her black eyes. "Be your usual calm, sweet, professional self and register Mr. McHune. I know it'll throw me late, but I promise you can leave as soon as he's in a treatment room. He really is a special case. With special needs."

As she turned with squared shoulders and head held high, he added, "Be nice."

She rewarded him with a toss of her curls, a red and white flash of lovely lips, and cooed, "I always am."

"Good receptionists are hard to find," beamed Mark Goddard. "Especially on Saturdays. Thank you, Melinda."

Before he entered the treatment room to see Gregry McHune, he called his wife. "I'll be tied up with some counseling. Don't wait lunch on me if you have something else planned . . . . No, it's no emergency. I've been manipulated into this most skillfully, but I know it and accept it. I don't have to arrange a commitment hearing or anything like that; it's mostly nondirective and listening . . . . I'll be home as soon as I can, but this is one not to be hurried. He's been rushed and pushed around too much in his life already . . . . I love you, too, Hon . . . . Thanks."

When he walked in after a perfunctory knock on the door, he briefly surveyed the lithe form in the chair, the even brown pelt above the watchful, waiting golden eyes, thought that the panther might be tamed, but only half-way, and cordially extended his hand.

"Good morning, Gregry McHune! It's good to see you."

The returning handshake, he noticed, had resumed its former impersonal flaccidity, was today nothing more than perfunctory acknowledgment of civility.

"Ain't morning no more, Doc; it's Saridy afternoon now. And how a man old as you what has worked his ass off all morning can come in here grinning beats a hog flying sideways. I been setting out front watching all them sick folks come in and go out like possums in a dead mule's ass, and I figured I wasn't gonna be met with no smile this day. You done fooled me again, Doc. Set your scrawny little wore-out butt down on that stool and blow a while afore you start in on me. I'n tell you without you picking up that blood pressure thing that I'm 120/80; Rose took it just before I left home."

"That's fine, Gregry; it checks perfectly with my instrument. How are you sleeping?"

"Like a baby, Doc."

"How's your sex life?"

"Like a rooster, Doc. No complaints."

"How's your drinking?"

"Dry as a chip, Doc. Don't even miss it. And before you quit doctoring and commence to meddling, let me settle something with you ahead of time. All nice and polite like, if you know what I mean. If I ever quit smoking I give you my solemn promise, before God Almighty, I'll tell you about it. You'll be the first to know. You won't have to ask. That way I won't be getting the red ass ever time you mention tobacco, and you won't feel like you're shirking your responsibility as a doctor. Know what I mean?"

"I think I can accept that, Gregry."

"Fine. Now, ain't you gonna ask me about the picnic?"

"How was the picnic, Gregry?"

"Couldn't a been better. We all had a good time. Sort of laid out on the grass and nothing planned for us to do. Had to act like a family and figure out our own entertainment. Me'n Rose wound up with sticks trying to see who could knock a hickey nut the furthest and the kids run around finding more hickey nuts for us. It was great. Now, ain't you gonna ask me about what happened next at Big T?"

"I don't think so, Gregry. Lest I cross that fine line between doctoring and meddling, I give you my solemn promise before God Almighty that I won't ask you any questions about your private life. I'll be glad, however, to listen to anything you want to tell me, and you seem to have this visit pretty well under control. Now. Do you want to tell me about what happened next at the Big T?"

"Don't matter how late in the day it gets, you're still sharp as a rat turd, Doc. And case you don't know it, that's pretty damn pointed. I reckon I can recognize when I been put in my place and, honest to God, I ain't trying to be contrary. Hell, yes, I wanta tell you about Big T. Leastways, part of it."

"In that case, I'd like to hear it." Mark Goddard rolled his padded stool back and leaned against the treatment table, relaxed but attentive.

"You see, I got sort of a reputation after I joined the WBC. The maintenance supervisor took me off the truck, said the warden and what all told him not to let me roam loose no more. Especially if they was any way I could get my hands on a pitchfork or some such. Put me back inside like any ordinary prisoner and all my special privileges was gone. The which I didn't fault nobody for that; they had a job to do and none of the guards was ever what I'd call less than fair to me. They wasn't very smart, but then if they had of been they wouldn't a been prison guards to start with.

"The Gingerbread Man was right about one thing—them black men were sure out to get me. I stuck close to the whites and we all managed pretty well—leastways we kept them from really hurting any of us, and I got to be sort of the

WBC point man about cracking heads on coons what got too close to us, if you know what I mean."

"I'm not sure that I do, Gregry. What do you mean?"

"Like I told you. They didn't have just one club like we did. If they had of, it don't take no genius to figger that seventy percent would of plumb overpowered thirty percent. But they couldn't get along amongst they ownselves, bickered and jowered and fought and one even got kilt while I was there. The different clubs they had hated each other 'most as much as they did us. It was like living ever minute of ever day in a war zone and you didn't know what might be coming at you from around the corner or what might just be on the prowl for somebody else.

"Mr. Metters had learned me on the farm and in the woods to watch every little detail and be particular if they was anything at all what had changed around you. 'Read sign' was what he called it. Well, turned out I could read them jigaboos like a first-grade primer. Something about they eyes. I could tell who they was after and pretty close when they would move. Gingerbread got to leaning on me for information like, and the WBC was getting along just fine. Ever time somebody tried to mess with us looked like we knowed about it ahead of time and whipped more black ass than you could shake a stick at. We was tight, and I was right on the edge of it and also in the thick of it."

"What did the guards do to prevent fights?"

"We was careful, both sides of us, to try and not let the guards know what we was up to. If anybody snitched to a guard, the unwritten law was that he was dead meat. You ain't got no idea how many broke arms and noses, or yet cuttings, was passed off as accidents that happened in the shop or in the kitchen or in the yard. You just didn't snitch to no guard no matter what happened to you. Course ever now and then they'd pull a lockdown and search for concealed weapons and all, but most of them guards was so damn dumb that they thought they was smart. Know what I mean, Doc?"

"I've encountered a few people like that, Gregry, yes."

"Well, like I said, I had built myself a reputation and the niggers was out to get old Secretary. Now, chill out, Doc. I know you object to that word and all like that; I can say 'Black' and even 'African-American' along with anybody else, according to what they wanting theyselves to be called this week; seems like they forever changing and can't settle down to one name. But let me tell you, whenever one or a bunch of 'em is coming at me, low-down and dirty, up close and personal, they's automatically a bunch of goddam niggers in my mind, and you'll just have to overlook the language."

Mark Goddard's voice was level and smooth. "I'm overlooking nothing, Gregry, but accepting everything. The big toe is as much a part of the body as the lung."

"Now what in the living hell is that supposed to mean, Doc? You forever running something under my nose what I can't even smell, let alone understand, till the middle of the next week. Toes and lungs ain't got a plague-taked thing to do with what I'm trying to tell you."

"Maybe they do, but forgive me for interrupting. Go ahead."

"Good thing you did interrupt, Doc; I was getting way off track there, wasn't I? What I'm aiming to tell you this morning is how I got myself classified as being 'violent,' put in solitary confinement, and had ever privilege you can name taken away from me."

"That sounds like a bad time for you, Gregry."

"You can take that to the bank. Remember me telling you way back yonder when we first was getting to know one another that I felt like I was on the edge of a pit looking straight into hell? Well, all of a sudden I was right in the bottom of it and I was lucky to get out of it and stay alive. You see, Big

Black Daddy come after me. His own self. One on one.
Just me and him. Rumor in the grapevine was that nobody
hardly ever lived through a personal interview with him
and if you did you wished you hadn't."

"Big Black Daddy?"

"Yeah. That was his handle. He was head of a club of the
meanest dudes at Big T. He'd kilt three men. Sent up for armed
robbery at eighteen and soon as he got out on parole, he kilt
his first one; leastways the first one he got caught at. Beat his
head plumb off, they said. Served some time and got paroled
again and then got put back in for robbing a 7-11 and shooting the clerk. She didn't die; lived to identify him. Then one
by one he'd kilt two prisoners. Both times in a fight, both times
hollered self-defense. Both times white guys. Got hisself a lawyer from the ACLU who sung that old sweet song of deprived
childhood and oppression and civil rights, and the court
never give him the big jolt like he deserved but did give him
two life terms without parole. He was in from now on and
he knowed it and, to tell you the truth, I think he liked it."

"Liked prison?"

"Yessirree-bob, he liked it. He was so mean he had about
ten or twelve dudes what was scared to death of him and waited on him hand and foot, fetched and carried, bowed and
scraped, done any and ever little thing he ever told 'em to. He
weighed right at 270 pounds and a heap of that wasn't fat.
He had two or three butt boys in his club and they use to brag
that he was big and black all over. If you get my drift, Doc."

Mark Goddard's voice was dry. "I'm comprehending
every word so far, Gregry."

"Well, one of his favorite boys had smarted off to me once
too often and I caught him in a private corner of the yard one
day and tended to him. Split his lips up pretty good and got
a couple of teeth whilst I was at it. Big Black Daddy told the
guards the dude had got careless and caught a basketball in

his mouth, but bout a week later he sicked this mean high yeller on me. I'd been watching and waiting for payback time so I was ready. Got that cream-colored bastard so hard his right nut busted plumb open, one of the techs said. Swelled up big as a volleyball and he laid up in the infirmary packed in ice for close on to ten days. Big Black Daddy told everbody to say that Candy Man had fell straddle of a sawhorse, but even the guards wasn't buying that, cause they wasn't no sawhorses in the corridor where they found him rolling around in his own puke.

"The WBC gathered in as close around me as they could and several weeks dragged by. I was as jumpy as a bushy-tailed cat in a roomful of rocking chairs from all the watching and wondering. Only time I could relax was in my cell, the which I didn't even trust that till I got locked down ever night cause I was in between two cells of blacks and my cellmate at the time was a little pussy of an accountant serving two years for fraud what was scared of his own shadow and would piss his pants if you said 'Boo!'

"One night I was setting on the edge of my bunk whilst he was off in the showers, athinking about Rose and how long before I could be with her again, when the door swung open and Big Black Daddy was in my cell before I even had time to move. Shut the door and stood between me and it and said, 'Payback time, you little white shitass of a mother fucker.' I opened my mouth to yell for the guards and them coons of his in the cells around me commenced to singing so loud you couldn't a heard it thunder. 'You sure don't look like much 'cept a tight-assed cracker son of a bitch, but way you messed up my two main men, ain't nothing going to satisfy me 'cept fixing yo clock and stopping yo watch my own self.'

"Doc, that was the biggest, baddest animal I ever seen in my life, and I don't mind telling you I was scared shitless. I was already holding the side of my cot and I managed to ease my shank from under the mattress, but I thought for sure my hour to die had come."

"Your what from under the mattress?"

"My shank. Everbody had one. Homemade weapons, Doc. Made out of a spoon if you could steal one from the dining hall, or a old piece of scrap metal, even a sharp piece of wood was better'n nothing. I had me one I'd been carrying for months. Made it out a piece of one them heavy plastic cutting boards they used in the kitchen that I sneaked out the garbage when I was on that detail. I'd spent weeks shaping and sharpening it when nobody was looking. It was only about three inches long but I had stuck on a piece of wood for a handle. It was sharp and pointed and it was all I had."

Mark Goddard realized that he was sitting forward on his stool and forced himself to lean back and appear relaxed.

"Marco Polo, that Big Black Daddy stood there blocking my way out and lined out what he was aiming to do to me whilst all them dudes in the next cells was singing 'Dry Bones,' and it was the tightest moment of my whole entire life.

"All of a sudden I remembered Mr. Metters taking me coon hunting. We had only took along one dog that night and he had run this old coon up a snag of a dead tree wasn't more'n six feet off the ground. He was circling the stump and jumping and the coon was circling the top of that snag and watching. That old redbone hound had the deepest voice you ever heard and he was splitting the night wide open telling that coon what he was going to do. All of a sudden he crouched down and they wasn't no doubt he could jump six feet and grab that coon. That was when the coon made his move. He jumped first. Landed right on that dog's head. Grabbed his nose between his teeth, commenced to raking his ears and eyes with his feet, and rode that hound what was at least six times big as he was plumb out the swamp.

"When Mr. Metters quit laughing he told me, 'Gee-boy,

let that be a lesson to you. If you ever in a tight, don't announce to your enemy what you mean to do. Just, by God, jump first whilst the other one is bragging.'

"Well, I looked at Big Black Daddy, and I knowed a three-inch shank wouldn't never cut to the hollow and hurt him bad. I knowed I'd have to hit hard and hit fast and I thought I'd concentrate on his neck where the blood veins run shallow. He was yet talking, 'Only thing I get a bigger thrill from than beating the stew out of a smart-ass cracker boy is what I do to him when they ain't no fight left in him. When I get done with you this evening, I ain't gwine be easy with my old John Henry. You ain't even gonna have no asshole left. You white-trash piece of shit, you gonna be bleeding from both ends.'

Mark Goddard marveled that Gregry McHune's voice had not risen; nor was there any more impassioned inflection of tone than commenting on the weather would have induced. It made the recital even more gripping.

"That's when I jumped, Doc. I come up off that cot right in his face and I swung my shank. I was aiming for his left eye but he jerked his head back and I split his nostril open clean from the bridge of his nose down through his upper lip and laid it open; it was flapping like two separate pieces of meat. He squeezed me with those big old arms of his'n, but I was high up and had my right arm free. I sunk that shank just above his collar bone and come up and out with it hard as I could, and blood come pumping out and slap covered both of us. Punctured his lung, too; you could hear it hissing like a tire going down. He staggered back and fell like a butchered hog, and the locked-up niggers quit singing and went to hollering for the guards. I mean they was singing a different tune. They thought I'd kilt him.

"Guards come rushing in and got him to the hospital in time to save his life, but they flung me in solitary and classified me as violent."

He paused, and Mark Goddard felt free to speak. "Did that surprise you, Gregry?"

"Surprise me? I was downright flabbergasted. Hell, Doc, I ain't no violent man. Me? Any time I have ever hurt anybody it was in self-defense. Hell, I was in my very own cell minding my very own business when that bugger come in on me, and we was both still in my very own cell when them guards hauled him out from under me. At heart, I'm a peaceful citizen what ain't never wanted but one thing out of life, and that is to be let alone by all of the shitasses in this world and allowed to run my own business."

"It's not unusual for one's self-image to be different from that perceived by other people, Gregry."

"If'n you say so, Marco. That sure sounds fancy enough to be gospel. But let me tell you something. That lawyer told me where to find justice, and he was right. It sure ain't in court, as he pointed out, and it sure as hell ain't in prison. You know what they done to me? They kept me in solitary for a whole month, and then they shipped me out. Me. Left Big Black Daddy right there in Big T like a royal king sitting on a heathen throne in the middle of all his ass-kissing lieutenants and shipped me out in maximum security with 'Violent' stamped all over my records. 'Violent.'

"That done it for any hope I had of time off or early parole. Any time anybody ever open that record that's the first thing they see. 'Violent.' And they mind right away snaps shut tight as a bull's ass in fly time. I had not adjusted to prison life, they said, and showed no sign of rehabilitation. Hell, only thing I had done was to defend myself and commit the unpardonable sin of being alive and in one piece. There ain't no justice, Marco Polo. Nowhere. I ain't followed that lawyer's advice, for I ain't never tried no whorehouse. But I bet you a thousand dollars you wouldn't find justice there, neither."

Dr. Goddard took a deep breath. "If there is no justice,

Gregry, I guess the only recourse left is to beg for mercy."

"Mercy? What the hell is mercy, Doc?"

"Well, one man wrote that its quality is not strained, that it falls like gentle rain from heaven upon the place beneath, and that it falls on the just and the unjust."

Gregry McHune's eyes were steady, as watchful as ever, but his voice was lightened. "Hell, Marco Polo, you really are a trip. Talking to you is like chasing a rabbit without no dog—ain't much chance of catching you. Bout the time I think I got you figured out and get to talking to you straight from my guts you double back up some side path and lead me off in the briers and bushes. They sure as hell wasn't no mercy in that prison and if they had of been it wouldn't of been falling like no gentle rain; and Big T, or any other prison in this state, would make a reasonable man quit ever considering they even being a heaven for it to drop from. Besides the which, I ain't never been no begging man, and to have begged for mercy in that slime pit would have set ever inmate and guard around me to laughing like devils in hell. Get real, Doc."

"I wasn't speaking just of prison, Gregry," responded Mark Goddard in level tone.

"Oh, shit," came the soft voice. "Here we go again. I'm supposed to put mercy in the sack with the big toe remark and study on it, ain't I?"

He lifted the edge of his shirt sleeve and looked at his watch. "Good God, look what time it is. I'm outa here." He rose but paused at the door. "What I don't understand is why all of a sudden I feel better. Can I come back next Saridy, Doc?"

"Certainly, Gregry. You must remember that another man wrote, 'The Kingdom of Heaven is within you.' He just may have been right."

The soft laugh bubbled over heavy wet leaves. "There you go; itching and preaching and meddling. I'll see you, Marco Polo."

Mark Goddard challenged his short-term memory and began dictation.

Next patient is Gregry McHune, medical record number 079214, who returns for follow-up. His blood pressure is 120/80 on no medication for it whatsoever. He continues his Prozac. He is having no insomnia. In parody of one more versed in obfuscation than I, let it be said that the medical world today still turns a considerable amount of focus upon the action-oriented clinical interplay between physician and patient, being ever aware that there yet remains a litany of specific issues in the health care environment and that it is not the listing of these issues that is so important but that the issues be clearly identified, albeit the health care industry is far from consensus on how to resolve these issues.

In view of these sentiments (whatever they be), I would say that Gregry McHune is much improved although the recall of his experiences with Big T and WBC trigger my recall of Housman and make me consider that Mr. McHune has been living the following words for years:

> *The laws of God, the laws of man,*
> *He may keep that will and can;*
>
> *Not I: let God and man decree*
> *Laws for themselves and not for me.*

This concludes my dictation for Saturday, May 31.

"And that," said Mark Goddard aloud as he removed the tape and wrapped it in the list of patients seen that morning, "ought to set them buzzing in Transcription." He grinned. "And, as the young people say, wad their panties and wrinkle old Bentley's shorts. We'll see."

When the administrator appeared several days later and

requested an audience, his presenting attitude was one of
respect, almost of deference. "You're busy as can be this morning, Dr. Goddard, and I hate to interrupt you, but could you
spare me just a minute or two between patients? I'll wait in your
office. No hurry. I have plenty of time. At your convenience."

Mark Goddard's thought was, "For what we're paying you,
I'm damned if I can afford much time for you to wait." Aloud
he spoke with as much smoothness as his petitioner. "Dennis, come on in the office now; I'm between patients and glad
to see you."

When the door closed behind them, the administrator for
once was devoid of bureaucratic harangue or word salad; his
words were simple and direct. "Dr. Goddard." He sighed. "I'll
overlook the obvious fact that you were quoting me, out of
context and in parody, and most inappropriately, but the thing
that brings me here is the poetry again."

"Now, Dennis, don't be upset. That poetry was very
appropriate."

"Dr. Goddard, it does not look appropriate on a chart."

"It is more appropriate than recording the conversation
that stanza recalls so vividly to my mind. Believe me, that
would require several pages of transcription and there goes
your shibboleth of 'cost effectiveness.' Besides, it's not all of
the poem, which goes on:

> *Please yourselves, say I, and they*
> *Need only look the other way.*
>
> *But no, they will not; they must still*
> *Wrest their neighbour to their will,*
>
> *And make me dance at their desire*
> *With jail and gallows and hell-fire.*
>
> *And how am I to face the odds*
> *Of man's bedevilment and God's?*

> I, *a stranger and afraid*
> In *a world I never made.*"

Dennis Bentley interrupted gently. "No more, Dr. Goddard, no more. Please. I must remind you again that I am merely trying to protect you and the partners. It would almost certainly be inappropriate for any of that poem to be read in a court of law from the official chart maintained by one of our more venerated and respected physicians."

"Dennis, I have observed judges whose pomposity grew exponentially greater with their tenure until they became fossilized right before my very eyes, their last vestiges of coursing blood and human compassion replaced by some thick distillate leached through the ever enlarging musty mountains of law and written rules by which they live until the last signs of movement about them are their powerful tongues, which grind like heavy stones and parrot only, 'I am important' and 'you are insignificant' as they announce one inappropriate recess after another, prompted only by their own convenience.

"I have seen one thick-necked, pot-bellied federal judge with a porcine forehead chew gum on the bench and actually go to sleep while evidence was being presented. From what I've seen of the creaking, antediluvian machinery of the court, I think a little poetry would be like opening windows in the springtime and letting fresh wind clear the must of cramped winter existence from a stuffy bedroom. A little Housman, about whom we are presently arguing, would probably blow some vindictive, manipulative, self-aggrandizing attorneys and that stuffed-hog, smirking judge into a corner like a pile of dried leaves and let truth shine out with enough light to cut jury time in half."

Dennis Bentley closed his eyes; his face as overly patient as his voice. "Dr. Goddard, I hardly think it is the mission or the responsibility of this clinic to revolutionize the court system of the State of Georgia . . . ."

"And, Dennis," interrupted Mark Goddard with excitement, "think what a little Edna St. Vincent Millay properly quoted could do for the feminist movement and the whole agenda of Women's Rights. She appreciated brains, beauty, and sex—and I'll guarantee you nobody ever pushed her around. I'll bet if you teamed her up with Emily Dickinson they could make mincemeat of an entire corps of judges and lawyers! And they wouldn't even realize they'd been decapitated until they tried to turn their heads."

"Dr. Goddard." The tone was weary now. "I'm sure this discussion would be very interesting, given a more appropriate setting, a better time, even a more appreciative audience capable of participating. But you are busy, I am busy, and the clinic policy about records is based on recommendations from the legal department of Mag Mutual Insurance Company. You are well respected in this group; you are our semi-official white hair; we all turn to you for wisdom in guidance; and I do not therefore understand why you are so blind, almost stubborn, about this one small issue."

"Now there you go, Dennis, being poetic your very own self."

"I beg your pardon? Not I, Dr. Goddard."

"Oh, yes, you are. You're pure Lewis Carroll. Listen:

> *"You are old, Father William," the young man said*
> *"And your hair has become very white;*
> *And yet you incessantly stand on your head—*
> *Do you think, at your age, it is right?"*

Dennis Bentley blinked, pulled his head back, tucked his chin. "Excuse me? I don't understand. I mean no offense, Dr. Mark, but I don't even really care for poetry."

"Ah, but Dennis! You do. You must. It is all around you. It supports you through fatigue, it carries you through the dark. Poetry, no matter the language in which it appears, is the queen of our language, the essence of expression between human beings, the result of communion between man and his God."

"Dr. Goddard, please!" There was almost a whimper. Dennis paused and swallowed, held out his hand. "Could I have your recorder? I hate to do this, but I am at my rope's end."

"No, no, no, no, Dennis. You cannot have my recorder. Not unless you are ready for me to quit, to walk out of this building and leave you immediately to deal with the long train of faithful patients who have looked to me and bolstered me for fifty years. You don't really want this tape recorder, do you Dennis?"

The hand fell, the shoulders sagged, the chest rose and collapsed in a sigh. "Not really, Dr. Goddard. But what am I to do?"

"Listen to the last stanza of the Housman poem that wrinkled your shorts so badly, Dennis:

> *And since, my soul, we cannot fly,*
> *To Saturn nor to Mercury,*
>
> *Keep we must, if keep we can,*
> *These foreign laws of God and man.*

"As far as Gregry McHune is concerned, that's exactly what this poem was evoking, for that is surely the direction in which he is headed; he just has not formulated the idea yet. As far as you and I are concerned it is equally appropriate, for I promise you of my own free will that I will obey your foreign laws. I swear to you that I will insert no more poetry into a patient's record until the day I am ready to quit this place, and that if I do it will serve as my official notice of resignation."

"Now wait a minute, Dr. Goddard; you're not thinking

of retiring, are you? Any time soon, I mean?"

"Retiring, Dennis? Hell, no! I may resign if things get too rough, but I'd keep on practicing medicine. Somewhere. Till the day I die. Retirement is a tremendous mistake, another fallacy, a materialistic myth that has been perpetrated on a money-grubbing society by the great god Mammon."

"I can count on that, Dr. Goddard?"

"As you young fellas say, Dennis, you can carry it to the bank. And now. Remember a minute ago you said, 'I'm busy and you're busy'? That's very true, and I have to get back to my patients. But before I leave, see if the last two stanzas from Lewis Carroll make you feel anything, have any meaning for you, make you laugh or make you think.

> *"You are old," said the youth, "one would
>   hardly suppose*
> *That your eye was as steady as ever;*
> *Yet you balance an eel on the end of your nose—*
> *What made you so awfully clever?"*
>
> *"I have answered three questions, and that is
>   enough,"*
> *Said his father. "Don't give yourself airs!*
> *Do you think I can listen all day to such stuff?*
> *Be off, or I'll kick you down stairs!"*

"Dennis, you are a wonderful administrator; I love you; I would buy a second-hand car from you; there are gaps in your education; and I am out of here."

The following Saturday morning went smoothly and uneventfully, a dazzling day beginning with a soft and early dawn that awakened to bird song and unfolded in such gentle air that no one was indifferent to the excitement or the beauty in it. There was just enough tingle to make shirt sleeves welcome. School was out and there was a significant diaspora of local families to early vacation at distant beaches. Everyone was in denial of illness on such a glorious day, and Dr. Goddard's census was lower than it had been in a month.

There was no sense of urgency in his welcome of Gregry McHune, but there was an ebullience in Gregry's response not noted before.

"Dr. Mark Goddard! Marco Polo, Esq.! Come in and set yourself down on that little old stool right there and act nonchalant while you're watching and listening and not fooling me one minute. You ain't ever missed a single trick, have you, Doc? We ain't discussing blood pressure this morning and we ain't discussing Prozac, though the truth of the matter is I ain't had none now for two weeks and so far I ain't missed it. We ain't going into any conversation atall about all those excuses and signposts we both been putting up in order to get me back in here."

Mark Goddard smiled with warmth but did not laugh. "Gregry, I have forty-five minutes. We don't have to have any conversation unless you wish. All healing, like a great many important things, ultimately comes in silence."

There was a vibrance in the voice, a timbre of authority, of active participation that was new to the doctor's ear. "Rose of Sharon may be right. She told me a good while back that you was a psychiatrist. I told her she was crazier'n hell, that we was working on blood pressure. She said in addition to BP you had also treated strep throat, pneumonia, depression, insomnia, and alkyhawlism in me, and all of 'em pretty damn successful, too. I told her I hadn't never heard of nobody being fool enough to go to no psychiatrist to get treated for pneumonia or strep throat, and then it looked like she was gonna twitch an eyebrow, swell up and sull on me like she does when I'm about to win an argument. The which, since you're married yourself, you know ain't very often, Marco Polo.

"That's when I hit her right between the eyes with the big one. I said to her, 'The big toe is ever much a part of the body as the lung, Rose.' I mean that'll stop anybody in they tracks, Doc.

"She jerked her head around at me and said, 'Say which?' I just looked at her like I knowed something she didn't and didn't say nothing. She walked off and terectly come back in the room. Stood with her arms folded between me and the football game, she did, and said, 'Gregry McHune, you ain't got goose doodie for brains if you think for one minute I'm gonna buy that as coming out of your very own head all by its very own self. That doctor put it in there, he did, and when you boil it down it means that ever thing happens to a person leaves a mark of some sort. Don't try to tell me he ain't no psychiatrist, even if he does charge GP fees and live on the south side of town.'

"Rose is smart, Doc, and I hadn't figgered out that big toe till she lined it out for me. I ain't tuned in to just exactly the same radio band you'n Rose are and sometimes it takes a while for me to switch stations. I believe, howsomever, that I have finely got there. A man has to accept ever part of hisself, don't he, Doc? And go on about his business. And use the big toe to walk, and the lung to breathe, and the heart to pump, and the brain to think. And they all got to work together, don't they, Doc? And not try to separate theyself from one another or else you gonna fall down and bust your ass if you leave the big toe out. It's deep, Doc, it's deep, but I think I'm into it. And Rose may be right. You may be a psychiatrist in disguise, for all I know. Disguised as Marco Polo."

Mark Goddard's mien was grave. "Labels are really not all that important, are they Gregry? I was taught by two very fine men, Dr. John Warkentin and Dr. Carl Whittaker, that when you categorize people and pack them neatly away in pigeonholes or slots of definition that you not only do them a disservice but restrict your own concept of them and narrow your personal capacity for expansion."

Gregry looked at him straight and level. "What the hell are you trying to tell me now, Dr. Mark Goddard?"

Mark Goddard gave a wide grin. "Gregry, if you think I'm opaque, you should meet our administrator. What I'm saying is that it doesn't really matter if I'm Marco Polo or a psychiatrist or a GP, they are all explorers, aren't they? Just in different fields and on different levels. I don't care what you call me as long as you feel better. Dr. John Stone says good health is whatever works—and for how long."

There was an intake of breath that was almost a soft snort. "If it's all the same to you, John Stone makes a heap more sense than them other two. And I sure as hell feel better, Doc. Now if you'll just quit hopping back and forth up them rabbit trails, I'll get around to the main thing I wanted to see you about today."

"Forgive me, Gregry. I tend to get carried away sometimes. What's on your mind?"

Then came the silence. It grew. Mark Goddard sat very still and so did Gregry McHune. Neither stared at the other; there was no eye contact, but the silence was a vibrant, pulsating presence between them, binding them, bonding them. Mark Goddard cleared his throat to keep from coughing, but Gregry McHune took no heed, did not move. His amber eyes with the golden flecks were fixed unblinkingly on some distant vista beyond the corner of the treatment table. He breathed so slowly that he seemed motionless.

The silence became comforting, warm, deep. Mark Goddard began feeling drowsy. He stole a glance at Gregry but said nothing. "The great cat is resting," he thought, "gathering his strength."

After long minutes, the doctor had the strange sensation

that the silence, like fog, was receding, growing thinner, admitting light.

Gregry McHune gave a long, shuddering sigh. His voice was thick, deeper than usual. "I reckon that ain't so damn important after all, Doc."

Mark Goddard had recall of Carl Whittaker puffing on his pipe with apparent placidity, and he remained silent.

Gregry raised his head and looked calmly at Mark. "I come in here to ask you how to get shed of a tattoo and to tell you how I come to have it on there in the first place, but I been setting here studying about my big toe and all of a sudden I have changed my mind. Ever thing that happens to a man becomes a part of him, don't it, Doc? And ever thing he is comes about because of the accumulation of all them things, good or bad, what has happened to him, don't it? And the knee bone connected to the leg bone and the leg bone connected to the ankle bone, and the big toe connected to the heart and the lung, and hear the word of the Lord! You see what I mean, Marco Polo?"

"I think I do, Gregry."

"I been living for years so ashamed of my tattoos I didn't ever want to take off my shirt in front of nobody. Not even Rose of Sharon, less'n the light was out. And I felt like I had to come and tell you about it because I knowed you had seen it and wondered about it, cause like I have said you don't miss a single trick."

"You've already told me about the tattoo, Gregry, and why you didn't get WBC put on the label."

"Not that tattoo, Doc. The other one. The one with the letter with my name on it what says, 'Moved. Left no address. Return to sender.'"

"Oh, yes. I recall that one."

"I reckon, by damn, you do. It'll blow the socks off any thinking man. I had this monstrous itch to tell somebody about

the shit that come down on me that made me come up with
the idea of it, cause to tell you the truth, what happened to
me after I left Big T was worse than everthing else leading up
to it. I mean, I earned that label of 'violent.' I was a terror.
Didn't get no good time atall and had to serve my full sentence. When we was setting here not saying nothing, I realized that you was accepting me just the way I am and that
Rose does, too; and all of a sudden I realized that tattoo ain't
bothering me no more. It's part of me. It can stay. I remembered you telling me you wasn't no tourist."

"I'm not."

"Well, I reckon I finely know that. So, Doc, what it boils
down to is you ain't got to have me show you Rock City or
Mammoth Cave or yet B. Lloyd's and the Grand Canyon or
take you to Six Flags, Stone Mountain or yet Disney World to
make you love America. There ain't a bit of need for me to line
out to you all the other horrors I went through in them other
prisons and the jaws of hell I squeezed myself through to come
out of there. I guess I can, by God, accept my own self."

Mark Goddard took a deep breath. "Thank God Warkentin
and Whitaker taught me to recognize an ending to therapy,"
he prayed. He smiled and extended his hand. "Whatever you
say, Gregry. I'll be here any time you need me if you ever want
to come back."

"I'm gonna count on that, Doc. I'll carry it to the bank."
He gave a big grin. "Now let me get all my toes, the big toes
and the least ones, limbered up and haul my ass out of here
so's you can go get yourself some dinner. Thanks for everthing."

"Thank you, Gregry. Check the blood pressure occasionally. See me if you need me."

Gregry paused at the door. "And the same to you, I'm sure."
He started out and paused again, turned to face the doctor
across the room. "You know what really caused all this
jello to set up, Doc?"

"What, Gregry McHune?"

"When you talked about the difference between mercy and justice and then told me the Kingdom of Heaven was inside of me. That's what. If a man gets to thinking hard on that, he's gonna quit blaming other folks and also things outside hisself for being miserable and realize he's got to stand up tall and make up his own mind how much control over his feelings he's going to let them have. So long, Marco Polo."

Mark Goddard was both exhausted and euphoric. He was replete with fulfillment but also a little poignant. He spent a few moments in thought and extracted his pocket recorder.

The last patient of the morning is Gregry McHune, medical record number 079215. Patient is having no further trouble with insomnia. He has had no alcohol in months. His blood pressure is 120/80 and he assures me this is the constant reading he obtains at home. He is no longer depressed and has discontinued his Prozac two weeks ago. In fact, he is on no medication whatsoever. He has dismissed himself from my care with the assurance that if he ever needs me again he will return to clinic. In his manifestation of independence he may be reminiscent of the proverbial hog on ice, but he also evokes the study of Dr. R. Browning of the effect on unseen listeners of a peasant girl as she passes them singing, "The lark's on the wing, The snail's on the thorn, God's in His Heaven."

End of dictation for today, and I will be here bright and early Monday morning.

He clicked off his recorder. "And that," he muttered, "ought to go over the head of anyone in the transcription department. Even if it should reach Bentley's desk, there is not a line in it that could meet his obvious conviction that all poetry must rhyme. I'm safe—I've neither broken a promise nor resigned."

He stepped out into the June noonday with happiness in

his heart. On the way to his car he recited

> *"Little Jack Horner sat in the corner,*
> *Eating a Christmas pie.*
> *He put in his thumb, and pulled out a plum,*
> *And said, 'What a good boy am I!'"*

If he had been absolutely sure no one was looking he would
have essayed a skip or two.

The rhythm of his life swept Mark Goddard along in gentle and accustomed current. His practice kept him busy
and his mind engaged. He worked through an epidemic of
strep throat that through his years of practice he had learned
to expect every July. In early August there was the press of
physical examinations required for returning busdrivers
and schoolteachers. The hordes of high school adolescents
waving applications for certification of enough physical
prowess to play football rose like a frenzy of feeding piran-
ha, briefly roiled the routine of the clinic, and were gone. Their
muscle-bound coaches manifested the attitude that attention
to these healthy young athletes was the absolute pinnacle of
civic duty for any truly dedicated physician and that the ser-
vices, by all rights, should be rendered without any pecuniary
obligation.

Mark Goddard did not acknowledge this bait. He noted
with wry amusement that the medical emigrants into his community now included a plethora of orthopedists, men who
were overly conscious of a new gold mine called Sports
Medicine and thereby made themselves available to collusion
with the coaches. Most of them seemed hungry for a Ferrari
or a Mercedes to adorn the garages of their opulent homes
and were well aware that the acquisition of such could be considerably accelerated by the repair of young bones broken,
or tendons snapped, or cartilages torn on the high school play-

ing fields, a steady flow of which could be assured by good will from the coaches.

Dr. Goddard did not feel at all competitive in this area; he had long since affirmed that football should be a game and had openly decried the community determination to make it a religion. Neither he nor the coaches missed the communion that had been forced upon them when he had been the only physician around who was willing to sit through the games.

In September and October there was the usual stream of older patients requesting flu shots and "while I'm here I might as well get a little checkup." Mark Goddard did not hear a word from Gregry McHune, and as the months slipped by let him slide to the back of his mind, his attention occupied by the ever-present parade of patients with new symptoms and compelling problems.

His dictation was now devoid of poetry, although he occasionally came up with a sassy insert, inconsequential and off the record, for the benefit of the transcriptionists. His typed records were models of decorum, his relation with Dennis Bentley harmonious and smooth.

This is number 231 settling in to toil and labor. This is Wednesday, the day before Thanksgiving, and while you young ladies are celebrating a four-day vacation from those electronic masters of yours, please pause to give thanks and show a little wonder that we live in the only country in the world that has a holiday specifically set aside, nationwide, for expressing gratitude to God. Having spent more years than any of you wallowing my way through the swamps of disillusion and also scaling the slippery cliffs of hope, I would admonish all of you to cling to this heritage, against the evil days when the Civil Libertarians, the atheists, the ACLU and the ADA band together to abolish Thanksgiving because it violates the separation of church and state. They might as well cut off our big toes. Now listen carefully while we get down to business and begin formal dictation on the first patient of the day.

Traditionally the hiatus between Thanksgiving and Christmas was one of decreased patient census, attributed by Dr. Goddard to the positive effect on the American immune system of excitement, anticipation, and joy. This year, however, the dreaded dragon of influenza came early, attacking first the adolescents of school age just as their vacation began. Mark Goddard was inundated by sick people. He worked at least twelve hours each day and was grateful anew that the younger doctors had relieved him some years previously from night call. On the last Saturday before Christmas Day, Melinda interrupted his whirlwind passage between treatment rooms.

"You'll never guess who has just come to my window exactly thirty seconds before closing time demanding to see you." Her eyes flashed in obvious disapproval.

"Lawsy mussy, Miss Melinda, I ain't got time this morning to guess," responded the doctor flippantly. "Who?"

The lovely lips tightened. "That man."

"Which one?"

"That Gregry McHune. Says to tell you the Secretary has to see you."

"Oh, no," Mark Goddard moaned. "Not today." He paused. "How many patients are ahead of him that I haven't seen?"

"Twelve," responded Melinda. "And two of them have been waiting almost two hours. I told him how busy you are and he said he was prepared for a long wait."

Silence fell between them while Mark Goddard reflected and remembered and juggled personal priorities.

"What shall I tell him?" prodded Melinda, hope in her eyes.

Mark Goddard sighed. "Melinda, go back to your window and lie like a Trojan. Tell Gregry McHune we'll be happy to see him. And, Melinda," he added in a lighter tone, "if you can force a smile and sound like you mean it, I'll dance at your wedding."

The teeth shone radiantly white. "I can handle it if you can." She looked at her watch. "Diana's coming to relieve me in thirty minutes. I'll think about you while I'm home eating lunch."

When Dr. Goddard eventually entered Gregry McHune's treatment room, chart in hand, he thought the great cat eyes were guarded, almost defensive. A cheery welcome, however, wiped away the months of absence and Gregry McHune responded with warmth.

"You're right, Doc, it sure has been a long time and I'm sure as hell glad to see you, too. Set down and give me just a few minutes; I won't take up much of your time today because I know you must be plumb wore out. How'n hell do you wade through all this mess of disease and sick folks that swarm through here and don't never get sick your own self? That has always been a wonderment to me. How do you do it?"

Mark Goddard laughed as he rolled his padded stool out and sank gratefully upon it. "Who knows? Maybe I'm just a Christian Scientist making a fast buck, Gregry."

The temporary blank stare that greeted this remark was dispelled by the golden leap of comprehension in Gregry's eyes and a following gurgle of mirth. "Gotcha. Same old Marco Polo, aintcha? Bouncing and twisting around like a rabbit on the run. But I'm on to you. Effen they's one thing you have learnt me, it's how to read between your lines. And that things ain't always just exactly what a feller thinks he's hearing when it first comes out your mouth. That one wasn't all that deep, though, and ole Gregry caught it right off. You're a trip without no suitcase, Marco Polo, and I really am glad to see you again. I been missing you."

"Likewise, Gregry. What can I do for you today?"

The man broke eye contact, studied his fingernails in silence, took a deep breath. "Doc, I have made one of the hardest decisions I ever made in my whole life and I waded through a heap of indecision before I come to it, if you know what I mean?"

"Are you talking about doubt, Gregry?"

"Not no more, Doc, although I have handled a heap of it for the last week. Doubt will drive you crazy effen you let it. You know that, don't you?"

"George McDonald said that doubt is not a good reason to do anything, but it is a bad reason for doing nothing."

"Huh? What you say? Run that by me one more time, Doc. I wasn't tuned in on the right track or holding my bat just right or whatever you call it when you whipped that one over the plate."

"'Doubt is not a good reason to do anything, but is a bad reason for doing nothing.'"

Gregry McHune's eyes were fixed on Mark Goddard's, lidless, unblinking. "Okay. I'm trying, but it ain't getting through. As the fellow said, 'I can hear you clucking but I can't find your nest.' I know what you saying but what the hell does it mean?"

"Perhaps it's a literary way of expressing what my father used to shout when he saw me nagged by indecision. 'Dammit, Son, do something! Even if it's wrong!'"

"Oh. Well, why didn't you just say so?" He smiled. "Same as Mr. Metters told me one time. You know Kentucky is big on basketball, Doc, and Mr. Metters started me off with a lard can what he had cut the bottom out of and nailed up on the side of the smoke house. After I got where I could hit that pretty good, he got a old wagon rod and had the blacksmith make a regulation hoop and put it up. Didn't have no net, but Mr. Metters said one would rot anyhow, out in the weather like that.

"When I got up in junior high, the which they call it middle school now, they had a little ole basketball team and Mr. Metters let me join even though it meant he had to come and get me in his truck ever day after practice. He even come to my first game, the which it was also my last. Turnt out basketball just wasn't built for ole Gregry; I'd rather run than dribble. I had the ball and this ole boy what was bigger'n me was guarding me so close I couldn't pass it off for hell. I heard Mr. Metters' hollerin, 'Shoot! Shoot! Shoot, Gregry, shoot!' But, Doc, I couldn't get through that thicket of arms and legs; seemed like that guard had a dozen of each; and I lost the ball.

"I'll never forget what Mr. Metters told me when we was walking to the truck. He was cutting off a chew of tobacco and said, 'Son, comes a time ever now'n then when a fellow just has to jump straight up in the air, shut his eyes, holler "Shit!" and shoot.' Now that's might nigh the same thing we're all getting around to in this here conversation, ain't it, Doc?"

"Probably so, Gregry. If George McDonald were still alive, I'd be tempted to write him and inquire, but I'm certain my father and your grandfather had something in common. Pardon the interruption."

"Don't matter. I done got a long time ago to where I expect that out of you, although I believe I'd call that one a whole new Sunday school lesson instead of just a interruption. Sometimes you underestimate yourself, Doc, if you know what I mean." The gray teeth flashed in a grin.

"Forgive me, Gregry. I have a tendency to intrude. Go ahead with what you want to tell me."

"Well, Doc, I got to fill you in first on a little background before I get around to what you really got to hear today. Since I seen you, I changed jobs, traded cars, and moved into a house instead of a apartment."

"You mean you're not working at Georgia Tech anymore?"

"Nope. I found a job what pays more money."

"What about benefits? Insurance?"

"Just as good, if not better, Doc. Ole Gregry didn't ride into town on no turnip truck; I didn't leave till I found myself something better. I got to studying on things after I seen you last. I was powerful dissatisfied in spite of all the feelings you and me had got thrashed out. It wasn't my marriage, it wasn't my boy nor yet them two twins what have now become my own boys. I was sleeping good and not drinking no beer but I was still restless as a red wiggler in a ant hill, and I finely realized that I hated my job at Tech. I got to studying on that Kingdom of Heaven we was talking about and how it is inside one's own self, and I recognized that it takes Gregry McHune to make Gregry McHune happy. Can't nobody else do it for him. I can't change nothing but me, Doc."

"That's a milestone a great many people never pass on the roadway of life, Gregry. Congratulations."

"Yeah. Well, this new job is driving a van and making deliveries all over town. Keeps me outdoors all day and I really like it. They like me, too. Give me a bonus at the end of six weeks and a raise in three months. See, Doc, they pay you on the number of deliveries you make and not just the hours you work, and anybody what has ever cut tobacco all day long in Kentucky is going to be some more good at something as easy as making deliveries through city streets. Paying folks by the hour has ruint this country, Doc, cause it's just human nature not to bust your butt if some slob next to you is fumbling and fiddling around all day long and taking home as much money as you. Anyhow, things was going good. I loved my job, my new bosses loved me and I was able to move Rose into a real house for not much more rent that we had been apaying. I even traded my old car just before it was time to file off the registration number, walk off with the tag, and leave it dead on the expressway. Hell, Doc, I also had a little money set aside in the bank."

"Gregry, that's great. I'm happy for you."

"Hold on a minute, Doc. Don't get carried away yet. About three weeks ago, I was taking a short cut, which I regular do and had got in the habit of, up one of the side streets off Stewart Avenue. Wasn't no traffic to speak of and I was clipping along pretty good. This car with two black boys in it come right over the center line dead at me and the only way I missed 'em was jumping the curb and hitting the sidewalk. It happened so quick all I could do was react to keep from having a wreck. I looked in the mirror and saw a big black finger jabbing up out of both sides of that car, but wasn't no chance of catching them, the which in that particular neighborhood it would of been a damfool thing to try to do anyhow."

Gregry's eyes narrowed slightly, his brow creased and he continued. "Well, sir, when I turned my van in that evening, one of the bosses said, 'Gregry, we had a complaint on you about reckless driving this afternoon.' I said, 'Come again?' 'Somebody called on the phone,' he said, 'and told us that you was speeding up Stewart Avenue and nearly lost control of your vehicle and even run up on the sidewalk.'

"'Who was it called?' I asked.

"'It was a male. Never gave no name,' my boss said.

"'Well, sir, how'd he know who to call?' I come back at him.

"'I guess he got the company name off the side of the van. He called you by name, too. Said he wanted to report Gregry McHune for driving all over the sidewalk and endangering lives and property.'

"'Hell,' I told him, 'they wasn't a soul on that street going or coming cept two sonbitches what deliberately run me up on that sidewalk. And they sure hell wasn't nobody on that sidewalk or I'd a seen 'em. And how in hell did they get my name? It sure ain't painted on that van.'"

Mark Goddard sat very still.

"Well, Doc, before I could ask any more questions or line out my side of what was going on, the boss got that tone in his voice what bosses get when they fixing to come down on you. 'Well, McHune,' he says, 'you admit you overran the curb. Were you also speeding?'

"'Well, hell,' I told him, 'I wasn't doing no thirty-five mile per hour like the signs say all over town, but I wasn't drag racing at sixty or seventy neither. I was clipping along at a reasonable rate of speed, but I wouldn't call it speeding.'

"'The witness called it that,' he said. 'And I am going to have to put this in your file.'

"Well, that sort of bowed my back up and I said, 'Ain't nothing else in the file, is they? And I been with you close on to six months now. I ain't no reckless driver and I take good care of your machines.'

"He said, 'You been a good employee, but . . . .' And, Doc, you can mark it down if somebody says you been a good employee *and*, it means you gonna get a raise or a bonus, but when they say you been a good employee *but*, you fixing to catch hell and get a reprimand, which nowadays they call a memo. I stood there and took my medicine and listened to all that stuff about public image of the company, safety of pedestrians, damage to company vehicles, and I don't know what all. Only thing I could do was say, 'Yes, sir, yessir, yessir.' That's because when you finely grow up and have a house note and a car payment and three younguns, you can't tell a boss to shove a job up his ass and jump his own self in behind it like you could of before. I took all the preaching he had to dish out, but all the time I was studying and thinking.

"When I had et all the humble pie he was hell-bent on feeding me and I was fixing to leave, I ast him, 'Was it a black male what took it on hisself to report this incident?'

"He looked at me sort of down his nose and said, 'How

could I tell? I didn't see him.'

"'Same way you knowed it wasn't no woman. You can tell.'

"He sort of raised an eyebrow and said, 'You're right, of course. Yes, McHune, I would say the caller was definitely black.'"

Gregry instinctively reached into his shirt pocket for a cigarette, recovered, and continued. "Well, Doc, I was so busy thinking about things when I left there and trying to puzzle them through that I had gone about three blocks before it come over me that somebody was following me, and it looked like the very same car what had run me off the road. I speeded up, slowed down, doubled back and forth and led them on a wild goose chase bout like a kill-dee leading a fox away from its nest. I finely got serious and lost 'em. Then I went on home. I never said nothing to Rose, but I was some more worried."

Mark Goddard involuntarily took an audible breath. Gregry McHune did not notice.

"Something commenced happening all the time. The very next day the air was let out of both back tires at one delivery and the valve cores throwed away. Now that'll slow up any man what works on the run, Doc. Same voice called the boss and said Gregry McHune would be late because he had parked the company van and visited a girl friend. Another day they starred one side the windshield with what looked like it must of been a ballpeen hammer. No phone call that day but I had to report the damage when I checked in. I was getting in deep shit with my bosses and I could tell they was getting close to the edge with me. Ever day it was something and ever day the snitch on the phone used my name. He knowed me.

"I took to toting my gun again, the which I hadn't done since I got out of prison, and I got so jumpy Rose asked me did I need to go back on my Prozac. I kept trying to get a good look at them two guys in that car because they would fall in behind me bout ever other night and try to trail me, but all I could tell was they was real big and real black and real young. I also realized they was smart as hell. I thought about the police but I couldn't go to them. First thing they'd do would be look at my record and that wouldn't be good. Then nearly ever police in Atlanta is black and they'd be sure to side with they brothers, as they call each other.

"I tell you, Doc, you just don't amount to nothing in this town anymore, and sometimes looks like in the whole country, less'n you're either black or gay. Especially if you're what they call a unskilled or a blue-collar worker. Besides the which I couldn't even identify nobody, let alone prove nothing. I kept wondering why them two was after me, but nothing fit. All I knowed was they was bent and determined to get me fired and to catch up with me after work and follow me home, and I was just as determined not to let them find out where I lived. All of a sudden the whole city of Atlanta had turned into a great big jungle and I was being stalked through it by a couple of hunters. I was nervous as hell, but I wasn't what you'd call scared because I knowed I was smarter'n they was and I could always lay a little ambush some evening and take both of 'em out. I even took to planning how I'd make it look like a gang war or a drive-by shooting and have the eleven o'clock news reporting another drug-related crime and the bleeding hearts piddling in their panties about tighter gun control. And no blame ever laid on me."

Mark Goddard's attention was too intense for speech. He became apprehensive about what he might hear next.

"I studied on it one evening and decided it was about time to jump up, holler 'Shit!' and shoot. But I wasn't about to close my eyes. Two could play the game they was up to, I told myself, and I'd just, by God, scare the living hell out of them, or at the very least find out who they was and get a close look at 'em. I seen 'em about a block behind me in the mirror and

I turned up a empty side street, gunned up it, spun my car around and when they come along I was laying across the fender on the driver's side with my pistol pointed dead at 'em. They let out a yell and tore out of there, but I got a good enough look at both of 'em I was satisfied I could pick 'em out of a line-up."

Mark Goddard could not resist. He had to know. "You didn't shoot?"

"Naw," answered Gregry. "Didn't need to. They scratched off so fast I never had a prayer of getting they tag number, neither, but at least I had let them know I was ready to fight any damn day they was. But you know, Doc, something new was worrying me now. You know some folks say all black folks look alike, but that ain't so, and that sure wasn't what made me feel like I had seen the one somewhere before what was driving. He was real big and real black and his face was some more familiar; but worry it around as I would, I just couldn't place it."

He paused, fumbled in his shirt pocket again, then nervously withdrew his hand. Mark Goddard spun around on his stool, procured an emesis basin from beneath the sink and placed it on the desk. "For God's sake, go ahead and smoke, Gregry. Nobody's in this part of the building but us, and that's the second or third time you've reached for a cigarette."

Gregry McHune gently pushed the receptacle aside. "No thanks, Doc. You got rules you live by and even if I don't apply 'em to myself, I respect you for having 'em. I just forgot where I was at." A wistfulness entered his voice.

"But thanks all the same for the offer." He added, "You sure you got time today for all this I'm laying on you?

"I am absolutely positive, Gregry."

"Good. Cause I ain't near done yet. The next day when I turned in my van, both bosses come out the back door into the compound and had the head mechanic with them. Said

they wanted to inspect my vehicle. I told 'em that was fine
with me, but it hadn't been giving no trouble at all. Well, sir,
they put in and took that van apart. Looked under the
hood, pulled up the carpet, felt behind and under the seat,
and after about thirty minutes of that I finely said, 'I ain't hauling no marijuana or nothing like that. Eff'n you'd tell me what
you looking for, maybe I can holp you.'

"'Fine,' said one of 'em. 'We had a report that you were
transporting firearms in a company vehicle and we had to make
a search, for that is completely contrary to company policy.'

"'Same black male voice on the telephone, wasn't it?' I asked.

"'I would say so,' he said.

"'Well,' I told him, 'that black male sonbitch was twisting the truth and lying just like he's been ever time he's
made them harassing telephone calls to you. Here's where I
tote my gun.' And I pulled up my britches leg and showed
it to 'em strapped to my leg. Well, sir, all three of 'em backed
off in a line together like they thought I was fixing to shoot,
and the senior boss said, 'How come you hadn't told us you
had that gun?' and I said . . . ."

"I know what you said," interrupted Mark Goddard.
"You said, 'Hell, you never asked me.' Right?"

There came a fleeting, abstracted attempt at a smile.
"That's right. Then they dismissed the mechanic—I will
give them that—and said they had to talk to me. Said for me
to come on in they office where we could set down and talk,
and I told 'em I didn't figger to be doing much talking
myself and I could listen just fine standing up outdoors
right where I was at.

"I was within a gnat's ass of getting mad, Doc, and then
I recollected what you had said about letting other folks have
control of my feelings, and I figured if I already wasn't
gonna let them control me enough to make me set down in
no chair that I sure as hell didn't have to turn over control

of my temper to them. I stood there with my arms folded so they wouldn't be nervous about the gun and listened them out. Just looked at 'em real steady and listened. You can't imagine how polite and calm I was. Hell, I don't even believe it myself and I was there.

"Course they went through all they crap about they responsibility to the company and morale of other employees and inherent dangers surrounding my continued employment and potential hazards to be avoided—all them big words which didn't mean a thing in this world except they was building up to firing my ass and couldn't do it without making they speeches and doing a few little war dances first. Seemed like the calmer I was the faster and louder they talked and the more they said the same thing over and over. As Mr. Metters would of said, 'They was as nervous as a hen on a hot hoe.' It come to me that, by God, at least for a little while I had control of they feelings and I decided I'd do a little preaching of my own. Not that I thought it'd do any good, but they was a few things they needed to hear, and effen I told 'em my ownself I'd always know they'd at least heard it oncet.

"I commenced to talking, talking soft enough to gentle a snarling hound, and, Doc, you shoulda seen how still and quiet they got. I said, 'You fellas ain't asked me my side in none of this and I guess my feelings don't really play no big part in what's best for your company and your bottom line and your peace of mind and all like that; so I'd be wasting my breath and your time to go into all of it. I don't know exactly who it is been making them calls, although I been trying to find out, but it's plain to me that the reason behind it all is to make you fire me. Now, y'all are holding the big stick all right, but let me tell you one thing and that is that you have grabbed it by the short end.

"'We living in this big grand city what's run by black folks and ever day we listen to all this stuff about violence and crime and corruption in government, and here you two guys cave in the first time a smart-ass jigaboo gets on the telephone and shakes you up a little and plays with your head. All this chain link fence with bob wire on the top what you have put around your plant to keep thieves out ain't gonna do you one bit of good if you let it come inside to you over the telephone and gnaw at your guts and turn your backbone yellow. Like I said, you're holding the big stick and you can use it to fire a man what ain't even got no stick, but remember you got ahold of the short end of it and you can't do much to defend your own self when all you're grabbing is the short end.'

"Well, sir, they stood for a second or two like they was froze, and then the senior boss pulled two checks out'n his breast pocket and started towards me. Before he could open his mouth I said, 'Well, I see your little minds is already made up ahead of time, even to having the secretary cut the checks before she left. I know one of 'em's for what time I got coming and the other one is probly for two weeks' pay instead of notice.' He never said a word, just held 'em out to me. I took 'em and looked at 'em and put the big one in my wallet, real slow and deliberate like. Then I give him back the one for two weeks and said, 'Tit for tat. Effen you don't want me to work out no notice, then I sure don't feel obligated to offer you no notice. I ain't never worked nowhere I wasn't wanted and I don't want nothing coming to me I ain't worked for. Lots of luck to you upper level types on your effort to maintain law and order and to restore family values in this town.' And I went and got in my car.

"Well, Doc, here come the junior boss in a trot. The old one was walking back inside, but the young one grabbed that check out of his hand and come over to me. I rolled down the window, and he said, 'Look here, McHune, you can't do this. Please take this check. You've earned it.'

"I said, 'No, I ain't. I know what I've earned and what I ain't, and effen you got it mixed up with money then you ain't gonna surround yourself down through the years with no great multitude of loyal employees.'

Then he come close to whining. 'Come on, Gregry,' he said. 'Take the check and make me feel better. It's the principle involved.'

"Doc, I looked him in the eye and told him real slow and real soft, 'I reckon you and me know by now that wasn't neither one of us put on this earth to make the other one feel better. The Kingdom of Heaven is within you and you got to tend to it your ownself. But since you done brought up this matter of principle, let me give you an example of principle. I know a lady what works for the Federal government; she's a secretary out at Fort McPherson. For years now they been shutting that place down tighter'n a bull's ass in fly time for Martin Luther King's birthday. That lady has got her own key to her office out there and she goes to work on that day just like it was any other. Puts in a full day, she does. Nobody knows it. She's the only one in the building. When I ast her how come she done it, she said it was because she didn't believe in MLK. Said she hadn't admired or liked the man whilest he was alive. Thought he was a self-serving troublemaker who preached nonviolence but everwhere he went he stirred up violence in other folks. Said she didn't think he was no saint just because some shortsighted evil fool had made a martyr out of him, and that she wasn't taking no money for setting at home doing nothing on his birthday. Now, that is what I call principle,' I told him."

Mark Goddard's foot was going to sleep. He needed to uncross his legs, but he was careful to do it unobtrusively.

"Doc, he just stared at me. His mouth was hanging half-open and he looked so young I almost felt sorry for him. I said, 'I feel moved to tell you something I hope you'll remember all your days. My granddaddy told me when I was a heap younger'n you and I ain't never forgot it.' He swallowed and said, 'What's that, Gregry?'

"'He told me,' I said, 'you know how to tell the short end of the stick from the long end, Son? The short end is the one what has got shit on it.' And I never changed my voice a bit, but I cranked my car and told him, 'In the case of you and the big boss, it's my personal opinion that it's chicken shit.' And I let the clutch out and eased away, didn't scratch off or cut no wheelie or nothing. Hell, Doc, for some reason I wasn't even mad."

Mark Goddard spoke. "Gregry, it is difficult to be angry in a moment of triumph."

"Yeah, I reckon. I'll study on that one later. Anyhow, I drove on home. Wasn't nobody behind me but I went roundabout to make sure. Et supper like nothing had happened, let my boy beat me in a game of checkers whilest Rose washed the twins, and was setting around waiting for her to tuck 'em all in bed and awondering how to tell her I had lost my job when the telephone rang. All I got to say was 'Hello.' This voice (and it wasn't a black, Doc, it was a nigger) said, 'We know where you live, you goddam white motherfucker. Now it's payback time. Goddam your soul to eternal hell.' That's all he said and hung up real quick before I could even get my breath. Let alone say nothing back.

"First thing I done was cut out all the lights in the front of the house, grab my gun, and slip outside behind a holly bush close to the sidewalk and wait. I didn't have no way of knowing what was coming down but I, by God, didn't aim to let it slip up on me. And whilest I was waiting I was thinking. I couldn't for the life of me figure how they had got my unlisted number. I knowed they hadn't followed me home, but if they was smart enough to get my number they sure as hell wasn't fooling about knowing where I lived. On top of that, something kept stirring in my mind about that fellow's face and all of a sudden I put it with the voice, which I hadn't yet heard before, and it come over me in a flash. 'Give me your money,' I heard ringing in my ears and it sounded just like, 'Now we know where you live.' Doc, it was the son of that dude I had blowed away on that Christmas Eve a long time ago.

"They wasn't no doubt in my mind no more. He looked like him and he even sounded like him. I had knowed the son-bitch had two boys, had even seen 'em once when they showed up with they mama at my arraignment. They was little then, but they was both sure to be growed up by now. Well, cold as it was, you can believe I commenced to sweating. Them boys was out to kill me and if they was going to all this trouble to harass and torture me first, they sure meant business, and on top of that was cocky as hell.

"I went pretty quick from being scared to being mad. I had killed one man in self-defense and everbody had called it murder. Now I was going to have to kill two of 'em and it was sure self-defense again, but the difference was that this time I wasn't going to get caught. I calmed myself down and went to planning."

"Oh, my God!" prayed Mark Goddard silently. Of a sudden he had a vision of Dennis Bentley's face when he would come to tell him that Gregry McHune's record had been subpoenaed. He said nothing.

"I went on back in the house feeling pretty sure of things. I figured if them two was doing all this staging and everthing and if it was in payback for they old man that they was aiming to do it on Christmas Eve. For sentimental reasons, if you know what I mean, Doc. So that give me a little time. When Rose jumped me about where I'd been I told her I'd been walking around trying to make up my mind how to tell her I'd lost my job. The phone rang at one o'clock and at three o'clock, but nobody said nothing and I told Rose it must be a wrong number. Wasn't no use getting her wind up till I had to.

"That phone went on like that ever night. I thought about having the number changed but, hell, effen they'd got it oncet, they could do it again. Most of the time they never said nothing, and I'd holler something about 'crank calls' or 'freaks or 'weirdos,' anything to keep 'em from realizing I knowed who they was. I was playing they game so they wouldn't tumble to the game I was playing. Rose got pretty pissed but I aimed to keep the truth from her long as I could. In fact, I didn't see no need in her ever having to know I had kilt two more men. You see, Doc, my back was to the wall. My plan was going to work and it was for sure and certain I didn't aim for nobody ever to find out about it. As much as I love and trust Rose, effen she didn't know nothing she couldn't tell nothing, besides which she is a tender-hearted person and it would of been a heavy load for her to tote.

"I wasn't sleeping much and I had plenty of time to plan. I wasn't working at no job and I had plenty of time to slip around and throw them two off my tail effen they tried to follow me. I found out they names, I found out they trail ever evening, I found out where they sold crack, I found out where they lived. Or at least I found out where they 'stayed;' I ain't never yet got no black person to tell me he 'lived' anywhere. I stole me a twelve-gauge shotgun and sawed it off, just in case the police had a match on my pistol somewhere. I had rubber gloves ready and I had the alley and the hour picked. I was ready."

Mark Goddard held his breath. He heard his heart thumping and felt that he was aging fast.

"I had 'em, Doc. One of 'em was in the phone booth, the other one was outside aleaning in. It was one a.m. They was laughing at each other and I knowed well enough what number they was dialing. I had double-ought buckshot in that gun and I had remembered to wipe the shells clean before I loaded it. Wasn't a soul in sight. I raised the gun and aimed at they chests. I wasn't three feet from them and they hadn't ever seen me. Then I let the gun down, eased back around the corner into the alley, and left."

Mark Goddard blurted immediately, "Were they still alive?"

"So far's I know, Doc. That was three nights ago and the phone is still ringing at one and at three."

"What are you going to do, Gregry?"

"I'm going to disappear, Doc. Me and my whole family. As far as Atlanta, Georgia, and all the scum in it, we're going to vanish off'n the face of the earth. That's how come I had to see you today. I come to say good-bye."

"Disappear? What the hell are you talking about? You can't just vanish. What are you doing that for?"

"I'm doing it to get away, Doc. Forever. I don't want to raise my three boys from now on looking over they shoulders to see what's sneaking up on 'em or else plotting and planning on payback they own selves. And I can vanish. I got it planned. I'm leaving no tracks that them two can follow, I don't care how smart they are nor how many of they kind they got helping them. They mean enough and smart enough to keep after me if I leave any track behind."

"If they're smart enough to get your unlisted phone number, Gregry, they're smart enough to track your social security number whenever you get another job."

"I done tended to that, Doc. I had a buddy in prison for something minor like bank fraud and maybe a little forgery, but he's had friends what knows the ropes in the protective witness program and all like that. I got a new I.D., social security number, driver's license and everthing. I got a hot pickup what I'm gonna load with what furniture we got to have. I done sold Rose's car and mine, too. Got the cash in my pocket. We loading that truck right after the one o'clock call tonight, and right after the three o'clock call comes through we leaving. I know where I'm going and I'll drive that hot truck back in two days, ditch it in Macon, and catch a Greyhound bus to our new hometown. They ain't a piece of paper, a forwarding address or nothing. We're going to vanish. I even aim to leave the lights burning in the house."

"I can't believe this, Gregry."

"You can believe it, Doc. The only reason I'm here is I had to say good-by to somebody, and I guess you're the best friend I ever had or ever will have. You been better to me than any man since Mr. Metters passed, and I know they ain't no way I'm ever going to find another doctor like you."

"Gregry, ordinarily I tell a patient who is moving that I will forward records as soon as we have a request, but that would be a trail, wouldn't it?"

"Right, Doc. See what I mean? Even now you're still trying to look after me. Don't need them records anyhow. I never let you run no tests or get no x-rays effen you will remember; so they can't be much on them records anyhow."

Mark Goddard's eyes did not flicker. "You're right, Gregry. They wouldn't be very illuminating to any other physician. I've never had another patient like you and I'm sure I'll never find another one. I'm going to miss you."

"Thanks. I was in hopes that you would."

He stood up, stretched thoroughly, and evoked once more the image of a giant feline. "Well, that's about it." He stretched forth his hand and clasped Mark Goddard's, looked long into his eyes, and said, "So long, Marco Polo. Thanks for everthing."

The doctor grasped the hand as hard as he could. "Thank you, Gregry McHune, O Cat That Walks Alone."

Suddenly Gregry McHune pulled Mark Goddard to him in a tight embrace, then pushed him back and laughed softly. "Whatever the hell that means. You won't never change, will you, Doc? I'm outa here."

As he ambled out of the treatment room and down the vacant hall, Mark Goddard hailed him.

"Wait a minute, Gregry." He walked close to him. "At the risk of your accusing me of being a tourist, I've got to ask this. Why didn't you pull the trigger?"

"I guess I'd of left here disappointed, Doc, effen you'd of let that one go by. It was the craziest thing; all of a sudden I heard Miss Lila's voice, and I had about quit ever even thinking of her. She said, 'Mr. Metters, two wrongs don't make a right.' And I heard Mr. Metters say, 'That's a crazy way to live when somebody's done you wrong, Miss Lila, but I guess it'll do till something better comes along.' And all of a sudden I realized that I was all twisted up in my thinking. I had really kilt that man in self-defense the first time and society had called it murder, and here I was fixing to murder two somebodies and I was calling it self-defense in my own head. Ever since I have knowed you I have tried to be honest with my own self, and I said, 'Shit, Gregry, this not only ain't self-defense, this is premeditated murder.' And I decided to back out, disappear and leave them two sonbitches and Atlanta to theyselves. They deserve each other."

"Thanks, Gregry. I needed to know. Go with God."

"Well, that's a crazy way to travel, Marco Polo, when somebody's coming after you, but I guess it'll do till something better comes along. So long."

Gregry Clark walked five steps, turned, and came back.

"You know the real reason I didn't pull that trigger, Doc?"

Mark Goddard waited.

"I remembered the hate in the eyes of they daddy. It's the worst look I ever seen in my life and I don't never want to see it again the longest day I live. Especially if I'm the cause of it. Not in no human being, don't matter what color he is."

He turned to leave, then turned back. "And all that stuff about Kingdom of Heaven? I reckon, Marco Polo, that what Jesus Christ tried His damn dead-level best to teach us is as good a way to live as any. At least till something better comes along."

He turned again and was gone. For good.

Last patient of the day is Gregry McHune, Medical Record Number 079214. As soon as this dictation is filed I want Mr. McHune's chart removed to the inactive file.

> *I caught this morning morning's minion, king-*
> > *dom of daylight's dauphin, dapple-dawn-drawn Falcon,*
> > > *in his riding*
> > *Of the rolling level underneath him steady air, and*
> > > *striding*
> *High there, how he rung upon the rein of a wimpling wing*
> *In his ecstasy! then off, off forth on a swing,*
> > *As a skate's heel sweeps smooth on a bow-bend—the hurl*
> > > *and gliding*
> > *Rebuffed the big wind. My heart is hiding*
> *Stirred for a bird—the achieve of, the mastery of the thing!'*

Add this memo:
TO: Mr. Dennis Bentley
I am reneging. I am not resigning. I am, rather, sending you this as an affirmation. If you ever have three hours to spare I will explain it to you, but in the meantime:

> *The world stands out on either side*
> *No wider than the heart is wide;*
> *Above the world is stretched the sky, —*
> *No higher than the soul is high.*
> *The heart can push the sea and land*

Farther away on either hand;
The soul can split the sky in two,
And let the face of God shine through.
But East and West will pinch the heart
That can not keep them pushed apart;
And he whose soul is flat — the sky
Will cave in on him by and by.

Yours for better medicine and for the poetry that lives in all of us.

> *Mark Goddard, M.D.*
> *a.k.a. Marco Polo*

HARMONY AIN'T EASY

IN EVERY FAMILY WORTHY OF THE NAME, THERE ARE especial stories that so early amuse, then later so tickle and tantalize memory that the phrase which recalls one of them becomes a shibboleth in the family. These are in-jokes, the use of which can leave an outsider so puzzled and bewildered in the presence of collective hilarity that explanations are in order, albeit convolutedly forthcoming.

At least three decades ago, such a story found its way into my family. The preciousness of it was enhanced by the fact that initially it was related to us by an older friend and neighbor. This was a man possessed of such innate dignity that we tended to regard him as inflexible; perhaps, though worthy, as a little dull; so dedicated to good works, so serious of purpose that he bordered on being a bore. Certainly, we never thought him possessed of that innate awareness of the ridiculous upon which any sense of humor is founded. "It just goes to show," we told ourselves afterwards, "that you never can tell."

My older sister, of course, remembered to say, "Still waters run deep."

An old farmer, the story went, arose at daybreak, dressed for the field and went to his kitchen for breakfast. There was no food on the table, no light on, and the stove was cold. He knocked on the door to his housekeeper's room to ask explanation and was answered with the plaintive wail, "I ain't cooked you no breakfast cause I'm too sick. I ain't even able to get out of bed. I need for you to go get me the doctor out here and that just as quick as you can."

The farmer sighed but went dutifully back to his room and changed from overalls into his suit in preparation for going to town.

When he went outside, he found that his old car wouldn't crank. He sighed, and by dint of much straining managed to roll it over a rise and down a little hill to jump-start it. He chugged on until he had to ford a creek, where he got off-center a little and the car was stuck.

He sighed, but patiently removed his shoes, rolled up his pants legs and managed with a prise-pole to free his car and go on his way.

A quarter mile down the road he had a flat tire. He folded his coat, with a sigh, changed the tire and put on the spare. A mile later he had another flat tire. He gripped the steering wheel and thought for a while. Then he removed the flat and with patience began rolling it before him toward town.

A half-mile from the car, the sky suddenly darkened. Rain began falling so heavily that the old man could barely see. Within seconds, he was soaking wet. He felt his shoes filling with water, he felt his only suit shrinking on his frame. He let the tire fall to the ground before him, raised his clenched fists to the heavens and howled at the top of his voice, "My God! Why do all these things have to happen to me?"

With that the rain stopped, the clouds parted, and a deep voice boomed down, "I don't know, Melrose; there's just something about you that chaps My ass!"

My children and I loved this story. My wife, Helen, who tends to regard repetition as an intellectual insult, laughed the first time she heard it, smiled dutifully the second time, shook her head the third or fourth time, and after that ignored it when she could.

Helen's niece, Jo Macon, in her early career as an artist, painted a seascape for Gloria Glass, a friend of ours who raised Golden Retrievers. It was a trade. Gloria was loath to part with cash money and Jo loved dogs. Since Jo was married to a Navy man at the time and moved around all over creation, we were coaxed into keeping a half-grown Golden Retriever puppy for her. That dog had feet as big as cathead biscuits, and what he couldn't dig up in the flower beds and foundation plantings, he chewed to ribbons. It was my professional opinion that he was hyperkinetic, suffered severely from attention deficit, and probably had a defect in his twenty-first chromosome. I lived in fear that he would become dehydrated, for his output in slobber alone surely exceeded his intake. He panted as loudly as a diesel tractor throttling down. On his registration papers he had a long romantic name with a hyphen somewhere in it, but after one week we named him Melrose. It was appropriate; he kept everyone chapped.

After six months, Gloria Glass manifested the candor found only between true friends and old friends. She confided in me, with just the charming hint of a stammer, that she did not like her painting and would really love to return it if she only knew how to approach Jo without embarrassment. She hated, she said, for someone who really liked that kind of seascape not to have it. I assured her with equal candor that all she had to do was take her goddam dog back and I would make things right with Jo. Which I did. I sent Jo a check for one hundred dollars and replanted ten square yards of centipede, four azaleas, two pittisporum, a Japanese maple and two gardenias. I put the seascape in the attic, Melrose's water dish in the city dump, and felt that all things considered I had come out ahead. I shrugged when I pondered on Jo and Gloria, but felt that each of them at least should have learned something from this Melrose caper and be the wiser for it.

That was three decades ago. Last summer, I had occasion to recall it. Ever since 1951 when we began a medical practice in Fayetteville, Georgia, my wife and I have taken Thursdays as our day off. We work on Saturdays, when it is difficult to get coverage, and Thursday consequently is our Sabbath. In a fervent attempt to keep it holy, we get out of town. A mountain range in North Georgia is our Mecca, an isolated cabin at the end of a dirt road on a ridge in Dawson County our Shangri-la.

My wife, through the forty-seven years I have known her, has without realizing it demonstrated herself to be the most unselfish and giving person I have ever met. So long as no violation of her principles is involved, there is nothing she would not do to please me. My responsibility has been to become ever easier to please, and also to acknowledge that she is possessed of more inviolable principles than any other person I have ever known.

In the presence of true nobility, a perceptive man who is blessed with both a modicum of intelligence and a deep desire for survival will attempt to emulate the unspoken demonstration of bedrock virtue with which he lives. This is a daunting challenge for a man of my plebeian defects, but I try. In recompense for my deficiencies through the week, I make a conscious effort on Thursdays to please my wife. In my mind I refer to our Sabbath as "Helen's day." I try. Often I fail.

In midsummer of last year, following a trying week at the office, Thursday at our cabin brought a seductive dawn and improbable sunrise across the valley over which our deck is suspended, and I arose from our bed in an entirely different world from the one I had quit the evening before.

Sipping my first cup of coffee, I watched the world awaken in silence until there was enough daylight to see the white splash of Amicolola Falls seven miles away. The tranquillity I coveted enveloped me; my cares vanished like the wisps of vapor that were rising to outline every hillock spread out below our deck; each nuisance I had suffered during the week was well-endured to have led to this moment. I exulted that a wonderful day, empty of duty, lay before us.

Helen likes neither to wake up nor to get up, but has principles that demand both. On Thursdays, I practice early morning stealth and leave the waking process entirely to her discretion. On that particular day, she arose only after the hum of bees had reached crescendo outside her window. The sun, however, was still low enough to anchor the trees with patches of crisp shade across the lawn; the opalescent sheen of dew-softened grass was still present in their shadows.

I poured her some coffee; I sliced her a mango. During her second cup of coffee, when I was sure she was awake, I suggested that we eat breakfast out on the deck. The yellow jackets were not yet out, I said, and there was just enough breeze to keep the gnats and the no-seeums away. I had prepared Mrs. Winners' biscuits left over from Sunday's dinner: halved, buttered, and toasted. I served them with slabs of fresh tomatoes from Lester Bray's patch and bacon cooked crisp and dry. As we ate suspended in overhang between heaven and earth, but equally conscious of both, I said, "It doesn't get any better than this. This is the best restaurant in the world."

In quiet voice still velvet from sleep she said, "I know. The menu may not be much, but you can't beat the decor."

I took this as at least a partial compliment and nodded. "What do you want to do today?"

"I don't know. Pour me another cup of coffee. I don't care. What do you want to do?"

My mind bounded around like a joyous dog just let off the leash, but I manifested leisurely nonchalance. "What about a little shopping trip, and make it a point to get back here by one o'clock for a drink and some lunch and a nap?"

My wife is a perpetual, accomplished and dedicated shopper. Her devotion to the process of discriminating selection pervades our lives. Price, quality, utility, appearance and acquisition are all fast-shuttling chips in the computer program of her daily existence. That computer does not shut down when she leaves Phipps Plaza or Lenox Square. A simple trip to the grocery store seems never-ending if string beans are on her list; each one is scrutinized carefully before being accepted or rejected. The mere process of arriving at a mall involves shopping for a parking space. "There's a better one over there."

A walk through the mountains means that I will, in spring or summer, return with a backpack filled with wild flowers that she uproots and packs in moss for relocation in our woods at home. In fall and winter she has an ever busy eye for, of all things, lightwood knots and logs. "Smell this one," she will say with joy. "It's really rich, it's almost pure turpentine."

I agree and compliantly carry it along. I have learned that sweating up a mountainside, laden like a donkey with a collection of potential kindling, is good exercise, costs nothing, and leads to eventual harmony. This depends, of course, on my being pleasant even when I cannot feign enthusiasm, and on my refraining from the observation that we already have a pile of lightwood behind our woodshed large enough for the seven dwarves to build a house.

I learned years ago that remonstrances in the ear of an accomplished shopper are totally futile and will produce only irritated rejoinders. I have also maintained silence about the subliminal obsession in my wife to shop. If she is not aware of it then I'll not point it out. Any change in that area might result in a subtle shift of balance somewhere else, other changes in unexpected areas, and I like her just the way she is.

"Shopping?" she replied on that memorable morning. "Are you out of your mind? Shopping for what? And where?"

"Well, I thought we might park on Highway 108 and hike to the north side of Burnt Mountain and shop for Turkscap Lilies. We found some blooming there last year, you know."

"They're on the endangered list, aren't they?"

"Maybe. Maybe not. But you and I know that it's only a matter of twenty-five or thirty years before some dollar-driven developer gets that land zoned for apartments, or some visionary in the highway department cuts a four-lane through there. It's really a missionary effort in ecology to move them and save them. If we don't do it, nobody will."

"Hummmm," she said.

I pressed the point. "Besides, it's not more than a quarter of a mile through the woods from there to that planting of Nodding Mandarins you found last fall, and you've been saying you'd like to get a start of that in our woods."

That was the irresistible bait. By the time we had laced our boots and gathered our gear, it had become a joint venture and a damned good idea. Oh, it would be a glorious day!

It was only five miles up the winding pavement to Highway 108, and since we had the road to ourselves we slowed to watch a hawk sail in hover above a ridge only to burst suddenly in glide-and-wheel over a deep valley, wondering at his effortless change of speed without so much as dipping a wing. I stopped the car so we could watch a wild turkey hen, in head-cocking, wary high step, shepherd her eight gangly poults up a wooded hill and out of sight. We involuntarily spoke in low tones. The hills of Dawson County inspire reverence.

We turned off the highway to the smaller 108 and followed it slowly uphill and around a curve, searching the bluff to our right for the telltale crimson flash of a Cumberland azalea that might be blooming late. We were in no hurry. Our mission was a leisurely one. Over the crest of Burnt Mountain and halfway down the other side, I turned into one of two roads that gave entrance to an exclusive development of mountain homes. Several yards from the highway each road was blocked by a locked gate. The one on the right was paved and stretched straight to the top of the mountain at a fifty degree angle, the traverse of which we knew from experience would produce shortness of breath, a pounding heart and the souvenir two days hence of sore calves and stiff hips.

Although each road ultimately gave access to our destination, we both chose without comment the lower. In addition to its gentler slope, it was unpaved and winding, overhung with trees, a softer path to the eye as well as the foot. A dirt road is always more alluring and seductive than a paved one, more enticing. It beckons with more promise of surprise, and more frequently rewards the traveler with some treasure of small adventure to be hoarded in his memory. On dirt roads, I have given relaxed snakes the right-of-way, watched quail dart with waddling speed ahead of me, disturbed a terrapin laying her eggs. I have never, on a dirt road, encountered a traffic light or a four-way stop sign. No one who has been smothered by dust and stuck in mud holes would choose again to live permanently on a dirt road, but, as is true in other manifestations of progress, there are some things that have been lost in the trade. Whenever we have the time and the option, Helen and I choose the dirt over macadam. On our Sabbath.

I nosed up to the gate, pulled over to the right, and reached to turn off the switch.

"You can't park here and leave the car."

"Why not? There are no tracks on this road since it rained, and that was two days ago. Besides, there's enough room on the left for somebody to squeeze by."

"I don't care. If I owned a vacation home down this

road, I wouldn't like it if I found some interloper blocking my road."

On Thursdays too many rebuttals can shatter serenity, can even earn the defamatory retort of, "You're being stubborn." I wanted none of that. Not today.

"I hadn't thought of that." I wagged my head and put the car in reverse.

In promise of security to prospective purchasers of over-priced lots, a tiny abandoned guard house stood just off the pavement. Shards of glass twinkled in vandalized glitter on its floor beneath shattered windows. Its front yard was gravel, albeit overgrown with grass and small weeds. With authority, I backed into it.

"What are you doing?"

"I'm parking. We're out of the road now; so we can't possibly block anyone's way. See, the wheels are completely off the edge of the pavement."

"I don't know about this. You are on a slant. I can hardly open my door. Do you think you can get us out of here?"

"No problem. Look. See the gravel?"

I popped the trunk open, got out the shovel and a supply of plastic bags and shrugged into my backpack.

"Don't you think you ought to put the telephone in the trunk?"

"I'll take it off its stand and put it underneath the seat. We're going to lock the car."

"Somebody might break in and steal it."

"If that's what's on somebody's mind they could break into the trunk, too. Don't worry. Nobody's ever bothered our car in these mountains."

"Somebody smashed the windows of this guard house to smithereens, and there's not even anything in it to steal."

"Aw, come on, Helen. Let's don't borrow trouble. I promise you everything will be all right."

And it was. She set the pace and I traipsed behind her down the meandering road. I watched in idle contentment as she moved from the high bank on one side to the drop-off on the other, eyes alert; shopping; exploring; seeking. Always shopping.

"Look at that spread of creeping cedar! You know it truly is a beautiful ground cover. Look how far up the hill it goes."

"I know. Ours at home has done well, I think."

"Sambo, look here. This is a whole stand of Doll's Eyes. Do you want to dig some or do you think we have enough?"

"Let's wait and see on the way back. No need lugging it all over the mountain when we'll walk right by it on the way back."

"You're right. Remember where it is, though. Listen! I hear an indigo bunting. Can you hear him?"

"No. I didn't put my hearing aids in this morning. I hear katydids in my left ear and July flies in my right one, but no indigo bunting."

"Well, I hear one. I know I do. Look, there he is! See him? Perched on the very tip of that poplar limb. See him? Right there."

"I see him. You were right."

"Oh, that has to be the prettiest blue in the world! Hello, baby! We're not going to bother you."

The bird was unimpressed by promises and flew in dip and dart through patches of sunlight across the road ahead of us, the sheen of its wings shimmering from light to dark, changing quickly from cerulean to Prussian blue and back again, a completely satisfying accent to the magic of the morning.

We swung to the right along the less-used, overgrown track that wound around the crest of the hill.

"Look at those ferns. They go on and on forever. There are a few Ostrich, but most of then are Lady Ferns. I don't think I've ever seen them any prettier than they are this year. We don't need any of them, do we?"

"Lord, no. They've come up as a fringe benefit around every azalea I've ever moved from up here. We sure don't need to transplant any Lady Fern."

"What about Ostrich?"

"We can always use more of them, but they're heavy as all get out. There are plenty growing close to the road at Nimblewill Gap. We'll get the truck some day and get a load we won't have to tote so far."

"I wish we could get the truck in here and get a load of these rocks. Just look at them. They're absolutely beautiful, and most of them are covered with moss. I love them when they have moss on them."

"I know. I think just ahead of you there, where that white oak is leaning over the bank, up the hill to the right is where I remember those lilies blooming."

"I think you're right."

The bank was more than head-high and loomed at a ninety degree angle. I threw the spade up the hill ahead of me, managed to grab a projecting root, and pulled myself up to the steep slant of this woodland floor.

"Here," I offered. "I'll give you a hand. You want to come up?"

"I don't think so. You hunt the lilies and I'll hunt an easier place to climb up. You know, I keep thinking if I look hard enough I can find and identify a ginseng plant. We have to be walking all over it."

With rare exception I had heard this statement every time we hiked in the woods. With comforting familiarity I knew exactly what she was going to say next.

"What we're going to have to do is get somebody who knows it to point it out to us."

"Which way are you going?" I said. "Don't get lost."

"I'm going to mosey on along this road toward the Nod-ding Mandarins, but I'm going to leave my jacket here; it's getting hot. We can pick it up on the way back."

"Don't get lost," I warned again.

There was a note in her voice, half fun, half asperity. "Don't you lose me."

I turned up the hill, its pitch so steep that I had to walk with my shoes dug in sideways in some areas; proof enough that the lilies require good drainage. I wanted to call after her, "How can I lose you when I'm staying put and you're the one who is wandering off?" I held my tongue, however, decid-ing that a joust in logic did not fit the time, the temperature, nor the terrain.

I mused that any well-seasoned husband who has not only gone through Basic Training in the career of matrimo-ny but has also experienced periodic advanced refresher courses and survived, with nothing worse to show than superficial scars from trench warfare, and even occasional artillery and air bombardment, should be a tenured, depend-able veteran. Such a husband is well aware that preparato-ry groundwork is constantly under way for anything that goes awry to be manifested as being his fault. He learns to side-step the minefields of puerile argument and reserve what ammunition he has for important controversy.

The fixing of blame, I had long since decided, is an idle, non-productive exercise. I could hear Dan Doughtery say-ing, "Don't sweat the small stuff." Dan is still living and still married. I could look farther back on my roster of friends and remember Everette Greer, who enjoyed till his death a tem-pestuous union, smiling at me when his wife, Kate, crowd-ed for space and pushed beyond her flash point, would berate him with skilled and sharpened tongue. With chest poked out and a tone of pride, he would declaim, "Just look at her. She's the cutest woman God ever wadded a gut in." He meant it, and Kate knew it. It served as the balm of apology from him, and for them it worked.

I turned with a smile of nostalgia for two long-dead friends and began my search.

Lillium Superbum, the native American Turkscap Lily, has a stupendously beautiful cluster of blossoms. They all face downward and are reminiscent of little girls, unaware yet of their innate beauty, who stand before strangers with faces tucked into shoulders, well worth a stooping peek or an upturning finger under the chin. The recurved petals are evocative of red and gold locks of hair gathered to the back of a precious head. The plants are not easy to spot before their splendid blooming occurs or when it is past, but some of us can do it. I cannot rattle off the identifying terms that botanists use with such precision, but then I can also, without conscious description of each and every feature, pick a beloved face from a throng of passers-by on Peachtree Street. I can identify a Turkscap Lily. With scanning imprint I surveyed the litter beneath the old hardwood trees around me. There were distracting drifts of Solomon's Seal, Spiderwort, Cimicifuga Racemosa, and Veratrum Veride, but in their midst I began discovering the treasures I sought.

"Here they are, Helen!" I shouted in exultation.

I shrugged at the absence of response and counted the plants scattered over the half-acre immediately around me. There were dozens of them, even three flourishing in a single clump. I rejected some of them because of difficult access, and two were nestled so securely in the fork of poplar roots that I feared damaging them if I tried to dig. The thrill of discovery settled into the fulfillment of procurement as I sank my spade with care, far out and deep, around the stem of each targeted plant. The soil was moist and soft, as black and crumbly as an earthworm bed. I had never encountered easier digging. With care, I lifted out a ball of dirt, the tips of the lily roots peeking forth like the curling tangle of coarse threads from a raveled bedspread; mute assurance that I had not harmed their bulbs. I scooped up great handfuls of dirt from the hole and made a nest in the bottom of the garbage bag before I gently slid the root ball from my shovel.

It was all so easily, so competently, so successfully done that I assuaged any feelings of guilt by visualizing the success of transplant and I procured eight of them, each with enough extra soil in its sack to guarantee establishment in a new home.

"I don't really think there'll ever be a four-lane through here," I muttered to myself, "but some asshole from the city just might buy this lot some day, bulldoze it smooth, and plant a fescue lawn."

I lowered my sacks of looted beauty to the roadside, nestled them in the shade of tall grass beneath the limb from which Helen's jacket hung, and swung down the woodland road.

"Complete with Bradford pears," I added, well content with myself.

A half mile later the breeze died and my shirt became wet beneath my pack. I was fanning gnats and frantically hallooing for Helen.

"She can't possibly have walked this far," I thought, "in the short time I was digging. She may have wandered too far off the road hunting ginseng, lost her footing, and be lying at the foot of one of these rock bluffs. That's why she doesn't answer me. Or," I added, developing irrational and fearsome detail in the scenario of my anxiety, "she may have a rattlesnake coiled so close to her broken leg that she's afraid to move or even yell back at me. She's scared to death of snakes."

I hastened my pace, my breath laboring as I mounted a steep incline in the road. "Damn that ginseng root," I muttered. I forced myself to trot, crested the hill, and howled at the top of my lungs, "Helen! Where are you? Helen!"

From a few yards around the curve ahead came a calm and

musical reply. "I'm right over here. Quit yelling."

I tried to curb my panting as I approached and I forced a conversational tone. "Why didn't you answer me? I've been calling you for half an hour." I realized that even with effort I sounded too accusing for the Sabbath and added wryly, "I was beginning to think I had lost you. In spite of what you told me not to do."

"I didn't hear you. You know how sound is in these mountains; it won't go around curves or over hills. I bet anybody down in that valley though could hear you a mile away. Look at all this Nodding Mandarin I've found. Isn't it beautiful? And lots of them have already set berries. What in the world is the matter with you? Your face is as red as a gobbler's snout. It looks like the blood is going to burst out of it, and there's not a dry thread on you. Here! You sit down and rest a while before you try to do any more digging; we're not facing a deadline."

She held out an uprooted plant. "Do you think this is ginseng?"

I took it from her hand. "No," I said.

"But look," she remonstrated, "this root is forked. All the books say that ginseng roots are forked like a man's legs. Don't you remember?"

I refrained from saying that this specimen would have to represent a mightly spindly man and one who had eight or ten legs. I also quelled the urge to observe that one can find anything one wishes in a Rorschach test. With a show of deliberation, I said, "I don't think it's ginseng."

"Well, what do you think it is?"

"I think it's one of the gentians is what I think."

"Gentian? For pity's sake, you know I recognize gentian when I see it. I think this just might be ginseng."

I resisted the urge to ask this loveliest of women, this most delightful and challenging of wives, why she had asked for

an opinion when obviously what she wanted was an argument. "You know," I said with studied calm, "what we're going
to have to do is ask somebody who knows it to point out some
ginseng to us."

"You're right," she said and tossed the plant aside.
"You've rested long enough. You're still red, but you're
breathing better. Let's get this Mandarin collected and head
back for the car. It's getting hot and the gnats are horrible if
you're not moving. I wish I had thought to bring insect
repellent."

I unzipped one side of the backpack. "Right here, your lady-
ship. At your service. I also have a couple of Diet Cokes in
here; let's drink them while they're still a little cool." A
rebound with a tip-in scores as well as a lay-up, I thought.

I remember the trek back to the car for its being uphill all
the way and my being laden like a donkey with earth-heavy
sacks of liberated plants. My breathing soon became labored;
the pulsations behind my eyes and in my ears were in tune
with the pounding hammer in my chest and were so force-
ful my vision gave little leaps and I heard every heartbeat. Helen
strolled unencumbered ahead of me, her hands dorsiflexed
and rotated laterally, arms and hips moving in rhythmic
counterpoint that could only be described as sashaying.
Unconscious of her gait, she kept peering into the woods to
see if she had overlooked anything. My admiration was
enhanced by relief that she had not been lost after all and also
that I had evinced the good sense to keep my baseless fears
to myself. I struggled under the weight of the treasures that
in triumph I was bearing and quickened my pace to keep her
in sight. "Queens have no need to carry shopping bags," I
silently averred. The morning had been a great success. I was
well content.

I approached the waiting Thunderbird-SC coupe with
admiration. Even at rest in the silent isolation of these

mountains its sleek lines bespoke speed and its heavy squat promised power as instant and thunderous as the haunches of thoroughbreds leaping from a starting gate. It was equipped with so many electronic conveniences and computer chips that I fancied the mechanic at Alan Vigil's Southlake Ford needed training under a Board-certified Neurologist to understand them. The instrument panel boasted flashing lights and warning signals worthy of a commercial air liner. I liked my car.

I pressed a button on my key chain and the trunk popped open from a distance of twenty feet. I tossed in the shovel and tenderly positioned my plants to protect them from jostling or bruising. I pressed another button and the doors unlocked spontaneously.

"Hop in," I called to my wife.

"I'll wait till you get on the pavement. I don't want to fight the weight of that door and I'd almost have to climb a ladder the way it's leaning. I just hope you can get out of there."

I made no reply, cranked the motor, and accelerated. The car moved forward, then stopped. I accelerated harder and gained a few more inches. I gunned it and heard gravel flying in fury behind me. The great chassis was motionless. I pressed harder, the wheels spun, the motor roared. Helen appeared suddenly to my left, bent from the hips, waving her hands back and forth with frenzy.

"Stop! Stop! Stop!"

I slid the window down. "I am stopped. You don't have to scream at me."

"Well, somebody has to, and I'm the only one around. You are going to burn every inch of rubber off those tires! And accomplish nothing!"

A thick black cloud was drifting from the rear, the odor of it just beneath gagging level. "You're right," I acceded, and got out of the car.

The spot where I had persisted in parking was indeed graveled. From disuse, however, that gravel was overgrown with a thick mat of crab grass and gave insufficient traction to a heavy car. I had managed to get the front wheels up on the pavement, but the rear wheels had dug themselves into strangling holes. If only Alan Vigil offered four-wheel drive in a Thunderbird, I thought, I would be in no predicament.

"Hindsight is always 20/20," I said aloud with an effort to sound concomitantly apologetic and confident.

"You're stuck," she said.

"You're right," I replied.

"You're really stuck," she added.

I clenched my teeth to prevent the ill-advised retort that the Declaration of Independence did not need rewriting and that I knew some truths were self-evident. I procured my shovel and began digging in front of the back tires.

The next half hour crawled like a snail, but not I. My activity was frenzied. I trenched. I sped forward. I reversed and came forward a little further, gaining thereby an inch or two. I trenched. Over and over. I inched forward, backward, forward again, over and over. I became wringing wet. Sweat stung my eyes, blurring my vision, but I remembered not to burn any rubber again. And I was winning. Maybe.

"You might as well call a wrecker."

"I don't think so," I gasped. "I've got the back tires. Five inches from the pavement. We're ten miles from the nearest town. Any hope of a wrecker. I'll come out. This very next time. You'll see. I'll get it out."

My voice was quavering. I was trembling all over, almost jerking. I realized that some primordial stimulus of suppressed rage, anxiety, fear, frustration, the Lord only knew what else, had overloaded my system with adrenalin.

"I think you ought to call a wrecker."

I knew that if I tried to speak my teeth would chatter in

time with my jerking hands. I wondered if humiliation was adrenergic. Not trusting speech, I willed my gaze to speak for me, to manifest apology, to explain frustration, and to plead for forbearance and, above all, silence. My eyes met the aquamarines through which my wife views the world and held for a long moment. I wondered again if beauty itself when seen through the jewels of her eyes was crisper, clearer, more alluringly delineated than the perception afforded me.

Her gaze shifted first. "You have worked yourself into a state over this, and a stuck automobile is not worth a stroke or a heart attack. There's no disgrace in calling a wrecker, but if you just must prove your manhood or something silly like that, go ahead; I'm going to wait across the road there. In the shade."

Her voice was calmly devoid of inflection or passion. I was exultant. She had received my message, had acted upon it. I, in turn, had received hers. "It's do or die now, old boy," I told myself.

I knelt beside each wheel, chunked the remaining grass pads aside, prepared a trench for the final rush to freedom. With confidence. This time would do it! Carefully, I shifted into reverse and backed down to get a good running start and hurl the rear wheels onto the pavement. I looked across at Helen, sitting in the shade, leaning against tree. I waved, gripped the steering wheel, and gunned the motor. Hard.

My next visual recall is of Helen disappearing. The only thing I could see through the windshield was the very tip-top of the tree under which she was sitting and a vast expanse of blue sky. In an instant I realized that I had neglected to move the gear out of reverse, but that I had reflexively slammed on the antilock brakes when the car had plummeted backward instead of forward.

When one has been laboring through a situation fraught with frustration, self-abasement, apprehension, worry, and the problem is resolved in a manner not the wildest imagination could have anticipated, then at such a moment, rarely, one may be visited by a strange and supernatural calm. The worst had happened. All my shaking stilled.

I switched off the ignition and with considerable force pushed my door up and back against the great weight of gravity. I stretched my feet down to the earth and stared in marvel. I had never before beheld the underside of a Thunderbird, certainly not tilted toward the horizon. It was an impressive sight. The front wheels were a good four feet above the ground; the great orb housing the transmission was half-buried in the soft lip of overhang; the rear bumper rested scant inches away from the trunks of two sturdy saplings which gave guarantee that my car would not slip and thereby slide to the bottom of the hundred and fifty foot slope.

"Are you all right?" No hint of acerbity, of acrimony, in that voice. Only concern.

I faced her, took a deep breath. "I think we ought to call a wrecker," I said. Then I laughed. I had to.

She walked in silence to the rear of the automobile, peered down the mountainside to the bottom of the yawning ravine. "You're right," she said.

"There sits our Thursday. I've sure managed to mess it up."

"That's not the important thing. You're not hurt, and I don't think the car is hurt. Yet. I could hike up this other road if you want me to. If Mr. McCollum is at home he'd let us use his phone."

"I don't want you to. Besides, we've got that phone in the car. Let me see if it will work."

"Do you think it's safe for you to get back in the car? It might slide on down the mountain."

"It's safe. Those two trees will hold it."

"Who are you going to call?"

"I'll think of somebody. We're on top of the mountain; so

maybe it will work up here. It sure won't when you're at the bottom of one of those hills."

"Call 911."

"911? That's only for emergencies."

I avoided the laser beam of her look, switched on the ignition, activated the telephone, and punched out 911. It worked. As competently as any telephone in the city. I gave silent praise to modern technology, and fleetingly withdrew previous disapproval of whatever sybaritic orgies among youthful geniuses in Silicon Valley that might have contributed to this modern marvel. On the very first ring a hearty male voice answered. It exuded youth and strength.

"This is 911. Can I help you?"

I introduced myself.

"Okay, Doc. What you got? Where are you?"

"I'm hanging on the shoulder of a road on top of Burnt Mountain. Backwards. On Highway 108. About a mile off Highway 136."

"Anybody hurt? You need an ambulance?"

"No, no, no." My response was hasty. "All I need is a wrecker. I hated to call your emergency number, but I don't have a telephone directory. Nobody's hurt. I just need a wrecker. Can you help me locate one?"

"You in Gilmer County?"

"No. I'm in Pickens County."

The voice of my wife intruded. From twenty safe feet away. In case the car began more downward slide. "Dawson County." I ignored it.

"You close to Jasper?"

"Not really," I answered. "About nine miles on 136 East of Jasper, I'd say."

"Sambo, we're in Dawson County. I'm sure of it. And we're ten miles out of Jasper." The wifely admonition was a little tart.

It has always annoyed me to be listening on the phone with

one ear and have my wife pouring directions, additions, definitions, codicils into the other. She knows this, for on rare occasions at home I have silently handed her the phone, departed the room, and left her to pick up my interrupted discourse with she knows not whom. That has never been more than a temporary deterrent, however, and the interpersonal side effects have not made it worthwhile. Since I was sure my helper could hear her as well as I, my temporizing answer was calm.

"We may be on the edge of Dawson County, but it's certainly near the Pickens County line. We're closer to Jasper than to Dawsonville."

"You've got Ellijay. We're in Gilmer County."

"Oh, I'm sorry. I just punched 911."

"Oh, that's all right. Pickens and Dawson ain't got no 911." I detected a nuance of satisfaction, of civic pride. "It rang through to us."

"Well, seeing as how I've got you, do you reckon there's any way you could send a wrecker out here to me?"

"Ain't no way, Doc. We ain't got but two in town. One of 'em's broke down and we just dispatched the other one to a pile-up out on the four-lane. Ain't no telling when he'll get done, besides the which you're a good twenty maybe thirty miles from us near as I can locate you, and he probably wouldn't want to come that far. We don't usually cross county lines."

"Oh." I had too much background in the county unit system to plead for violation of such territorial propriety.

"Tell you what, though. Let me give you the sheriff's number over in Jasper. I know him; he's a nice fellow. He'll do anything he can to help you."

"Oh, would you? I'll sure appreciate it. Like I told you, I don't have a directory in the car."

"You got something to write with?"

"Sure." I fumbled in the door pocket and fished out a ball

point pen. I grabbed for a piece of paper, came up with a parking stub.

"It's 692-5714."

"692-5714. Thanks a lot."

The pen would not write. I scrubbed it furiously on the paper
surface. It refused any mark.

"Lots of luck, Doc." He was gone.

I pushed "End" on the telephone, muttered 692-5714 repet-
itively and started to finger the instrument again.

"Who are you calling now?"

"The sheriff in Pickens County."

"Who have you been talking to?"

"911. But it was in Gilmer County. They don't have 911
in Jasper."

"Well, why didn't you just have them send a wrecker
from Ellijay?"

"They were all busy, it's too far, there are territorial priorities involved, he gave me the number of the sheriff in Jasper."

"Why didn't he just give you the name and number of a
wrecker service in Jasper?"

"Why don't you be real quiet so I can call the sheriff before
I forget his number."

"You don't have to get short with me. Why didn't you write
it down?"

I held my peace. I did not even sigh so that it was discernible.
I cuddled the phone and tapped in 692-5714. I know I did.
To this day I swear that I did. 692-5714.

After seven long pealing rings a female voice came through.
"Hello," it quavered.

"Hello. Is this the sheriff's office?"

"I can't hear you. Speak up."

"Is this the sheriff's office in Jasper, Georgia?"

"Say you the sheriff from Jasper, Georgia?"

"No, ma'am; I'm trying to reach the sheriff!"

"He ain't been nowhere around here since the week before election."

"Could you, please, ma'am, give me his telephone number?"

"You'll have to speak up. I'm a bit deef. Who'd you say this was?"

I obediently shouted. "I'm Dr. Sams. I'm stranded on the side of the road and need some help. I'm trying to get the sheriff."

"You a doctor?"

"Yes, ma'am. Could you give me the sheriff's number?"

"What'd you say your name was?"

"Sams!"

"I heered that all right. What's your last name?"

"That's it! That is the last name! My car's in a ditch and I need to call a wrecker to get me out. Could you, please ma'am, give me the sheriff's number?"

Her drawl was painfully slow. "I never heered of nobody by that name. You ain't from around here, are you?"

"No, ma'am. I'm from Fayette County. About a hundred miles away. I'm stuck in a ditch and I'm calling from a telephone in my car."

"Well, I swan. Ain't nobody been shot or hurt, is they?"

"No, ma'am. I'm trying to get the sheriff so he'll help me find a wrecker to pull me out. Can you please give me his number?" It is difficult to sound wheedling and pleasant while yelling but I was doing my best.

"I think we got it wrote down summers around here. Let me look. I'm glad ain't nobody hurt. Hold on a minute."

I heard furniture scraping across a floor, a chair perhaps. Even that sound was exasperatingly drawn out.

"Paw!" The voice was loud but without inflection, rolled out into flatness through years of straining to hear. "They's somebody on the phone claims he's a doctor in a ditch.

What's the sheriff's number?—Ain't you got it wrote down?
—Paw, can't you hear?—How come you don't answer
then?—Say where's he at?—He's in a ditch.—Say where's the
ditch at?—I never ast him.—But he's got a telephone in the
ditch right there in the car with him. Don't that beat all? He
wants to call the sheriff. Where'd you put that number?—
Naw, ain't nobody hurt. I done ast him that.—Say who is it?—
I disremember his name, but he ain't from around here."

There was silence. Then I heard a shuffle, then the chair
scraped again. "Hello. You still there? I know we got that number summers, but it's mislaid. Just keep holding on till we can
dig it up for you."

Silence again. Did these people not keep a directory by their
telephone? Or perhaps they could not read? Maybe they only
knew numbers and not their letters. I thought of Jay Hort-
enstein who had regaled us once with his account of stopping
to offer a ride to an old lady standing along the side of a country road.

"Could I give you a lift, lady?"

She cupped an ear in her hand. "What'd you say?"

"I said, 'Would you like a ride?'" roared Jay.

"Say you killed a hawg?" came the reply.

"No, ma'am," he yelled as loud as he could. "I said, '*Do
you want a ride?*'"

"How much did he weigh?"

Jay was young, his hair was red, his patience thin and sharp;
so he had sped away in his truck.

I was old and my patience had been thickened by the scars
incurred over many years in my bouts with impatience,
wounds that healed but not without bleeding. Basic politeness dictated that I hang on to that telephone until the
woman who had interrupted her routine to help me returned.
I curbed my anxiety, dismissed the thought of how much this
call was costing, and waited. I took slow deep breaths,

recited two sonnets in an effort to stop the trembling that had recurred, and waited. I waited so long that I thought the connection had been broken, but I could still detect an occasional shuffle of furniture, a distant voice shouting some unintelligible question. I abandoned any hope of help from these strangers, but telephone etiquette was too deeply ingrained to let me abandon the conversation in rudeness. I waited.

Finally I began shouting into the telephone. "Lady! Lady! Hey, Lady! Where are you? Please come back to the phone! Lady!"

No response. I whistled, I yelled, I whistled some more. In vain. I hushed and held the phone away from me, staring at it.

Helen appeared at my window. "Who in the world were you screaming and whistling at? And why are you sitting there staring at that telephone?"

"How much did he weigh?" I reflexively responded.

"What in the world are you talking about? Answer my question!"

"I don't know! And that's the answer to both questions." I punched the "End" button on the phone and with no farewell sent 692-5714 into oblivion. "It sure wasn't the sheriff."

"Why don't you call somebody else?"

"Like who?"

"Like our office."

"I'm not calling anybody from home to come get me!" My voice had become shrill, almost falsetto.

"Listen, Sambo. I want you to calm down. You look like a wild man, you're shaking like a leaf, and the last thing I need is for you to have a stroke or a heart attack on me way up here on the side of this mountain!" She started to reach through the window, thought better of it, backed away, and looked at the car. "And me with no way to get out of here. You calm down!"

Through the years I have noted that when two people get

into a bare-bones, down-home, trash-moving argument, reason and logic are not prominently present. When the argument gets really hot, when voices begin to rise, one of the participants will admonish, "Now, don't get excited." Invariably the response, delivered in ever increasing decibels, will be, "Who's excited? I'm not excited! Don't *you* get excited." To an outsider, a nonpartisan observer, so to speak, such an interchange had ever seemed futile, puerile, leading to even more poorly controlled outbursts that culminate in walk-outs and slammed doors; the resultant mandatory apologies. Love always seemed not only dredged up later with difficulty but also grudgingly tendered; I decided long ago it ain't worth it.

"You calm down," I said, without thinking, and felt rage instinctively rising in rebellion at being addressed like a four-year-old. I felt it just in time. I considered my current level of frustration, the personage addressing me. "She's right," I told myself. "Again," I appended. I took a deep breath, swallowed, rested my head briefly on the steering wheel, then met her gaze. "Okay." I said with exaggerated calm.

As she began a schoolteacherly nod of approbation, I felt impelled to manifest some last-ditch exhibition of mangled and generic defiance. "Just goddam 692-7412!" I bellowed.

She completed her nod as smoothly as if I had been mute. "Now, listen. You can get on that phone and call the office. Get administration and ask Ellen or Charlie or David to find us a wrecker somewhere. There's no use in our clinic having a senior management team if they can't rescue the two senior partners."

"You're right. I'll try that." I picked up the telephone.

"Tell whoever you get to call the Chamber of Commerce or something in Jasper and get the number of any wrecker service and then send one of them to us. Or they might try Dawsonville."

I replaced the telephone, forced myself to unclench my jaw and I spoke in controlled, adult tones. "Helen, you have convinced me of the error of my ways and have told me what to do. I am going to follow your instructions. I've got to tell you, however, that I have reached a stress level that is not going to accommodate your standing over me and supervising every move I make, especially when I know that the minute I get somebody on this phone and start talking to them you will also start talking and telling me what to say to them."

I took a deep breath. "I want you to do one of two things. Either get in this car and use the phone yourself, or go sit down on that nice soft mossy hammock under that tree across the road."

She opened her mouth, thought a moment, and spoke. "You couldn't raise enough money to get me in that car." She turned away and then said over her shoulder, "Good luck."

Some thirty minutes later, my frenzy finally abated, I sought her out to give an accounting. While fighting the telephone I had watched her sit for a time and fan gnats, then stroll around and peer with purpose up the forested hill. I was sweating but not shaking. The heartiness in my voice was only partially forced.

"Well, success at last! Help is on the way."

"Who did you get? Ellen?"

"No. She's not back from lunch. Neither is Charlie. Nor David."

"Who did you talk to?"

"Sabrina. Nobody was in administration and the phone rolled over after six rings to Sabrina. She's answering for them."

"What did she say?"

I reflected for only a brief moment. "At first she said, 'You've got to be kidding,' but after I explained the second time exactly what happened and exactly where we are, she quit snickering and became her usual efficient self. She's looking after us and we can quit worrying."

"What's she going to do?"

"She's going to find a wrecker service in Jasper and send them to us."

"How?"

"She's going to call information or City Hall or the sheriff or somebody and then she personally is going to call the wrecker and send them to us."

"How will they find us?"

"I told Sabrina to tell them to go 136 toward Amicalola Falls, turn left at 108, and we'd be the first car on the right in the ditch. They can't miss us."

"I just hope they don't turn on old 108."

"They can't. It's blocked off. Remember?"

"The sign's still up. I hope you haven't gotten them confused."

"I haven't. Trust me. Just relax."

"How long will it take them to find us?"

"Gosh, I don't know. I guess it depends on how soon they can start."

"You mean we are not even going to know if Sabrina gets anybody?"

"That's right, but I've got faith. That Sabrina is great. I promise you she'll bulldog it until she gets us some help. One way or another. You can trust Sabrina."

"I don't see any sense in having a telephone in the car if we can't do better than this. She could at least call us back."

I gave a little cough. "Well, she did ask me the number of the car phone, but I had to tell her I don't know it. It's not written on the phone anywhere and nobody's ever called us on it."

"Sambo Sams, do you mean we've had that phone all these weeks and you don't even know the number?"

I answered defensively, "I've never had an occasion to need

it before." I swallowed my guilt, considered for a moment, and cleared my throat. "Helen."

"What?"

"Do you know what the number is?"

In a tone that I would describe as one of mildly impatient hauteur she answered me. "I don't have the faintest idea."

Before I could open my mouth or even savor the moment, she added, "But it's ringing."

"What?"

"The telephone. It's ringing."

"Are you sure?"

"Of course I'm sure. What's the use in going to all the trouble and expense of getting hearing aids if you're not going to use them? Of course I'm sure. You'd better hurry and answer it before whoever it is hangs up."

I sprinted across the road and snatched the phone from its stand.

"Hello, Sabrina!" I exulted.

"No, this is Rhonda. Sabrina got tied up on something else and asked me to call you."

"How'd you get this number?"

"Sabrina gave it to me."

"How'd she get it?"

"I don't know."

"What is it?"

"Sir?"

"Never mind. I don't have anything to write with anyhow and it's getting to where I can't trust my memory. I'll get the number later."

"Yes, sir. Sabrina said tell you that she has spoken personally with Andy's Towing Service in Jasper and they will be on their way shortly."

"That's great, Rhonda! You don't know how much I appreciate this. Tell Sabrina."

"Yes, sir. Andy wanted to know if your car was functional. He means is it hurt? Can you drive it away? You know; whether it was just stuck or whether he needed to bring a carrier."

"No, no. The car's fine if we can just get somebody to pull it back on the pavement."

"All right. I'll call him back and tell him. We're all glad you're not hurt. You be careful."

"It's way too late for that, Rhonda, but you can be sure that I will approach what remains of this day with a greater than ordinary measure of caution. Thanks again for looking after me."

Back across the road I went, both my step and my heart springy once more.

"Great news! The wrecker is coming. Sabrina and Rhonda have taken care of it. I tell you, Helen, we work with a great group of people."

"When's it coming?"

"Right away. I should think it'll take about an hour, but at least we know the end is in sight."

"I think I'll walk up the hill to the top of the mountain."

"Okay. I'll go with you."

"You don't think somebody should stay here with the car?"

"Who's to hurt it? In the fix it's in?"

I fell in behind her and we began the steep ascent of the paved driveway leading to the cluster of vacation homes above us.

I sought to ingratiate myself. "Isn't that an indigo bunting? You reckon it's the same one?"

"That telephone is ringing again."

"What? Are you sure?"

"Of course I'm sure."

I bounded down the mountain and caught the phone.

"Hello. This is Andy's Wrecker Service in Jasper. You the fellow got his car in a ditch?"

"Yes, sir! That's me all right."

"I was calling to check and see if your vehicle is damaged or not so's I'll know what to drive out and get you. Am I going to need to tow you in or just pull you out of a ditch?"

"The car's fine. It's just stuck. I sure appreciate this. How long before you get here, do you think?"

"Where you at now?"

"About nine miles out on 136. Maybe you'd better make that nearer ten. Turn left on 108 and I'm up over the hill on the right. On the down side of the mountain. My girl was supposed to have given you all this information."

"She did, but I thought I better check and be sure. Women folks are bad to get things mixed up and they sure ain't no judge of distance or direction. Plus they don't know nothing about machinery. Know what I mean?"

I wondered briefly how my own knowledge of distance, direction, or machinery would affect my gender scale in this man's eyes, looked cautiously across to be sure Helen was out of earshot and with noncommittal flippancy replied, "I know what you mean. How soon you think you'll get to us? My wife'll want to know."

"Oh, I dunno. Not much more than an hour. Hour and a half or forty minutes. I ain't familiar with that part of the county."

"It's right off the main road from Jasper to Dawsonville."

The reply was still bubbling with cheer. "Don't many folks born and raised in Pickens County have much call to ever go to Dawsonville. Know what I mean?"

I considered both time and place inappropriate for my engaging in a discussion of either priority or turf. All I wanted from Andy was a service and that as rapidly as possible. "Know what you mean," I parroted. "I'll be on the lookout for you, Andy."

"Oh, I ain't Andy," came the hearty rejoinder. "My name's

Ed. I been working for Andy though ever since I was in the tenth grade and got my driver's license. He's sure been good to me, too. Only one I knowed what didn't fuss at me when I dropped out of high school. Know what I mean? I hurt my knee so bad they wouldn't let me play no more football and didn't seem like I was going to ever need no diploma just to help Andy with his business."

I had an urge to interrupt and ask if he lived at home and if his mother was deaf, but subdued it.

"And I ain't," Ed continued. "Andy pays me pretty good and tell you the truth, I make most of the calls for him now. All the ones at night. Don't you worry none. I'll look after you and be there soon as I can. Andy has always wanted to go to Florida and he finely took off this week, him and his wife both. The which she's his third one. Wife, I mean. Left everthing with me and I been pretty busy. Just got back an hour ago from a wreck out on 575. I'm on my way to you soon as I get gassed up."

"I'll be watching for you, Ed," I promised.

Clambering out of the car once more, I started the climb up toward my wife.

"Who was that?" she called down to me.

"Ed from the wrecker service, just checking. He's on his way."

"How soon?"

"An hour and forty-five minutes or two hours," I yelled back. Give old Ed plenty of leeway, I thought, and me as small a margin of time as possible to deal with marital impatience.

"The phone is ringing."

"What?"

"I said," she cupped her hands around her mouth, "that phone is ringing. Again."

I raced back to the car. "692-5714," I said briskly into the phone. Enough was enough. Reality is often more palatable when seasoned with levity.

There was a long pause before a voice replied. "Dr. Sams? Is that you?"

"It is," I answered. "That is the one thing I'm sure of right at this moment."

"Well, this is Sabrina. I was just calling to be sure you're all right."

"We're fine, Sabrina, and I'm more grateful than I can tell you for your bailing me out of this mess."

"The man at the wrecker service promised he'd get to you right away, but I wanted to be sure you and Dr. Helen were okay and that he was looking after you. After all, he's a stranger. And you know how some men are."

"I know what you mean," I said with some sincerity, "but this one is named Ed and he swears he'll be here in an hour. Thanks for giving him this car number. Thanks again for everything, Sabrina. Bye."

I hurried to overtake Helen, who had been mounting steadily away from me during my last conversation, but about fifty feet up the entrance to the subdivision I had to pause for breath. A small battered Toyota station wagon came over the hill on the highway below me and slowed noticeably as it approached the abandoned guardhouse and the equally abandoned automobile. I thought for a moment it would stop, but its driver's curiosity apparently reached satiety and the car resumed speed and fell away down the mountain, taking curve and hill with enviable competence and grace. Before the sound of its passage could dissipate, I heard it returning.

I stepped to the edge of the roadbank so that I would be clearly visible to the driver, who now had an uphill panorama. Better to prevent than to interrupt vandalism, I thought, in case this was a teenager with a yen for hubcaps.

There were two people in the station wagon. The driver was obviously a woman, with large melon breasts and an amply rounded abdomen. Her seat belt gave interesting and constricting delineation of these parts. The person in the passenger's seat appeared to be a teenaged boy, who sat with his hands in his lap. The lady slowed again and leaned out her window to peer at my car. She had long, muddy blonde hair that capped her ears and hung in a ponytail. I thought perhaps that she was a hippie gone to fat. The boy punched her shoulder and pointed to me. She looked up, met my eyes, and pulled the station wagon along the highway until she was at my level and stopped.

"Hello," she said. "Are you in trouble?"

She seemed like a nice lady, her English free of accent.

"Well," I said, "you see that car hanging over the edge of the mountain? In a very stupid move I put it there. Personally. Against what turned out to be very good advice. You see that lady walking ahead of me way up there? That's my wife. She's the one who gave the good advice. I'm trying to catch up with her to find out whether I'm in trouble or not. So far I've been too busy trying to get help to gauge exactly how much trouble I may be in. I have an idea it may be considerable."

If she smiled, I didn't notice it. "That your car?"

"Yes, ma'am."

"You're in trouble."

"You could say that, I guess."

"Both front wheels and your right rear wheel are off the ground. That's trouble."

"But it could be worse. If it weren't for those two little trees holding against the rear bumper I'd probably be another fifty feet down that ravine. I guess I'm pretty lucky."

She looked at me. "If you want to call it that, I guess that's one way of looking at it. You want I should help you?"

"Thank you, ma'am, but I've called somebody. Help is on the way."

"You've called somebody? You're not from around here, are you?"

"No, ma'am, but I have a phone in the car. Only had it a month or six weeks, but I've managed to locate a wrecker over in Jasper and he'll be here, he said, in about an hour."

"Where you from?"

"Down south of Atlanta. You're not from around here yourself, are you?"

"Born and raised not twenty miles from this very spot. What makes you say that?"

"You don't have the slightest trace of a Southern accent. It's sure nice of you to stop and offer to help a perfect stranger. I appreciate it."

She leaned over and turned off her ignition, said something in an admonitory tone to the boy, who had apparently protested. He sat quietly thereafter, more than a little chubby himself, a study in passive patience. The lady leaned further out the window, twisted around to face me, forearms extended, wrists relaxed. She wore no wedding band.

"Listen. You're talking to someone who's been in trouble herself. I broke down on the side of the road in Washington State one time and nobody came by. Finally it got dark and I thought I was going to have to spend the night in that old heap I was driving at the time. I'm as good a mechanic as you can find and I had done everything to that car you can think of and couldn't get it started. I mean I was out on the backside of nowhere.

"A car finally came along with two guys in it. They got out and did everything I'd already tried. Of course, I kept my mouth shut and didn't tell them none of it was going to work, that I'd already tried everything they were doing. You know how some fool men are, think a woman can't even understand the combustion engine, let alone have sense enough to repair one. Well, anyhow, they insisted on giving me a lift to town, said I'd freeze to death out in that desert along about two or three in the morning. I guess I would have, too. Ever since that night I've always stopped when I see somebody stranded."

"I think that's wonderful, ma'am. What a nice story."

"I travel prepared, too, you can betcha. I've got a complete set of tools I don't ever go anywhere without."

"You're a remarkable lady," I offered.

"I've even got a tow chain in the back. I'll be glad to pull you out of there."

I looked at the little Toyota, the massive Thunderbird, and promptly decided that such an effort might be not only futile but even dangerous. I felt that, although this Samaritan's knowledge of machinery obviously exceeded mine, I was as proficient as she in estimating weight, and that enthusiasm alone was not enough to overcome mass and momentum. If she did happen to succeed in dislodging the heavier T-bird, there was real danger that its slide into the ravine might pull both her and her station wagon behind it. I had, of course, more discretion than to voice it.

"I've already got this man on his way from Jasper and it wouldn't be right for me to snatch a job right out from under him when he's nice enough to accommodate me. I reckon I'll just wait."

"You sure?"

"I'm sure. But you were really nice to turn around and come back to check on me."

"Oh, I was headed back this way anyhow. You see, I deliver papers. Amongst other things. I got a customer about a mile on down the road here and he was the last one for today. I started to stop on the way in, but I didn't see anybody around the car until I was coming back up the hill and spotted you."

She had not moved her elbows or otherwise manifested any signs of departure. Helen, never overly patient with my tendency toward chitchat with strangers, was still plodding slowly along, studiedly ignoring me. I saw no reason to eschew entertainment just because I was stranded, thwarted and frustrated.

"What were you doing traveling alone through Washington State?" I asked.

"Oh, I lived out there for a little over ten years. Started out in California and that got a little too much for me when I came to my senses; so I sort of drifted to the Northwest. I liked it there well enough and would still be there, I guess, if it hadn't of been for my health."

I had been right about the hairdo. I had visions of teenage rebellion, marijuana, LSD, orgies, communal living.

"Your health? You don't look like you've ever been sick a day in your life."

"Oh, I'm healthy as a horse ever since I got back to these mountains, where folks have got some sense about how to take care of themselves. They settled into these hills and learned from the Indians all they knew about plants and herbs, and then learned even more on their own. They been dosing and curing themselves for close on two hundred years in these parts, and we live a long time and stay healthy while we're at it. We don't have much use for doctors in these parts."

I accepted this without a rejoinder other than a nod of the head, wondering, however, why the good Lord had failed to bless the forests of Pickens County with a herb that would prevent deafness.

"I been back home for eight, no nine years now, and I haven't had so much as a head cold. And energy? I got more energy than two teams of mules, and can work any man in the county down. No sirree, I haven't been the least bit sick, not one minute, since I took my gallbladder flush."

This conversation, I thought, was developing twists that promised some interest.

"Gallbladder flush?" I encouraged.

"Yes. You never heard of it? Most folks don't live in the hills haven't and heap of those that do haven't, if they've never themselves borne the curse of gallstones. Nowadays you'd be surprised how many folks who build those things up inside of them take them to town, lay down to let some butchering doctor whack them wide open, and then lay up in bed for six weeks getting over the cutting."

"Down our way," I interposed, "I hear tell they're taking the gallstones out with laser. Through a tube no bigger than your finger. The patient doesn't even have to stay overnight in the hospital and is back at work in two or three days. So I've heard."

"Well, I'm not denying that may be true," she said affably, "but, Mister, I've lived long enough, and from the looks of you, if you'll pardon me saying it, so have you, to know that you can hear anything. Back when I had my attack, and it like to have killed me I can tell you without exaggeration, the only thing doctors knew to do was to lay you wide open and help themselves to whatever they could find. And even if they are doing it nowadays the way you say, it still isn't necessary, and I'll bet you a dollar to a doughnut they're charging every bit as much or maybe even more."

There was a note of triumph in her voice which I felt no compulsion to resist. "I wouldn't know."

"Well, have you ever heard of doctors' fees going down? Every time they discover a new way to do something they commence to charging you more for it. Reminds me of a cute thing I heard the other day. You know what unnecessary surgery is? It's operating on somebody when the doctor don't even need the money. That's a good one, isn't it?"

"It's a real hoot," I said. "I'll have to remember that one.

What does a gallbladder flush cost?"

"Not a dime!" she pronounced. "Well, not a dime paid out to any doctor. You have to pick up a few odds and ends here and there, but they don't amount to enough to shake a stick at."

"And it works?" I prompted.

"Does it work? Does it work? I've got a little time and looks like you do, too; so, Mister, let me tell you about it."

The boy beside her had not moved but apparently he muttered something, for the lady turned her head. "Hush your mouth," she said. "We'll go when I'm good and ready." She turned her attention back to me. "I was sort of like this kid here when I was growing up, wearied about hearing things over and over, not realizing that I should of been listening and learning. You see, my mother had gallstones and my grandmother before her, and I used to sit around at night and hear them going on about how they had cured them in themselves and in various neighbors and about how it might be coming up on time to take themselves another gallbladder flush, and they'd get so wound up in the recipe for it that I'd get to nodding and nearly fall off the porch.

"Well, sirree, when I got my growth and ripened off and fleshened out like a true woman will, the gallstones came aknocking at my door. I was staying a good ways out in the country from Seattle at the time and they hit me in the middle of the night like a ton of bricks. I mean I was drawn double with the pain and was heaving worse than a puking dog, throwing up things I couldn't even remember putting down."

This was a simile that was new even to my ears. "My goodness, you were sick."

"As they used to say on TV, 'You can bet your sweet bippie' I was. I thought I was going to die before I got to the hospital, and then after I got there I was sure of it. They gave me a shot for pain all right enough, and it did ease me off a little bit for a little while, but then they commenced to talking about cutting. About four of them, all doctors of one sort or another. Gathered around me and every one of them said, 'Cut!'

"I was high as a Georgia pine on that morphine or whatever by then and my mouth was dry as cotton wool, but I still had sense enough to ask them what was the matter. The oldest one, the one that seemed to be the boss doctor or whatever they call themselves, said, 'Well, madam, we are all agreed that you have an acute surgical belly,' and me, being one to always keep my spirits up no matter how bad things get, I came back at him, 'If you think it's so cute now, you should of seen it ten years ago.' And, Mister, I think to this day that was a pretty good one to come floating up at you from the death bed of somebody who's had a double shot of morphine, but you know not a one of those sober-sided peckerwoods even smiled? I knew right then and there that, as the youn-guns say now, I was in deep poo-poo.

"I've no use atall for the medical profession in general and for doctors in particular. They're all a bunch of money-hungry birds of prey just watching and waiting to rip somebody's guts apart so they can holler 'modern technology' and drain 'em of every last dime they got in the world. Only difference in a surgeon and a buzzard is that one of 'em takes off his wingtips at night. But just double damn any doctor who's got no sense of humor, and here I was surrounded by four of them. You can bet I was scared. Then I realized they might of thought I was ignorant and that I had said that about the cute belly because I didn't know any better, so I got my old thick tongue going again and said, 'I was just trying to be funny. What you think is causing it?'

"And then that ringleader patted me on the shoulder and says, 'The most likely underlying diagnosis is an impacted gallstone, but regardless we have to operate. You have symptoms already of peritonitis.'

"Well, sirree, you can be sure and certain I was scared half to death by that. 'That stuff can kill you,' I told him. I didn't aim to be operated on for anything that serious, I didn't care how bad it hurt. Then the boss doctor says, 'Exactly,' and he stops right there and waits. Doesn't say another mumbling word.

"And all of a sudden I thought back to Mama, who I hadn't even seen in ten years. 'How come you don't just give me a gallbladder flush?' I asked, and I looked around at all four of them even if I was having trouble getting both my eyes to move along together.

"Those four grand and glorious men of medicine swiveled their grave and serious heads around and stared at each other for all the world like a row of hoot owls on the same limb. One of them says, 'We never heard of a gallbladder flush,' and he sounded like if they hadn't heard of something then it had to be of no consequence.

"'My mama had gallstones and she took the flush, and my grandma had them and she took the flush and neither one of them had to have an operation; passed those stones and was done with them,' I told them. One of them turned to the others and says, 'Now we have heredity to add to her criteria of "female, fair, fat and forty,"' still with that condescending, talking-down-at-you tone of voice, he was. Well, sirree, if there's one thing I hate it's the word *fat*, and nobody's going to say it about me just because I'm a ripened-out figure of a woman. Not and get away with it. Not as long as I got a tire tool in the trunk, they're not. But you hate to let somebody know they've touched a nerve, if you know what I mean."

I nodded in obvious agreement but did not speak.

"'I ain't forty,' I snapped at him, 'not by three years yet. And nobody's gonna cut me open till I've had a gallbladder flush.' The old one was trying to smooth my feathers and make up for the other one ruffling them. He says in a different tone of voice, 'Just what is a gallbladder flush?' and I had to tell him I didn't remember the exact recipe but that I knew it called for yellow root and olive oil and lemon juice, but that I could get my mama on the phone and she could tell them. And then one of them who hadn't had much to say before spoke up, and he sounded like he might have been from Harvard or Stanford or some snotty place like that. 'Yellow root?' he says. 'Yellow root? My good woman, we do not have the time nor the inclination for an experiment with folk medicine. You are seriously ill and surgery is your only option.'

"With that I fired up. Sick as I was. I was fed up with them treating me like I was an ignoramus. After all, I had finished high school and I hadn't forgot everything I learned. I laid there and I looked him dead in the eye and I says, 'There are more things in heaven and earth, Horatio, than are dreamt of in thy philosophy.' That comes straight out of Shakespeare, I'm sure you know. Wellsirree-bob, be blessed if they didn't do the hoot owl swivel again. 'Don't you ever think I don't have but one option,' I told them. 'I got three that I can line out for you four stiff-necked professors right fast. I can let you cut, I can lay here and die, or I can put my clothes on and get myself out of here with what dignity you pompous priests of science have left me. Right now. And that's what I aim to do. You have that nurse bring me my clothes right this very minute and I will not be taking up any more of your valuable time.'

"Then I got 'my good woman'ed again. By the same jackass, if you'll pardon the expression. 'My good woman,' he says, 'I cannot allow you to leave. I realize that you are distraught, but you are seriously ill and this is a matter of grave consequences. We'll give you another injection for pain and discuss this further when you are a little calmer, but it is quite out of the question for you to leave the hospital. I will not allow it.'

"Oh, you could tell that old Lord Cut-you-open was used to having his own way and nobody daring to dispute him! I wasn't about to let him shoot me up to the point I lost what little judgment I had left. I'd been down that road already on more than one occasion and always lived to regret it. I looked at him and I says, 'You better wake up and smell the coffee, Buster. You must of been behind the door when brains were passed out and Rights were invented.'"

I was puzzled to the point of interrupting. "Rights were invented?"

"Sure. I can remember when there weren't any Rights. Everbody just went along and did what their ma and pa told them. And the schoolteachers. And the police. And the preacher. And the government. And if you didn't, you got whipped or flunked or put in jail or damned to hell, and things were pretty orderly all in all. Then here came all the Rights. First it was Civil Rights, then it got to be Students' Rights, Women's Rights, Gay Rights, and even Children's Rights. Sounded like the whole nation was broke out with Rights. You couldn't move without stepping on some. Seemed like the worst thing you could do in this country was violate somebody's Rights. They'd slap you in jail in a heartbeat.

"I told those four doctors, 'I've got Rights and you needn't think I don't know what they are. You get my clothes to me or I'm calling the police.' And I opened my mouth wide as I could and hollered out, 'Help! Police!' Right there in their emergency ward, I did. They did the hoot owl routine again, and the boss says, 'Nurse, this woman is signing out A.M.A. Bring the necessary forms to her.'

"And I says, 'Nurse, this woman ain't signing nothing. You just bring the necessary clothes. Any forms need signing these four cotton-picking hoot owls can do it. I'm outa here.'"

"And you left? Without signing?"

"Nosirree-bob, I didn't sign. I got myself to a phone and called my mama. Hadn't talked to her in over four years, I hadn't, and that had not been what by any stretch of the imagination you'd call a pleasant conversation. But I was hurting and I was scared and I didn't waste any time making up. When she answered, I just said, 'Mama, can I come home?' and she said, 'Of course you can, Baby Sister. Where you at?'

"And I said, 'Seattle,' and she said, 'How come you crying?' And I told her it was on account of gallstones and the doctors wanted to cut and nobody had heard of the gallbladder flush, and she said for me to get myself home as quick as I could and she'd have everything set up and ready. And she did and I did. My mama not only gave me life when I was born, she saved my life when I was grown. I moved a trailer in down below her house because you know the old saying there ain't no house big enough for two women, and I been healthy as a horse and happy as a dead pig in the sunshine ever since. I'll never leave these hills again."

Helen had stopped to rest and was looking down on us from a considerable distance. "I was beginning to have that same feeling about these hills until I got hold of the wrecker," I said. "But you still haven't told me what the gallbladder flush consists of."

"Why, so I haven't. Takes me forever to tell my way around to something, it does. You sure you got time and aren't bored?"

"I can promise you I'm anything but bored," I rejoined. "And there's nothing for me to do until that wrecker comes."

"Well, you start off for a day and a half you don't put anything in your mouth but apple juice. Drink all of that you can hold but no water or anything else. Not even a soda cracker. Mama said Grandma used to have to fix it by hand but nowadays you can get a gallon jug of it in most any grocery store. You stay on that at least thirty-six hours, and forty-eight is better if you can handle it. Cleans your system out, if you know what I mean."

It seemed that everyone in these mountains sooner or later used that phrase. "I know what you mean," I replied with sincerity. "I know exactly what you mean."

"Well, that's just leading up to it, getting ready and on the mark and set to go, so to speak. Then along about four or five o'clock in the afternoon you drink down three cups of olive oil as fast as you can."

"Three cups? Olive oil?"

"Yep, and it's better if it's extra virgin. You know, olive oil comes in regular, virgin and extra virgin, and there's no question the extra virgin goes down better. I know it stays down better. Now, give that about thirty minutes to be sure you aren't going to lose it and then you follow it with three cups of fresh-squeezed lemon juice.

"Some folks mix the olive oil and lemon juice and drink it down together, but it takes a strong stomach and a strong will to keep from throwing all that back up soon as it hits. If it's mixed, it's a real load. On top of that you have to squeeze the lemon juice by hand and three cups of that is hard work; so you don't want to lose that if you can possibly help it. Besides, if you do throw up lemon juice, it has a tendency for a heap of it to come back through your nose and it stings like the very devil. So I always swallow down my three cups of extra virgin olive oil straight, let it get settled down and greased all around real good and then chase it with the lemon juice. Now then. Soon as you are sure that has become a permanent resident, you take the yellow root."

"Yellow root?" I said. "Yellow root?"

She laughed. "You sound like those dumb doctors in Seattle, Mister. Don't tell me you don't know what yellow root is. It grows all over these mountains."

"Of course I know yellow root." My answer was a little

imperious. "It grows about knee high. Has a soft, fimbriat-
ed leaf, little panicles of tiny green flowers, and the Indians
used the roots to dye their baskets. I just didn't know people used it for medicine."

"Yessirree-bob, they do. You get the roots and that's
where it gets its name from, for they're yellow as a lemon rind.
You wash them real good, then boil them in a little water for
about an hour, and the tea is a good stomach medicine.
Like I was saying, after you've got the olive oil and the
lemon juice fixed in place, you take two tablespoons of yellow root. Then you go to bed and lay down and go to
sleep."

"I wouldn't," I interjected, "not a minute."

"Sure you would," she answered heartily. "Then you get
up real early the next morning . . . ."

I was impelled to interrupt again swiftly. "Now, that I believe
with all my heart."

She ignored me. ". . . . and take the laxative of your
choice."

"Laxative?" I almost yelped.

"That's exactly what I said, Mister. It doesn't really matter which one. Folks are some more divided and opinionated on the subject of laxatives, in case it's never come to your
attention. Some won't take anything but Ex-Lax while others swear by castor oil. It makes no difference long as it's one
that'll really work you. I myself prefer a good dose of Epsom
salts; seems like it cuts the grease better. But the laxative, like
I say, is where you can express some personal preference.
You've got some leeway of your own there. Like some folks
put a little pinch of sugar in their turnip greens, which to my
way of thinking is a sissified thing to do.

"But to get back to our subject. Now you're ready. And
you better not have anything else planned for the day. I
mean, you're going to be busier'n you've ever been in your

whole life all morning, and weak as a kitten all afternoon. When it's over all you gonna want to do is lay around and feel relief from being rid of your gallstones."

"How do you know you are? Rid of them? Do you go get x-rayed?"

"X-rays?" Her look was tolerant. "X-rays? Get real, Mister. A hundred dollars or more plus an unnecessary trip to town just to prove to some dim-witted, doubting, money-snatching sawbones that you're cured? Nosiree-bob, Mister. You don't need any x-rays. You can feel those things passing. There's no doubt in your mind. Why, they went through and came out of me like buckshot. Just exploded out. And not just one at the time, either. I mean it was a rejoicing feeling. I was hollering, 'Praise the Lord,' and Mama was patting my back between trips. I'm here to tell you that, if you'd been able to count them, there was hundreds of them. The chickens had a field day."

I could not help myself. "Chickens?"

A defensive note crept into her voice. "First time I took the flush after I came home was before we got a pump in the well and we still had to go out. But we always put our chickens up for a week before killing them. To clean 'em out good. If you know what I mean."

I assured her hastily that I did. "You talk as though you'd taken this treatment more than once. Did your gallstones come back?"

"Not on your life." She laughed. "The chickens got 'em." She paused to be sure I knew what she meant but mercifully refrained from asking. "I've never had a trace of trouble since, but I take the flush once a year just to be sure. That night in Seattle is the most horrible thing in my life and I don't intend to ever go through anything like that again. Not me." She paused. "And you know those things run in families. Did you know that? They sure do." She jerked her thumb over her shoulder. "And soon as this little gal gets another couple years on her, I'm gonna flush her gallbladder every year. Just to keep her from having to endure what I have."

I was shocked. I had assumed her corpulent companion to be male, a lonely boy who watched too much TV, ate too much and never exercised. From where I stood I could not see much of the face above the chin, but the legs, the thick-wristed arms, the shorts, the tee-shirt all looked androgynous. The hands were still folded in the lap. Were the nails bitten? I couldn't be sure, but it would fit. If the child winced at the mother's declaration I did not detect it, but I winced for her.

"Well, I better run before this kid here has a squealing worm or they think I'm broke down somewhere. You sure I can't help you?"

"No, ma'am. But I want to tell you again how much I appreciate your offer. It's not every day an old man runs across a big-hearted person like you."

"Well, like I say, you ever been in trouble yourself it gives you a sympathy for others. What'd you say you do for a living? Or are you retired?"

My answer was as smooth and rapid as any lie ever uttered. "I sell burial insurance. And I'm not about to retire." Neither was I about to confess to this mountain Valkyrie, who possessed a feeling about doctors that might activate the tire tool she always carried, that I was a physician. "You need some?"

She shook her head. I knew she would. "Got no use for it. Don't aim to die. Not any time soon; and by the time I get around to it the government'll probably be paying for it anyhow; then I'd of wasted all that money. But I wish you luck. You're a nice man." She cranked her car, leaned out the window once more. "Tell your wife I said so."

"Thanks," I laughed.

"Wait a minute, Mister. I didn't catch your name. What'd you say it was?"

I was ready for her. I had a friend from college and med school, a boisterous, bumptious, sometimes bellicose person with whom I enjoyed an interesting relationship. "Darnell Brawner," I called down to her. "Darnell Brawner. If you're ever in Savannah, look me up."

"Darnell Brawner," she repeated. "That's easy enough to remember. You take care, Mister."

I waved good-bye and turned to Helen, a very private person, who was coming down the hill.

"Who in the world was that?" she demanded.

Glad to have her attention deflected from me, relieved to detect interest and purpose once again in her demeanor, I replied, "That was Baby Sister." I thought a moment, "And Baby Sister, Junior. History is sure as hell going to repeat itself there. To the third and fourth generation. Soon as the hormones kick in."

"What in the world did they want?"

"They wanted to help me."

"How?"

"She offered to pull me out. She carries a tow chain in her car."

"Well, I hope you had sense enough to tell her we have a wrecker coming."

"Trust me. She's gone, isn't she?"

"Well, she took long enough about it. What in the world was she mouthing about all that time?"

"Her gallbladder."

"Well, you deserved it if you had poor enough judgment to tell her you were a doctor."

"Believe me, Helen, I didn't. We just got to talking, and one thing led to another, and first thing I knew she was telling me about a gallbladder flush."

"A gallbladder what?"

"Flush. Gallbladder flush. Let me tell you about it. It prevents surgery and you may want to use it on some of your patients some day."

"Fat chance," she snapped. "But tell me about it anyhow. Or do I want to know?"

"Probably not. But I want you to know; I've got to tell somebody. First you get a gallon or two of apple juice, then three cups of extra virgin olive oil. Then . . . ."

"The phone's ringing."

"What did you say?"

"You know very well what I said. That phone's ringing again. This is as bad as trying to stay home on our day off."

I dutifully bounded back across the road to lift the receiver.

Some minutes later as I left the car, Helen had descended to the roadway. "Who was it that time?"

"Ellen. She had a luncheon meeting and had just gotten back."

"What did she want? Nothing's the matter, is there?"

"Nope. She was just checking to be sure we were all right." I glanced at my watch. "I told her the wrecker should be here in about another hour and not to worry."

"Okay." She developed a calculating tone in her voice. "You don't happen to have a container of any sort in that car, do you?"

"What sort of container?"

"A box, a bucket, anything. When I was up on that hill I thought I saw some blackberries across the highway and down a little ways."

"I may have just the thing. Let me check." Hoping I had not completely depleted my store of bags for plants, I rummaged under my seat and returned with an unused Zip-Lock freezer bag, gallon size. I presented it in triumph.

"Wonderful," she said. "This is perfect."

Perfection may seem an inappropriate accolade for a simple plastic bag, but I was grateful to hear it voiced. It denoted a swing from frustration and annoyance to a more normal mood level. It carried an unspoken hint of forgiveness, perhaps a tentative offering of the connubial olive branch. From the slough of guilt in which I was mired, I reached out eagerly.

"I'll go with you. Maybe we can get enough for a pie."

There was a touch of acerbity in her crisp reply. "You'd better stay here and catch the telephone."

"Why? Everything's taken care of. All we can do is wait for Ed from Andy's. Who would be calling us now?"

"That what I've wondered every time the thing has rung." She paused. "One of us needs to wait here for the wrecker."

"Why? We can hear him coming a mile off and there's sure no other traffic on this road."

She shrugged. "Come along, then."

We found some berries. Late in the season, wizened, bitter; nevertheless they were blackberries. I dutifully began picking.

"The ones down here in the ditch where they get a little shade are not as dried-up as those you're fooling with.—Be sure you don't pick any that are too ripe and soft; they'll ruin before we can get home with them.—There's a nice bunch right there over your head.—No, behind you to the right.—You finish this little patch; I think I see some more farther down the hill."

Sweat was soon stinging my eyes, gnats were invading my ears, briers were pricking dark drops of blood that pooled on the backs of my hands, and my back was aching. I looked downhill at Helen, who seemed to be contented and unruffled. Her hands were swift and busy; she reached with grace between the brambles; her demeanor was as queenly as that of any matron at Phipps Plaza. She was shopping. On this isolated, sweltering roadway, in the midst of

a ferocious brier patch she was shopping. Selecting, reject-
ing, and gathering.

The only thing I was enjoying was watching her. After some
thirty minutes of this, I called to her, "I think I'll go back to
the car."

"Why? There are plenty of berries yet and we don't quite
have enough for a pie."

"The telephone might ring."

"I would hear it."

"The wrecker might come, and we're a pretty good ways
from the car."

"Is it time for him?'

My fingers, grimy from the harvest of lilies and Nodding
Mandarin, were now stained purple with berry juice. I picked
a brier from the back of my hand with my teeth. "Almost."
I was itching all over. "I think I'll go wait by the car." After
a pause, I added, "If you think you'll be all right."

"Of course, I'll be all right." She responded with just the
soupçon of indignation I had intended to raise. "You go on
back if you want to." There was the very faint sneer in her
voice for a quitter, which I had also anticipated. "I'm going
to keep on until I get enough for a pie."

I trudged up the middle of the highway. A grasshopper
hung in whirring suspension four feet in the air. A July fly
screamed from somewhere in the blue shade of a poplar tree.
A box terrapin bumped across the rough pavement, paused
in caution to crane his neck, but did not pull in his limbs and
snap shut the doors of his tiny fort. I could not stand so much
serenity. I turned and shouted down to Helen, "Watch out
for snakes!"

I sat down on the mossy bank and leaned against Helen's
tree. I realized that I was ravenously hungry, that I was
trembling again, that I was exhausted. Where in the hell was
Ed? He had said an hour and a half at most. It had now been

two. I began to worry. Activity of some sort became imperative. I began to regret denying Baby Sister's offer. I surveyed my car once more and recanted the regret. Frustration grew. I walked down in range of Helen's voice and shouted, "I'm going to walk up the road to 136."

She put a handful of berries in her sack. "Why?"

"To be sure he doesn't miss the turn-off. He's late."

"Why don't you first call and see if he's left?"

"I don't have the number."

"You could call Sabrina and get it."

"I'd rather die," I howled.

With the back of a berry-stained hand, she pushed her hair away from her forehead. "You look here. You're getting in a dither again. You've done all you or anybody else could do. You've got to just calm down and relax and wait. Have a little patience, for goodness' sake."

I roared,

> "*'Patience is a virtue,*
> *Possess it if you can.*
> *You'll find it in a woman*
> *But never in a man.'*

You'll be all right here. I'm going."

She gave me a long look and stooped to a laden berry cane. "Be careful," she said.

Without reply, I turned and began my climb. I waited for her perfect riposte of "Watch out for snakes!" but it did not come. My wife is a much kinder person than I.

Minutes later, sweltering and panting, I began to deal with the creeping despair I felt at my folly.

The fiasco of the automobile.

The ruin of the afternoon.

It is difficult to be mature when faced with cataclysmic self-stupidity.

I concentrated on Ed. Was he lost? Had he taken another call, an emergency, after he talked to me? Was he ever coming?

I crested the Burnt Mountain road and began the descent of 108 to 136. It was further than I had thought. I began to regret my pilgrimage. What was I trying to prove anyway? I looked at my watch. Two hours and fifteen minutes.

Then I heard the motor, far away in the hills but definitely in the direction of Jasper. I began running for the intersection, but before I could round the curve, I heard the motor throttle down and then turn with a full-throated boast of power to come climbing toward me. Exulting within, I stepped sedately into the roadway as the wrecker moved into sight and gave an ever so nonchalant wave of my hand to flag it down.

I had to yell above the roar of the broken muffler. "You must be Ed."

His grin was restorative. "You got that straight. You the doctor what's in the ditch? Climb in."

"I'm the damn fool what's in the ditch, and am I glad to see you!"

Within minutes, this excellent young gladiator had efficiently assayed the situation, threaded a cable around the tree under which we had been sitting and winched my car back to its place of proper function, a paved surface. With joy I paid Ed, quieting his protestations that the price was exorbitant because the distance was great with assurance that the fee was most reasonable because the need was so great.

I opened the door for my wife and gently placed her bag of berries on the floor of the back seat.

"Be careful. Don't smush them."

I refrained from commenting that their own weight had already thoroughly smushed that arduously garnered fruit, as evinced by a good three inches of juice across the bottom of the plastic bag. I fastened my seat belt, gunned the T-bird, and soared up Highway 108 to crest out like a bird newly released from a clutching hand.

My wife sat in silence in her seat. I, also in silence, reviewed the events of the morning and, mentally but manfully, castigated myself for my stupidity, my ineptness, my helplessness.

I waited.

Silence.

After a mile or so, with no recriminations forthcoming from Helen, my mood lightened. I turned to her and said quite simply, "Thank you."

"For what?"

"For not beating hell out of the obvious and telling me what a fool I have been."

"You're welcome." A note of gentle amusement crept into her voice and she very softly, very evenly concluded, "I figured I owed you one."

She owed me? For what. What possible event in the past could have preordained forgiveness for my ignoring her parking instructions, imperiling not only the car but our own lives, and then chewing up a completely wasted five-hour chunk of her Sabbath with nothing to show for it but a trunk full of plants? And a half gallon of late-season, bitter blackberries which I had better sense than to ridicule?

Then in a flash, I remembered.

Oh, I remembered totally. Despite the adventure not having been mentioned between us since its occurrence, I could recall every detail.

It had been a bitter cold evening three years previously. It was early January when the days are dismally short and the skies more often than not low-ceilinged and gray with gloom. We had headed out after office hours for our holy day in the mountains, anticipating a roaring fire in our hilltop cabin, a time of relaxed seclusion, of non-demanding intimacy. We approached Smyrna on the interstate.

"You want to go by the House of Chan and eat supper?"
I asked.

"What time is it?"

"Six-thirty."

"If we get there before seven we won't have to wait.
Sure. Why not? We don't have any deadline."

The House of Chan is one of our favorite restaurants. The
food is excellent and the service impeccable. They always have
very fresh fish, which delights Helen. They also have a lady
of aristocratic thinness and carriage who glides around
replenishing water glasses and occasionally removing dishes. She delights me. Her features are finely chiseled and delicate. She never speaks and she never smiles. It is fun to watch
her. I imagine that she is some Mandarin empress in exile who
is being sheltered and protected by Mr. Chan and that she con-
descends to officiate in his dining room out of boredom. She
is beautiful, aloof, exudes noblesse oblige, and is marvelous
to behold.

We had a bowl of sizzling rice soup that really sizzled, and
sipped a glass of wine while we waited patiently for our steamed
snapper to be prepared. We knew it would be served whole,
with sightless eyes intact. It would be deboned at our table
by a friendly Oriental waitress who was an artist with chop-
sticks. It would be well worth the wait. While we relaxed in
idle chit-chat I drank lots of water so that the aging Chinese
princess would regally replenish my glass.

The snapper was excellent; the tea was comfortingly hot;
we dawdled over dinner, even munched the fortune cookies
that always remind me of tiny vaginas fashioned from spun
sugar and egg white. It was almost eight-thirty when I started to the cashier, bill in hand.

"You're not going to the restroom before we leave?"

"No, but I'll wait for you."

"I don't need to, but I haven't drunk all the water and tea

you have. You certainly were thirsty. I think you'd better go."

"Helen, I really don't have any urge to. Come on."

"There may not be anything open farther up the road tonight."

"I'm not three years old. I can manage. Let's go."

Fifty miles later I was squirming. She was right on two scores. There was no roadside facility open on the stretch of road we had chosen and I definitely had to go. Urgently.

"Sambo, you're driving entirely too fast! You'd better slow down or that picayunish patrolman named Shadrick will get you again. You know he patrols this part of Pickens County and you know how nitpicky he is."

I unfastened my seat belt to remove as much external pressure as possible. If it helped, I couldn't tell it.

I threw myself on the mercy of the court. "Helen, I was a fool not to make myself go to the bathroom back yonder. Now I'm getting into an emergency situation."

Her shopping circuitry immediately became activated. "I'll find you a place. There's a filling station in Jasper that I think stays open until nine-thirty or ten. Can you hold on till then?"

"I'll have to. There's too much traffic on this four-lane to stop by the side of the road."

The filling station she remembered was long since closed. I zoomed through Jasper, desperate but determined.

"I'll find you a place. Just hang on."

I clenched my teeth, decided that even that activity increased the pressure on my throbbing bladder and forced myself to relax.

"I've never seen so much traffic on this road this time of night," I moaned.

"Slow down. You're going to kill us. The shoulder is too narrow for you to pull off now. I think I know a place a little further on."

"Forget it, Helen. I'll make it to the overlook this side of Burnt Mountain. That'll be an ideal place. No spooners will be parked up there on a night like this with the wind blowing like it is."

"I know it. Thank goodness it's not raining."

The idea of any more water anywhere made me wince. "It's too cold to rain. It's down in the twenties up here, I'm sure."

"Well, I hope it doesn't sleet. Sure you can make it?"

"Maybe I can. If we just don't talk about it anymore."

Traffic disappeared. When we arrived at the overlook, I pulled smartly off the highway, parked at the very edge of the graveled strip overlooking the town of Jasper far below, left the motor running for Helen's comfort and leaped from the car, racing for the rear while zipping my fly open. With the satisfied fervor of delayed salvation, I relaxed my sphincter and ejected a veritable torrent. As my pain lessened with the deflating bladder, I had a tremendous urge to pass gas. The wind was shrieking through the mountain pass and besides there was no one around to hear. I let it go.

It was not gas.

With instant horror I accepted the unwelcome warmth and grasped for a solution that might keep everything confined to my underwear. Stiff-legged and spraddling I swung from the hips and maneuvered my way to Helen's window. I tapped on the glass.

She opened the door.

"What is it?"

"Look around the glove compartment or the console or the floor of the car or anywhere you can think of and see if you can find me some paper."

"Paper?"

"Yes. Paper."

"What kind of paper?

"Any kind you can find. Newspaper. Paper sack. Prescription pad. Anything."

"For what?"

"Helen, for God's sake, I have messed my britches and I think it's beginning to set up and freeze on me. Any kind of paper. Sand paper!"

"Oh, bless your heart! I know where there's a whole box of Kleenex!"

With this she leaped from the car, groped for a moment along the floor of the back seat, and then pressed a button on the door handle. I heard the two locks thump into place as dooming and definite as bolts in the Bastille, but before I could utter a sound she had slammed the door shut.

I howled in anguish, "No, Helen, no!"

It was, however, done. My wife and I stood on a freezing mountainside beside a toasty warm car with its motor and heater running, its lights on, and we were locked out of it.

With effort I kept my voice soft, level, without recrimination, but I had to say it. "Helen, you are Phi Beta Kappa and AOA." I added gently, "Why did you lock that car?"

"Oh, my goodness. Have I locked it? I was trying to pop the trunk open. I think that's where the Kleenex is."

"The button for the trunk is inside the glove box."

"I know that." The implication was that I was engaging in unnecessary conversation. Her tone became solicitous. "Are you all right, darling?"

"I'm as all right as any grown man can be who has just made a plumb fool of himself. I'm not sick, if that's what you mean." I reconsidered. "Except when the wind changes. I feel like Keats and his knight-at-arms.

> *And this is why I sojourn here*
> *Alone and palely loitering,*
> *Though the sedge is withered from the lake,*

And no birds sing."

"Oh get real, Sambo. What in the world are we going to do?"

"We are going to break a window, get in that car, and drive five miles over this mountain to our cabin."

"You're not going to break a perfectly good window in that car!"

"Oh, yes, I am."

"Maybe we can find a coat hanger somebody's discarded. Or a piece of wire."

"If we did, who's going to use it? I know very well I can't. What about you?"

"Break the window."

I began looking around for a rock. She added, "But just a little hole. So you can reach in and unlock the door."

"Right."

I kicked up a rock with my shoe, started to bend over for it but was sharply reminded that any stretching of my trousers accentuated my loathsome predicament. I knelt with stiffened spine and groped with my hands. I stood back and hurled the rock against the window. It bounced back. I searched for and found a larger rock. A good five pounder. It bounced. I threw with all the force I could summon. The rock rebounded to my feet.

"I never knew a damn car window was so hard to bust," I said.

"Use your rock like a hammer," she said. "But be careful. Don't cut yourself." She paused. "You really need some gloves."

"I really need a lot of things I don't have," I said and swung the rock.

The result for a moment diverted my attention from my perineum. The window did not shatter. It exploded. Or rather, it imploded. Tens of thousands of tiny glass cubes filled the seat and covered the floor, shimmering like diamonds in the light from the dash. I gaped in wonder and then pressed the unlock button.

"Hop in, Helen. Let's go."

In the corners of the window frame, sheets of glass, slivered and minutely crackled, hung like old rags. When I opened the door, the motion jostled most of them loose and they fell in tiny globules alongside the car, like a line of sleet.

I pondered for a moment, pulled my jacket sleeve protectively down over my hand, swept enough glass from the floor to free the brake and gas pedals, and surveyed the seat. I was able to brush some of the glass from it but tiny mullioned bits glittered like prisms. I groaned and heaved myself into the car, plopping with resignation into shattered glass and worse, accepting with what fortitude I could muster the inevitable shift within my trousers.

"This is a front seat in hell," I moaned. "I never in my wildest dreams could have conceived of anything like this."

I slammed the door and heard the last bits of glass tinkle down within it. The window frame was stark and bare.

"Can't you stuff something in that window? We'll freeze to death."

"Not in five minutes we won't," I said. "And that's how fast we're going to shelter. Hang on."

Awesome Bill from Dawsonville never drove better than I, and he never leaned forward bolt upright, rigidly gripping his steering wheel, with his pants loaded and freezing wind whipping around his head.

The cabin was a more welcome sight than ever before. Heretofore it had been a playhouse for escape, a luxury; now it loomed as a dire necessity. I stopped at the water cut-off in the edge of the yard.

"Why are you stopping here?"

"I have to turn on the water."

"Of course. I had forgotten that."

I got back in the car.

"Thanks for breaking the window out on your side of the car."

"It never occurred to me to do anything else."

I pulled the car up to the steps, left the lights on so that I could find the house key, and fumbled with the lock. My teeth were chattering, I was shaking like someone with the ague. I clutched the key with both hands lest I drop it and have to bend over to pick it up.

Helen called from the car. "Turn the gas heater on. I think we'd both freeze before we got the fireplace going."

"I will." By now I was so cold I was jerking as uncontrollably as Elvis in the midst of a song. I found a switch and flooded the yard with light. Helen turned off the car lights, prepared to follow me inside.

"No need to lock it," I called.

"I know that. You go turn on the hot water heater."

Like a dog that has been sprayed by a skunk and is so conscious of the resultant stink that he slinks around the edge of the yard, cowed, eyes rolling, lip pulled back from one side of his teeth in a grimace of apology, sneezing in revulsion, I sought with diffidence a place by the blazing gas heater. Of a sudden I could bear it no longer. I bolted for the bathroom.

"Where are you going?"

"To bathe. I can't stand myself another minute."

"You are stark raving crazy! It'll take at least twenty minutes for that water to get hot."

"I know it."

"You wait!"

"I can't."

"You'd just better."

"Helen, you've heard that time and tide wait for no man.

Believe me, I'm in a position where I'd rather die than wait for hot water. Hand me a bunch of those newspapers by the fireplace."

I stripped. Gingerly. I rolled my defiled clothing into newspaper. Multiple layers of it. I gritted my teeth and stepped into the coldest shower of my existence. I soaped and rinsed, soaped and rinsed, soaped and rinsed. Uncontrollably I yelled and wahooed, but I forced myself to continue until I was squeaky clean.

Scrubbed dry with a rough towel, I huddled naked before the small space heater, so close I had to turn frequently like a chicken on a spit.

"You're going to get blistered."

"I don't think so. As soon as I get my clothes on, I'll build you a fire."

When I had the blaze roaring I announced, "I don't know about you, but I could use a drink."

By now she was curled up on the sofa, feet snuggled beneath her, a blanket over her lap, reading. "That would be nice."

I fixed the drinks, carried the heavily wrapped bundle of clothes outside, sat down in the rocker.

In a very few minutes, I spoke again. "I don't know about you, but I'm going to have another drink."

"I'm fine." She looked up from her magazine. "Don't you overdo it."

But I did; I poured a stiff one. Then I settled into the rocking chair, faced the fire, and began to feel delightfully warm. All over. Inside and out. Warm and clean. Warm and clean and dry. I reveled in physical sensation that heretofore I had taken for granted. I became aware that I was nodding, that I had nearly let my glass slip from relaxed fingers.

"Helen."

"What?"

"I know it's early, but I'm falling asleep in this chair. I think I'll go to bed."

She closed her magazine. "Are you mad at me?"

"Mad? Of course I'm not mad at you."

She put down the magazine, pushed aside the blanket, uncurled her legs and came over to me. She placed a hand on either arm of the rocker and leaned above me. She looked into my eyes, straight and deep. "Are you real sure you're not mad at me?"

"I'm absolutely certain I'm not mad at you," I expostulated.

Long ago, I had noted in this beauteous creature that merriment can turn aquamarines almost into sapphires. Now I saw the eyes become a darker blue, their corners crinkle. She leaned over and kissed me. Softly.

"In that case," her voice became gentle. I waited. "Good night, Melrose."

That is the only time in my life I ever laughed myself to sleep.

I remembered that evening in a flash of detail as we drifted now down the south side of Burnt Mountain. I looked over at Helen.

"I had forgot. I guess you do owe me one."

She smiled and we coasted in silence for a while.

"Helen?"

"What."

"I love you."

"I love you too, darling."

We turned on the dirt road leading to the cabin.

"I sure do like being married to you."

I thought for a moment she was not going to reply. Then it came. "It sure is a good thing you do."

We both laughed.

As we turned into the yard I noted that it was four-fifteen.

There was still a remnant of our Sabbath left. I turned to
Helen and, in as courtly a voice as I could summon, inquired,
"Where would you like me to park?"

"Anywhere you please," she said. "But just be sure to take
the keys out."

It was a glorious day.

RELATIVE & ABSOLUTE

THEY SAY THAT DOWN IN THE COLORED CHURCH EVERY Sunday Jack Glass prays, "Lord, it's getting late in the evening for me." Well, I guess that's my case, too. What Jack and I mean, I reckon, is that it's coming up on time for us to get in line and take our turn. Like flowers closing up at night, or old leaves falling off a post oak to make way for bloom tassels and new shoots. To tell you the truth, though, I hadn't particularly studied on that till those young folks came swarming in here asking all those questions. I've been too busy living.

Lord knows I don't feel much older than I did twenty, thirty years ago. Oh, my back gets stiff as a board and my knees and hips ache when I overdo in the garden, but that's natural for anything that's about worn out. Then, too, I have to use the slop jar three or four times every night now, but from what I hear there's some that's younger than me that have to get up even more than that.

While I'm at it about that part of a man's anatomy, I'll just remark that for several years now I have added another item to the list of things that I don't take as plumb stomp-down truth in Holy Writ. I mean that part in Deuteronomy about Moses dying when he was a hundred and twenty and his eye was not dimmed nor were his natural forces abated. Well, I admit I can see well enough for my age. Soon as I get my glasses on every morning, anyhow.

But if they mean what I think they do about natural forces, then I don't hold with that at all and haven't for several years now. I side more with old man Pat Monroe, who had eighteen children and told John Cole that eighty will cut you clean as a knife. I think that holds pretty true for most men. Unless, of course, you're a Senator from South Carolina.

From me living long as I have and observing my fellow men pretty dad-blame close, there's another thing I doubt. I just do not believe that Lot was that drunk. He may have fooled his Uncle Abraham and most of his neighbors, but the Lord knows same as I do that was a lie he and those gals of his told, and how it ever got set down in the Bible as the truth is more than I can understand.

But then it's like I wanted to tell that young girl who was quizzing me about religion the other day. We're not supposed to understand everything. If we did, we wouldn't need religion.

What got me started on all this remembering and thinking about age and all was that trio of seniors from the high school here in town. They kept pestering me to let them come and interview me for a little book they get out every year. They've been doing it for several years now. They go and talk to people about what it was like in the old days and write it down in book form and get a grade on it. In their English class, I think. The taxpayers are footing the bill, I guess, and the teachers are calling it an education.

I don't understand, but I guess education is like what I told 'em about religion. If you understood it, you wouldn't need it. I've seen a couple of those little books they put out, and to tell the truth they're a pretty poor go. Needed a heap of punctuation and grammar correction, they did, and would have been a credit for seventh graders but not for seniors in high school.

All this came about from that fellow moving into the North Georgia mountains and putting out those books called *Foxfire*. Created a tremendous big stir, those books. Made a play out of 'em and put it on in New York City, the Yankees did, and everybody set the little fellow, young as he was, up as some sort of newly-risen authority on education; had him teaching at the University of Georgia and I don't know what all. Supposed to shed new light on how to get the interest of students and make them creative and productive and all like that. Well. I watched that fad grow and put it down as another modern example of spoonfeeding instead of true teaching. Made for lazy teachers and lazy students, to my way of thinking.

Anyway, in spite of my misgivings about the whole kit and caboodle, I eventually let those children wear me down and I told 'em they could come and interview me. If I hadn't it had got to the point where it would have looked like I was an old crank that hated young folks. Or else they might have used that old tactic of newspaper reporters who say so-and-so was unavailable for comment or refused to return telephone calls or some such sly little dig to make their readers think somebody is hiding something, instead of just plain not giving a hoot whether or not that reporter gets a story.

Anyhow, here they came.

Two girls and a boy.

They weren't much to look at. Most of the young people today aren't; one of the girls had too much hair with way too much curl in it. Just a mess of tangles halfway down her back and all around her face so you could hardly see it. Looked like she had spent an hour or so in front of the mirror making that head of hair look like there never had been a comb put to it. And a flouncing and flinging it around every time she turned her head.

The other girl didn't have enough hair and didn't have a bit of curl in what little she did have. You could see too much of her face. Looked like she had just given up and was saying this is all God gave me and I can't do much with it.

The girl with the hair had on too much paint, especially on her eyes. Looked like a raccoon peeking out from under a brush pile, she did. The girl without much hair didn't have on enough make-up. I wanted to tell her that a little coat of paint makes even an old barn look better, but it wasn't my place to give any advice. To either one of them. That's a painful awkward age and most of them will come out of it all right if you just let 'em alone. I right off put my money on the plain one to come out ahead of the pretty one when they grew up. Real pretty girls, seems to me, tend to rely on their looks to the neglect of other virtues that last a heap longer. And every blessed one of them has an ugly girlfriend that makes them look even prettier by contrast.

That boy was another case and something else. He had on a baseball cap turned backwards and an earring. His shirt and pants were way too big for him and the end of his belt hung down a good eighteen inches and his shoes were untied. I know the sloppy look is what's in fashion right now, and I recognize that it's not my place to give advice even if it's to members of my own sex who are, after all is said and done, supposed to be representatives of American manhood. I would have said nothing if I had met him on the street, but here he was in my own living room with a tape recorder in his hand and a pencil stuck behind his ear.

"Young man," I said, "if you will give me your cap, I'll hang it up for you."

Just as cool as a cucumber, he said, "I can't. If I take it off, I'll like, you know, have hat hair."

I gave him a polite smile, but I put a no-nonsense tone to my voice. "If you have a problem with your hair, I can let you have the loan of a comb and a brush, but gentlemen do not wear their hats in the house."

He tried to hold firm. "I really don't want to take it off, Mr. McEachern."

"My name is not pronounced 'McEeechern'," I said. "It's spelled that way, perhaps, but the correct pronunciation is 'McKaren.' It's Scottish and my branch of the family has never given in to popular usage and changed it."

That set him back a little, and he said, "Yessir."

"Now," I said. "The hat."

I reckon my disgust at seeing grown men wear their hats inside, and even come into restaurants nowadays and eat with them on their heads, had finally come to the surface. You can't just walk in a restaurant and start yanking hats off of strangers. If you didn't get into a fist fight, you'd at best get put away for being mental minded. I know a lady down in Thomasville; she put it straight, and I'll go along with her. "You reach a stage in life when you find yourself tolerating much more than you condone."

That doesn't mean you have to like it, though, and this young spriggins, after all, was in my house. And I was the one doing him a favor; I hadn't wanted this dad-burned interview in the first place.

"Young man," I told him, "the only excuse I know of for a man wearing his hat in the house is if he is an Orthodox Jew in the Temple. Even if you are Jewish, which I strongly doubt, this is not a synagogue. It is my home. I regard your cap as an insult to the memory of my dead wife and all of the other gentlewomen who have influenced me. You are perfectly welcome to stay, but the cap has got to go."

I held out my hand and be blessed if he didn't very slowly take that cap off his head and hand it to me. I saw right

off what he meant by hat hair, and I very nearly handed him
back his cap in sympathy. That boy's hair was cut real short
up to about three inches above each ear and then it looked
like a neglected mule's mane on the top and in the back, all
long and mashed down in some spots and flapping around
in others. It was a plumb mess and I couldn't fault him for
wanting to cover it up. But then I thought to myself that no
barber had held him down and forced that haircut on him.

I said, "Thank you," and hung the cap on the hall tree. I
never even mentioned the earring.

Seemed like that settled all three of 'em down. I kind of
thought little Short-Hair-Plain-Face had a giggle she was trying to keep from letting out, but old Ring-eyed-Pretty-Girl
looked a little startled. Why, she never even popped her
gum for about fifteen minutes.

They explained all about their project and their little book
and that they were dedicated to preserving the local stories of
how things used to be in our town and county, and they
would get graded on their efforts and they would be sure to
bring me a copy of the booklet with my interview in it when
it was all printed up. Then Ring-eye said it was a privilege to
interview the oldest citizen in the county and they really appreciated it; it was most kind of me. You could tell somebody had
told her to put that last part in for good manners, for her voice
had a sing-song that showed she had memorized it.

Mule-mane asked me was it all right and would I mind if he
recorded our conversation, and right off swung that machine
of his up in the middle of the table. He tinkered with it for
a minute and then clicked it on before I had time to answer.

That kind of got my dander up. I have heard all of my life
that youth will be served, and I have watched several generations go through their wild oats before they settled down
into respectable citizens. After Reconstruction and World War
I and during Prohibition, I saw young Southern girls turn them-

selves into what they called flappers. They bobbed their
hair off, pulled their eyebrows out and drew different ones
back on, smoked cigarettes, and took to wearing short
dresses that showed their knees. Those dresses were as
loose-fitting and bob-tailed and long-waisted as guano
sacks. After Kate Taylor's daddy got her a job in the tag department in Atlanta, she finally settled down and got married.
But she told me one time that she had learned how to drink
liquor out of a fruit jar on the back seat of an A-model Ford
and had kissed might nigh every boy in the county who
brushed his teeth every day and didn't wear overalls. I think
she tried to maintain that record till the day she died. Kate
was a sight. I miss her.

Then after World War II I watched the flower children come
along and the hippie colonies spin off from the Vietnam storm
like little tornadoes dipping out of a thundercloud. They wrecked
as many families just as completely as a tornado could, too,
and some of them are just now repairing the damage. I
guess I had more trouble with them, come to think of it, than
any other group. They deliberately talked gibberish, were always
saying, "Like, man, you dig me?" and "Far out." That all came
on right after the duck-tail haircuts and the shirts unbuttoned
halfway to the navel and the shirt sleeves folded back two times,
and probably wouldn't have amounted to much more than
that if the hippies hadn't taken up with the drugs. They had
LSD and marijuana and such as that floating around in
their systems until you never knew what was making them
stumble around and have visions in their heads. Always
plumb nasty looking, too.

They came in here from everywhere, seemed like. Camp-
ing in cow pastures and doing what infrequent bathing
they condescended to do in little farm ponds and doing all
kinds of scandalous sex acts right out in broad daylight, not
seeming to care who was watching. They upset this community

and, to tell you the truth, I suspect the whole nation was torn up and bleeding about it. Nothing gets to you like your children going to hell in a hand basket right before your very eyes, unless it is your child running off with the hippies and you've got no idea where he or she is. They drive you crazy when they're underfoot, but you grieve when you can't find them.

Our police did the best they could, but it didn't amount to much. We didn't have but three in the whole town back then, and the mayor called them in and talked to them about these children dropping acid and explained that they should be locked up for their own protection but not whipped like common criminals, even when they were acting crazy and being abusive and yelling. June Edenfield was one of the police at the time and I'll never forget his coming in my store with his lips real tight and thin.

"I don't care what the mayor says," he told me. "I'm on night duty by myself, and if them damn fool younguns give me any trouble I'll just plain put the coitus on 'em."

I kind of choked and said, "June, I think you mean 'quietus.'"

"Whatever," he said. "Them damn younguns just better not give me no trouble."

James Weaver was the sheriff along about then and was 180 degrees away from the mayor; he had the same philosophy as June. Called the doctor one night, he did; pretty late, too; good ways past the turn of the night; said, "Doc, my deputies have hauled in a whole bunch of hippies from out around Adams Pond and I can't tell male from female. Would you come down to the jail and sex 'em for me? I be goddam if I'm gonna lock 'em up in the same cell."

James always put on sort of a grumpy tone of voice, especially if he was going on with what in anybody else you would have called foolishness. He was in my store the morning after they had arrested one of the hippies for urinating on the sidewalk by the courthouse and right across the street from the jail. The whole town was talking about it; so of course I mentioned it to James.

"Mr. McEachern," he said, "I had more trouble with the magistrate than I did with the damn perpetrator. I told him I wanted a warrant for public nuisance and he stood me down it oughta be for indecent exposure. We jawed around till I got sort of hot and told him, 'Kenny, you're wrong. Old maids a block away saw him plain as day and I could see it from the jail without my glasses on and the windows not washed. It wasn't indecent, it was magnificent exposure, and they ain't a goddam case on the law books of Georgia to cover that.'" James was sure a sight; I still miss him.

I never did comprehend what got into young folks during that period; that urge to expose and exhibit their privates. One of 'em came in my store one day when I had gone home to lie down for an hour after lunch. The doctor had told me to do that for my health. I sure laugh at old Doc; he is something of a sight himself. I had hired this lady as cashier; came from Great Britain as a war bride; ran into one of the Gooches when he was overseas with himself in uniform and cleaned up and talking big. She thought all Americans were rich and that she had landed herself a prize. Came over here pregnant and found out she had to live in a remodeled chicken house that still had a dirt floor. The British are plucky, though, and I never heard her complain. When I got back to the store that day, the police were just driving off and Mrs. Gooch explained what had happened. This hippie came in and asked for a pack of cigarettes. She got them and turned around to give them to him and she told me, "There he stood, with his nastiness laid out on the counter right before my eyes."

I said, "Oh, my word, Mrs. Gooch, I'm sorry. Did you scream?"

"Most assuredly not," she said. "That's probably what the bloke wanted, don't you know? I snatched up the fly flap and gave the beastly thing several truly good whacks, I did. He's the one who began screaming. He ran out the door holding his wretched self and I called the bobbies to him. They brought him back for me to identify and have just left the premises. Will you go by the jail and prefer charges, or shall I?"

"Oh, I'll tend to that, Mrs. Gooch." I looked at the fly swatter. It was one of those old wire ones with ragged edges. I should have thrown it out long ago but you know how you just keep putting things off. "I guess I'd best take that fly flapper along with me. They may want it for evidence. We'll be needing a new one anyhow, after this."

"Right you are," she said. "I'll finish cleaning the floor. There's a drop or two of blood I've missed. Just there. Near the door. Mind you don't step in it."

I sure miss Mrs. Gooch. She moved off after her husband left and I lost track of her. Don't know what became of her, but she was evermore a sight.

Like I said, I've heard all my life that youth will be served, but maybe that's a little like praying. You don't always get what you ask for, and sometimes you get it but it comes in a form you don't like at all. I know I myself quit years ago praying for anything but strength to take whatever the Good Lord sends my way. At any rate, that youth standing in my house with his mule-mane and sloshed all over with so much toilet water that he smelled like a French fancy woman was cocky as a young jaybird in a chinaberry tree, and you could tell he thought he was something extra special. He was sort of tolerating an old man, and his English teacher, and even those two girls he was with; and he probably ruled the roost at home by scaring his parents with what he might do if he didn't get his way.

So when he said, "You don't mind if I record this conversation, do you?" as though it was merely a formality and only an idiot would have objected to anything he wanted to do, I summoned up my strength by shutting my eyes just a minute and said, "Isn't that a tape recorder?"

He sort of talked down to me. "You betcha," he said, real cheerfully. "Like, you know, the best one money can buy."

"I certainly do object to it, young man. If the three of you together can't take notes or remember in your heads what goes on in this interview, then you're not getting a proper education. I've even heard lately about them letting you carry calculators into math exams, and I don't approve one bit of substituting machines for human minds. Education is sinking low and teaching laziness when they give up diagramming and also quit making students memorize the multiplication tables. I don't condone any of that, and in this house I don't have to tolerate it. Turn it off."

He looked at me like I had dropped into his presence from another planet. His jaw was plumb slack.

"Better still," I said, "take it out of here."

"Take it out?" he said.

"Right. I don't know enough about these new-fangled machines to tell whether that one is turned off or not, but I do have sense enough to learn from things that have happened in the past. Do you realize that one of the biggest scandals in this country, even if it was, to my way of thinking, a tempest in a teapot, came about because of one of those infernal tape recorders? One of those machines was responsible for drumming the President of the United States out of office. Did you know that? A president who, for all his faults, had the common sense to get us out of a hopeless war and to recognize the existence of the most populous nation on earth?"

I turned real quick and pointed at Little Miss Ring-eye. "You know which one that was?"

She blinked real hard from under all that hair and shifted

her wad of gum to her jaw. "Was it Jimmy Carter?" she said.

So help me, she said it. I grunted and said, "Not teaching you much history, either, are they?"

Then I turned back to Mule-mane. "Make haste and take that thing out of my house and let's get on with this. You can set it on the front porch."

"But somebody might steal it. Like, you know, we're talking big bucks with this machine."

"Not off my front porch, they won't," I told him. "But if you're worried, lock it in the trunk of the car. Just get it out of here."

While he was gone I turned to the girls. "My full name is William Henry McEachern. I'll give a quarter to whichever one of you can tell me the president I was named after."

Little Miss Short-hair pops back quick as a flash. "Harrison?"

While I was fumbling out my change purse to get her quarter, she perked up and said, "Tippecanoe and Tyler, too," and grinned at me. She wasn't nearly so plain when she smiled.

When that boy came back in and sat down, I felt like I had pretty well demonstrated that I was going to be in control of things in my own house and now I could afford to settle back and be nice, a gracious host as some might say. I laced my hands over my stomach and said, "Now then, what can I do to help you young folks?"

Be blessed if it wasn't Miss Ring-eye who took the lead. "Tell us, Mr. McEachern, what it was like in this county when you were a boy."

"What do you mean? What *what* was like?" I said.

"Oh, you know. Life. Times. Things like that."

"Pretty broad subjects, young lady. How long you got to listen?"

"Oh, Mr. McEachern. You know. For instance, were times hard? Were you very poor?"

I harked back to my childhood. I could see my daddy plain as day. Seems like every time I think of him I see him outside. Chopping fast with a hoe in the everlasting cotton; slapping a plowstock back and forth in his hand going down corn middles; swinging an ax or mattock in new ground; bent over with a mule's foot between his knees, filing a hoof and shoeing him; standing up on the wagon hauling wood for the fires. I reckon that's because when he was in the house he was usually so tired out he went to sleep early. Soon as he had prayers after the dishes were washed up. Always outside, I remember him. And always working. Scrabbling out a living for his wife and nine children from rocky soil that wasn't the richest in the county by any means. And getting the name for being a gentleman farmer because he always wore shirts and pants. All the other farmers wore overalls, but my daddy never did. He was a Civil War veteran and didn't talk about the War much, but he did say to me when I asked him why we couldn't have overalls like everybody else, "Will Henry, overhauls are blue. That's the onliest color they come in. And blue was the color of the Yankee uniforms and you'll never catch me wearing that color. Not as long as I remember my friends in gray that died when I didn't."

He looked way off for awhile like he was studying something and held his ax real still. "When you and your brothers are grown men on your own, you can wear overhauls if you're a mind to, but complete forgiveness has not come to my heart yet. Let's finish this load of wood before dark. You've got to milk."

None of us ever lacked for something of some sort to eat, and our clothes were patched and handed down forever, but we were always clean before we lay down to sleep. I remembered my daddy's thick, hard hand and looked at Little Ring-eye.

"Times were hard, but we weren't poor. What else you want to know?"

"You weren't poor, Mr. McEachern? I thought every-body was. Way back then."

"Child," I said, "*poor* has several meanings. The one that usually comes to mind is that of sorrow. Like, 'Poor Mrs. Lindbergh, she lost her little boy.' Or of pity. Like, 'Poor Mrs. Roosevelt, she's got those buck teeth.' Or, 'Poor Miss Mitt; her husband was brilliant, but he drank himself to death.' And we use the word to sort of comfort ourselves because we're better off and nothing that bad has happened to us. Yet. And we need to be careful how we use the word like that, like Jesus got on the Pharisee about for praying, thanking God that he was not like other men. Watch out all your life how you use that word *poor*.

"Now if you're talking about lack of money and mater-ial things, everybody across the whole South was poor when I was a boy. I grew up during the tail end of Reconstruction and there wasn't any money. And you know something? It's hard to miss something you've never had. No. We weren't poor. You got another question?"

Little Short-hair cleared her throat and said, "What about schools, Mr. McEachern? Was it hard to get an education when you were young? Here in our county?"

Now that for sure and certain carried me back. I hadn't thought about that subject for years and years. When Papa first came home from the War, there hadn't been any schools. None at all. The children ten twenty years ahead of me didn't get any schooling except what their own parents could give them in the evenings after the farm work was done or on days when it rained. Soon as they could, folks out in my district hired a schoolmarm for six months out of the year. Paid her by subscription from those willing to do without so their children could learn. Taught them letters and numbers. And the proper way to put them together. When you get right down to it, that's all math and writing boil down to in the long run, putting things together correctly.

I mean we paid attention in school back then and learned. If the teacher ever whipped a youngun at school, that wasn't a circumstance to what happened when that youngun got home. Mr. Pepperwood ran a school down in Inman, for years and years. He came in here from Merriwether County and set up as a lawyer, but he took on a school to make a living till he could get on his feet.

Barlow Bayne and all his brothers and sisters and a passel of his cousins went to him. He was supposed to be a good teacher, they say, but a better disciplinarian. Barlow told me one time that about the second year under Mr. Pepperwood he wrote a note to Little Robert Mask and slipped it to him. The note said, "At recess I am going to pee in your hat."

When Mr. Pepperwood rang his dinner bell to let out for recess, Little Robert Mask took off running and Barlow said it took him two turns around the schoolhouse to catch him and, wrassle as he would, he never did get the cap off Little Robert's head. On top of that, Mr. Pepperwood caught up with them and whipped the both of them for fighting. Sent notes home to their parents, of course. Barlow said Little Robert Mask took another licking from Mr. John Mask, but old man Jim Bayne didn't lay a finger on Barlow. Told him that he'd flay the hide off him if Mr. Pepperwood ever whipped him for lying, stealing, or cheating, but that Bayne men had it born in 'em to fight. About one thing or another. Told him just always to be sure he wasn't picking on somebody littler'n him. And it would usually be a help if he was on the right side.

Out around Ebenezer, I was in another section of the county, and we never had more than twenty, thirty children in our little school at a time. Miss Lizzie Moffat was a distant cousin of mine and the parents hired her to teach us. Young and pretty as she was.

Miss Lizzie made it a point to collect books from anywhere she could get 'em and was said to spend nearly every dime she made buying new ones. Every Friday she would send a book home with a child from every family in her school so the parents could read it and send it back the next Friday. It was, I guess, the first circulating library ever heard of in this county.

I was only two or three years shy of being as old as Miss Lizzie and so were two other boys in the school, but she was real patient and understanding of us. We all thought she was a saint, and believe you me she never had the least bit of trouble with discipline. Not long as we were there. We were always glad to build fires and tote water for her, too.

Wasn't but one room to the school and the children were all bunched together on benches; we didn't have desks. She'd hear one group do their lessons and then another and then another. All in front of the whole group. When you got up to the level of what we'd call the seventh nowadays, I reckon, that was all Miss Lizzie could teach you, and that was the end of your education. Unless your parents could spare you from the farm and could also afford to send you off to boarding school. Then you could get a high school diploma and maybe have a chance to go to college.

They had good boarding schools around, but none in this county. There was one at Locust Grove and Barnesville and way down in Greenville and one over in Newnan, but only a handful of children could afford to go. Most of us had to settle for what we'd learned from Miss Lizzie and use that as a foundation to build on. Which was what she told us to do.

"You can read," she said, "and you can figure real well, Will Henry. Do some of both every day of your life and make it a point to add to it week by week as long as you live, and you will wind up a well-educated man, even if the world does not recognize it."

One of the Huddleston boys was my age and he said, "Miss

Lizzie, much as I been looking forward to it, I almost hate to leave school. I told Paw that you must be the best teacher in the whole wide world. I told him that if a body come in here and didn't know nothing that you'd learn him something if he just set in your room and listened at you."

"I'll never forget Miss Lizzie Moffat. She said in the most gentle voice you every heard, "Harmon, Jr., everything in life can be a learning experience and should be. You are a good boy. You keep on listening and be sure to keep your heart open and you will do fine. There is more to an education than is available in books.""

Then she looked at me. Real straight, for just a second. It was the perfect place and time for a wink, but Miss Lizzie was a lady and wouldn't think of such. I'll never forget that she said *heart* when the ordinary person would have said *mind*. She gave a lot to a heap of people. She didn't tend just to the children; she educated a whole community and was an example to us all. She was sort of a poor Martha Berry, I reckon, who didn't have the opportunity to meet Henry Ford nor the antebellum mansion to entertain him in. Miss Lizzie was a sight and everybody misses her.

"To answer your question," I said to Little Short-hair, "book learning was a heap harder to come by when I was coming along, before they put in public schools and compulsory education, to say nothing of free textbooks. We had the Blue Back Speller, McGuffey's Reader, and a few more old standbys and that was about it. We were considered pretty advanced when we got to where we could read out loud from the Bible to the old folks who couldn't see, especially when you could do it without following your finger along for a pointer. I only had one schoolteacher in my whole life; she carried me from the first through the seventh grade in three years. Taught me to read and to figure and how to keep building on that. To this day, I read everything I can get my hands on."

Mule-mane butted in. "I thought you said you weren't poor. Now you're telling us like, you know, you went to a private tutor and there weren't any public schools. I'm like, you know, a little confused. What did they spend their taxes on?"

"It sure wasn't on schools," I told him. "At least not for a long time after the War. Why, they didn't even spend taxes on public roads. A body was supposed to keep the road that went through his property in good repair himself, and if he didn't then the County would come and do it for him and slap a fine on him. But in those days nobody thought about levying taxes for schools and then forcing children to go to them. Most of the folks around here thought book learning was important enough for them to do without so their children could have it. The North had whipped us down to where we couldn't afford to give our children much of anything, let alone an education, and then they come along even to this day and make fun of us for being ignorant."

That boy looked like he was a little dubious about what I was telling him; so I thought I better give him another stout dose of reality. "Son, it wasn't until after World War II that enough prosperity hit this part of our nation so's a parent could buy his kid an automobile when he hit sixteen. Or a fancy tape recorder. Or up-to-the-minute stylish clothes." I looked at his head. "Or ten dollars for a haircut. Every civilization has to build on what has been laid down and given them by those that went before. And in the South we've had the special opportunity of having to build around what was taken away from us in the past. You think on that for awhile."

He squirmed a little and I could tell I might as well have suggested he spend a long weekend on the moon.

Little Short-hair brought us back on track. "Mr. McEachern, do you have any idea, or can you tell us, how much it cost to go to one of the private schools in your day?"

"Just a minute, young lady," I said. I pulled myself up and

went over to the secretary in the corner and rummaged around through my old papers that I didn't need anymore but wasn't about to throw away. I found what I was looking for and brought it back to them. "Y'all look at this."

Georgia, Clayton County. 1861
Article of agreement between Morgan B. Dorman of the first part and we the undersigned of the second part. The said Morgan B. Dorman does agree to teach a literary school in the neighborhood of Mr. Wesley Souter and others for the term of ten months. He does agree to teach spelling, reading, writing, English grammar, and arithmetic at the following prices: One and one half dollars per scholar per month for each scholar. He does agree and promise to keep good order and pay strict attention to the students during school hours. We the undersigned do agree to and promise to pay the said Morgan B. Dorman or bearer the above mentioned price (with board included) and to pay him at the close of school.
Names of Subscribers

The writing was full of curlicues and was heavier on the downstrokes than the upstrokes. You could tell it had been written long before anybody ever heard of a fountain pen. It was most probably done with a goose quill, although I had seen my daddy take a turkey feather, slice the end off it on a sharp diagonal and then split the point with his knife and write with that. It was almost like drawing with it. I never said anything to those youngsters, though. I myself had never heard anybody talk about a turkey quill pen and they would probably have been bored with all that. Plus, it would sure lead to one of them asking me when the fountain pen had been invented, which I didn't have the faintest idea of in the first place, and in the second place the question had been about how much an education cost.

"The ink sure is faded, Mr. McEachern. It's a wonder we

can read it at all," said Little Short-hair. "But it's fascinating. That was not but fifteen dollars per year per child.
That's hard to believe."

"Some things," I told her "never change. You can see for
yourself that schoolteachers never have made much money.
But you know, it was not till after World War II that I ever
heard any teachers grumble about their salaries. I guess
they'd all believed Proverbs back in the old days, that a
good name is to be preferred over great riches. Although that
contract was written thirty years before I was born, I doubt
very much if prices had gone up much by the time Mr. Pepperwood and Miss Lizzie came along. Times were hard and
money was tight in '61, too, you know."

They were passing the paper around amongst them and
I will give them credit for the way they were handling it. With
respect and care. Like every one of them automatically
knew any paper over a hundred years old was delicate and
might crumble in their hands or tear if they snatched it.

"This is like, you know, a contract, isn't it? Like, you know,
a real sure enough one," Mule-mane asked when it got to him.

"You could call it that," I told him, "although I'm sure no
lawyer wrote it up. One of those subscribers might have been
doing what they called 'reading law' back when I was a boy,
but if it had been drawn up by a sure enough certified
lawyer it would have had his name on it as having prepared it and more than likely a seal on it.

"I can't answer for the time before I was born, but when
I came along you didn't have to go to law school to be a lawyer.
All you had to do was pass an examination and get admit-
ted to the bar. Most folks did it under the supervision of an
already established lawyer, but it was not unheard of for a
fellow to venture out and do it by himself. If he could get a
hold of the law books and codes and what all."

Mule-mane acted like he was warming up. "I've thought

about like, you know, being a lawyer myself," he said. "But like, you know, it takes seven years out of your life after high school and like that's a lot of time. I'm not sure yet."

Since he was sort of relaxing and branching out, I decided the least I could do was follow suit and that I would give the three of them a little parable from my own experience.

"I recollect my father laughing about Old Man Webb Hosey. I reckon I was about ten when Old Man Webb got sued for stealing a mule. It was too wet to plow; so Papa wasn't as put out for being called for jury duty as he would have been during good weather. Mama told him to go on to town and enjoy it and quit making like he didn't. Papa sort of grunted and Mama told me later that menfolks all enjoyed court and politics and the Masons and she wasn't really all that sure about war. Mama was a heap younger than Papa and pretty quiet and reserved, but when she did come out with something it was worth listening to.

"She was right about court and politics, too. Up until we had paved roads and radio, the two highest forms of entertainment we had around here were court week and election night, and folks that went talked about it to folks that didn't till next term of court. Papa said everybody in the county knew Old Man Webb Hosey hadn't stole that mule. The Hoseys were bad to drink and fight and had been hauled into court more'n once for the white liquor they made and sold now and again, but it was unheard of for the Hoseys to stoop to stealing. Old Man Webb was butt-headed, unlearned, poor as a church mouse, and wasn't always too particular about shaving and washing before he came to town, but Papa said stealing just wasn't in him. Everybody around the courthouse knew that, and Old Man Webb knew that everybody knew it.

"On the other hand, everybody knew that Mr. Hulon Cranford, for all that he wore a celluloid collar and necktie and carried his head high, was tight as a tick and as mean-spirited as a striking snake. Got it from his mama's side; Papa said all the Hulons had their eyes set too close together and folks knew to watch out for them. They were bad to lie, too, when the truth would have served them better.

"To top it off, Mr. Cranford had hired Lamar Forrester as his lawyer. It had been the talk of the town the winter before when the marshall had set out a watch because the coal pile at the courthouse kept going down more than could be explained by legal use, and he caught Mr. Forrester sneaking down around midnight and loading up not one but three scuttles of coal in the back of his Model-T. They never made a case against him because he was so prominent and a big Methodist who didn't drink or smoke, but it got out on him anyhow.

"One of the lawyers in town, Mr. Dean Pepperwood, it was, the son of the old schoolteacher, said that it just went to prove that every man needed an acceptable vice. Said if Lamar Forrester had ever smoked a cigar or held a hand of poker or taken a drink of liquor or even stepped out just once on Miss Mamie, then maybe he would of been a man of honor and never taken up stealing. Said all the lawyers in town knew where half of the courthouse records and law books ended up when they disappeared and that was in Lamar's library at home. Mr. Pepperwood said that Lamar never seemed to have a fountain pen, and he had learned whenever he borrowed his to hand him just the pen and hang on to the cap if he wanted to get any of it back. It was his opinion that if ever a man needed a vice, Lamar Forrester was that man.

"Anyhow, Papa said here you had a thief representing a liar against an unwashed honest moonshiner, and he settled back in the courtroom to watch it. Our county is on a circuit and we've always had a traveling judge. You couldn't expect him to know folks and families the way all of us did, but he knew Old Man Webb Hosey all right enough for him having been in court so many times before. He said, 'Mr. Hosey, who is your attorney?'

"'I'm going to represent myself in this case, your honor,' said Old Man Webb.

"The judge looked down from the bench and over his glasses and said 'Mr. Hosey, have you ever read any law?'"

"Everybody in that courtroom knew Old Man Webb had to sign his name with an X and that he couldn't read a lick; so they got real still and quiet and waited. Old Man Webb came through for them. 'No, sir, your honor,' he said and shifted his tobacco cud to the other jaw. 'But I've sure had a heap of it read to me.'"

I stopped for them to laugh, but they were all three staring at me as if they were waiting for me to get to the point. Mule-mane's mouth was even about half open and you could hear him breathing. That story had been one of my father's favorites and I don't share it with just everybody. Besides, it's nothing but good manners when somebody has gone to the trouble to lay out a good tale like that to laugh just a little bit, even if you don't think it's all that amusing yourself. So I let out a couple of chuckles to let them know it was supposed to be funny and also just a little bit in memory of Papa.

Then I said to Mule-mane, "Old Man Webb Hosey won his case, too. On top of that, the judge made Mr. Hulon Cranford pay court costs."

I thought I'd try those kids one more time. See if I could jolt 'em loose or something. So I told 'em, "What had actually transpired, and Old Man Webb got it into the court record, was that Mr. Hulon Cranford had bought this old mule from old man Webb. Didn't give but thirty-five dollars for it when it was easy worth seventy-five, but old man Webb was hard up and needed some cash bad; so he took the money and Mr. Hulon's manservant came and led the animal to the Cranford barn. Next morning about sun-up when he went to catch the mule out to plow, it was stretched out in the stable. Stone cold dead. Stiff as a board. Couldn't bend the legs nor the neck. Had to knock the boards off a whole wall to drag him out.

"Mr. Hulon went tearing over to the Hosey shack and found old man Webb sitting on the porch. 'Webb,' he hollered, 'that infernal mule you sold me yesterday afternoon died last night!'

"And Old Man Webb rocked back on the hind legs of the little kitchen chair he was in and hooked his thumbs up in his overall galluses just as calm as you please and said 'Hulon, you don't mean to tell me! That sure is strange. You know, that mule never done that whilest I had him.'

"And the judge dismissed the case. Said that wasn't stealing and that old man Webb could keep the thirty-five dollars."

Well, that set them off. Little Ring-eye started it. Sort of snickered in the back of her nose, she did. Then Little Short-hair tittered just a little and then be blessed if Mule-mane didn't come to the party. He threw back his head, which helped a lot about straightening out that haystack he called hair, and just plain whooped. That really made me feel better about this whole younger generation. I had worked hard telling them that story, and if they hadn't finally laughed I was to the point I was going to fake a sinking spell and terminate our association.

But they had listened. Close. Like I had when I was a youngster and your entertainment didn't rush in on you like lightning flashes out of a box and you could change channels if it didn't just exactly suit you. On top of that, they gave every appearance of having enjoyed it. In fact, I thought for a minute Mule-mane was going to need pounding on the back to keep him from choking on his own laughter.

I said to him, "Son, that just goes to show you that common sense will stand a man in as good stead as book learning. Like Mr. Pepperwood told me once out of his own mouth when he had got old and independent enough to say whatever he pleased and not worry anymore about whether he'd lose a vote for the legislature, 'I'm going to contribute to our church fund to send the preacher's son to college, but I don't in any manner of speaking regard it as bread upon the waters, nor do I expect to have it returned to me in good measure, packed down and running over. You can educate a fool, but when he graduates from college he'll still be a fool. You can mark my words, Will Henry McEachern, that preacher's boy will bear me out. I may not live to see it manifested, but you're young enough so that you will.'

"And I did, son, but that's another story, a long one, and we started out talking about contracts, didn't we?"

"Yes sir. I believe we did. And, Mr. McEachern, I'm not like trying to dis anybody, you know, but this paper seems pretty cheap to have a contract written on it. It's thick enough, but it's got ruled lines on it like, you know, it might of just come out of somebody's old notebook."

"Well, young man, you may be right. Look at the date on it. 1861. Now ask your young friend, the historian sitting over there, what was going on in this part of the world in 1861."

I turned to Little Short-hair, and quick as a wink she said, "The Civil War?"

"Right," I said. "Or the War Between the States, as the UDC wants you to call it. Or even as I heard one lady of the landed gentry say, 'the Late General Unpleasantness.' My father said that particular lady was more landed than she was gentrified. That he had fought in it and 'Civil War' was as good a term as any. Although he did allow there hadn't been very much civil about it. Except the way Lee conducted himself. Especially at Appomattox.

"But let me tell you young folks what they told me was going on in 1861. All sorts of things were scarce and not only did they not throw anything away, they used up every little bit of whatever they had. It was surely to goodness a matter of

'waste not, want not' in this part of the world for going on
the next fifty years. Why, when I came along some thirty years
later or so there still wasn't any waste, and thrift was defined
as what your pappy left you. We didn't have paper napkins
or wrapping paper and we didn't have notebooks in school
until we got on up to where what we wrote might have some
significance; used to write on slates, we did. They made
paper out of rags back then; not pine pulp. It was worth more.

"We didn't have the plastic civilization back then that we
have now. Until after World War II, the which, to my way
of thinking, has contributed to a lot of our problems. I tell
you this, son, when I was coming along there wasn't any concern about landfills and garbage dumps. We didn't have
any garbage to worry about in those days; we fed it to the
pigs and the chickens.

"And seems to me that nowadays a heap of folks have taken
up 'no deposit, no return' as a creed; a way of getting along
with other people. If you don't put much into a relationship
to start off with, then it's no dilemma whatsoever to throw
that relationship on the garbage heap when you're done with
it. Use them up and throw them away. And that, to my
way of thinking, just might even apply to the way parents raise
their children nowadays. Plastic toys, lots of them. Plastic
automobiles, the fancier the better. Even got plastic money
now. Give the kid a credit card. Indulge him with a plastic
telephone of his own. Then with all these bright material things
you have discharged your duty as a daddy or a mama, and if
the kid doesn't turn out all right then it's no fault of your own
because you have given him, free of charge, every one of what
this society today fools itself into calling modern advantages.

"Well, that's just plastic love, it is, and it hasn't taught a
youngun a thing about duty, responsibility, honor, how to work,
or the sweat of his brow. I say, 'no deposit, no return.'

"But to answer your question, yes. That paper probably

did come out of a notebook. More than likely a bound one. Where family records were kept. And then when somebody died and inheritances had to awarded, some contract or such would be written in the book. Then when Baby Sister, or Little Brother, or whoever, inherited that particular thing, the record of it would be cut out and given to them."

"But, Mr. McEachern," Mule-mane said, "this is a contract to teach school. Nobody would inherit like, you know, a job, would they?"

"I sure wouldn't think so, son, and that's a telling point. You've got a good head on your shoulders. Remember about 'waste not, want not' and remember the Civil War is just getting cranked up. Gathering and growing and growling like a tornado building strength before it sweeps down and destroys everything in its path. Then turn that paper over and read these young ladies what's written on the other side."

And he did. He had to study the faded ink and the Spenserian penmanship a while, and then he looked plumb puzzled. But he read it out for the girls to hear. The way it was written without any punctuation and with sort of convoluted wording made it come out of his mouth as stilted and labored as I imagine it had been written.

Georgia. Clayton County. Know all men by these presents that we grant bargain sell and convey to the said Bogan Mask a Negro man named Charles twenty-seven years of age for and in consideration of the sum of twelve hundred dollars to them in hand paid warranted to be sound this the 20 day of December 1860.

A. F. Guice, J.P.	*Daniel McLucas*
J.P. Frances	*John Lamb*
I. W. Hills	*E. V. Ball.*

*A. Chambers, James A. Chambers as trustees
for Joseph V. Chambers*

Mule-mane quit reading out loud, but then he went back over it to himself. You knew because his lips were moving and his forehead was wrinkled up. Also he had commenced to fiddling with his earring. You could tell he was concentrating. Both the girls were still as church mice; Little Ring-eye wasn't even chewing. I just bided my time and waited. Sure enough he picked up on it. There was a brain in that head after all.

"Mr. McEachern, this is dated 1860 and the school contract is 1861."

"What do you reckon that means, son? Or what does it indicate to you?" I asked.

He shook his head. "I'm not sure," he said.

"Well, any of us would look foolish being absolutely sure about something that old and about two transactions that went on over a hundred years before any of you were born, wouldn't we? We weren't there and we don't have any of those people to speak to us. But they did leave the scrap of paper, didn't they? What do you girls think? About those dates?"

I was expecting Little Short-hair to come through for us, but be blessed if Little Ring-eye didn't get her chin off the table and hold herself straight. She reared back and grabbed a fistful of that frizzed hair with one hand and yanked it over to one side and all of a sudden the raccoon had come out of hiding. You could actually see her face. At least the biggest part of it. The bangs still came down so low that every time she batted her eyes the top of her head jumped, but at least you felt like she was finally with us. She even reached up with two fingers and pulled something less than a quarter pound of bubble gum out of her mouth, and that made a world of difference. You could actually understand what she said. At least most of it. Seems like all young girls nowadays tend to talk too fast. Also they don't open their mouths wide enough and they speak to their own adenoids instead of out front to the folks who are straining to listen. Getting the gum out helped Little Ring-eye, though.

"One was dated before the Civil War and the other a year later, after the war had begun."

"Yes?" I said.

"Well, maybe, just maybe. Like you said, none of us really knows." Now that kind of caught my attention. Miss Lizzie had drilled into us that *none* is a contraction of *not one* and is singular, but an astonishing number of people nowadays who ought to know better persist in making it plural, even when they're writing for the newspaper where all the world can see it.

Little Ring-eye went on. "Perhaps it illustrates that after just one year of war things had changed so much that people who were desperate to educate their children couldn't afford even a good living wage for a schoolteacher."

"And perhaps it doesn't," said Little Short-hair, and her voice was more than a little sharp. She took a deep breath and you could tell she was getting ready to make a speech, but I didn't turn and look at her yet. Without letting on that I was watching close, I was waiting to see what Little Ring-eye did with that wad of gum. If she popped it back in her mouth, that was her own business, but if she so much as moved like she was going to stick it under her chair or under the top of my table, then that would automatically be my business and I was prepared to give her what some would describe as unshirted hell. But you know, she wrapped that mess in a piece of Kleenex like it was dough getting ready to rise and tucked it down in her handbag? The girl had more raising than her appearance would indicate. It is nice to get surprised like that.

Little Short-hair had taken her text. "That piece of paper is a contract to buy a *slave*," she was saying. "It's down there in black and white that those awful people were selling a fel-

low human being to some awful person named Bogan Mask.
It even names the price they got for him. And then just
coldly guaranteeing that he's healthy! It's like buying a dog
and getting a certificate that he's had his distemper shots and
has been wormed. The very idea! It's awful. They didn't even
give him the dignity of a last name. Just 'Charles.' I don't care
how hard up and needy people were, they had no business
selling other people for money."

She stopped to get herself another breath and kind of glared
at me. You could tell she wasn't near through.

I never shifted in my seat nor unclasped my hands. Just twid-
dled my thumbs a little. Real slow and easy like. And that's
the way I kept my voice, too. "Makes a body think, doesn't
it?" I said.

"Think?" she said. "Think?" There was something about
the way she looked right then that brought up the vision of
Carry Nation swinging her ax in a saloon.

"You know what I think, Mr. William Henry McEachern?
I think it's disgraceful to preserve that piece of paper. I think
you ought to burn it!"

Be blessed if that didn't bring Little Ring-eye to her feet.
Yes, sir. She jumped up like a jack-in-the-box. In addition to
all that, just quick as a wink, she reached up with both
hands and tied all that long hair in a big knot on the back
of her head and got it out of the way. She had the least little neck you nearly ever saw. Sort of made her look like a king
cobra rearing and spreading its hood. Especially with those
black eyelids. I was somewhat impressed.

"I am surprised at you," she told Little Short-hair. "Of
course, that's a record of slavery. I would call it more of a deed,
though, than a contract. A deed to a man named Charles,
and nobody in this country condones slavery anymore. We
all deplore it. But it happened. You can't change history. You
may rewrite it or try to twist it to suit you, but you can't change

it. It would be a tragedy for Mr. McEachern to burn that paper. It needs to be preserved. It has made not only slavery but education more real to me than ever before. I don't believe in burnings. I don't believe in burning Joan of Arc, or Salem witches or books. I don't believe in 'Burn, baby, burn.' But I believe all of those things have happened, and it's not going to make me or you feel any better by pretending they didn't."

Little Short-hair cut her eyes at me real quick. I pretended I was nodding off and not very interested. When you're old as I am you can get away with most anything, including staying out of a ruckus you have your own self stirred up.

She bristled right back at Little Ring-eye and for one so young she sounded considerably haughty. "I'm as entitled to my opinion as you are to yours, and I still think that creature named Bogan Mask was an awful person to go out buying a man, a grown man, like he was a horse or a cow or something. And I'll have you know that I don't need to be lectured to by the likes of you. After all, I'm already in the National Honor Society."

I opened both my eyes and broke in. "Y'all started off real good there for a minute or two, young ladies, but sounds like all of a sudden you've quit thinking and commenced to getting personal."

I turned real quick to Mule-mane. "What are you thinking, young man?"

He was holding my paper down with two fingers flat on the table and was sort of slouched back in his chair, "I've been sort of shocked, too, I guess. It's hard to believe that a whole group of people looked down on another group of people, like, you know, as sub-human and bought and sold them and really owned them. But here," he tapped his fingers, "we've got proof from the past that like, you know, it was really true. I guess I feel like both the girls. It brings slavery home to me and I don't like the way that makes me feel, but I sure don't think you ought to burn this." He lifted the paper up real carefully. "In fact, I think you ought to frame it. Or else give it like, you know, to a museum or something like that. Like it sure, you know, needs to be preserved."

I kept quiet and the girls did, too. "But, you know, Mr. McEachern, what I was really sitting here thinking was like, you know, like what would of happened if he like, you know, Charles had died that night in his bed, or his stall, or wherever Bogan Mask kept a slave, like you were telling us old man Webb Hosey's mule did. Well, I know it sounds weird, but I was wondering if Bogan Mask, well, like, you know, would he have sued the same as Mr. Cranford did? Seems to me like, well, you know, after all he did have himself a written contract and it does say that this Charles was 'warranted sound.' And like, after all, twelve hundred dollars is considerably more than thirty-five.

"Maybe the reason I'm thinking along those lines is like, you know, my mama just got off jury duty. Had to miss a whole week of work and she had some like what she thought were some important conferences, and she spent what time she had at home that week fussing about the trivial cases that folks clutter up the court calendar with. The whole time you were telling us about that thirty-five dollar mule I was hearing like, you know, in my mind, what she'd have to say about Mr. Hulon Cranford, even if it did turn out to be funny enough to make it like worth your time just to listen to it."

He was getting serious enough, I thought, that maybe his speech pattern might improve. Just maybe. At least I had hopes for him. I couldn't be real sure just exactly where he was headed, but at least the boy was thinking. Maybe that wasn't going to turn out to be a ten dollar haircut on a twenty-five cent head after all. I just waited.

He looked at the girls. "But, you know, there's a like considerable difference in a thirty-five dollar mule and a twelve hundred dollar slave, and if anything like that had of like, you know, really happened, which this is like, you know, just speculation, I guess you might call it, then would it of been a stronger case for Bogan Mask than for Hulon Cranford? Or would the Chambers family have got off by telling Bogan Mask nothing like that ever happened while they had him?" He shrugged. "I don't know. What do you think?"

Little Short-hair had a fire lit in her boiler; I wouldn't have been too surprised to see a little puff of steam blow out of her ears. "I'll tell you what I think, Lathrop Bulineau Featherstone, IV. I'll tell you just exactly what I think. I think you are perfectly awful. I think you are awful to think there might be any semblance of your loathesome male humor about that dead mule in a situation where one human outright owns another human. And you are wrong when you say there was a considerable difference in a thirty-five dollar mule and a twelve hundred dollar slave. The only difference I can see at all was the price. In the eyes of those people who sold him and that horrible Bogan Mask who bought him, both of them, the mule and the man named Charles, were livestock and both of them were regarded as private property and both of them were treated like animals! And you sit there and quibble about little hypothetical legal points. It makes me sick at my stomach!"

I figured it was about time somebody gentled that little filly down before she kicked the whole back end of the barn out. "What the three of you are really discussing, seems to me, is right enough the theme of morality, but then that brings us to that old question of whether morals are relative or absolute, doesn't it?"

Little Short-hair quit glaring at Mule-mane and twisted her head so sharp toward me it made her straight hair flounce out for just a quick minute like a bullfighter's cape or that Cybill Shepherd who advertises shampoo on television in slow motion. Except thinner. "What do you mean by that?" she said, but her tone was gentler.

"I went to a chautauqua once a long time ago, up in Tennessee at the Monteagle Sunday School Assembly. Had to ride the cars all day to get there and change trains twice. Stayed at a boarding house there for three days and heard speakers from all over the country holding forth on various things. But this one that talked about morals being relative has always stuck in my mind. He was a smart man. Didn't hand you out any answers in a spoon, but he sure made you think."

"What exactly are you getting at, Mr. McEachern? What are you trying to tell us?" asked Little Ring-eye.

"Well now, young lady," I told her, and I was right glad she was the one who had broken in and asked, for Little Short-hair was still puffed up and blowing like a bellowsed bull, "I reckon I'm not trying to tell you anything. Leastwise, not any cold, hard facts. And I reckon what I'm getting at is the business of retrospection, or hindsight, or what they call arm-chair quarterbacking nowadays."

"I'm not sure I understand," chimed in Mule-mane. "Like, you know, all of a sudden this is getting pretty deep."

"Yep," I said. "That's a good word. Deep. Opposite of shallow, it is. Life's a little like that, isn't it? Like wading in a river. You can be scuffing along in water less than knee-deep with the sun warm on your back and the water cool on your feet. The honeysuckles are smelling sweet and the birds are singing. Everything seems simple and calm and almost perfect. All of a sudden you step off in a suck hole ten feet deep and the current grabs you and if you aren't prepared, or if you can't swim, you can drown in all that muddy water. Best to feel your way with your forward foot and be a little cautious and wary. I've always tried to do my thinking like I was wading in a river and not come out with any real firm opinions until I was pretty well convinced I wasn't in over my head."

I had their attention, but they were probably wondering

if my mind wasn't wandering. They were still looking at me like I was a relic from the distant past and that suited me just fine. Not a one of 'em said a word.

"You can start on just about any subject you want when you start thinking on morals being absolute or relative," I went on. "The man at the chautauqua used killing as an example. I'll never forget it. The Ten Commandments, he told us, were the basis of our moral code today as well as our legal system. 'One of them,' he said, 'is "Thou shalt not kill." That's all it said when it was handed down and that's all it says today. Four words. "Thou shalt not kill." Period. It doesn't have any modifying clause that starts with *except* or *unless*. It just says very simply "Thou shalt not kill." How many of you people believe that? I want to see a show of hands.' And, young people, every hand in the room went up. I was sitting at the back and I could see.

"Then that man wanted to know if it was all right to kill if some thief was threatening your own life. Or if your wife or daughter was being raped. Or was it all right for young men to go to war and kill on a wholesale basis for their country. The Lord on Sinai hadn't even mentioned the term *justifiable homicide*, he told us.

"Then he lined out, scripture and verse, instances where those people who were told simply 'Thou shalt not kill' had later on been given not only specific instructions when to kill somebody else but directions on how to do it. Death by stoning was pretty cruel, but it was in use officially for hundreds of years. 'Smite them hip and thigh' was the order for the army and sounded a sight nobler, but it sometimes carries instructions with it not to leave a man, woman, or child alive. The same God had handed down to the Jews what sounded to him, the man said, like conflict in moral principles.

"The whole crowd at chautauqua had stilled plumb down and half of 'em were looking at him with their mouths open and the other half with their mouths clamped. The tight shut ones also had their arms folded. But there wasn't a sound. And I'll never forget how he ended that talk. 'Ladies and gentlemen,' he said, 'in closing I want you to ponder a bit on the fact that the Lord chose as the recipient of this law from on high, this commandment "Thou shalt not kill," a man named Moses who was himself a murderer and a fugitive from justice. Is morality relative or do we have any morals at all that are absolute? Do not leave here with the assumption that I know the answer. I do not. But remember some words of Paul: "If there be any virtue, and if there be any praise, then think. Think on these things." Thank you for your attention.'

"He bowed and left the podium and that was the expected time and place for applause, but you know he got plumb out the door and nobody even offered to clap? Everybody just sat there in dead silence. Half of those folks never even unfolded their arms. When they did break up and leave, they were hardly talking to each other at all. It was right spooky, it was. I've never forgotten it and I've spent my life ever since trying to think things through before I advanced a truly deep-seated opinion."

Little Short-hair took a real deep, sort of shuddering breath. Filling her bellows, she was, in preparation for a speech. Smooth as I could, real soft and gentle, I headed her off.

"Now let's the four of us sit back and look a little bit at this business of slavery that has sort of got us all hot and bothered here all of a sudden. Examine it with our minds and let our emotions rest a minute."

She took it well. Let her breath out slow and easy and never said a word. Little Ring-eye untied her knot and let her veil fall again. Mule-mane did his best to sit on the back of his neck. But the three of them were looking straight at me.

"I guess we've had it around as long as there has been any history recorded," I told them. "The Jews in Egypt were slaves;

started off with brothers selling one of their own. Then later on they themselves had slaves. In the writings of Paul a millennium later, you'll find him advising slaves to obey their masters. Right along with 'Women, obey your husbands.' And that right there would be another topic of relative morality we could consider some time, especially if we could get Betty Friedan and Phyllis Schlafly to take it on the chautauqua circuit.

"The Greeks and Romans had slaves. The American Indians, north, central and south, had slaves. When you get to reading around, you'll even find it referred to as 'the institution of slavery,' sort of accepted and confirmed; like nowadays we say 'the institution of marriage.' I guess nearly every culture in the world has had slavery of one sort or another at some time or another."

I looked at Little Ring-eye. "You were dead right when you said nobody believes in slavery or condones it anymore. Of course, I keep reading that it still exists in some areas of North Africa, but certainly our country wouldn't tolerate it. Every now and then you read about modern day peonage in our country and folks getting fined for mistreating immigrant labor, but no, sir, we won't put up with slavery. Not in the United States of America, we won't. Why, we have reached the point where we even quit giving our money away to other countries if they violate what we call human rights nowadays. That, of course, is exactly the kind of persuasion that was going on in international affairs back in 1863. Abraham Lincoln abolished slavery by presidential fiat at the time he did purely and simply to placate Great Britain and keep her from coming into the War on the side of the South. Did any of you know that?"

Little Short-hair nodded her head and started to speak out, but I didn't slow down. "Today we know that slavery is evil, but one hundred and fifty years ago a majority of folks didn't think so. It's easy enough to judge the generations that went before us from our level of enlightenment now, but the question that keeps teasing me is that business of relative and absolute morality. What is absolutely wrong now wasn't considered so back then."

I slowed a minute and couldn't help but look at Mule-mane's earring. "And some things that were absolutely wrong when I was a boy don't seem to bother folks today. You see, a heap of things change, young people, but do morals change? And if so, which ones?"

Little Short-hair couldn't stand it any longer. She had forgot she was on a school project, she had forgot I was the oldest man in the county, she had forgot everything except her righteous indignation. "Mr. McEachern," she said, "I never heard of and can't imagine anybody being *relatively* a slave."

I thought of some married folks I had known, both male and female, and could have argued that point, but, shucks, I had her flustered enough already; so I never interrupted her.

"Slavery," she said, "is an evil. It is an absolute evil. It always will be and it always has been, and nothing you can say will ever convince me otherwise."

"Oh, I'm not trying to convince you of anything." I said. "I was just trying to make you think. But it appears like you've already done that. At least to your own satisfaction. A made-up mind is like a made-up bed; it's smooth and slick till somebody sleeps in it again and wallows around in it all night. Then it's all to do over again. I'm wondering how you account for the fact that a great many men of high morals owned slaves."

"I'm not!" she snapped. "If they owned slaves then their morals were weak. We've got living proof of it right there on that piece of paper where it's recorded that a man named Charles was purchased for twelve hundred dollars by that horrible Bogan Mask."

I almost chuckled. I had been hoping she'd get back to Bogan Mask. Enough rope comes up quicker for some folks than for others.

"Bogan Mask," I told her, "was a preacher. I've seen a license for him to exhort in the Methodist Episcopal Church, South. It was dated 1848."

"Preachers aren't saints," she said, "and I guess that's been proven over and over lately. Bogan Mask was a scoundrel to own slaves and Abraham Lincoln was noble to free them and he still remains the Great Emancipator, in my mind!"

I mean she was hot. "Little lady," I said, "it didn't cost Abraham Lincoln one red dime out of his own pocket to free the slaves. He never owned one."

"What's that got to do with it?" she said.

"There's a record in the courthouse dated December 22, 1861, that says Bogan Mask grants freedom to a negro man named Charles, age twenty-seven years, who shall be known henceforth as Charles Cofield and is owned by and bound to no man."

"What?" she said.

"That's right," I told her. "You can look it up for yourself when you've got time. There is no mention in it of whether slavery was right or wrong; it just sets Charles Cofield free. Two days after he was bought. Makes you wonder what Reverend Bogan Mask thought of slavery, doesn't it? Twelve hundred dollars was a heap of money in 1861, young lady; a heap of money to take out of your own pocket and put where your mouth or your heart was, and Bogan Mask did that two years before Abraham Lincoln did. How do you feel now about morals being relative or absolute?"

She sort of fell back and blinked, but then she recovered, and there was yet a little defiance in her voice. "I'm still glad the South lost the Civil War," she said.

"Oh, I am too," I told her. "I am too. But don't any of you

for one minute ever think that war was fought over slavery. Slavery was just a side issue, and folks who set out to write history books can be just as biased as anybody else. Do the three of you know that Lee freed all of his slaves before the War started and then got in there and fought his heart out for the South? Or that Ulysses Grant still owned slaves when he accepted Lee's sword at Appomattox?"

"But Mr. McEachern," Mule-mane put in, "I thought like, you know, Lincoln freed the slaves before the War ended. Like, you know, that's what I thought you said awhile ago. How could General Grant still have owned any?"

I'd been hoping one of 'em would ask that question. I was liking that Featherstone boy better by the minute.

"Because, son, Lincoln's proclamation applied only to the states that had seceded—or were what he called in rebellion. He wasn't about to alienate any more folks in the North than he could help. He was too good a politician for that."

"Politician?" Little Short-hair was still up on her dew claws. "Abraham Lincoln was a leader, a statesman, Mr. McEachern."

"Statesmen have to get elected, little lady," I said. "I'm not trying to take anything away from Lincoln. He had a rough job on his hands. There's a fellow named Benét who wrote a book called *John Brown's Body*. He's got a section in there where Lincoln is agonizing over the slaves, and projects that in Lincoln's praying over the situation he questions whether he's being influenced by God's will or Horace Greeley's will. You recollect Horace Greeley?"

"Wasn't he the one who said 'Go West, young man, go West'?" I mean it was fun to deal with Little Short-hair. She'll be keeping men on their toes all the rest of her life.

"That's him, all right," I said. "But that's not all he said. He was a front line, hell-for-leather Abolitionist, right in there with Harriet Beecher Stowe. On top of that he was a very influential newspaper editor, and if presidents don't pay attention to those folks, they wind up like Mr. Nixon. Why, even the president we have now knows that. Watch how he hops and skips around like a flea on a hot griddle and does what little governing of the country he's managing to do according to what various newspaper editors advocate on any particular day. I agree with you that Lincoln was a statesman and a leader. Contrasts can sure illuminate a person's mind, can't they? I'd like to recommend *John Brown's Body* to the three of you. I believe you'd like it."

Little Ring-eye chimed in. "I've read it, Mr. McEachern, but I'm afraid I skipped the part about Lincoln. I loved Sally Dupre."

"Oh, I do, too," I told her. "'Eyes not black and eyes not gray/Why do you haunt me night and day?'"

She grinned and chimed in, "'Her feet beat fast but her heart beat faster. She was the daughter of the dancing master.'"

It would be fun to watch Little Ring-eye grow up. "Go back to it and don't read just the girl parts," I told her. "I believe you'll like all of it."

Little Short-hair must have been feeling left out, for she piped back up and this time she sounded calm. Plumb mollified, she was. "Mr. McEachern, what do you think the Civil War was all about if you're going to insist that slavery was not as important an issue in it as I do?" She still had her chin poked out a little. That is one more strong-minded little girl. You can't help but like her.

I shut my eyes a minute before I answered her. "Liberty," I said.

"Liberty?"

"Yes, ma'am. Now I can only answer for the McEacherns and their neighbors, but it's my conviction that's what it was all over the country. My folks have always scratched and scrambled for a living and fought for liberty. Plus, like it says in the Declaration, 'the pursuit of happiness.' You can't have the one without the other. McEacherns never owned any slaves and the majority of farmers who fought from Georgia never did either. It was drilled into us. My granddaddy really was opinionated about slaves, although from a little different viewpoint than most."

I stopped like I was done, and she came through for me. "A different viewpoint?"

"Yes, ma'am. He came over here from Scotland in the early 1820's all by himself when he was just a lad of a boy. He was strong as a young bull but didn't have two pennies to rub together. He found work right enough, but he said it blame near killed him. The big plantation owners in south Louisiana were hiring poor whites to work in the rice fields because their labor was cheap and it was better to pay out wages than to lose expensive slaves to yellow fever and malaria. Your talking awhile back about Bogan Mask treating Charles like livestock is what brought my granddaddy to mind. He said the white laborers were treated worse than the slaves or the mules or the cows, because if they got down sick they just died. Nobody would spend money getting a doctor for them. It wasn't good economics.

"Now how does that make you feel about absolute and relative morality? I know it still keeps me, old as I am, studying on it." I wagged my head a little. "I told y'all my father never would wear overalls because they were blue. Well, his father never would let anything but grits be served at his table; hated rice all his life. Said it reminded him that the people who raised it thought he was less valuable than a black slave. Also he said those slaves in Louisiana looked down their noses at him, and he didn't have much truck with them or anybody else thought they were better than he was. Maybe you're right about slaves being treated like livestock, but when you get human beings treated even worse than livestock, seems like to me things are really turned upside down. Don't you agree that's a different viewpoint?"

She just looked at me with her mouth a little open and never said a word. I'm afraid I was about to wear her down. I sure wasn't worried any longer about her kicking out the side of the barn.

"So you see, all my folks fought the Civil War over liberty." I stopped long enough to reach in my pocket and get my handkerchief. I didn't have a cold. It's just that my plague-taked nose started dripping years and years ago. When I was about eighty or eighty-five, I guess. Not running all the time, more like a slow leak before the valve in the faucet goes out on you. Gets a big drop right on the tip end that just gathers and hangs for all the world to see. I guess it's what Shakespeare called the rheumy nose of old men, but I'm particular about it. I have a horror of getting so old I get careless about personal appearance, let alone hygiene; and a drop of water falling from your nose is plain an embarrassment to me, and to those young folks would be what they call "gross." I sure didn't want to gross Mule-mane out. Especially since he had cooperated so well about his cap and his recorder.

"Now before we get into any sort of quibbling about some complicated definition of liberty, let me tell you that to the McEacherns who were first and second generation immigrants to this country, and had managed to settle and hang on to fifty acres of land and make their own hardscrabble way, liberty boiled down to being let alone. They didn't want anybody from way off in Washington messing with them. They just didn't think it was right for the federal government to be passing so many laws that it took a whole firm of Philadelphia lawyers to keep up with them and interpret them. They believed in as little government as possible and that folks on their home territory should be allowed to provide their own laws and run their own business through the state government. Folks like my father felt so strongly about it that they volunteered to leave their little farms and go fight about it.

"My father fought hard, too. Maybe in a sense, come to think of it, he might have been fighting over slavery after all, because he was fighting for everybody to have individual freedom, and the slaves got more out of the War, some would say, than my father. There's no way any of you could have known him, but my father was looked on all over the county as a remarkable man. He lost an arm at Shiloh, a whole arm. Took it off at the shoulder socket, they did. He never let any of us talk about it, and he never gave in to it one bit. Wouldn't let Mama help him dress and wouldn't accept a pension when they finally got around to handing out one to disabled Confederate veterans. 'I'm not disabled,' he said. 'Give it to somebody with no legs.'

"He harnessed and plowed his own mule and worked in the field same as any other man around. Had a sling he rigged up to go round his neck to the off handle on his plow and even could use that sling and manage to push a wheelbarrow. Any of you ever tried to balance and push a loaded wheelbarrow? He was some more man to watch and he is some more man to remember."

I looked at Little Short-hair. "I'm right in there with you when you say you're glad the South lost the War. This is a great country. Robert E. Lee loved the United States of America and I love it. But when you look at Washington, D.C., nowadays it sort of makes you think that the McEacherns of this world were right nearly a hundred and fifty years ago about what would happen if they didn't leave home and go fight. It all boils down to my thinking the other day that, try as I will, I cannot identify one single individual who is willing to stand up and say that he trusts the federal government to do what is right. Now that is a pretty come-off after all these years.

"Of course, I'm glad the South lost the War, but when I study on that mess up there in Washington I can't for the life of me help grieving for her.

"And as for slaves, I honestly think we'd have gotten around to that before long anyhow. Don't forget Robert E. Lee and Bogan Mask. They were leaders and not politicians, and I suspect everybody else would have followed their lead eventually."

Little Short-hair was holding her lower lip real tight and blinking too fast, but her words were sweet. "Mr. McEachern, please forgive me for snapping at you a while ago. You're making history so much more real for me than it's ever been and I'm sorry I jumped before I listened." She managed a smile. "I'm going to remember what you said about a made-up mind."

Her voice didn't tremble even the least little bit. I had been right after all when I put her down as having class. I looked over at Mule-mane. "Son, we have really wandered around. You started all this by asking if that wasn't unusually cheap paper for a contract to be written on." I turned back to Little Short-hair. "And you, young lady, had opened it all up when you asked how much education cost when I was a boy. My, my, but you young folks have led me a merry chase and got me to talking in circles. You sure are experts at making an old man think. I'm afraid I've gone all the way around my thumb to get to my elbow. We tend to ramble when we get old. But, to answer your question," I looked straight at Little Short-hair, "Education didn't cost much when I was a boy. Not in money. It was relatively inexpensive."

Then it was Mule-mane's turn. "And to answer your question, young man, you are absolutely right. That was cheap paper. But it was all they had."

I reached in my pocket and dragged out my Waltham watch. "My goodness, it's past time to take my medicine and stretch out for a little nap. The doctor has a fit if I don't keep to my schedule."

I was lying. I don't take any medicine. I see my doctor once a year and he believes medicine is like government: The least you can get by on, the better off you are. Says more old folks have been hastened than slowed up on the road to heaven by well-meaning doctors writing a prescription for every ache and pain they have. I had to go to the bathroom was all I had to do, and the last few years the urge comes up in an awful hurry. It's that gland is what it is. The doctor checks it every year and I don't have any cancer; it's just overgrown. From age, he says.

When I grunt while he's checking it, the doctor says that if anybody lives who doesn't think the good Lord has a sense of humor he should just consider where he put the prostate gland. Doc's not but seventy-five and I tell him that's well enough for a young whippersnapper like him to proclaim, but from the level I've reached it's not so dad-blamed funny. Doc is really a caution. I'm going to miss him when he retires.

At any rate, I didn't feel like announcing my real reason for leaving the room to those students. In the first place, I didn't want to leave them alone. Children have always been bad to plunder around in things that don't concern them if you're not there to watch, especially if they're in an unfamiliar place, but the real reason was I don't like for anybody to realize how long it takes me to go to the bathroom nowadays. I tell you, that gland of mine is a sure enough booger.

When I stood up they did too. "I hope you've been able to glean and scrape enough from this interview to get your project done," I said. "I don't feel like I answered but just a couple of questions for you and those maybe not too well, but you young folks sure know how to draw an old man out. I've thought about things I hadn't considered for years."

Little Short-hair said, "Mr. McEachern, you've raised

more questions than you've answered. And I've thought about things I've never considered at all." She shook her head with a little quick jerk that made her hair look like it was rattling. "Would you mind awfully if we came back?"

Little Ring-eye swayed around a little. "Please, Mr. McEachern?"

Mule-mane joined in. "Like, you know, there's got to be some other things we need to ask about. Like, you know, I forgot to take notes and like, you know, I don't have everything organized in my mind."

Well, now. I figured that was one of the most honest statements I had ever heard. I looked at him a minute. All over. It came to me that if I had been named Lathrop Bulineau Featherstone IV, I might have dressed worse than that. "What do they call you at home, son?"

"Bulineau," he said. "It has rotated around. It was my dad's turn to get Lathrop."

That didn't help much. Then right away he blurted, "But the guys at school call me Chuck." He grinned. "Like, you know, they had better."

I was really beginning to cotton to that boy. "Well, Chuck," I said, "you are perfectly welcome to come back. And I tell you what I'll do. If you'll strike the phrase 'like, you know' out of your speech pattern, I'll let you set up your tape recorder next time."

He sort of blared his eyes for just a minute, and I heard Little Ring-eye snicker a little. Then he stuck out his hand. "Deal," he said. He grinned again. "But no cap, right?"

"Right," I said.

I started to tell him that when he did have that cap on his head he'd be better served to wear it straight. Nobody but a catcher has any business with one on backwards, and even he looks like a fool when he takes the face mask off. But I figured I'd already hit him a pretty good lick; so I said good-bye and told 'em I'd see them next week. I tell you, that boy would have driven Miss Lizzie up the wall with that 'like, you know' business. She wouldn't have put up with it as long as I have. I sure do miss Miss Lizzie.

Over the next week I found myself missing those students a little, too. Or if not missing them, at least looking forward to seeing them again. In spite of the way they looked and the way they talked, they were bright and young and I had enjoyed myself. At least I felt like they had found out I wasn't as backward and ignorant as they had probably thought I was before they started. Maybe they had had a good time, also. Same as I did.

I even took to studying on what they might ask me next time. It wouldn't hurt a thing to anticipate them and sort of be prepared. The more I thought about it the more I figured that they would pop up with "family values."

Everybody likes to keep up with trends and be in fashion about things. Leastways till they're old enough to have seen everything come around at least twice. That movie actor, of all people, the one who got to be president, took to drumming on family values a little, but then that little pretty-faced vice-president who came after him as president really took it up. It was his answer to crime and sex and abortion and drugs and most anything you could mention. I personally thought he was as sincere as a hog on ice about the situation; wasn't a thing in the world against that boy but his looks. Maybe his brain pan was just a tad shallow, but he couldn't help that any more than he could that straight nose.

But here came the newspapers and the TV commentators like coon dogs baying a hot trail on a slow night or else laughing like hyenas around a fresh carcass. Had to pull somebody down, they did, just to keep their hand in, and they hadn't spilled any fresh blood in a week or two. When they got through with their editorials and their sly digs, they had that poor man looking like a namby-pamby mama's boy and the general impression was that "family values" was about as unfashionable as wearing white socks and brown suede shoes to a funeral.

Yes, sir, I thought, "family values" was dead as a hammer, especially after the last election when that mean-spirited, jug-eared, beady-eyed little billionaire chewed up our bone-weary, indifferent incumbent who wasn't but halfheartedly campaigning anyway, and we got the nation saddled with another Southern governor that we have been reduced to accepting as our president. Now, you want to talk about a mama's boy, we got one for sure and certain this time. He even married himself one; we're talking about a mean mama, too. Hyphenated herself soon as the election was over. But I didn't expect to hear "family values" out of either side of either of their mouths. Especially after she got her fingers burnt talking about staying home and making cookies.

But it just goes to show you never can tell. He slips around like a three-year-old with that kind of soft voice sounds like he's been eating chalk, and when lying won't get himself out of something, he spreads his hands and looks innocent right into the camera and I keep expecting him to say, "But I didn't go to do it." Please the majority today and keep the squeaking wheel greased, and the nation and the whole world will go on a steady course and things will get better and better. Oh, yes. Like the chicken business in Arkansas.

Well, some poll must have shown something that caught his eye, because I'll be blessed if he and that careful-talking vice-president, who speaks real patient and condescending, haven't commenced talking about family values themselves here of late. And he ought to be. Far as I can tell, the poor boy never had any of his own. However, you've got to give him credit. I'll bet a buffalo nickel nobody who knew him when he was showing out in college about Vietnam and all would have ever thought he'd wind up where he is today. I just wish he could train himself to quit smirking and grinning all the time when he's discussing things and answering questions. Sometimes I'd like to snatch him right out of that TV set and ask him what's so consarned funny. I, for one, never thought the country would wind up scraping the bottom of the barrel like we have for leadership.

Of course, I knew I wouldn't be able to say any of this to those young people. Folks have to be let alone to figure things like that out for themselves. You have to have faith that they can still think, although that faith is rarely rewarded when it comes to politics. I decided some sixty years or more ago that folks vote with their glands instead of their heads, and if you're going to fall out with everybody who votes different from you then, sooner or later, you're going to be left with a very weird circle of friends that gets tighter and tighter. Whenever somebody asks me how I voted in any election, I always say, "I'm an American; I voted a secret ballot." To tell you the truth, it seems like in most elections lately, I go to the polls thinking, "A pox on both their houses." And then I vote against the worst one instead of for the best one; we have come to a pretty pass.

What I wanted to hand those young folks when they came back and popped me with "family values" was a twist on the subject that has been tantalizing me for some years now and which I have never mentioned to anyone else. If it makes me wonder and think, then it ought to set them to thinking, too. I'm not talking about reading the Bible and having meals together. I'm sort of like the author of the Declaration on that score; "We hold these truths to be self-evident." Also I'm worn out with hearing "The family that prays together, stays together." You can run anything in the ground.

Several years ago now I got to studying on just what a family is. You hear about nuclear family, extended family, surrogate family, and all such as that. I finally got so puzzled I went to the dictionary. Newspapers and TV can do that to you. They'll use terms you've been familiar with all your life but in a different way than you've thought they were meant. Or even pronounce words differently. I learned long ago that it's worthwhile to check on them. You get the occasional reward of discovering that Bryant Gumbel was wrong. Or Sam Donaldson. Or Barbara Walters. And you were right. Then you can sit in your own living room and realize they aren't as smart as they'd have you believe. That is a real reward for a trip to the dictionary, and it sure helps your perspective when you can satisfy your suspicion that Miss Lizzie knew more about some things than a heap of folks who present themselves as authorities.

When I got around to looking up *family*, be blessed if Webster didn't have twelve definitions: eleven for the noun and one for the adjective. That's a sure sign we've used any word either too much or too loosely. About anything can be called a family that shares a common lodging, and if you don't believe me you go look it up for yourself. So I'm on solid ground when I talk about old maid sisters who live together by themselves as being a family unit.

You used to see a lot more of that than you do nowadays. I could tick off a sight of 'em without stopping long to think about it. Miss Lee and Miss Beauty Tarpley, Miss Sadie and Miss Fannie Mae Burns, Miss Alice and Miss Exor McLean, Miss Lorraine and Miss Mary Lou Lawson. Of course, Miss Lorraine had been married a while but not long enough to get the old maid out of her. Miss Mattie Mae and Miss Lois Grantham. Now they do say Miss Lois wasn't married but about thirty minutes after the dust settled from her wedding and I've never doubted it for a minute. Miss Gray and Miss Dodge Murdock. Addie and Madelyn Rivers, although it has always been my opinion that Madelyn was more what you'd call a bachelor girl than a true old maid.

No proof, you understand, and really not a whole lot of hearsay; that's just a feeling you get about folks. A real honest-to-goodness old maid in my day wouldn't even think about letting a drop of liquor cross her lips.

Now those old maid units were a sure enough rock bottom repository of family values. They held on to what Mama and Papa and their grandparents before them had entrenched in them, and they never budged an inch or changed a bit. They couldn't. It was born in 'em. That's why the most of them were old maids in the first place.

In the usual circumstances, it would turn out that one of them was sort of the head of the house, the father figure, you might call her, at least the dominant personality. She got out more in public, was the one who drove the car, wrote the checks, went to the bank and such as that, and wasn't scared of the devil himself. The other one usually did the cooking, most of the dusting and sweeping, and always had a plate of tea-cakes ready for nieces and nephews when they came by.

And believe you me, they came by. There has never been anybody in this country more looked up to, pampered, cosseted, and sometimes just plain fawned upon than old maid aunts. Especially if they had outlived their married brothers and sisters and had most of the family property in their hands. Young folks might get feisty and rebel against their parents, but they were always docile and obliging around the old maid aunts who could change a will by just cranking the telephone. And that was a great stimulus for keeping the nieces and nephews in line. They minded their P's and Q's in this town. Having their parents find out something on them wasn't near as bad as having it get back to the aunts.

And get back it would. Those old ladies had an information network that would put the FBI and the CIA to shame. If Miss Dodge saw or heard something going on with a young lady that didn't look genteel, she wouldn't tell the girl's own aunt. She'd pass it on to Miss Gray, of course, who'd then hand it on to Miss Exor and from there it would go to Miss Beauty and on to Miss Lula and finally get back to Miss Mattie Mae, who was the one who really needed to know in the first place. By dinner time, Miss Mattie Mae would have her niece on the carpet and be holding court, gentle but firm. Suggestions and kind advice. Very effective. Old maid aunts who wore several diamond rings to be passed on, to say nothing of real estate and a right smart bank account, didn't need to go beyond hints and indirect questions with young folks. They were all very sure of themselves and they held firm on what was allowed in their families, but I never heard of one yelling and hollering at anybody.

Except, of course, Miss Lois Grantham. She had red hair and a .45 pistol to reinforce her temper when she let it loose, and she was quick enough on the trigger, with both the gun and the temper, that nobody messed with her.

Funny thing though, she never to my knowledge showed out at anybody but menfolks; slapped the sheriff full in the face once right on the courthouse square. And another time she ran old smartmouth Herman Malone plumb off his motor grader when he was scraping the road in front of their house and gave her some sass. Shot her gun and hit the blade of his motor grader and Herman ran all the way back to City Hall. Said pieces of that bullet were zinging around his ears like honey bees.

Miss Lois didn't yell and holler at her nieces; she saved all that for the men that crossed her path. I always have wondered what happened to that fellow she married so briefly, but he wasn't from around here and nobody knew his folks. Old maid sisters sure aren't going to discuss family concerns with outsiders; so we've never found out. Old maids are bad to close ranks and pretend things didn't happen. Why, Miss

Earle Griggs wouldn't even let anybody say the South had lost the War. I can hear her now. "You'd better hush," she'd say. "You just stop right there now."

Janie Lou Bridges said her Aunt Martha was the one who taught her to balance a checkbook and look out for bad boys, but her Aunt Sara Jane gave her a teacake recipe and taught her and all her sisters to walk up on their toes like ladies. Old maids were peculiar, but they were supposed to be. I tell you one thing, they flat out knew how to run a family and how to make a whole passel of kinfolks toe the line and hold on to their principles. Family values have just not been the same since apartments and nursing homes sprang up all over the place and old maids have disappeared, at least from public view. For the life of me I can't point out sisters anymore who are maiden ladies that live together in the family home and look after each other.

Those ladies were always, seemed like, dried to match their wrinkles. Their voices trembled but their words were stout. They smelled peculiar, too. It was a sure enough mixture. There was always the clean flat smell of fresh-pressed starch in their dresses and a little drift of mothballs in their shawls, but some of them also might have a little fragrance of snuff. Although you'd never get any visible signs of such and it was always masked by rosewater and glycerin. Sometimes there was a little underlying whiff of something else I never could identify that wasn't quite so pleasant. When you mixed all that together with a little talcum powder, you had a smell a man wasn't likely to forget. Not one to get him all stirred up. On the contrary, I guess all in all it would calm you down and back you off. Maiden ladies stayed behind the scenes, but they ran this country. They're gone forever, I guess, and I sure do miss them.

I wasn't sure I could make those young folks understand precisely what I meant by old maid families and their hold on family values, but I aimed to give it a try.

And you know what? It never came up. When those three showed back up I almost forgot my manners and stared.

Little Short-hair had on lipstick and a little bit of stuff around her eyes. Just a little bit, but it was a big help. On top of that, she had polished her nails.

Little Ring-eye had done away with all the black from around her eyes and that sure made a difference. Of course, she had substituted pink and lavender but it was not quite so startling, and at least the raccoon resemblance was gone. So were the bangs. She had all that mess of hair tamed down into what they call a French braid and was carrying her head on that slender neck like the Queen of Navarre or at the very least Audrey Hepburn. She looked like she'd rather die than chew gum in public. Those two girls were stomp-down pretty.

But Mule-mane was the marvel. No hat. Not on his head, not in his hand, nowhere in sight. He had the top roach of his hair trimmed down to within an inch of the rest of it, his shoes were tied, his shirt and pants actually fit him. His belt was tucked into the loops, and he looked so clean-cut I couldn't believe it. And be blessed if the earring wasn't gone. I don't know where it was, probably in his pocket, but it wasn't in his ear. All you could see was the little hole where it had been. I hadn't commented on that earring when it was present, and I sure had sense enough not to mention its absence. That boy looked so good that for a brief moment it washed over me that I wished he was kin to me. Of course, I had more sense than to mention that either. All I said was, "I'm glad to see you young people again. Come in and sit down and make yourselves at home. Did you bring your tape recorder, Chuck?"

He held it up and set it on the table, and Little Short-hair said, "I brought some cookies I made for you, Mr. McEachern." All of a sudden I felt so comfortable and at home with those three that I had to blow my nose.

Chuck fiddled around with his contraption a few minutes and then announced it was ready. I looked around at them and said, "Who's got the first question? What y'all want to talk about today?"

Little Short-hair cleared her throat and said, "We thought we'd like to start out this session on race relations."

"Race relations?"

"Yes, sir."

"But I thought we pretty well covered that last time," I told them.

"That was just about slavery, Mr. McEachern."

"Why, child, race relations were woven all through that discussion. In and out. From the rice plantations of Louisiana to the Civil War. Maybe the subject wasn't stamped with a painted label and fed to you out of a spoon, but it was pretty well covered, to my way of thinking. You know, I sort of thought y'all would come in here today and want to discuss family values."

Little Ring-eye patted her braid. "Pooh," she said. I swear that's what she said. I hadn't heard that word out of a young mouth in thirty years. "Pooh! The group last year did some interviews on family values. We don't want to duplicate anyone else's work. Besides, Mr. McEachern, to tell you the truth, I'm about fed up with all this talk about family values. Everybody bears down on divorce or the absence of a father figure and the difficulty of child care in a single-parent family, and we kids wind up thinking it's all our fault. The only solution people seem to get around to anyhow is reading the Bible more. I've heard 'The family that prays together stays together' so much that I associate it with the radical Right and it just automatically turns me off."

I just sat there and stared at her for a moment. I was thinking that you could still find something in common with the most improbable looking people even across the better part of a century, but before I could say anything, Mule-mane spoke up.

"What we mean when we say race relations, Mr. McEachern, is like, you know, how the people of the two races interacted with each other when you were young." I cut my eyes at him real sharp and then without a word I looked over at the tape recorder. He swallowed and grinned. "Let me rephrase that. What we're interested in, Mr. McEachern, is how the races interacted with each other when you were young, what their real feelings were. We've studied separate water fountains and restrooms in history class, and we've studied the civil rights movement and school desegregation, but we really don't have any idea of what it was like on a day-to-day basis, with blacks and whites living together like everybody says they did in a small rural county like this one was back when you were young."

Little Short-hair butted in. "Did you ever get any idea, Mr. McEachern, about the real feelings black people had when all that horrible oppression was going on?"

Well, so much for family values. I can quit worrying about school teachers spoon-feeding this particular trio. "Young lady," I said in the real flat soft voice I use when I want to set somebody back without riling them up, "it seems to me that you have a talent for editorializing when you ask a question. You're liable to make a name for yourself on TV someday. When you grow up." I smiled but she didn't smile back. Just waited, she did. That girl is a wonder for her age; she flat out has the poise.

"If you're talking about the Jim Crow laws and all, which Chuck seemed to be alluding to a while ago, I guess by the time I came along everybody pretty well took them for granted and did not think about them one way or another.

Black and white, near as I can remember. That's just the way
things were, and we all lived and worked around them.
Everybody was so busy trying to scratch a livelihood out of
the dirt and fight the boll weevil hard enough to have a little cash money for Christmas that I don't remember anybody
talking about being oppressed."

I thought a minute. "Remember us talking about relative
and absolute? And judging the past by the light of the present? That sure keeps flying up in our faces like a loose board,
doesn't it? From where we sit now, those laws and rules don't
look so good, but back then I can't remember a single black
person complaining about them. That's just the way we
lived and we spent our worry time on things of greater
importance. Like enough to eat. Like survival."

I thought I might be sounding a little preachy and ought
to tone it down a little. I shrugged my shoulders and spread
my hands. "Course you have to understand that in this
county a lot of things that stirred folks up around the rest of
the country just didn't apply to us. I don't recollect ever seeing a water fountain in this town; so that couldn't have
bothered anybody. We had water buckets with a dipper
that we drank from and usually a jelly glass we dipped
water into for any colored person wanted a drink, but
nobody commented on it.

"The only public restrooms were two in the courthouse and
they were labeled men and women. Not white and colored.
On top of that, no woman would go in theirs because the
bad town boys had bored peepholes through the walls. The
men's room was so dirty that nobody ever went in there anyhow unless it was a dire necessity. Except the bad town boys.

"And there wasn't then any public transportation, no
more than there is today. If you had a car and passed somebody walking, black or white, you stopped and offered
them a ride. Unless it was a woman. Be she black or white,

we were pretty particular about that. 'Avoid the very appearance of evil,' you know.

"But oppression? Let alone 'horrible oppression?' We
didn't know we had it. Poverty was the horrible oppressor
and those of us living here didn't even know we had that.
Because everybody was afflicted with it. 'Times are sure
hard,' we said, but nobody ever went around saying, 'This
county is a stinking sinkhole of poverty.' Some folks had a
little more money than others, all right, and we referred to
them as well-off, but in this day and time even they would
be regarded as 'below the poverty level.' Which is another
catchword of modern times. Back when I was younger we
weren't paying out tax money for somebody in Washington
to gather up all those figures and then put a ruler on them
and draw a line so they could call it the poverty level. We all
knew that we were in it deeper some years than others, no
matter how hard you worked, and we grumbled some but
we kept on working. You had to if you wanted to eat. Black
or white."

I smiled over at Little Short-hair. "So, honey, you're right.
We did have horrible oppression, but it came from the Yankees who kept those railroad tariffs so high that they got rich-
er and we got poorer. But we were so concentrated on farming or running country stores or sawmilling that we couldn't
see the forest for all the trees we kept bumping into, and I
never heard a living soul, black or white, say 'I can't buy my
children new shoes this year because the railroad tariffs are too
high in the South.' Tariffs are relative, I guess. Bread and meat
and dollars are absolute. Am I making any sense to y'all?"

It was Little Short-hair's turn to smile at me and she did
it the sweetest you ever saw. "You're making perfect sense,
Mr. McEachern; you always do. It sure seems to me, though,
that you're evading the subject." That girl is a caution.

I glanced over at Little Ring-eye with my eyebrows raised.

She tilted her head sideways on that little neck like she was thinking on which sandwich to pick from a tray at a tea party and said, "I agree with Melanie. We ask about race relations and wind up hearing about poverty and railroad tariffs. Of course, I think all that is perfectly fascinating, and we've all learned a lot from you. You did just ask a moment ago if you make any sense to us, though, and of course you do. I think you're doing this on purpose."

"Doing what on purpose?"

"Not discussing the specific question. I get the feeling, and it's just a feeling, Mr. McEachern, that what you really wanted to talk about today was family values. If I put you off about that, I sure didn't mean to."

Dad-blame if I wasn't as transparent as a glass of water to those two. It's sure hard to fool a female. At least when one has got her head in gear instead of cavorting around on gland-control. I twisted around toward Mule-Mane, waiting for his two cents, and it was pretty readily forthcoming.

"Looks to me like us men ought to stick together, Mr. Will Henry; so I'm not going to say you were evading a question. I learned last week that you talk all around an issue before you get down to specifics. I'm sure you're going to get around to race relations for us. In your own way. In your own time. I'm in no hurry myself."

And he turned it loose. Didn't say another word. Put that baby in my lap and sat back as relaxed as if he was eating popcorn in a movie he'd already seen once. I was beginning to have more respect for that fellow who had come up with the idea of *Foxfire*. These three kids I was dealing with had certainly developed some skills. I took a deep breath.

"To tell you the truth, we didn't have them," I said.

The two girls looked at one another and Little Short-hair said, "Pardon? You didn't have what, Mr. McEachern?"

I almost grunted at her. "Race relations."

Little Ring-eye took a breath and I thought for sure and certain she was going to say "Pooh" again. But she didn't. That girl has got some sense of what's appropriate and doesn't seem inclined to run anything into the ground. Except maybe eye makeup. "Mr. McEachern, I think you're teasing us now."

She rolled her eyes and any male, even one so old he was beyond being really red-blooded, would have enjoyed teasing her. Then she got earnest. "You see, we don't have much interaction with black people. We look at TV and most of them seem either mad or prickly or hostile, and we get the impression that they are still rebelling about the way they used to be treated. That's what Melanie meant about 'oppression.' We don't have but a handful of blacks in our class at school and it seems like, just between us, that we are all making such a conscious effort to get along that we have an automatic wall of politeness between us. Nobody relaxes and acts naturally. Honest. None of us has lived under segregation, and I guess what we want to hear from you is what it was really like before racial integration. Were the black people angry? Were the white people mean?"

"Well, child," I said then, "from what I can see and read in the papers and even watch in this town, we were more integrated in my day than y'all are.

"And we lived together and we got along together. At least we did in this little town. Without any trouble between the races. The reason, I think, was that we all knew each other. Personally." I shut my eyes and studied a while. "To answer your question, I don't guess I can right this minute recall a single time back before integration when I thought any black folks were hostile toward white folks or angry. If they were, they sure didn't show it. Course they would every now and then get into a regular melee amongst themselves—as often

as not on Sunday afternoon on their church grounds—and
get to fighting and cutting one another. The sheriff and the
deputies would have to go out and tend to them. Their boss
men would come to town and pay the doctor and go their
bond at the jail, and everybody would be back in the field
on Monday. Those that were able.

"Of course, to be perfectly bare-bone honest with you, I
suspect that the white people kept the black folks pretty well
cowed down. Back in those days, I used to hear a lot of talk
about nigras staying in their place and not being uppity, and
I was used to seeing them stand aside and let a white person
go ahead of them in my store. That's just the way we lived,
and if anybody thought it was wrong they didn't let on.

"They had race riots occasionally, but that was always in
the big cities. I recollect once back in the twenties they had
a fierce big one in Atlanta. Can't quite recall what triggered
it, but it was famous. Whites went on a rampage and took
to beating or killing any man on sight that was colored. Every
train that came through here, freight or passenger made no
difference, was loaded with black people. They were hanging on the steps, riding underneath on the rods, some were
even laid out flat and holding on the top of the cars for dear
life. They didn't have any clothes or baggage with them; they
were just getting out of Atlanta to save their lives. Of course,
everybody went down to the depot to watch. Including me.
It was one more awsome sight, and I never have been able
to understand why most of our men and boys were laughing and pointing.

"I got what bread and potted meat I had in my store and
tried to hand it out to those poor scared people, but it wasn't
a drop in the bucket. Some of them were too fearful of los-
ing their hold on the train to take it from me. But you
know, all I saw in those faces was the fear. I didn't see any
anger. Our own black folks were mighty scarce around the

depot, but old Uncle Edmund Arnold, who wasn't scared of even lightning storms or snakes, came up to me and said, 'Mr. Will Henry, the Lord will bless you for this.'

"One of the Detwilers was standing next to us and said, 'Yeah, and the Klan might put your name on its list, too, Will Henry McEachern. I'd be cautious about pampering those animals they've run out of Atlanta, was I you.' When I looked around, Uncle Edmund had vanished. I never said a word to Lamar Detwiler, but for seventy some-odd years I've regretted I didn't lay him flat. A thrashing couldn't possibly have helped a Detwiler, but it would have been a considerable satisfaction to me."

Those kids were staring at me so hard they were forgetting to keep their lips closed. "What I'm getting at is that I saw hostility and anger from whites toward blacks when I was young but never the other way around. On the contrary, young folks, I saw a lot of patience and acceptance. That's just the way things were. They couldn't afford anything else.

"Of course, now and then they could get in their little digs and get you told off in a way you couldn't take exception to. A case in point was Deacon Kilough. He was coal black and had been brought into our county by old man Sommers Hunnicutt. Mr. Sommers got him off the chain gang on parole and made a house boy, yard man, and body servant out of him. Didn't have to pay him any cash money, just house him and feed him. Most white people using that program got extra cotton hands that way, but Mr. Sommers owned the bank and didn't have to raise any cotton. Old Deacon had it pretty easy and it wasn't long before he had Mr. Sommers convinced that he couldn't get along without him. When his sentence was up, he kept Deacon on. Paid him a little wages and let him have one of his tenant houses and get married.

"Deacon married a local gal who was almost black as he was and already had three or four yard babies, and it wasn't any time before he was a fixture in our colored community. All of them were scared to death of him. First of all, it got out that he had cut his first wife's head slap off and that was why he was on the gang. Then, second, it was his personality. He didn't mix and mingle much. Hessie Mae, his wife, went to church and all like that, but Deacon kept to himself. Got up at daybreak and went off to Mr. Hunnicutt's house to fix his breakfast and build his fires, and then he pretty well just strutted around town and did what he wanted after Mr. Hunnicutt went to the bank.

"Nobody, white or black, messed with him. He had real red gums and real white teeth and he could flash a smile on a white man and call him 'Boss-man' in that deep voice of his that would make you feel important for the rest of the day. He always went out of his way to use the word 'nigger' when he talked to white people. 'I'm Mr. Sommers Hunnicutt's nigger,' he would say.

"He also took pains to use the word when he talked to black folks. I'm sure you've probably heard that it's all right for black people to call each other that, but white folks better not do it. Not true. Not when it was Deacon Kilough calling them 'sorry high-yaller mixed-up nigger trash' or saying, 'you stink like a sho-nuff nigger.' He even referred to Buris Youngblood, who had inherited some insurance and drove a Buick and had a mink stole and even voted and was said to have joined the NAACP, as a 'squash-nosed, duck-butted, uppity nigger wench.' He got away with it because he worked for Mr. Hunnicutt and also because he carried two straight razors in his bib pocket and everybody would think on his first wife. But don't you imagine for a minute they liked him. Or that it was all right with them the way he talked.

"One time he was in my store when nobody else was there but a couple of colored men who were real deacons and who were properly respected by everybody. They had been home-grown in good families, and he said right in front of them, 'Mr. Will Henry, do you realize me and my wife are the only true pure-blooded Africans in this whole town? Look how black we both is. All these other niggers ain't nothing but a mixed up bunch of colored trash that has come about from obliging every yellow dog that come through the yard.' I was glad when the real deacons eased on out without disputing him.

"Another time he came in when we had waked up with snow on the ground. Miss Gray and Miss Dodge were there to lay in some extra lamp oil and rations. They never bought much of anything at any one time; had a dread of dying with extra groceries in their pantry. Miss Dodge hadn't been able to hear it thunder for years and years in spite of having wires hanging all over her like lights on a Christmas tree and extra batteries tucked in every place imaginable. Deacon had his feet wrapped up in croker sacks against the snow and swept his hat off his head and bowed and scraped and said 'Howdy, Missy,' so deferential anybody could tell it was faked.

"I said, 'Good morning, Deacon,' and he said, 'I'm glad you white folks think it's a good morning, Bossman. This sure ain't no nigger weather.'

"When he left, Miss Dodge turned to her sister and said in that real flat voice she had, 'What'd he say, Gray?' And Miss Gray got right in her ear and yelled till you could have heard her at the courthouse, 'Nothing of any consequence, Dodge. The man is despicable.' Course Miss Gray probably had that opinion of all men, but with Deacon she was free to voice it."

Not a one of those children had even shifted; so I figured I could ramble on a little longer. "But to show you how a black person could get in a dig and shift 'staying in your place' around to the white person and still abide by the rules we all observed, let me tell you about Wayland Hunnicutt. He was old man Sommers Hunnicutt's son and stayed in the family business by virtue of his birth, but he didn't turn his finger to do a thing. Grew up a party boy with a raccoon coat and a flivver automobile and never got over it. Thought the Tech-Georgia football game was not only the social event of the year but was also more important than Christmas or Easter. He ran into Deacon one day and said, 'Deacon, my wife keeps complaining to me that she wants your wife to help her around the house but that Hessie Mae keeps making excuses and won't come. Can you fix that up for me so's I can keep my womenfolk happy?' And Deacon gave him that smile and scratched his head and shuffled his feet, but what he said was, 'Lord God, Mr. Wayland, I know what you mean; I can't keep mine happy neither. You know you done called this to my attention before but I can't do nothing with her. We both got to face it, Mr. Wayland; try as I will, Hessie Mae just ain't in no shape, form or fashion a Hunnicutt nigger.' You know, young people, I think Wayland Hunnicutt went to his grave without knowing he'd been insulted.

"That wasn't the case with Mr. Rainbow. He was the principal of the colored school back before integration and a man of some presence. Everybody but the most diehard crackers called him Mr. Rainbow, some of them sardonically, because he was so dignified he was plumb pompous. But he ran that school with an iron hand. One time Deacon Kilough had cranked up his old car and given Claudine, who was his youngest daughter, a ride and let her out at school because it was raining and she had a bad cold. She came home that evening with her lips poked out so you could ride to mill on them, said Mr. Rainbow had the front door locked and had made her walk through the rain to the side door. Next morning it wasn't raining, but Deacon drove her to school anyhow, and he marched into the principal's office where they were having a teacher's meeting and smacked his hand down on the desk. 'Rainbow,'

he said, 'I want to know what sort of school is you damn niggers running down here!'

"Mr. Rainbow stood up real straight and formal and
said, 'Mr. Kilough, I will have you to understand we are not
niggers.'

"And Deacon said, 'O.K., then, Rainbow, what sort of school
is you damn Ethiopians running down here?'

"And Mr. Rainbow said, 'Mr. Kilough, we are not
Ethiopians.'

"And Deacon fired back, 'All right, Rainbow, if you ain't
niggers and you ain't Ethiopians, you tell me what you is and
I'll call you that before I tell you that the next time you make
my baby girl walk in the rain when she already got a head
cold, I'm gonna slice you till you trip on your own tripes when
you commence to running.'

"You asked me if I saw any hostility or anger on the part
of black folks toward white folks, and the answer is 'no.' But
I sure saw a lot of anger and hostility on their part toward
Deacon Kilough. Although it was certainly repressed and covered over. They might let me see it, but they were very careful not to let him see it."

"How awful," said Little Short-hair. "He was a perfectly terrible person."

"There you go again, little lady. Judging the past by the
present. Deacon Kilough, I now think, was probably defying
the system we had in the only way he could at the time. By showing contempt for those who were content to live under it,
including, perhaps, himself. He wore an old cast-off overcoat
that came within two inches of the ground and a felt hat that
was on the verge of crumbling and that you could smell ten
feet away, but there was something about the way he toted his
head that made me see a royal prince in a leopard hide. Coal
black skin. Barefooted. Feathers around his ankles, voodoo
powder in a pouch, wearing a crown, laying about him and

keeping order in the community. He put up with a lot from the Hunnicutts but he made up for it. I sure do miss him."

Little Short-hair wasn't going to turn it loose. I tell you that little girl had given up getting by on being cute a long time ago and had set her head to amount to something. Probably a lawyer. Although I never knew one to bake cookies. She is an interesting little piece of humanity.

"Mr. McEachern," she said, "I can't buy into your assessment of this Kilough man being a person of any principle. He still comes across to me as crude and cruel. What about the poor black people that he insulted? He even badgered and harassed them, to hear you tell it, and went out of his way to do it. He degraded them. How did that make them feel, do you suppose?"

"Well, young lady, I was using Deacon to illustrate the anger and hostility y'all asked me about, but like a heap of other things in life that have more layers than a hen yard, it does get to be a complicated subject."

"Hen yard?" she said.

"Yep," I said. "Let me tell you about another black man in town who comes to mind. He took a little different approach to situations and to life in general. He was what today we would call an alcoholic, but since we didn't know about such as that back then, we all just shook our heads and said that Dump Simpson was 'bad to drink.' Mr. Mullins Mayfield was Dump's bossman, or patron, or champion, whatever you wall to call him."

I shot a quick look at Little Short-hair. "Certainly we didn't say Mullins Mayfield owned Dump, for slavery was long ago a thing of the past, but he sure stood up for Dump and looked after him. Mr. Mayfield had four boys, and Dump, in turn, looked after them. Changed their didies when they were little, then later walked them to town to buy a ice cream cone and taught them to ride bicycles and

cut grass and milk the cow. All the things town boys had
to learn how to do."

"Milk the cow?" said Mule-mane. "Town boys?"

"Sure. There weren't any dairies around here making
home deliveries then, and we didn't carry anything but con-
densed milk in the stores. Every family in town had a little
pasture and a barn and a milk cow. No Board of Health back
then to lay down laws about animals in the city limits. The
Mayfield boys even kept a Shetland pony, and Dump taught
all of them to ride. He could cook good biscuits, too, and was
handy to help Miss Myrtis Mayfield in the kitchen and the
garden and around the house. When he was sober.

"Mullins Mayfield, Jr., who was called 'Buck' by the
whole town, came back from World War II all shot up and
disabled. Wasn't able to work. And be blessed if Dump
wasn't still living and he set in to look after Buck. Not waiting on him hand and foot; Buck wouldn't have put up with
that. More buddying around and keeping him company.

"And you know what? It got to where Buck was trying to
look after Dump. In a way. He hadn't as a child been overly concerned about Dump's drinking; you know children take
folks as they are and either love 'em or hate 'em ; they don't
try to change 'em. But the day he found Dump straining rub-
bing alcohol through a loaf of bread, Buck put in to do a little preaching.

"'Dump,' he said, 'you can't drink that alcohol; it'll kill
you for sure.'

"Dump told him, 'Hit won't kill you. Course you gotta proof
it down just right, and that's what I'm a-doing; but hit
won't kill you, Buck.'

"Buck waited till Dump came off that spree and then he
tackled him again. Lined everything out to him and honed
in on him about his health and all. Dump listened real
politely to each and every word and never interrupted even

once. But when Buck had run through everything he could
think of to say, Dump told him with a considerable amount
of patience, 'Buck, everybody dies. Them what drinks dies
and them what don't drink dies. But when them what drinks
does die, hit's the liquor what kilt 'em.'

"The day after Dump's funeral Buck came in my store on
his crutches. Said he couldn't get his last fishing trip with
Dump off his mind. They had gone way down in the lower
part of the county on Whitewater Creek a little ways before
it runs into the river and had fished nearly all day. They were
using mostly red wigglers for bait, but Buck had also brought
a dozen shiners. They caught a bunch of bream, one catfish,
and a couple of bass, and both of them were feeling relaxed
and good. Dump hadn't had a drink in a week and Buck's
stump wasn't even hurting.

"A little past middle of the afternoon, Buck said they'd better go. Dump said, 'Buck, what you want to do with this here
one little ole shiner we still got in the bait bucket? Take him
home and try to keep him alive twell next week?'

"Buck said, 'No, I don't think so. Just turn him loose in
the creek.'

"Dump squatted down and eased the little fellow into Whitewater and watched him while he circled around in the shallow water for awhile and then darted off into a deep hole under
the bank.

"'Do you think he'll live, Buck?' Dump said.

"Buck told him that if no big fish got him he stood a good
chance of living and even growing up and finding a lady
shiner.

"Dump was still squatting on the bank looking in the water,
and he got this real dreamy tone in his voice and said, 'But
he won't never be nothing but a shiner, will he, Buck?'

"Buck had tears in his eyes when he left my store. You see
what I mean about layers in a hen yard? It's so complicated

not just everybody can understand it, but I have always regarded Deacon and Dump as men of similar dignity. Just manifesting it differently."

I glanced over at Mule-mane's machine and it was still running away. I was being recorded for posterity of some sort, I suppose, but I had become so interested I didn't care. These kids were making me bring up things for consideration that I hadn't bothered with in years.

"But you know what I noticed most a long time ago about the black folks in this town and their reaction to things that nowadays would make headlines in the newspaper and talk shows on TV? They laughed. They always have. Things that you or I would get so swelled up about and let fester inside of us until our whole system was full of poison might upset black folks at first, but within a few days—and sometimes within a few minutes—they'd be laughing about them. It's their sense of humor that brought them through the lean years and up out of Egypt. I hope they never lose it and I hope we can get a little more of it ourselves. They laugh at white folks, they laugh at themselves, they laugh at anybody trying to put on airs.

"After we had integration of the schools, I heard Molcie Blackshear explaining to one of her daughters about the importance of getting an education. Molcie had gone through our colored school system and had got on with the post office in Atlanta. Rode back and forth before day and after dark, held her head up, raised a house full of children and never considered moving off and living anywhere else. Her little girl was complaining about somebody being mean to her on the school bus and also about not being elected as a cheerleader. Molcie told her to quit whining about things that didn't amount to a hill of beans and concentrate on her books. Told her that she and her brothers and sisters had lived two miles out from town and didn't have a school bus.

Used to walk through the pouring rain back and forth to school on muddy roads and get splashed by every automobile that went by. Said they used to wish that big yellow bus full of white children would stop and give them a ride but their mama said to forget that. Then she laughed.

"I was getting hot in the collar and feeling a little guilty because we white folks had done that to little children in the old days without ever thinking about their feelings, but Molcie stood between the paper towels and the potato chips and laughed. 'Child,' she said, 'you don't know what we went through to get a little schooling when I was coming along. My sister and I got to laughing about it the other day. It wasn't the books and it wasn't the studying that was rough. It was getting to school and then back home that we thought would kill us. We stayed up north of the peach orchard past where they're putting in that new shopping center now, and walking was some more mean when it was wet or cold. But Sis got to laughing and said she thought it was worse when the weather was pretty. Said she might every now and then manage to sneak past the Dorsey's front yard and Dr. Dorsey's old bulldog, but she never did make it past the Bishop house with them Bishop boys throwing rocks at her. Said anybody who could run fast as she did could qualify for the Olympics today. You shut your mouth and ride that bus and count your blessings.'"

I looked around and none of the three was even smiling. I hadn't figured they would. Little Short-hair looked suspiciously like she might start crying.

"You see? They were able to laugh at things we don't think are funny. Let me tell you about Elenda. She's from one of the old established families around here. She nor her sister ever married. Both of them did day work and managed to scrape and save enough to build a little house for themselves that they owned outright. Looked after some sorry brothers off

and on and helped raise some nieces and nephews who
have long ago moved off to various parts of the country and
done very well, to hear Elenda tell it. Elenda's like me. She's
been left all alone. Every now and then she comes by to check
on me and we get to visiting."

"You've known each other a long time?" said Little Ring-eye.

"Well, at least we've recognized each other for a long time,"
I told her. "I always knew who she was, who her parents, her
grandparents, were, and Elenda and I would pass and repass
for, oh, sixty or seventy years, I reckon. But it's only been for
the last five, ten years I've really come to know her. She's a
fine person. I'm not sure she can read and write but that does-
n't keep her from being a good friend and having good
sound judgment. We've gotten to be real close. We can let down
our hair with each other and not pretend.

"When we get to talking about the old times, we don't have
to explain things like we're having to do with each other right
now, because we both lived through them and each one
knows where the other one's coming from. I love to see
Elenda coming.

"She's a great, tall, raw-boned, broad-shouldered woman;
always, even as a child, big for her age. They grew up in a
little house across the patch behind the Moselys, and Elenda said Miss Tiny Blue Mosely used to ask their daddy to let
Elenda or her sister come across the patch to play with the
Mosely boys and keep them entertained while she did her
sewing. Elenda and her sister did it to be neighborly; there
was never any money changed hands, and baby-sitting had
not yet been invented.

"One evening they were playing ball and Frank Mosely had struck out every time he came up to bat and had finally commenced to bawling his head off. Elenda said it was
her turn at bat and she was watching the pitcher real close
and nobody was paying any attention to Frank because he

was forever crying about much of nothing anyhow. All of a sudden Miss Puss Jones, who was Mrs. Mosely's mama and blind as a bat but spoiled all her grandchildren rotten, yelled out so's you could hear her all over that side of town, 'Tiny Blue! Tiny Blue! Tell the nigger to let Frank hit the ball.' Elenda said her folks raised her not to pay any attention to white folks nor talk back to them, but about that time the ball came over the plate. Said she laid into it so hard it went across the road, plumb over the roof of Mr. Mouse Todwiler's house, and nobody has found that ball yet."

I looked at the two girls. "I'm just telling you that to illustrate the point I was making about laughter and how a real sharply developed sense of the ridiculous can carry some people through troubled times and comfort their wounds.

"Elenda even chuckled now and again about her daddy talking at the supper table on weekends when they'd had enough extra cash to buy a little meat down at Alice Fulton's meat market. Said when the meat was all gone and the plates sopped clean, her daddy would laugh and say, 'Hope everybody's belly is full, cause ain't nothing left in the pot now but Miss Alice's thumb. We done paid for it over and over, but there ain't much nourishment in that white woman's thumb.'"

Mule-mane smiled, but you could tell it was a polite smile; he didn't really think it was funny. "Mr. McEachern, does Elenda think everything is funny? Like, I mean, you know . . . ." he swallowed and grinned wider and reached over to pat his boom box. "Excuse me, I forgot. Are there things that happened that she doesn't laugh at?"

I looked at his instrument and grinned back at him. "Well, Chuck, she never has laughed about Miss Sally Hamilton. Miss Sally was old man Dorman Hamilton's wife. He got ready to get married and Miss Clyde Sims wouldn't have him, so he rode over to Douglasville because he heard Judge Ivey had a marriageable daughter. Wasn't much to look at, they said, but she was ready to get married. Old man Dorman proposed and brought her home without ever having what you younguns would call a date. Miss Sally did not ever get to be what anybody could call popular in this town, but for all her life she was never short on opinions or directions. She was a sharp-tongued female and used an unnecessary amount of energy both walking and talking.

"Elenda's mama ironed for her. Miss Sally had a washerwoman who came to her house but she didn't iron to suit; so Elenda's mama would go get the clean clothes, carry them to her house, sprinkle them down, iron them and carry them back. Once, after a fresh rain, she sent the clothes back by Elenda and her sister. Elenda says she'll never forget it. Miss Sally met them at her back door, snatched two pillowcases off the top of the pile and hollered, 'Look at the wrinkles your maw done pressed into the borders of these pillow slips! They got to be washed again before those wrinkles will come out. Your maw's getting as sorry as all the other niggers in this town. You tell her to wash these herself and iron them over and you tell her I want them back tomorrow!' And with that she flung the pillowcases down in the red mud and slammed her door.

"Elenda says she and her sister cried all the way home. Elenda told me when Sally Hamilton died, 'I know we ain't supposed to speak ill of the dead and I know she ain't even been put in the ground yet, but, Mr. McEachern, I don't care if she is laid out in a solid copper coffin up the street and covered over with flowers, that is one mean white woman. My mama told me and Sister not to be disrespectful or ever say nothing back to Miss Sally. Ma said, "She got her ways, children, but she white and we colored and we need the money. Besides the which, ain't no way it can be easy being married to a Hamilton. We don't know what all may be troubling that white woman's soul." I can't help it, though. That woman was born mean; she lived mean; and she died mean. I don't believe nobody can preach her into heaven neither, even though everybody says the family has got three preachers lined up to try.' No, sir, Elenda doesn't laugh at everything. And Miss Sally has been important in her life. You can tell because she's told me that story at least four or five times. You know how old folks are about repeating themselves."

I considered Mule-mane's machine sitting there in the midst of us recording like crazy and decided I wouldn't go into just how lowdown and mean some of the white folks had been, which made it even more remarkable that the black folks had hung on to their sense of humor and hadn't wound up hating everything walking around in white skin. It, of course, was because we were close enough in the community that everybody knew everybody and there wasn't anybody, black or white, who expected Forrest Sawyer to amount to anything, but the colored knew we weren't all like that. Everybody kept hoping Forrest would step so far over the line that the law would put him away and give him his comeuppance.

The Sawyers were good people. They were more than a little land poor, but they held their heads up, worked their cotton and paid their bills. They shined their shoes, looked up to their womenfolks, and washed their automobiles before Sunday; just all around good stock. All his brothers and sisters were solid, respectable people and were raised right by the same parents who failed so miserably on Forrest. You see enough of that through life that you realize everything can't be environmental, there has to be a heap to heredity. Any good farmer could have told you that Forrest Sawyer was a throwback, that some scrub bull somewhere back along the line had got in with the Jerseys.

Forrest wasn't only baby chicken head-yanking mean, he had a warped and twisted sense of humor. He could snicker and cackle that laugh of his until a grown man would want to vomit. He was single-handed probably responsible for more black folks packing their families up in the middle of the night and in the middle of a crop and sneaking off to Detroit or Cincinnati than any other one white man in the county. He ran off so many plow and hoe hands that no decent black person would hire on with him for a crop; all he could get was the leavings. Then he would be sure enough crazy mean to them.

He came strutting in my store one day to settle an account one of them had run up for a little lard and self-rising and sow belly. Shoved his hat to the back of his head and said, "Mark this one off, Mr. Will Henry, he's long gone from here." I never bothered to ask him what had happened because, to tell the truth, I didn't want to know.

But Forrest was going to tell it anyhow. "I've known some sorry lazy niggers in my time, but I believe he was the worst one I've ever tended to. Times have got to where you can't find nobody to help you whip one anymore, so a man has to make out the best way he can. I couldn't keep that lazy rascal in the field to save my life. Here it is the middle of June, the cotton's knee-high and I couldn't get him to work. He took his mule out for dinner day before yesterday along with everybody else, but at one-thirty he hadn't showed back up in the field. I went looking and you know where I found him? Curled up on his front porch, barefooted as a yard dog, sound asleep with his head on a wadded-up guano sack. His mouth was hanging open and he was sleeping so hard the flies were crawling in and out and not even disturbing him.

"I called him and he never even grunted. Just kept sleeping away. I said, 'You black sonbitch, I bet I can wake you up.' He still didn't move a muscle. I pulled my gun out and shot one of his toes off. You'd adied a-laughing. He come off that porch and run on all fours plumb across the yard. Never straightened up till he jumped the ditch and hit the big road. I knowed I'd never get no work out of him now for sure; so I put a bullet in the road behind him just to keep him running and told his wife to get the baby and their stuff outa my house before dark."

He looked over in my meat case and said, "Whilest I'm paying up, just wrap up that roast of beef. I'm tired of hawg meat and chicken, and a little beef for Sunday dinner will tickle my wife."

I said, "I'm sorry, Forrest, but I'm holding that for Miss Laura. She and Miss Jess came by and it's promised."

When he left, Idella sidled up to me and said real low, "Mr. Will Henry, I was cleaning up for Miss Laura this morning and they taking dinner in Jonesboro tomorrow."

I said, "I know that, Idella, but that roast can lie there and rot before I'd sell it to Forrest Sawyer. Can I wrap it for you? Free of charge?"

"Thank you very kindly, Mr. Will Henry, but I guess it'd do better to rot. I don't believe I could stomach sitting there watching my chappies eat nothing that reminded me of that trashy Mr. Forrest Sawyer."

Course even Idella and most other people in the county never realized exactly what trash that white man really was. Word got around on him so widespread that he couldn't get anybody to put in a crop and he had to give up farming. He sold enough of his land to build a honkey-tonk back in the river swamp. Hired a big old fat mean woman with thick lipstick and bottle blonde hair to run it for him. She lived in an apartment he had built up above the honkey-tonk. Called herself Princess. No telling what her mama had named her.

Wasn't any time before she was driving a purple Cadillac and those that knew, plus some that didn't but liked to make you think they did, said all the furniture in her apartment—sofa, chairs, cushions, rug, bedspread and sheets—was all the same shade of purple. I don't know about that, but

I do recollect that you never saw her in that car or out of it without she was wearing a purple blouse and purple slacks and about to bust loose out of both of 'em. Front and back. She was a sight to behold.

Old Doc told me one time, in strictest confidence of course, that he had treated her for a female complaint, something involving a great deal of unseemly itching. Said there were lots of treatments available but the one he chose for Princess was gentian violet. Said he never used it ordinarily, save on the most severe cases or on babies with thrash, because it was bad to stain clothes and you couldn't get rid of it off your skin for weeks. But he swabbed her down good with it and then gave her some to douche with at home for a month. Told me it gave him some degree of satisfaction to consider how color-coordinated she was. "Pseudo-royalty to the bottom," is the way he phrased it.

That was before he threw Forrest Sawyer out of his office. Nobody but he has ever known why, but old Doc said he had to tell somebody. Forrest came in with a drip to get himself a shot of penicillin and got to cackling at Doc about the treatment he had rendered Princess. Told Doc that, when she told him about it, he had dubbed her Princess Purple Puss until she got her blackjack out and threatened to lay him out.

Went on then and told Doc how accommodating to him she was. Said a young couple from over in Polk County had come in one evening and got to drinking real heavy. Prettiest little girl you ever laid eyes on, Forrest said. More he looked at her the more he couldn't keep from looking. Finally he told Princess he'd really love to have a little of that.

Wasn't any time till Princess had put something in the girl's drink made her sick and pass out. Then she got all sympathetic and told the girl's date she'd take her upstairs to her apartment and let her lay down till she got to feeling better. Princess and a heap of others need Miss Lizzie to straighten them out about the difference between *lay* and *lie*; I've about given up. Then she slipped around and told Forrest to go up to the bedroom, she had a little surprise for him.

Forrest told old Doc he walked into that purple bedroom and Princess had that little girl stripped buck-naked, laying back on purple pillows with her legs drawn up and all spraddled out. "And, Doc," he said, "Princess had laid a little red silk handerchief right over that sweet little thing's sweet little thing. I'll never forget that sight the longest day I live. I was in and out of her and she never even knew I'd been in the room with her."

Old Doc said he'd already given Forrest his shot and couldn't think of any way to get it back; so he no-charged him and told him not to ever come back in his office. Told me that even Hippocrates would have sat in judgment on Forrest Sawyer. Told me, "He is so contemptible he makes me feel dirty to be a man."

I told him, "I know what you mean. He makes me feel ashamed to be white."

"He can lie in a ditch and die before I'd lift a finger to help him," old Doc said.

"I know what you mean," I said again. "He could starve to death before I'd sell him anything to eat."

And he did. Lie in a ditch and die. And starve, too, I reckon. Trussed up like a Christmas turkey and been there for days before they found him. That was years and years ago and they still don't know who did it.

The funeral, they say, was a mob scene. Everybody wanted to know how the minister was going to preach Forrest Sawyer into heaven. But he never even tried. Just read some scripture. It was a real short service. The scripture was "Vengeance is mine; I will repay, saith the Lord." Nobody cried except Forrrest's wife and that just a little bit. That scripture was elaborated on by the minister to be a comfort to the family and he counseled them to forgive, to leave bitterness out of their hearts. But I always thought that preacher was making a pronouncement because he ended it up with "The Lord moves in mysterious ways his wonders to perform."

Miss Gray said that is the only funeral she can remember when they didn't read "In my Father's house are many mansions." Miss Gray and I both had a great deal of respect for that preacher and I was saddened when he was called to a bigger church. He was a Baptist, but he was still a loss to the community.

"Mr. McEachern, are you all right?"

It was Little Ring-eye. I'd been staring at that tape recorder so long without saying anything I guess they thought I was dozing off or having a spell or something. There wasn't any way in the world I could have told those young-guns about Forrest Sawyer. I stand solid on the premise that you can't change history, but on the other hand you sure don't have to record every scrap of it, either. Makes you ponder on how absolute or relative history that gets written down must be, but that was a little deep for me and I sure didn't want to throw it out to those kids. Besides, if Little Short-hair thought Deacon Kilough was horrible, I certainly didn't have any desire to acquaint her with Forrest Sawyer. It was getting too close to supper time.

"Mr. McEachern," Little Ring-eye said, "we were all born after the schools were integrated. I'd be interested to know how the actual process went on in our community. Was there any trouble?"

Now that was a subject I would love to have recorded. "Young Lady," I said, "it went smooth as silk. Completely and totally. First grade through twelfth. All the same day. No fuss. No ruckus. No fights. We were held up in Washington, D.C., as a model of how to do it.

"The reason, like I have touched on before, is that in this

place we all knew each other. There wasn't any way white parents were going to let their children be mean to the children of their maids and cooks, and on the other hand there wasn't any way black children were going to be disrespectful to the teachers their mamas had been working for.

"So you see, we had what they nowadays call peer pressure working for us. Also we had a sheriff who had put the quietus on the hot heads around town. There were some, of course, who beat their chests like dancing Indian braves and hollered 'Nigger,' but Sheriff Jeter had already announced that he would personally beat the hell out of anybody that caused trouble and then lock 'em up. 'White or black,' he said. 'Don't make no difference.'

"Which was the way the sheriff had operated for years. He had hands as big as pork shoulders, and he could slap a man so hard he wouldn't know what day it was. Which he routinely did if anybody crossed him. White or black. Made no difference. I've wondered lately if we'd had TV coverage back then like we have today, how Sheriff Jeter would have stacked up alongside Singapore. We had law and order around here, too."

I glanced around at all three of them. The girls were round-eyed and still, but Chuck slipped me a wink. I tell you, I believe that boy's going to turn out to be all right.

"Of course, some people were indignant over it; nobody likes being told you have got to do anything. But it was basically accepted with good humor. Magnolia Dewberry laughs a lot about much of nothing, but since she has all her lower teeth and none of her uppers, it's hard not to laugh along with her no matter what has turned over her tickle box. She told me, 'Law, Mr. Will Henry, you shoulda been with me up to Miss Tiny Blue's house a while ago. She can't afford no help but I like to check on her now and then just to see how she getting along. You know, she come from quality way back down the line somewheres, and a woman can't always help who she marry. Besides the which we the same size and she always save her old dresses for me when she done had a cleaning out and throwing away.

"'She make out she might glad to see me. "Magnolia," she say, "come in this kitchen. I just took a pot of fresh turnip salad off the stove and a pan of cornbread. Set down here and eat some with me." They was good greens, too.

"'Miss Tiny Blue, she know how to season, she ain't scared of a little boiling meat like some these white folks has done got to be. I'd bout finished my greens and was drinking my buttermilk and we'd done bout visited out; you know how womens is. We had talked about nearly everbody both of us knowed. Miss Tiny Blue leaned back and say, "Magnolia, how you feel about this here school integration?" I never said nothing for a minute, thinking about how all her boys done growed up now but she got a bunch of grands and maybe two or three greats in school now. They all time playing on our side of town whenever it suit and just as cute as they can be. She say, "You know what I mean. I talking about mixing of the races in the classrooms." And I say, "Law, Miss Tiny Blue, to tell you the honest to God truth, I don't see nothing atall wrong with little black children going to school with the white." And Miss Tiny Blue flang down her fork and holler out, "Damn your soul, woman, I hope them turnip greens chokes you!" Then she bust out laughing and I did, too. That Miss Tiny Blue a sight.

"'I have laugh myself plumb across town so hard I think I done weakened my kidneys. Could I kindly use your restroom? Ain't no way I can make it home; I just gotta let off a little water.' Magnolia has known me all her life, of course, but she'll talk real open and frank to anybody else, too. She gets away with it because she has a sense of what's ridiculous. So does Tiny Blue, for that matter."

The girls were looking at each other with smiles on their

faces, but Mule-mane was right solemn.

"Mr. McEachern, did things go on smoothly afterwards? In the schools when they started out?" Then he added, "And if so, why?"

I declare, that Chuck can set things up so quick for you that he'd have made a good pin-boy in a bowling alley—back when we had pin-boys instead of those electric robots.

"Now that you bring that up, son, we'll look at your first question on both a relative and an absolute basis, and the answer on both counts is yes. Things stayed very smooth, especially when you compared them to Jacksonville and Boston, the only difference in those two places, to my mind, being the presence or absence of that meddling Mrs. Peabody.

"We were relatively a Sunday School picnic. We maybe had a few little bumps in the road, but on the surface, far as we in the town could tell, everything was absolutely smooth as pond water. You ask, 'Why' and I've already lined out for you the attitude we had from parents and community leaders. But the folks who caught the ball and controlled it, took it up and down the court and scored the points, as far as I was concerned, were the teachers.

"Oh, we had an occasional one with either a chip on her shoulder or genetic incompetence, but those very quickly had their attitudes adjusted for them or were kind of smothered till they could be moved on out. Most of our teachers were dedicated women who didn't have but one purpose for being in any school, and that was to teach. Miss Tommie Lee Colvin, now, was a case in point and a good example. I'm sure all of you young people have noticed that generalities go down better if they're accompanied by some specifics.

"Miss Tommie Lee was born and raised here and she taught high school English for something less than a hundred years. She revered the English language and had tremendous respect for its rules. She was an authority on literature, both prose and poetry, and she wouldn't hesitate to sniff and label something 'trash,' even if it had won a Pulitzer Prize or some such.

"She loved her subject and she knew her subject and she loved to teach her subject. She also loved her students. Now she wasn't any hypocrite. Y'all know as well as I do some students aren't lovable, and Miss Colvin didn't pretend they were. She just went at them with a lot of patience, firmness, and interest until the unlovable modified their behavior and became lovable. Usually took till about Christmas every year. Then they could all learn.

"She came from a long line on both sides that was what the papers would have called 'white supremacist.' Her folks didn't know they were nor talk about it; they just lived that way and never bothered anybody unless they got bothered. Miss Tommie Lee had no background of interchange with the colored on any other basis, but she came through like a thoroughbred.

"We were discussing those days a year or so before she died. She had brought me a book she thought I'd enjoy and took time for a little visit. Got to talking real reflective. Real personal too. For Miss Tommie Lee Colvin. She said, 'You know, Mr. McEachern, I will have to confess to some prejudice. I am well aware that there was no basis at all for it, but I had the deep conviction that if I touched a black person the color would come off on my hand.'

"I chuckled and told her that was sure true of some of them back then and also of a heap of the whites. Things have evermore improved around here since all the people got running water and soap. Miss Tommie Lee went on to say that she kept her mouth shut and just felt her way along through that uncharted sea during those first days of integration. You know they integrated the teachers, too, don't you? Miss Tommie Lee said she took her cue from them. None of them called her by her first name and so she used courtesy titles for them.

She quoted Robert Frost at me, 'Good fences make good neighbors,' she said.

"But then she started interacting with her black students and the teacher in her really came out. Some were dumb and some were bright. Just like her white students. Some were eager and some were lazy. Just like the white.

"She always had been a strict disciplinarian, and she didn't let up on anybody just because of social changes. When the black children saw how Miss Colvin could wither a white girl with a look or cut a white boy to the bone with a word and also leave the whole class laughing, the word got around that nobody better mess with Miss Colvin. It has always seemed to me that most teen-agers will go to any length to keep their fellows from pointing their fingers at them in ridicule. Laughter can be wounding as well as healing."

"I know what you mean, Mr. McEachern," put in Little Short-hair, but she shut up when Little Ring Eye looked at her.

"Miss Colvin was always fair. And I don't mean just about dishing out grades, although she meticulously gave a kid exactly what he made. Didn't shave any points. All you got if you complained to her about a test score was sympathy and the encouragement to work harder and do better next time. No, I mean she was fair and conscientious about trying to understand each student. When she had senior boys who grumbled that they never had liked poetry she'd have them read Robert Service or Rudyard Kipling out loud and say, 'See? You just haven't liked poetry before because you misbehaved in the tenth grade and Mr. Booth gave you the choice of memorizing "Thanatopsis" or taking a paddling.'

"She had some paperbacks of Louis L'Amour on hand that she'd pass out to those same boys when they claimed they didn't like to read. Wouldn't be long before she had the class eating out of her hand and paying attention. I mean, she kept order in her class. Same as you will remember Morgan B. Dorman was required to do in that contract he signed back before the War. Same as Miss Lizzie did when I came along. If you stop and think on it, teaching is a long line of unsung heroes.

"She was more than somewhat prepared then when Vernisha Jones showed out in class one day and complained about an assignment. She had already had a set-to with Vernisha the second day of school and had put that girl down with real expertise, to my way of thinking. Vernisha had raised her hand and with a bold voice said, 'Miss Colvin, I want to know one thing before we get started. Have you got race prejudice?' Miss Tommie Lee didn't hesitate a minute or even bother to look over her glasses. 'Of course I do, Vernisha. So do you. Everyone does to a greater or lesser degree.'

"Vernisha said, 'What you talking about? I ain't got no race prejudice.'

"Miss Colvin was calm as she could be. 'Of course you have, Vernisha. If you didn't, all you could see would be a teacher standing up here and not even be conscious that I'm white.'

"Somebody snickered and Miss Tommie Lee cut him down with a glance and bore in on Vernisha.

"'No one can help prejudice or any other feelings that he has. We can, however, move to modify our feelings and we can most certainly maintain control over what we let those feelings make us do. I would hope that neither you nor I would let race prejudice get in the way of your getting the best education of which you are capable. Do you have any other question?' Vernisha said, 'No'm,' and ducked her head, and Miss Colvin hit her another lick.

"'This is an English class, and I would encourage each of you to polish your use of our language as we go through the school year. Vernisha, I am sure you have heard repeatedly that "ain't" is not a word. That is not, however, as offensive to my ear as a double negative. Try to remember that when you're talking. The correct way of speaking would be to say, "I don't have any prejudice." Remember that. Maybe somewhere along the road you and I will both say it. Not just grammatically, but truthfully.'

"Of course, Miss Colvin had already been teaching for years when that happened. There was a male teacher on the faculty with her. He was a young fellow, not from around here, only been teaching a year or so. He had bought into this notion that showed up a little later on in Congress as what they called affirmative action. He had the conviction that black folks ought to be treated with extra special consideration and not have as much demanded of them because they had been oppressed for generations. Of course you mustn't call that attitude 'paternalism' because paternalism was practiced just because someone was black. Affirmative action is different because that is based on oppression and comes under the heading of what they call justice. But it still exists just because someone is black. Wouldn't Lewis Carroll have fun with all that if he were living in Georgia today?

"At any rate, this Mr. Monroe fancied himself as an enlightened liberal, and any label like that can get tedious when you're very young and, as Mr. Nick Willis said, 'ain't yet learned sooey.' But Miss Colvin said all the other teachers liked him because he was such a hard-working, dedicated teacher himself and had so much enthusiasm. The two of them got to be friends, one of the reasons at first being that neither one of them smoked and couldn't stand to sit around in the teachers' lounge and cough. So they had ample opportunity to visit while they were drinking their coffee in a little side office.

"Mr. Monroe took a shine to Miss Colvin and would pick her brain about her teaching methods. One day he jumped her about Vernisha Jones. 'Miss Colvin,' he said, 'I need to

talk to you about that girl. I lean over backward trying to accommodate her. I spend time with her after class. I take time during class to explain things to her. I promise you I am the soul
of patience with her. Yet she continues to have this attitude
of belligerence, of hostility, toward me.

"'You know, the child has had a very poor background and
because of that she does not test well and consequently
makes poor grades. Giving her the benefit of every doubt and
even not counting off as meticulously as I do on other students, Vernisha is failing in my class. Every time I hand
back a paper she flounces up with this sullen look and slaps
it down on my desk and says, "Mr. Monroe, how come you
give me this here F?"

"'And I, as patiently as I can, go over the paper and
explain to her every point I've taken off. And each time she
snatches her paper back and says, "You doing it just cause
I'm black," and marches off in a huff. I know that you
have gained not only her respect but that of all the black students. Do you have any suggestion?'

"And Miss Colvin very gently explained to him that he needed to devote his attention to something that was in the present and right before him. She told him there was not a thing
in the world he could do about Vernisha's background but
that he could address her attitude. Miss Colvin didn't line out
any specifics for him, she's a much wiser woman than that,
but she did tell him, 'Vernisha's doing much better for me.
She flared up at me in literature class and said, "Seems like
all we studying in here is what was wrote by a bunch of dead
old white men." As soon as I corrected her grammar, I
introduced her to Countee Cullen and Paul Lawrence Dun-
bar and made her memorize "The Turning of the Babies in
the Bed." Then I had her recite it, in dialect, for the class, and
she's been a lamb for me ever since. Vernisha does not enjoy
memorizing.'

"A few weeks later Mr. Monroe looked her up after school and said, 'I sure feel better, Miss Colvin. I just had another encounter with Vernisha and I think I'm making progress. She flung her latest paper down on my desk and said, "Mr. Monroe, how come you give me this here 40?" I just shook my head back and forth and in a real weary tone of voice said, "Because you're black, Vernisha, because you're black." And you know what she did? She threw her head back and laughed and said, "Don't you jive me, Mr. Monroe, don't you jive me." And then she stomped out of the room as usual. But this time she was laughing and the stomp was a happy stomp. I feel good. I think I may have broken through.'

"And Miss Colvin laughed and patted him on the back and told him she thought he might very well be right. Her theory was that you had to recognize education as an institution, all right enough, but that you have to modify any institution occasionally to fulfill the needs of a particular person. White or black. No, Chuck, we didn't have any trouble here. You see what I mean when I say it was mostly on account of our teachers? Also you see what I mean about the importance of good humor? Either of you have any other questions about race relations?"

Mule-mane spoke up first. "No, sir, I believe that about covers it, Mr. McEachern. Or at least you've given us more material already than we can condense into a paper."

Then Little Ring-eye piped up. "Oh, pooh," she said. "Pooh on the old paper. I had almost forgotten that's why we were here." She was sitting up straight and had a gleam in her eye. "Mr. McEachern, I want to thank you for sending me back to *John Brown's Body*. I've been reading it ever since we left last week. Parts of it over and over. When you were telling us about Elenda and Deacon and Dump a while ago, all I could think of was Cudjo.

'Cudjo watched and measured and knew them,
Seeing behind and around and through them . . . .
He couldn't read and he couldn't write,
But he knew Quality, black or white . . .'

"Benét was really getting into the heart and soul of a lot of people, wasn't he?"

"That's why it's a great book," I told her. "I thank you kindly for paying attention to an old man and reading it."

Be blessed if Little Miss Short-hair didn't jump in then, feisty as a Massachusetts chihuahua. "Well, that's all very well and good, Mr. William Henry McEachern, but while we're at it, I'd like to pin you down about something. Personally. You've pulled us up pretty short about judging the past in the light of the present, and you even put me to thinking about relative morality. I'd just like to know your personal feelings about segregation and integration. How you, as the son of a Confederate soldier, the oldest person in the county, really feel about the Civil Rights movement and what has come out of it. No varnish. Pure truth. Don't blow any smoke up my skirts."

Well, you can be sure that got my attention. I cannot condone most of the things young people are doing to our language, but I have to admit that some of their phrases are not only pungent but picturesque. So I let it pass. At least she was grammatically correct and certainly her meaning was clear. She wanted honesty. I gave it to her.

"I am completely recovered from my shame," I said.

That startled her. "Shame?"

"Yes. Shame. I think a lot of people in the South realized down in their hearts that legal segregation of the races, regardless of the validity of the social pressures that spawned it, was wrong. We went along with it and lived under its rules because of custom and tradition. Also because of inertia. If any of us had ever considered spearheading any meaningful change in the way things were, the prospect of the firestorm and mares' nests to follow would have scared us off.

"My shame comes from the fact that it took a bunch of Yankees, who, I might point out, have themselves not come to the table of racial integration with clean hands, to line out for us through the federal courts that we were wrong. I would not return to the days of enforced segregation for anything."

There was still a little edge to her voice, and I swear one shoulder was just a bit higher than the other. "You are using the terms 'legal segregation' and 'enforced segregation.' Could you clarify?"

I was so cordial butter wouldn't melt in my mouth. "Most certainly. I was in hopes you would pick up on that. You know, it seems like in the history of man things go in cycles and we keep repeating ourselves. Consider Guinevere, Anne Boleyn, and Jackie Onassis. They say Jackie is the closest thing to royalty America has ever had; so I guess you could say they were all three of them queens. They were all wealthy, and each of them was an unfaithful consort. One went in a convent, one was beheaded, and the other one has been anointed by the Liberals in this country as a model for feminine behavior. Not to worry, I say. All tides ebb and flow and things eventually get washed up on the beach.

"After Cromwell died and the Roundheads lost power, up sprang the Royalists and Cavaliers again with their shocking ways as though to say, 'Look what we can do now, since there's nobody to stop us.' Then came Victorianism. Then we had flappers. Then we had rigid work ethic coming out of the Depression. Then here came the flower children and the hippies. Then after them we're having a resurgence of fundamentalism. All that's as natural as the pendulum on a clock swinging back and forth to mark the passage of time.

"To get back on track. Slavery and segregation were both

legally abolished after the Civil War and those laws were
enforced in the South. At one point by an occupying enemy.
Not in the North, mind you. The South. Then the whites
got back in political power and we had legal segregation.
Rigidly enforced in the South. Not in the North. Then we
had legal abolition of Jim Crow and enforced integration
in the South. Along with riots and demonstrations and marches. Brought out the worst in both races, seemed to me. On
the one side we had fire hoses and police dogs and secret
burial. On the other side we had rape and fire and pillag-
ing and using coffee urns in restaurants for slop jars. 'We
shall overcome' was the anthem of Civil Rights, but 'Burn,
baby, burn' was its slogan. We watched riots and fires on
TV while we were told that everything was nonviolent.

"Heroes were known by initials. MLK, JFK, RFK. The
blacks have never cottoned up much to LBJ, although he's
the one who really pushed Civil Rights through and he's got
good initials, too. No matter. It happened. It needed to happen and it did. None of us liked it, but it happened.

"Now we have legal integration, enforced integration. On
the books. In the courts. And what do we have in reality? Voluntary segregation. Whites swarm out of the cities to estab-
lish elite subdivisions most black people cannot afford.
Blacks, after raising all that sand to get the schools integrated
so they could get educated with white people are now, forty
years later, demonstrating on college campuses for all-black
dormitories and black student centers. Today you young people are having to ask an old centenarian what black people
are really like because our society is probably more segregated
than it has ever been. But it's all voluntary. By choice. Black
and white."

I looked straight at Little Short-hair. "Missy, do you
know what bothers me most about all this? I'm afraid the South
is getting like the North. All of you have heard the old saw

that Yankees love the Negro race and hate the individuals and that the South hates the race but loves the individual. There's a lot of truth to that. It's rooted in history. I worry about Farrakhan and the militant blacks today and what they are doing to their people."

Little Ring-eye gave an eager interruption. "Mr. McEachern, this is reminding me of the Prologue to *John Brown's Body*, you know when the slave trader turns south with his wares because the northern merchants have no economic need for slaves. And you remember he speaks of how he got his cargo in the first place. From tribal wars in Africa. The blacks sold other blacks to slave traders. Captives from wars among themselves. That can't happen in America today. They wouldn't do that to themselves again, would they?"

Before I could think up a reply, Mule-mane cleared his throat. "I don't particularly, like, you know, want it to get around on me, but I read a poem, too. One I liked so much I learned it.

'*They set the slave free, striking off his chains . . .*
Then he was as much of a slave as ever.

He was still chained to servility,
He was still manacled to indolence and sloth,
He was still bound by fear and superstition,
By ignorance, suspicion, and savagery . . .
His slavery was not in the chains,
But in himself . . . .

They can only set free men free . . .
And there is no need of that:
Free men set themselves free.' "

I watched that boy and I was plumb spellbound. The longer I live the more I learn that you can't always judge a book by its cover. I looked across at the girls.

"I like that," said Little Ring-eye.

I turned to Little Short-hair.

"It's all right," she said. "I guess. But, if you really believe that, then the Civil War was completely unnecessary."

"Exactly," I said. "And do we believe it? I think the black people finally believe it. Most of them. It took a hundred years after Lincoln, but finally they did it. They set themselves free. And maybe all that ruckus, including their repulsive behavior about the coffee urns, was a necessary part of it. Even if they did put Loeb's Restaurant out of business and backlashed Lester Maddox into the Governor's mansion. They had to do it for their own self-respect. They couldn't just sit back and let the white man give it to them.

"My concern now is that we don't become cold toward each other. Alienated. We need to reach out and be concerned. About individuals. The Yankees have Boston and New York and Philadelphia. They are welcome to them. We have Atlanta. It is the Phoenix City. It has risen from the ashes. I hope we can prevent the pendulum swing back to ashes."

I was getting into some pretty deep stuff, but they had started it. If these kids didn't want to think, then they shouldn't ask penetrating questions. I looked at Little Short-hair. "You got any more questions on how I feel about segregation?"

She swallowed. "No, sir. It seems like the more questions I ask, the more questions pop up that aren't answered."

"That's growth," I said. "It never stops."

"I'd love to stay," she added, "but it's getting late. I have an Honor Society meeting."

"I have to cook supper," said Little Ring-eye, and looked at her watch.

"And I have baseball practice," said Mule Mane. "I finally made starting catcher this year." I cut an eye at him but he wasn't pulling my leg. "We surely do appreciate your time, Mr. McEachern."

"Well, it's turned out to be a real pleasant experience for me," I said. "Are you young folks, by any chance, coming back next week?"

"No, sir," he said. "We'll have to have this interview ready for the paper by Monday and we'll be pushed to make it."

Then Little Ring-eye put in, "But before we leave, Mr. McEachern, I'd like to know something. As profound as I've watched you get about questions you hadn't anticipated, I'm curious to know what you'd have come out with on something you'd thought out ahead of time. What were you going to tell us about family values?"

"Do you have an old maid aunt, young lady?"

"No sir," she said. "I have two who have divorced. One of them twice. But no old maids."

"Then what I was going to propose wouldn't be relevant." And I winked at her.

Be blessed if she didn't lean up and kiss me. Just below my ear. "Mr. McEachern, I just love you. Can I come back and visit you some time this summer? When Elenda is here? I'd like to meet her." She giggled. "And let ole Frank hit that ball." Then she was gone. French braid, eyelids, hips, and all.

Mule-mane stuck out his hand and the way he shook was sort of like one brother to another, strong grip and swinging sideways. Back and forth. Not one of those put-on, fake handshakes that teen-agers and athletes try to push on you nowadays. That handshake made me feel young again. No more than eighty or so.

"Mr. Mac," he said, "I can't thank you enough. I've got a full summer. Have a job to save up money for school. Like, I'm going to the University next year. Pre-law, I think. But could I, like, you know, pick you up some time and carry you to a Braves game? I'd like to hear more about Miss Tommie Lee Colvin. I wish I could have known her."

I didn't bother to correct his language. Besides, he'd already taken the tape out and was headed for his car. Way I felt right then, he could say "like, you know," till Kingdom Come and I wouldn't open my mouth and say a word. I know that all young people have to make the trip over Fool's Hill and that Mule-mane and Ring-eye still have a ways to go, but they made me feel like maybe the journey would be just a little bit safer for them on account of me. I'd never considered myself as a seat belt before, but then there are a lot of things I haven't thought of yet. That's what keeps me going.

I turned around for Little Short-hair to tell me good-bye. She was standing up right enough as if she was ready to go, but she hadn't picked up her book bag or even her car keys yet like she was in a hurry. I have in my day seen enough Southern women drag out a farewell to know she had some visiting yet left in her. "I hope you're not going to be late for Honor Society," I said.

"I've already missed it. I was only using that as an excuse to get Tiffany and Chuck moving."

I just looked at her. Of a sudden it hit me that I was all alone with a determined young female who had already demonstrated that she held some fairly strong opinions, and now here she stood manifesting pretty shrewd manipulative skills. I wondered if she was going to grow up and be an ACLU lawyer. Then I thought about the teacakes she had brought and relaxed. I do not believe that dedicated liberal feminists bake cookies for old men. I sort of raised my eyebrows but I didn't say anything.

"My grandfather died ten years ago. He lived with us, and although I never had much opportunity for conversation with him, I watched and listened around the house and learned a little something about old men. You run along to the bathroom, and I'll wait right here till you get back."

Her tone was crisp and efficient, had an authoritarian ring

to it, but wasn't the least bit officious or hostile. It never occurred to me not to mind her. I already needed to go, but her mention of it made it a matter of considerable urgency. About halfway through my business I thought, "That girl may turn out to be the sort who has an old maid aunt." Then just as I finished I thought, "If not, she may be well on the road to being one herself; she already talks like one."

I returned with dignity and more than a faint curiosity. She was seated with her hands in her lap like she was in her parlor instead of mine. "You certainly are in good health for a person of your age, Mr. McEachern. I apologize for imposing on any more of your time, but I wanted a minute alone with you and I can't come back later. I'm leaving right after graduation."

"I'm at your service, young lady." She just sat there; so I said, "Where are you going?"

"New York. I have a scholarship to Julliard. My hands don't look like it, but I can span an octave plus two, and I intend to be a concert pianist."

I noted that she pronounced the word correctly and not like something reminiscent of male anatomy. My respect went up a notch or two, but the cookies still didn't fit.

"I have worked hard. Real hard. All of my life." Seems like the younger a person is and the less life he's lived, the more portentously he can use that phrase. All of my life, indeed. But I didn't figure this was the moment to comment on that. "When the other little girls were skipping rope or playing hopscotch or paper dolls, I was practicing on the piano. When the big girls were dating or having slumber parties, I was studying or practicing. I'm the Star Student this year and the valedictorian of my class. Also I have this scholarship."

I sat real quiet. "I'm about to graduate from high school." She swallowed. "And I've never had a date. Nobody has ever asked me for a date."

I was careful not to change my expression, but I thought of Miss Saphronia, who was kind and sweet and loved by all. A much younger person asked her in my store one time why she hadn't ever married. I never heard a more accepting tone in anybody's voice; Miss Saphronia told her, "Well, child, when I was a maid all the young men went off to the War and so many of them were killed that the few who came back could have their pick of the girls. And nobody picked me."

Little Short-hair was beginning to touch my heart. She was on the road to being an old maid, right enough, but it was attitude in her case and it wasn't for me to speak. Josephine Floyd, who never married, looked around at the gaggle of husbands at her fiftieth college reunion and said, "The only thing worse than being an old maid is to wish to hell you were one." But Little Short-hair was too young to find either comfort or humor in that. I held my tongue.

Her voice got that defensive, sort of prickly tinge to it that I had come to associate with her. "Mr. McEachern, are you a bigot?"

Well, you can believe that nearly made me jump. I didn't, though. Just sat there with my hands on my stomach and my eyes shut and was real careful to breathe slow and even. Where in the world was this child headed?

"Mr. McEachern, you're not asleep. I said, 'Are you a bigot?'"

I opened one eye. "I don't think so." I kept my voice calm and peaceful. "But you are, aren't you?"

It was her turn to jump and she hadn't had as much practice as I have in quelling it. She also sat up real straight and gave a little yip. "I most certainly am not! Whatever gave you that idea?"

"Well, Missy, you know sometimes we hear a word used so frequently in one particular sense, so tossed around on TV and in the newspapers, that we come to accept it in their context and forget the true meaning. Reach up on the second shelf in the corner behind you there and hand us down that dictionary. The print's so small, I'm going to let you look up the word and read it out loud for us if you don't mind."

And she did. "'Bigot,'" she said. "'Noun. One obstinately or intolerantly devoted to his own church, party, belief or opinion.'"

"You see? I don't believe I am devoted to anything obstinately or intolerantly. I've spent a century watching and learning and bending. Came from getting my fingers burned so often. And so early on." I took time to put in a little sigh. "Only the very young are always right. About everything."

She had some fire to her; she stood her ground. "Mr. McEachern, I am not trying to insult you. It's just that you and Chuck have been laughing about things I don't think are funny. You and Tiffany even seem to have a bond between you, and in my book that girl is a total space queen. You've been talking about good humor and you can't change history and judging the past by the present and what's absolute and what's relative, and I haven't quite figured you out. I guess what I mean is, are you a racial bigot? Inside? Deep down?"

I didn't bother to give that question enough importance to sit up any straighter in my chair. I did look at her real straight, though. I thought to myself that if I'm a racial bigot, why have I stood up for the governor about wanting to change our flag? Of course I never wanted the Stars and Bars put on there in the first place; I regarded it as a desecration of the Confederate battle banner, just like I do most of the other uses folks have put it to. My father would have a fit. But I distinctly remember that it was put on there in defiance by an impotent legislature that was determined to thumb its nose at integration. Regardless of what some of them try to say now. The governor was right and should have stuck to his guns. I mean, politics can change right to wrong in the blink of an eye, and it sure wreaks havoc with human nature.

On the other hand, I have little patience with the young blacks yelling and dancing in the streets for the TV cameras. The Jews are busy calling attention to the Holocaust and building museums about it, and here the Blacks go trying to wipe out all reminders of their bondage and things that they are angry about enduring. Next thing I'm expecting is a move to change the carving on Stone Mountain.

I didn't mention the flag to Little Short Hair, though. I decided to answer her question on a more personal basis. "Young lady, three years ago when my gallstones shifted and got me blocked off, my doctor gave me the choice of dying at home or dying on the operating table. Said he'd never heard of anybody my age being operated on and living through it, but it was the only chance I had. You know who I made him call in as my surgeon? Dr. Charles Kilough Cofield, that's who."

"Cofield? Kilough? Charles?"

"That's right. He's Deacon's grandson on his mama's side. And on his daddy's side the great-great-great-grandson of the slave that Reverend Bogan Mask bought and set free. A proud young man and a smart young man. He graduated from high school the year after we integrated, and I loaned him the money for his first year of college till he could get the help of available grants and scholarships and such like that make it possible for any determined young person to get an education nowadays in this country we live in.

"He paid me back, too. Every dime. From working nights and summers. Paid me back before he finished his third year of college. I was real proud of him. Went on to med school and specialized and is one of the pioneers of this new-fangled laser surgery in our state. Kilough will operate on anybody. White or black, makes no difference. Anybody who needs it, that is; he's not in it just for the money. He kept me in the hospital only one night and that was simply because of my age.

"It was with more than a little pride that I went by his office the next week for a check-up. 'C. Kilough Cofield, M.D.' it says on the door. And that's in one of those big profession-al buildings in Georgia Baptist Medical Center. When he was a little barefoot, shirt-tail youngun running around town dusty-legged and snot-nosed, we all called him 'Charlie-K,' but when I mentioned that to him he told me that he dropped the Char-lie and took up the Kilough when he got to med school. In memory of his granddaddy, he said, who he remembered as a rough man but a man of dignity.

"I told him I imagined the first Charles Cofield was also possessed of dignity, although he passed on before I was big enough to remember him. You know what Charlie-K told me? He said, 'Mr. Mac, my granddaddy Kilough is the one who told me when I was six not to never let anybody call me "nig-ger." Black or white, he said to me. "Don't make no differ-ence." Then he said, "And, son, you be careful you don't never be one." I want my name to honor him, Mr. Mac.'"

I slowed down to see if she was going to take all this in and you know what she said? "Mr. McEachern, I don't believe I can take another example of relative and absolute right now," and she had that shoulder up again. I declare, womenfolks are hard to figure out, and I'm not sure I'll do it if I live anoth-er hundred years. A man can't afford to let one get too far ahead of him, though.

"Well, young lady, let's get back to your question, if you please. And I'm going to let you be the one to answer it. Am I a bigot?"

Well, sir, that got through to her. She bowed her head and studied the polish on her fingernails a minute and then she said, "Mr. McEachern, the only reason I brought this up to you is that I need to talk to somebody. And don't tell me to go to the school counselor. If I wanted my business talked about all over school I'd put it on the bulletin board and not strain it through a show-and-tell in the teachers' lounge."

I had sense enough to realize she was getting serious and going deep; so I kept my mouth shut.

"My mama would have a fit if I went to her. Besides, she has an executive job with AT&T and a lot on her shoulders. My father flies for Northwest and lives in Minneapolis with his third wife and their children; I hardly know him. I need to talk to somebody and I thought maybe you wouldn't mind."

She wasn't being bossy now and directing me to the bathroom. She wasn't sounding arrogant or prickly, either. Both shoulders were sort of slumped, and all of a sudden I could almost visualize her in the kitchen making those teacakes from her grandmother's recipe. I nodded my head at her. "Go ahead."

"Well, you see, like I told you, I've never had much to do with boys. About two or three years ago I began wondering why none of them ever paid any attention to me. That Tiffany Burkhalter has been covered over with them ever since we were in the seventh grade. Like butterflies on a dog turd."

That one pulled a grunt out of me. I couldn't help it; it just came up before I could stop it. She said, "Forgive me. My grandfather used to say things like that. Which is one of the reasons we didn't ever talk to each other much; I thought him unduly coarse. But that simile has always seemed appropriate for Tiffany and her friends, and, to tell you the truth, I've enjoyed thinking it when I would feel miserable about boys ignoring me.

"The more none of them looked at me, the more I wanted them to. The more I wanted them to, the more I would pretend that I didn't and would keep myself aloof. I'd go home after watching Tiffany laugh and roll those eyes and pop that stupid bubblegum and play 'Flight of the Bumblebee' as loud and fast as I could and call it 'Flight of the Butterflies.' Then I could be nice to her at school the next day. Mr. McEachern, except for the studies, high school has not been easy."

"I suspect Tiffany might agree with you about that. On her own account. Or Chuck. On his account. It's a time of change and indecision for most of the young folks I've been privileged to observe. Comes down to a conflict between what they've always been told they should stand for and what they're willing to jettison in order to be popular. It's even worse with those who already don't like themselves so bad that they're dead set on making other folks like them. Just to prove something to themselves. A heap of folks go through that. It hurts, but most of them get safely through it, find out who they really are, and go on with their lives. It's refreshing to see somebody be as open and honest about the process as you."

That's what I said out loud. To myself I was saying, "Dog turd? That's not the Tiffany I've met," but I had sense enough to realize she didn't need me for a champion. Good thing, too, for here came that shoulder back up and the fire back in those eyes.

"Mr. McEachern, I have not said for one minute that I did not like myself. I am very aware of all the folderol that's written about teen-agers and all the buzz words the pseudo-professionals use; I want you to know that I have a very good self-image and more than my share of self-confidence."

I wanted to say that I could sure agree with her but that wasn't exactly what I'd call it. I was back again to wondering about those teacakes. Then her shoulders slumped again and her eyes got big.

"Except with boys." She sighed so deep it made her frame rattle. "For the last few weeks this boy I've known all through school has started talking to me and confiding in me. I can tell he really likes me. He's always been a loner himself. Walked around swaggering and sneering and I couldn't stand him. Neither could anybody else. He's a body builder and works out with weights all the time. But he won't go out for any sports; tells the coaches and football players that he can't stand dumb jocks, and he's big enough to get away with it.

"He makes straight A's in math and science and then bounces from A's to D's in English. He's read Camus and Sartre and torments the teachers with smart alec questions and snide remarks. He moved over here from Alabama when he was in the sixth grade and nobody can stand him."

I was so far tending to side with that particular majority.

"Except me," she went on. "Mr. McEachern, I've fallen in love. I'm sure I have. I don't have any sense left at all when I think about him, and I think about him all the time. When he touches me I almost jerk away like you do from an electric shock and my knees get weak and my insides turn to water."

"Oh, Lord," I prayed, "don't let this complicated Little Short-hair be pregnant and come up here asking me what I think about abortion. You haven't let me live this long for that have you, Lord?" Although, I thought, I'll have to admit it would be a good launching pad for considering absolute and relative.

I made my voice as dry as possible for her. "That's called glands, young lady. Happens to everybody, usually sooner than later, and it's not to be trusted. You'll do well to keep on jerking. Away from it. That's not electricity, it's a magnetic field; and it can grab you up in it so tight you lose control. Maybe you have already."

"If you mean what I think you do, Mr. McEachern, I most certainly have not!" Her voice softened. "Not yet."

I waited. The only thing that made this better than a soap opera was that I was in it. She shifted back to softness.

"Although that's about to come to a head. I know it. He wants to come to my house some afternoon and have me play the piano for him. And I want him to. I'm scared because I know what will happen later, but there's a part of me that wants it to happen." She wouldn't look at me straight. "What do you think I ought to do?"

Well, now, what sort of position did this little minx think she was putting me into? And what right did she have coming in here and putting me there in the first place? Teacakes can carry you only so far in this world, even if, after all, she did say she had made them herself.

I didn't even take a deep breath. "I think you ought to do what you want to."

She looked sort of shocked. I had counted on that. "You do?"

"Yes, ma'am. I sure do." Then I took that breath. A real deep one. "Course I think it would behoove you to put the bridle of your Honor Society, Juilliard brain on that hormone horse of yours before you start riding it out across the countryside, jumping fences and ditches and getting all lathered up just for some moment of fancied ecstasy."

"Mr. McEachern!"

"Well, you asked. Before any of us do what we think we want, it's a good idea to look at it from all sides and be dead sure it's what we really want. And whether it's worth the consequences. And from what I've observed in the last few years with young girls throwing caution to the winds and their morals on the garbage dump because they think they're in love, it usually turns out they were in lust. Or in heat; like young heifers. And that is neither enduring nor endearing."

I figured that with somebody this smart and this opinionated it was about time to throw in a little scripture. It might not help, but it sure couldn't hurt.

"Some say Solomon wrote *Ecclesiastes*. I'm not so sure about that, but it doesn't really matter; it got written. I've not thought before about applying this to a female, but now it seems like it might be appropriate. 'Rejoice, O young girl, in thy youth, and let thy heart cheer thee in the days of thy youth; and walk in the ways of thine heart and in the sight of thine eyes. But know thou, that for all these things God will bring thee into judgment.'

"I'm not preaching at you. That's just a fancy way of saying 'Look before you leap.' You have to do what you want to do, but you need to be real sure exactly what it is you want. Later on as well as right now."

I wasn't real sure she was listening. She sat there a moment and then the chin came up and she looked right at me.

"Mr. McEachern, he's black."

I gave a little toot. I couldn't help it. One just popped out. When you're my age you can't always be in control of everything about yourself, try as you will. I ignored it and so did she. She'd probably experienced it with her grandfather.

"Does that change your opinion?" she asked, and her voice was tight and as sharp as lemon juice. The Lord, I thought, has sure enough let me live so long I'd have this put on my plate. Then I thought I was in the middle of a case of nevertheless His will, not mine, be done.

"Oh, no. I still think you ought to do what you want to do. Within exactly the same parameters." She wasn't going to catch me off third base that easy. "How does it affect your opinion?"

"I don't think it should make any difference at all."

I bore in on that real quick. "But it does, doesn't it? Else you wouldn't be having this compelling urge to talk about it. And with an old fogey you think is going to advise you against it."

Her chin by now was so tilted she was having to look down her nose. "Well, aren't you?"

"No," I said. Then I decided to use one of those phrases that young folks have adopted, one that is designed to shock, and one that, although I have thought it very expressive, I have never previously let cross my lips. "You don't want advice. You just want somebody else to be as aware as you are that you are fixing to step on your own meat." I shut my eyes a minute. "What you want and what you need are two different things."

She was still as suspicious as an unbroken filly. And almost as fractious as one in season. "And what would you suggest?" she snapped.

I shut my eyes again and commenced to studying on what in the world I had to offer this child. We didn't have much time to speak of. She was headed off to New York; and as for me, I've been surprised every morning for the last ten years when I wake up and am still on this side of the Jordan.

I needed to move quick, but I needed to move soft with this young colt of a woman. You can't gentle one by yelling at her. The more I studied on it the more I felt like I was eating chitlins; the longer you chew those things the bigger they get and the harder they are to swallow. I thought and thought, and I guess maybe I did get to breathing a little heavy.

"Mr. McEachern, are you snoring? I believe you really have gone to sleep on me."

I opened both eyes. "Maybe I did drop off for just a minute, but you asked me a pretty hard question when you inquired what I suggest you need." I waited, but she never said a word. "What church you go to, young lady?"

She gave a little pretend laugh. "You're not going to suggest that I turn to the Lord, are you? Or read the Bible for answers to all my problems? I'll have you know that I'm a regular communicant in the Episcopal Church. I am not a theological ignoramus, Mr. McEachern."

That was even better for my purpose than if she had been a Baptist, but I didn't smile. Talk about intolerant and obstinate. I'm of the opinion there's as high a percentage of bigots among so-called liberals as there is among the Ku Klux Klan, and I have little enough patience with either.

"You see that little red book behind you? Two shelves down and a little to the right of the dictionary? It's that one with the gold end papers and the leather covers. Hand it down to me if you don't mind, but be extra careful of it; it's so old the binding is crumbling.

"This is a special book. It was printed in 1899 and brought to me from England by a lady who had luckily missed the *Lusitania* and had to book passage on a later boat. It has meant a lot to me. I am going to give it to you. For your very own. It may not be what you want, but in my obstinate and intolerant opinion, it's sure as tarnation what you need. It's called *Sesame and Lilies* and was written by an Englishman named John Ruskin.

"I want you to take it home and read it. But before you do, I want to read a little out of the preface to you. Just so you'll get an idea and a feel about it.

"Listen to this and see if you think it might apply to you. In more ways than just religion.

"'Questions have arisen respecting the education and claims of women which have greatly troubled simple minds and excited restless ones. I am sometimes asked my thoughts on this matter, and I suppose that some girl readers may desire to be told summarily what I would have them do and desire in the present state of things. This, then, is what I would say to any girl who has enough confidence in me to believe what I told her, or to do what I ask her.'"

I looked over my glasses at her and she was paying attention.

"'First, be quite sure of one thing, that however much you may know, and whatever advantages you may possess, and however good you may be, you have not been singled out, by the God who made you, from all the other girls in the world, to be especially informed respecting His own nature and character. You have not been born in a luminous point upon the surface of the globe, where a perfect theology might be expounded to you from your youth up, and where everything you were taught would be true, and everything that was enforced upon you, right.'"

I checked to be sure she was listening. You had better believe she was; and watching me close as a chicken snake.

"'Of all the insolent, all the foolish persuasions that by any chance could enter and hold your empty little heart, this is the proudest and foolishest—that you have been so much the darling of the Heavens, and favorite of the Fates, as to be born in the very nick of time, and in the punctual place, when and where pure Divine truth had been sifted from the errors of the Nations; and that your papa had been providentially disposed to buy a house in the convenient neighborhood of the steeple under which the immaculate and final verity would be beautifully proclaimed. Do not think it, child; it is not so.'"

I stopped and looked at her again. She seemed to be taking it in. And also taking it pretty well.

"'This, on the contrary, is the fact,—unpleasant you may think it; pleasant, it seems to *me*—that you, with all your pretty dresses, and dainty looks, and kindly thoughts, and saintly aspirations, are not one whit more thought of or loved by the great Maker and Master than any poor little red, black or blue savage running wild in the woods, or naked on the hot sands of the earth; and that, of the two, you probably know less about God than she does; the only difference being that she thinks little of Him that is right, and you think much that is wrong.'"

I closed the book and handed it over to her. "This has been one of my treasures. I want you to have it."

She took the book right enough, but she didn't back down one little bit. That child is as dedicated as a pit bull, and if anybody ever needed to read Ruskin, she does.

"Mr. McEachern, I know that you wander around a lot to make a point, but for the life of me I cannot see the relevance of religion to the problem on the table."

Well sir, I started to tell her that it takes one to know one, for I was having a little difficulty seeing how my agreeing to an interview for a school paper had wound around to getting me involved in an interracial romance, but I didn't. I already had her so high up on her dew claws it wouldn't have surprised me if she had arched her back and started spitting.

"Count Leo Tolstoy, young lady, defined religion as the way an individual relates to the great universe around him. I know you're an Episcopalian and I know you can profit from Ruskin. What church does your boyfriend go to?"

"He's not my boyfriend!"

"Yet," I said. "But it appears to me that both of you are bent and determined for him to fill that role. At least temporarily. This boy hasn't got much else going for him, and his church affiliation is something you ought to investigate."

"You don't even know him!"

"Neither do you," I shot back. "But let me line out what I do know about him. And I learned all this about him in the last several minutes. From you.

"I know he is black. That is not the do-all and end-all of existence, and he probably puts even more emphasis on it than you and I.

"I know that he is very insecure and feels inferior and unsure of himself. Else he wouldn't be a smart alec and a show-off as early as the sixth grade. Also he feels physically inferior, or he for sure and certain wouldn't have taken up body building just to be what you young folks call a hunk and not for the purpose of playing football.

"I know he's highly intelligent or he couldn't read Camus and Sartre. I also know that he's got poor taste and misguided direction of his intelligence or he wouldn't bother with those two. At least with more than just a little dip to find out they amount to nothing. Like James Joyce.

"I know he came from Alabama and that he ought to regard this area as paradise; so I know he probably had that chip on his shoulder before he got here.

"What I don't know, child, is his religion. You haven't told me his name, and I don't need to know it, nor do I particularly want to. But let's just speculate for a minute.

"Here we've got a little black boy who moved over here from Alabama. If his name was Leroy or Willie Hugh, then we can assume he was raised a Baptist and is a Christian. If he changed his name to Mbangua or Quotagu or some such, he's not anything at all any more except mad as the devil, and he may revert to animal sacrifice before he dies.

"If he is now called Muhammed or Khalim he has really and truly changed religions and I don't see how any sensible female could get caught up in the inferior role she would have to play in that sect. The Prophet may have had some splendid ideas about morality and integrity and God, but the rules he laid down for women are even worse than those of the Orthodox Jews.

"So you see, religion, or how an individual spiritually relates to the universe around him, is very important. I wasn't just wandering. I'm trying to help you to help yourself find out what you really want to do. Before," I couldn't help adding, "you get the bit between your teeth, your leg out of the traces, your tail over the dashboard and fly away over Fool's Hill so fast you tear up your own buggy."

I had her attention. She had got round-eyed and sweet again. "What do you suggest I do, Mr. McEachern?"

"Go to his church with him before you go to the bushes with him," I said. You can believe that made her sit up straight.

"Don't take him to your bed before you've taken him to your church. And the whole time you're sitting there, remember that electricity can be cut off like a light switch and then there's nothing but the dark. Remember that love is enduring and steadfast, but that lust is as ephemeral as the Great Northern Lights and not to be trusted.

"Remember what Ruskin says about your thinking much about God that is wrong."

Her eyes had got moist. I think she was pretty close to crying on me. "And just what do you think about God that you know is right, Mr. McEachern? Absolute, now. Not relative. What do you really *know*?"

Well, now, that jerked me up short. There's a heap of bottom to that Little Short-hair and you can't help liking her no matter how contrary she gets at times. This was the most honest question she had asked and it required the most honest answer I could give.

I thought about reciting the Apostles' Creed, and letting it go at that, but that seemed more than a little evasive. I shut my eyes, but not for more than a minute or two.

"During my time, I've done some reading here and there. About all the more prominent religions in the world, but more especially books about Christianity. And the Lord knows there are rooms full of them. Christian theologians are bad to sit down and write for hours about various theories and doctrines; they have written books by the ton. No man could recall all of them, which is all right because the great majority of them aren't worth reading.

"Tolstoy was a Christian, but even he did a lot of unnecessary intellectualizing; Kirkegaard's titles were better than his books; Karl Barth could get you as confused as a boxwood maze and is about as tedious as Calvin himself. After a lifetime of reading and thinking, young lady, I guess I know only one thing about God. Beyond the shadow of a doubt. I know that Jesus died. That is enough."

I was through and I stopped to give her a turn. She never said a word. Just sat there. Still as a mouse. She was the one had her eyes closed this time.

After a while I said, "All the rest is faith."

I waited some more. "He does say, 'Rejoice!'"

Her eyes were still closed, but her head was straight up. I couldn't believe it, but I saw a tear trickle out and down. I put a real light, sort of frivolous, tone in my voice. "Would you Episcopalians think I'm a theological ignoramus?"

She opened her eyes and very carefully ran one finger up the side of each cheek. Then she wiped her nose with the back of her hand. I wanted to offer my handkerchief but remembered in time that it was soiled.

"Ignoramus?" she sniffed. "You know what I think, Mr. Will Henry McEachern? About religion?"

"What?" I said.

She stood up and so did I.

"We don't know shit!" she shouted.

I jumped in spite of myself. Like I have said, these young folks can sure throw phrases at you that will startle you. I made like it was an intentional jump though and yelled back at her, "Right on!" I have managed to learn a move or so my own self. Just to keep current.

She held up her octave-and-two hand with the palm out and we did what they call a high five. Right there in my living room. For a minute I felt young again. "That's as good a starting place as I've ever heard," I told her.

"Thanks for the book." She grabbed her car keys and her purse. "And thanks for the bridle. I think I can keep this horse out of magnetic fields. At least for a while longer. I'm going home and pound the daylights out of my piano. Alone."

She headed for the door. "I'll check on you before I head for Juilliard. Enjoy the cookies." And she was gone.

Like Jack Glass says, it is indeed getting late in the evening for me, and I've got sense enough to know that the very young can have good intentions but often as not don't get around to fulfilling them. I had wound up enjoying every one of those three students, but I doubted seriously that I would ever lay eyes on a one of them again. Despite those good intentions, most young folks are too busy with their own affairs to pay much attention to old folks. It doesn't really matter. By now I've got more friends on the other side of the Jordan than I'll ever have here anyhow.

Tired as I was, I walked into my kitchen. I looked at those teacakes and decided I'd save them for Elenda. A man couldn't make it through an afternoon like this on cookies. Especially when they didn't fit the personality of the one who made them.

What I needed was a drink. Old Doc and Kilough Cofield don't know everything.

Neither does Jack Glass; maybe it is getting late in the evening but there is always the hope of another dawn.

Youth will be served, but age has its privileges. I grabbled around under the sink behind the Windex and Comet, came up with my bottle and dusted it off.

I poured me out a good two fingers in a glass and held it up to the light.

The sun was setting, and it shone through that bourbon like the blood of Christ.

"Here's to *Foxfire*," I said, and drank it down. Neat.